A TASTE OF WITCHCRAFT

PATRICIA FINNEY WRITING AS PF CHISHOLM

Patricia Finney Books, an imprint of Climbing Tree

Books

CONTENTS

SATURDAY 24TH FEBRUARY 1593, WIDDRINGTON

Young Hutchin was just trotting into the large stable yard at Widdrington Castle, carrying a bucket, when one of the Widdrington cousins stepped out of an empty stall and slashed at his face with a heavy girthstrap. Young Hutchin ducked just in time and threw the water at him. He kept hold of the bucket though, turned fast. . . Oh yes, two more boys . . .

He picked Wattie, the biggest one, and swung the bucket as he sprinted towards them, took it round his head once and slammed the wooden bucket into Wattie's face so he dropped, googly-eyed. He caught Barney's arm as he tried a wild punch, slipped on a turd and fell over but took the other boy with him crashing to the ground. He accidentally head-butted the other boy and got a squirt of blood on his jerkin which really annoyed him so he butted again properly, heard something crack and a wail of pain from under him.

Somebody grabbed him round the neck from behind and the wet told him who it was so he rammed backwards with his elbow and beat with his fists on the other boy's codpiece.

The water made him slippery so he turned in the arm, bit something, got his fists up and punched Jamie's Jock hard in the pit of his stomach. The Widdrington gasped and slid to the floor, rolled and scrambled away. Young Hutchin had his knife out by then and was just going after him to finish him off when he heard the sound of a person clapping.

He stopped and turned away and found he was cawing for breath.

At first he thought it was the Courtier, with such fancy clothes and a gelding well-worth the reiving under him. It wasn't though and the face made Young Hutchin freeze on the spot.

It wasn't the Courtier, although it was a courtier. It was in fact Lord Spynie who still sometimes turned up in Young Hutchin's nightmares from last summer, smiling as his men grabbed for Hutchin and he fought for his honour in the little room at the best inn at Dumfries. Behind Lord Spynie was a bunch of men in smart jacks that had henchman written all over them and among them a bald man with an iron expression and a dark robe a little like a minister on a very handsome black gelding who looked unhappy with his ears back.

Young Hutchin spotted his statute cap lying in a puddle, grabbed it, pulled it down to hide his blue eyes and golden hair.

But Lord Spynie hadn't recognised him. Maybe?

"Ye're a good fighter, lad, wad ye like a place wi' my henchman?"

Young Hutchin crushed the impulse to say, "Ay, I am, I'm a Graham and ye're Lord Spynie, so die!" That would never do. There were far too many henchmen standing about.

Lord Spynie was taking his embroidered gauntlets off. "Ah should probably tell yer master but then ye'd get a beating, so I won't."

Young Hutchin was covered in mud and dung. He didn't realise how much he had grown in the last year and had plenty more growing to do yet since his hands and feet were so large. His hair was still golden under the filth and his eyes were still blue but one of them was swelling from a blow he hadn't felt at the time. And his jaw was lengthening into a true Graham chin which would probably make him handsome again in a few years, but not yet.

Sir Henry was limping across the yard, his face wreathed in smiles like a happy gargoyle.

Young Hutchin looked around for the idiots who had attacked him. The wet one, Jamie's Jock was almost out of the yard, hunched up; Wattie, the one he had hit with the wooden bucket, was still sitting on the ground holding his head and Barney was at the horsetrough, trying to wash the blood off while more was flowing freely from his nose.

Jesu, the lummocks were so stupid. Young Hutchin actually felt embarrassed for them.

Sir Henry was welcoming Lord Spynie loudly, shouting orders for grooms to come and take Lord Spynie's horses and since Hutchin was the only one standing, he went and took the nice horse Lord Spynie had just jumped down from. He took the other from the grim bald man and took them both over to the best loosebox, where he evicted three hobbies and doubled them up in a loosebox with a hole in the roof. He untacked the new horses quickly, gave them water and fodder, took the tack to the tack room and put the saddles on the hooks for guests. Then he came back and groomed them and found the bald man's horse tended to shy a lot, took the burrs out of their tails, gave each a handful of grass as a thank you for co-operating, except that the bald man's horse didn't want it.

The lads he had battered were dealing with the other horses Spynie's men had brought. One was shaking his head occasionally as if to clear it, one was sniffing and the other was still wet and limping, looking at Hutchin sidelong from the corner of his eye and clearly hating him.

That was the boy calling himself Head Lad. Young Hutchin went over to him and stood there smiling as his eye swelled up. "Ye lost," he said to Jamie's Jock Widdrington conversationally. "Three of ye on me on a surprise and ye lost."

The other boy cringed and carried on curry-combing. He was a year older in age than Young Hutchin.

"Ye canna beat a Graham in a fair fight, much less an unfair fight," said Young Hutchin with great satisfaction. "Ye just canna. So stop trying. I'll be the Head Lad here now."

"What will Sam the Man say?"

Sam the Man was the Head Groom, a wizened old man of at least 50 who had a bad arm from an old injury. He was wise with horses but drank a lot.

"Wilna care, one way or t'other," said Young Hutchin, hoping this was true. "So long as the nags are looked after right. And they will be nor better than under ye, what's more."

Young Hutchin had been in the Carlisle castle stables since he was around eight and thought he knew how a proper stables should be run.

"So I get the perks as well. I get yer bed by the window, ye hear? So when ye've finished here, ye'd best go clear it."

He looked in on all the other lads, only three out of four were there but Toad had disappeared as he did when there was trouble. He'd turn up later. Young Hutchin went up to Wattie and tapped him on the head to remind him of the bucket.

"Dinna let Jamie's Jock lead ye astray again," he said and Wattie shook his head. "Ah'm Head Lad, any problems?"

"Nay," said Wattie, "Ye're Head Lad, Young Hutchin Graham."

"Good."

The other one was still sniffing every few seconds which Young Hutchin found annoying, so he grabbed him and pulled him backwards.

"Whit?" he demanded. "Whit have ye got tae say to me?"

Barney hunched his shoulder and muttered.

"Nay, ye've got to say it loud and clear."

"Ye're the Head Lad, Hutchin Graham."

"Thank ee."

With enormous dignity, Young Hutchin let go of him and marched out of the yard and when he was sure no one could see him, punched the air once.

Then he sauntered round to the dairy and hung around the back door into the small yard until Jane Fenwick came out, carrying two full buckets of water and a round bundle of cloth perched on her head. Her square face was concentrated and Young Hutchin enjoyed the look of her breasts which were big to match the sturdiness of her body. Her woad blue kirtle was old and a little too short for her and her cap grubby on her brown hair but somehow she looked like a princess in silk and velvet to Young Hutchin. He had made no progress with her at all.

Suddenly he got a brilliant idea and as he had learnt from the Courtier back in Carlisle, he put it into action immediately.

"Can Ah help ye," he asked. She stopped dead and stared.

"Are ye foolin' wi' me?" she asked in her attractive Northumbrian accent.

"Nay," said Young Hutchin, offended, "Which would ye like me to take?"

She put down both buckets and stepped out from between them since they weren't on a yoke. Young Hutchin picked them up, quite relieved, because carrying water buckets was something he did all day while balancing a bag on his head would be tricky.

"We're ainly going to the corner of the laundry yard," she said, "where the lye droppers are. I'm to wash the cloths and leave them to soak in the big copper and then later boil 'em up and hang 'em on the gooseberry hedge."

"A'right," said Young Hutchin, enjoying the way she walked, striding along with her hobnailed boots kicking up her kirtle in front of her and the bag still balancing comfortably on her head.

"How old are ye, Jane?" he asked. As far as he knew he was about 13 or 14, nobody was sure.

"Ah'm around 15, me mam said I was borned in a good summer, which would ha' been 1578, and I've done dairying since I wis 10. You?"

"Somewhere around that," hedged Young Hutchin, "Where d'ye sleep?"

Her eyes narrowed with suspicion and she scowled. "None o' yer business," she said, taking the buckets off him with a sniff, "And nowhere ye can come at me."

Young Hutchin could have bitten his tongue, he was so annoyed with himself for letting that slip out. He did his best to look innocent which was hard. "Who said anything about that," he protested, "Ah only thought..."

"Ah, I ken verra well what ye're only thinking.Ye can stop it now."

Young Hutchin decided to say nothing more but soon asked "What will ye do now?"

For answer she poured the bucket into the little copper, then carefully got a bowl full of lye from under the third lye dropper and poured it in, put the bowl back under, poured the other bucket into the big copper and stirred with a wooden stick. There were already cloths in there, swimming about like strange sea creatures.

"If ye meant it about helping me," she said shrewdly, "ye can go and get me four more bucketfulls from the well and pit 'em in the big copper here."

"Ay mistress," he said with a wink and trotted to the well with the buckets over his arm, dropped the well bucket down, pulled it up again as fast as he could, poured twice and started back.

He poured both into the big copper, where Jane was lighting the fire under it with charcoals from the kitchen and a couple of faggots crossed. He went back and forth again.

"Ye spilled a bit," she said critically.

"I didna!"

"Well Ah'm no' paying ye."

"Only wi' a kiss," said Hutchin, shutting his blue eyes and braced for the slap which often followed this kind of boldness.

It didn't come. Instead he felt a soft mouth delicately brush his cheek and his eyes flipped open in shock.

"Ye kissed me!" he shouted.

"Ah did no'," said Jane with composure, "It was a butterfly."

"Ye did!" crowed Hutchin and then thought of the Courtier who harvested so many women and what he might do in this situation.

He struck himself on the chest and made a wide gesture with his other hand. "Och God, my heart is broken, how can I bear my life when my mistress is so cruel..."

It was quite a good imitation of the Courtier's funny southron accent as well though he didn't expect her to get the joke.

However, Jane giggled and blushed. "That's Mr Carey," she said, "Ye're a good mimic."

"Och, when did ye meet him?" said Hutchin astonished.

"When he stayed here the year before the Armada when he wis on his way to Scotland to tell the King of Scotland that the Queen had executed his mam."

That sounded exactly like the sort of crazy thing the Courtier would do. "He did that?"

"Well, he didn't, see ye, because all of the Scotch surnames wis angry that the Queen of England had chopped off the head of their ain Queen that they all wanted to chop the head off of her theirselves. So the Scotts and the Kerrs and the like were waiting to waylay and kill him and the King of Scots wouldna let him cross the Border so he waited around at Widdrington for a couple of months."

"And that's when he fell hard for Lady Widdrington?"

She grinned shyly, "Ay, it is." Her face clouded. "Though it's done 'em no good, for Sir Henry soon spotted whit had happened and he's bin beating her worse every year." Jane scowled again and her fists were clenched. "Ah hate Sir Henry, so I do. I hate the bastard and if I could find a way, Ah'd kill him meself."

She sounded like she meant it. He stared at her. "Ye would?"

"Ay, I would," she said. She untied the bag and dumped more dairy cloths into the little copper and started stirring them round and round while singing a very rude song about a pestle and mortar.

"But what if they hang ye? Or burn ye for petty treason?"

"They willna," she said, "but if they do, well, it wilna matter so much for Lady Widdrington will be safe."

"Och," said Young Hutchin, "If ye come tae it and ye need a man, I'll help ye wi' that too."

"Ye will?"

"Ay."

"Though ye're not a man yet."

Young Hutchin shrugged. He thought and hoped that the courtier he had stuck with his dagger in the little room in Dumfries had died, but he didn't know it for a fact so he said nothing about it.

She was still stirring the cloths in the nasty smelling liquid.

"Ye'd best get back to the stables afore Jamie's Jock notices ye're gone."

Young Hutchin spat and grinned. "Disnae matter. I'm Head Lad now."

"Oh aye," she said, "how did that come about?"

"Ah fought and bested all three o'them, except Toad this morning and Toad disnae count."

"That where ye got yer black eye?"

"Aye, it is – though you should see the others."

"Hmf."

"But ye're right," he said, "I should go back and mek them do summat about the dunghill, it's a right mess so it is."

She had started singing again as she stirred and dunked the cloths. He looked at her pretty ear, all neatly half-hidden under her cap. She was the same size as him, or maybe now he was a mite taller and so, greatly daring, he leaned over and gave it a kiss.

She clapped her hand on it and he leaped out of the way of the clout.

"It was a butterfly!" he shouted, and then squeaked at the end, damn it.

She dissolved into giggles and didn't hit him again.

Young Hutchin sauntered away feeling pleased with himself and into the stableyard where he shouted at Jamie's Jock and Barney to get the dung hill tidied up.

Toad was already in the yard, carefully filling a bucket at the well, breathing through the mouth heavily and concentrating. He looked up anxiously and froze so that the well bucket overflowed his own bucket and he only noticed when it splashed his legs.

Toad was a grown man though not very tall but he talked and acted like a seven year old. Old Sam the Man had something to do with Toad because he never beat Toad, even when he'd done something daft. Toad had a round moon face and squinty little eyes, hence his nickname. Toad had long ago forgotten what his own real name was, he wore hand-me-down homespun and a hemp shirt and ancient cracked boots.

So Young Hutchin swaggered over to him and Toad looked frightened and tried to escape, but was too slow because Hutchin grabbed his arm and locked it.

"I'm sorry, sorry," said Toad in his mushy squeaky voice, "Ah wilna do it again!"

"Who put ye up to it?" shouted Hutchin.

"I didn't, I never, I didn't do it."

"But ye said ye would?"

"Yes, no."

"A'right," said Young Hutchin, "What were ye to do?"

"Hit you with the bucket. Jay Jock give me a shiny thing for it."

"Ay." Young Hutchin thought about beating Toad up because he could, since Toad never fought back and he found Toad really annoying. But why? Better save his energy for another fight with Jamie's Jock which was clearly brewing. "A'right Toad, go cuddle a horse and stay oot of the way for a bit. Will ye do that?"

Toad nodded. "You won't hit me?"

"Nay son, not this time," said Hutchin very lordly. "Ye didna hit me with the bucket, did ye?"

Toad frowned and thought. "No," he agreed. "Yutchin, can I show you something?"

Young Hutchin hesitated. It could be a trap, but if it was he knew it so he drew his dagger and said, "Ay o'course."

Toad took him to the secondbest stall where there was a large black gelding standing with his head down. It was the Minister's horse, the one that kept shying. When they came in, the horse tried to shy again but Toad mumbled and chucked to him and gentled him with his big square hands and the horse quivered and stood still for him, sighing deeply. Toad put his arm around the animal's neck and nodded to Young Hutchin.

"Look in his mouth."

Hutchin got a grip on the nag's chin and after a struggle got the mouth open. It smelled ugly, the lips were cut and grazed, the tongue had a great welt across it that looked an ominous yellow white.

"Jesus Christ," said Young Hutchin.

"He wilna eat, just drinks."

"Ah'm no surprised. Let me look at his bit."

Hutchin strode to the tackroom, found the fancy bridle that the Minister had ridden in with, tested the bit with his finger and swore.

"Ay," he said in disgust as he came back, "The bit's sharp. Nae wonder."

"But why?"

"Dinna ken," he said, although he did. Some nobles liked a sharp bit because they made the horse foam at the mouth and even bleed, which they thought looked good, and also made the horses more sensitive to the reins. Young Hutchin thought that if you needed a sharp bit to ride you were a pretty useless horseman. Young Hutchin could ride anything at all, with no bridle or saddle.

"Is Sam the Man sober?" he asked Toad who shook his head. "The horse needs a leech now. That thing on his tongue needs draining, poor lad."

Toad put his arms round the horse's neck and started snuffling. "Poor horse,"

Was the man actually crying because the horse was in pain? Jesu, how strange. Hutchin watched for a minute, honestly nonplussed. The snuffling soon stopped and all Hutchin could hear was soft muttering and the horse blowing through his lips, almost as if they were talking.

"I'll go talk to him," said Young Hutchin because after all it was his job to do it as he was the Head Lad now.

SATURDAY 24TH FEBRUARY 1593, WIDDRINGTON

Lord Spynie sat in Sir Henry's chair with his boots on Sir Henry's parlour table. He was wearing his black cutwork jerkin over a tawny brocade doublet and was only slightly drunk. Two of his men at arms were at the door and a third was in the passage. The others were all in hall getting fed.

Sir Henry was bringing a tray of wine with his own hands, and behind him came his younger son, Roger, in a plain stuff scholar's gown and with a new sprinkling of spots on his face. There was a nicely chased silver jug with three tall silver goblets and a silver cup, all with different patterns of chasing, incised crosses and angels and suchlike.

The man sitting bolt-upright in a chair to Spynie's left glanced at the goblets and then looked again. He had a face that looked as if it had been carved from stone, a sallow complexion and he was completely bald, also lacking eyebrows and eyelashes. His falling band was snowy white and he wore black brocade and well-made riding boots with sharp spurs. Over everything he wore a long minister's gown made of silk grosgrain and a fashionable beaver hat on his bald head.

Sir Henry hobbled over, wincing a little, and poured wine into the fanciest goblet which he offered to Lord Spynie. Roger Widdrington served the man in the minister's robe and picked up the cup. Sir Henry then raised his own goblet and gave the toast: "Confusion to the Spanish!"

"Confusion!" answered the Minister promptly and Spynie took his feet off the table and repeated the toast.

"May I present Mr Anthony Lindsay to you, Sir Henry?"

The bald man bowed gravely in his seat, sipped the wine and put the goblet down delicately. His brown eyes caressed the goblet with its chased angels around a circled cross.

"Oh, is he a kinsman of yours?"

"I'm not sure," said the man in a deep flowing voice. "That's my surname certainly, as to being a kinsman of my lord, I don't know." His voice sounded English, perhaps with a slight flavour of something else?

"Ye don't sound like a Scotchman,"

"I am though," said Lindsay, with a smile. "I was born in Scotland but my mother was married to a Spaniard and moved to the continent after the Reformation in Scotland."

"Then ye're a Catholic?"

"I was. I am no longer, since I saw the light ten years ago and became a Protestant. I studied theology at Cambridge."

Sir Henry grunted.

"For instance, these rather beautiful goblets were chalices used in the Mass. A Catholic would say it was a sin to drink from such sacred objects. I however regard that as superstitious nonsense and am pleased to drink from such beautiful plate."

Sir Henry looked at them again. He hadn't noticed that before; he had reived them from someone many years ago, so long ago he had forgotten who or even their surname. And no doubt whoever it had been had reived them himself from a church.

"They are pretty," he said, with surprise in his voice. His big toe gave a twinge and he winced. He was taking a decoction of crocus bulbs which was supposed to help his gout. The trouble was the medicine made his stomach hurt which added to the cacophany of pain throughout his body: in his back, in his fingers and toes, his knuckles, his knees, even his ears for God's sake. And his privy member. That hurt all the time now, so he had to take laudanum for it at night. The unfairness of it made him angry.

He sighed, moved his foot carefully, got another twinge.

"You have gout?" said Lindsay.

"Ay," sighed Sir Henry.

Roger Widdrington had sat down on a bench with his own drink, listening to them all.

"Have you tried avoiding red meat and wine as being too hot for your complexion?"

Sir Henry suppressed another sigh. One of the worst things about being ill was the way everyone wanted to advise you. At least Lord Spynie didn't do that.

"Tried that," he grunted, "most boring week of my life. If I can't eat meat and drink wine, what can I eat?"

"Pot herbs and water?" said Lindsay, then smiled to show it was a joke. The smile seemed to take considerable effort and didn't quite work. "I have also studied a little medicine," said Lindsay, "although I must confess that I was expelled for heresy from Pavia."

"Because you were a Protestant?" asked Spynie with interest.

"And because I do not regard Galen as the last word in medicine, less still Hippocrates."

"So what do you say is causing my God-damned gout?"

"Witchcraft."

Sir Henry sat up. "What?"

Spynie didn't seem surprised. "Hear him out, Sir Henry, I think you may find it interesting."

"Go on,"

Lindsay tilted his head. “Witch craft, or should I say, witches, are the cause of many illnesses, either by using the Evil Eye or by means of such methods as making a wax doll in the appearance and nature of the victim and sticking pins in it, writing curses out on a lead tablet and dropping them in a well, or by incantations.”

“Och,” Sir Henry stared at him.

“Of course, all kinds of witchcraft involve summoning a demon, sometimes Satan himself,” Lindsay continued. “Except for the Hermetic wisdom, there can be no magic without some kind of devil involved.”

“Somebody put a spell on me?” asked Sir Henry. He was frightened at the thought but also suddenly hopeful. If his pain had a human cause and he could find out who it was...

“Maybe my uncle?” he said, sitting forward, “He cursed me, the bastard...”

“When did your gout start?”

“Years ago, before the Armada.”

“And when did your uncle curse you?”

“Last autumn. He was a Papist monk and he’s still hanging on in the old abbey of Jedburgh...”

Lindsay shook his head gravely. “I think not, although he may be worth investigating. You should look for someone close to you, whom you first met a year or two before the gout started.”

Sir Henry was silent because he had suddenly had a realisation, a moment of utterly limpid clarity. Of course. Of course! Who else could it be? Who had made him miserable by being tall, being redheaded, being infuriatingly submissive to him while yet ruling Widdrington castle with a rod of iron? It had to be her.

“Elizabeth!” he whispered, “Of course.”

Spynie and Lindsay exchanged glances.

"Perhaps," said Lindsay smoothly, "but we must look at other possible suspects too. For instance, does your wife have a particular favourite lover?"

Sir Henry hammered his fist on the table and stood up. "Ay, by God, the filthy bitch," he shouted. "Sir Robert bloody Carey!"

A small smile was hovering around Lord Spynie's full lips. "Of course," he agreed softly.

***

Young Hutchin crept into the Chief Groom's small chamber hard by the tackroom. It looked very comfortable with a small fireplace and a cupboard bed, a table covered with bits of tack, several lumps of cheese and some mysterious bottles. In a chair with arms, Sam the Man sat slumped, breathing loudly and dribbling. There was a leather bottle in front of him and a horn cup half-full of something brown. Young Hutchin sniffed it, funny smell, tried some and found it weirdly smoky but also comfortingly fiery so he drank the rest.

After consideration, Young Hutchin picked up a lungeing whip and prodded Sam the Man with it. Sam came to with a splutter and a punch thrown at random.

"Sir, sir," shouted Hutchin, "One o' the horses needs a leech bad, sir!"

"Whuffle."

"Ay sir, he's bad, Toad's wi' him and ah... Toad's upset too."

Sam blinked swollen eyes at him. "Whut?"

"It's the Minister's horse," shouted Hutchin, still well out of reach, "He's bin badly used, sir, will ye come and look?"

Sam was now conscious enough to feel his hangover and moaned, covering his eyes. He reached for the cup, found it to be empty and chucked it in the corner, took a suck from the bottle.

"Will I run tae the buttery and get ye some ale?" asked Hutching with a winning grin.

"Ay, there's a good lad. Where's the... ah... where's the horse?"

"Second best stall, sir."

"Urgh." Sam steadied himself and stood up, took the lunge whip with him and tottered out of his chamber where he winced at the watery sunlight. Leaning on the whip, he walked across the dung and straw-strewn yard, kicking lumps of shit out of his way angrily. That was another thing that had to change, Young Hutchin thought.

Young Hutchin sprinted to the buttery and got a quart jack of mild ale from the barrel on the counter which he tasted cautiously. It was still drinkable though sour from the vinegar fly. Young Hutchin shook his head as he walked back carrying it carefully. If Lady Widdrington were there, the ale would be sweet and fresh, but everything went to hell when she wasn't there because the steward was useless and Sir Henry wouldn't allow Lady Widdrington any women he didn't know to come and learn huswifery from her. Sir Henry hated hearing the twittering of women and was suspicious they would plot against him with his wife, and so the women were mostly his elderly cousins and unable to think for themselves.

Young Hutchin came to the second best stall and found Sam giving the Minister's horse a good checking over, moving slowly and painfully himself and sighing a lot.

"Here sir, here's yer ale."

Sam the Man was preoccupied, reached a hand out for the jack, ignored the proffered cup, and drank the whole quart down in one. Young Hutchin was impressed. "Did ye find the bit?"

"Ay sir."

"Get some bread and cheese while ye're at it."

"Ay sir."

Hutchin sprinted back to the buttery and nearly rammed into Jane who was also fetching ale, bread and cheese for the dairy's dinner. Jane went quite pink when she saw him.

"Now then, Young Hutchin."

Och, he loved the warning tone of her voice. Progress! He bowed to her. "Ay," he said, "Goody Fenwick!"

She giggled at him. "Ah've to go back now," he said, belted over to the tack room, found the sharp bridle and brought it to Sam in the stall where the horse was drinking thirstily from a bucket with leaves in it. Sam stuffed a bit of cheese into the penny loaf and started munching it.

Sam felt the bit and let Toad feel it too. Toad's little slitty eyes went as round as they could and he hugged the horse again.

"Now then," growled Sam, "dinna take on so."

He gave the bridle back to Young Hutchin and said, "Ye're tae find a file and use it to blunt down this bit so the horse don't feel it, understand? And dinna let the Minister catch ye doing it either." Young Hutchin knuckled his forehead. "Ah canna send for the leech wi'out asking the bailiff for more money so I'll clean the abscess maself and file his teeth as well."

Young Hutchin wanted to see this, but Sam waved him away. So he philosophically went into the tackroom, took the sharpened bit off the bridle, locked it in the vice and started filing. He was listening for a ruckus – by Hutchin's reckoning that was a three-man job right there, not an old drunk and a booby. But no, there was some snorting and whuffling but no horse screams. Had they given the beast laudanum? Surely not, the stuff cost a fortune. He left the bit in the vice and looked out the door. A bit of seafret would have been nice, but of course not.

He climbed out of the window into the back yard where the chickens were, climbed up the chicken coop onto the back of the stable roof. From there he eeled carefully along to the end because the thatch was old, pulled some of the thatch apart and looked down into the stall.

The Minister's horse was lying flat on his side, with the gag in Sam used when he wanted to give a horse a drench. Toad was sitting cross-legged by the horse, his arms round his neck, singing something soft. Sam was working with a knife and scraper on the horse's tongue.

The hairs went up on Hutchin's neck. The horse's eyes were half-open, as if he were dozing. He wasn't hobbled or trussed up. Nothing but Toad hugging him.

Young Hutchin shook his head, put the reeds back, squirmed back to the chicken coop and got on with filing that bit blunt. A while later he heard the unmistakeable sound of a horse getting up and shaking himself. Then Hutchin brought the bit to Sam who felt it and nodded.

Toad smiled at Hutchin. "He's better now," he said, "the horse."

"Ay," said Young Hutchin cautiously, "Will ye speak to the Minister about it..."

"Nay, I wilna," said Sam.

"Why not, master?"

"Cause it'll do nae good."

Ye're afeared ye'll lose yer place, thought Young Hutchin contemptuously, and looked at Toad who was staring at the ground.

Young Hutchin felt hot in his stomach and angry for the horse. He was nobbut an animal but what was the point of using a sharp bit just because ye were shit at riding? He took breath to protest and met Sam the Man's gaze which was like running headfirst into a brick wall.

"Shut up," said Sam through his teeth. "Ye know nothing." Then he turned and went.

MONDAY 26TH FEBRUARY 1593, EDINBURGH

Lady Elizabeth Widdrington was enjoying herself, sitting at a large table in Queen Ann's parlour at Holyrood, helping to embroider a huge bed curtain in colourful crewel work. The fabric was stretched on a large tenter-frame which made it much easier to sew and she liked the variety of stitches and the different effects you could get. Lady Schevengen had shown her a new filler stitch and she was using it to fill in a poppy petal with red and black silk.

A page came clattering in, grabbed his hat off, bowed to the Queen and then went over to Elizabeth.

"Lady Widdrington, Mr Widdrington asked if you could meet wi' him, please?"

Elizabeth raised her eyebrows as she finished her thread, and tilted her head at the faint crack-booms audible in the distance. The page grinned. "Ay, ma'am," he said, "They're at it again."

Elizabeth stood and curtseyed low to the Queen and then hurried from the Queen's Parlour into the gardens at the back of Holyrood Hoouse.

Young Henry was exactly where she expected him to be, across the gardens, through the orchards, right down beyond the archery butts to the place surrounded by high earth banks like a faery fort. More loud booms sounded from it and clouds of gunpowder smoke swirled up like dragons breath. It had taken a lot of convincing to persuade the King to put up a rough target range suitable for firearms. The high earth walls were the King's own idea to prevent the usual numbers of accidental casualties. He had some excuse: one of his ancestors had been killed by a bursting cannon.

As she came round by the opening in the turf walls, she saw Henry standing with a couple of friends of his, aiming a caliver at a target at what seemed a ridiculous distance. His spotty face was concentrated and set. Elizabeth waited for his shot, not to spoil his aim. There was a loud echoing boom and then two more from Henry's friends. They immediately set about cleaning, reaming, loading and priming again, doing it themselves rather than have servants complete the fiddly bits for them. She rather liked that about them.

Elizabeth walked up to Henry, smiling. They were all young men who had just crossed the border into adulthood like Young Henry himself. One was remarkably handsome and she wondered if Lord Spynie had spotted him or did he have a family powerful enough to protect him.

"Mr Widdrington," she said formally because of the other lads. "It's a pleasure to see you."

Young Henry didn't answer and she reached up and tapped him on the large shoulder. He spun, hand to his swordhilt, and then relaxed and smiled and bowed to her. Then he took what looked like a torn wad of perfectly good shirt out of each ear.

"Sorry, my lady," he said, sounding surprisingly Scottish, "Ah couldnae hear ye."

Lady Widdrington blinked at the wads the other lads were fishing out of their ears. "What a very good idea," she said.

"Yes," said Henry, "Every gunner I've met over the age of 40 is as deaf as a post, so it's worth a try."

"Is it hard to learn to load and prime a gun?" she asked. "It does look very complicated."

"The more often ye do it the better ye get at it," said the handsome one with blue eyes and black hair. "Will I show ye how it's done, yer ladyship?"

Some adventurous part deep inside herself shoved past her daylight self and said, "Yes please."

"It's ay good for me, too, ye ken," said the young man, "teaching somebody else."

Young Henry elbowed the young man who stopped, made a lovely Court bow and added, "Ma name is Johnnie Carmichael, ma'am."

The short broad lad next to him stepped back. Lady Widdrington liked the graceful way the young man had made showing her the art of loading a gun into a favour to himself.

And it was complicated. He showed her first, slowly, explaining at each turn. Then he had her do it, reaming, cleaning, measuring the powder with a rather clever little gadget that had a spring in the lid to give the right amount, tamping, wad, ball, wad, tamping again, tapping the milled powder into the pan and then trimming the bit of match held in the clamp and blowing on it to make it hotter when he fired. Then she tried without his instruction, though she still didn't have the courage to fire the weapon. The fourth time, Johnnie Carmichael made her teach him to do it and he made her laugh by pretending to be terribly stupid and slow and doing it all wrong.

That last time he had her aim the caliver herself and squeeze the trigger and she nearly dropped the whole thing at the incredible bellow and flare of the slowmatch in the powder pan.

Her hands were shaking and her ears were hurting but somehow she found herself taking the caliver, swabbing and loading it with another half charge and aiming and firing at the nearest target. She was astonished to see that she had actually hit the target, probably by sheer chance.

"You should take up shooting, ma'am," said Young Henry judiciously without a trace of a smile. "Ye could be good at it."

She laughed a little because that was ridiculous. "I don't think Sir Henry would like that."

"No," said Young Henry, "ye're right, he wouldna."

Still she felt exhilarated somehow, as if she was somehow bigger than she had been when she found them at their shooting.

"I'm sorry, I completely forgot to ask you what you wanted to speak to me about, Mr Widdrington."

He reached into his doublet breast pocket and pulled out a letter, written in the cramped secretary script of Sir Henry's cousin and secretary, John Widdrington. She read it carefully a couple of times and then handed it back to him.

"You're to go immediately to meet my Lord Maxwell at Caerlaverock and collect four wolfhounds as payment of a bet. It seems all right."

"I really don't like Lord Maxwell. And he's a Catholic."

"I think it's a good opportunity to meet him yourself – you might have to deal with him when you're the Deputy Warden of the East March. Go and admire his hunting dogs and... oh yes, make sure you take him a little present as well."

"What should I..."

"Brandy is always very welcome. You could probably buy a small keg from the buttery here at Hollyrood, and if not, one of the Edinburgh merchants will be delighted to help you."

Young Henry nodded seriously. "I was thinking I should take five men..."

Elizabeth shook her head firmly. "Ten at least," she said, "and supplies would be polite as well. The Maxwell has old-fashioned views: the more henchmen ye have, the more respectable ye are. I didn't realise it at the time, but that was part of the reason Sir Robert had such trouble with him last summer: Maxwell just could not take him seriously since he only had three men with him."

Young Henry nodded, "Ay," he said, "that makes some sense of it. I'll go and talk to the Sergeant-at-Arms..."

"Good idea," said Elizabeth, "And take the Sergeant – you can't take the banner with the Widdrington badge because you're not the headman yet, but I'm sure he can find a way to look impressive."

Young Henry smiled and kissed her on the cheek. "Ay," he said, "Thank you, ma'am."

She saw him off that afternoon, looking very fine indeed: his Sergeant riding ahead of him, Young Henry in his Widdrington patterned jack and polished morion, all his men by two and two behind him, also in Widdrington jacks and helmets, and a boy behind them with two packponies. He had decided against remounts for everyone since they weren't in a hurry and just took two spare horses for himself and the Sergeant. The only thing marring the picture was the magnificent new spot on the point of his chin, battling hard against the perennial spot on the end of his nose.

TUESDAY 27TH FEBRUARY 1593, EDINBURGH

Elizabeth didn't sleep well that night for some reason. She was a little sad at Young Henry being gone, but truth to tell, she rarely saw him when she was on duty with the Queen and when she wasn't on duty, she preferred to stay in Edinburgh than go home to Widdrington Castle which had never been more of a home to her than it was her prison. She felt at home and comfortable at the Scots Court despite all the formality and backbiting that came with being a Court, though there was much less of that than there was at Queen Elizabeth's Court down in London. Young Henry was staying with her to get some of the Courtly polish Sir Robert had in such abundance, and also to make friends that would be useful for the future. She wondered how he would do with the Maxwell, who was a robber baron through and through. Mind you, she was a little surprised that the Maxwell had the time for Sir Henry's wolfhounds since he was presumably getting ready to fight the Johnstones in their endless feud.

When she finally fell asleep she dreamed she was in a dark wood, full of grabbing thorns and brambles, catching her shoulders where Sir Henry's belt had left scars. She was stumbling along in only her white linen shift which was stained and smelled horrible.

At last she came to a place where the path forked but the night was black as pitch. Fog blew around her and seemed to make holes in the world through which she could see brightness and demons.

She gasped when she saw the little sharp toothed devils and for a moment thought of turning tail and running. But she didn't want to go back through the thorns and brambles and tear more holes in her ragged smock. She tried to peer through a hole in the world – the devils were hanging over the edge, shouting in rough and squeaky voices at her and clawing for her.

She heard some kind of animal howling and screaming and wondered what it was.She knew she had a choice to make, a choice of path, but it was as if the fog was wrapping round her head and stopping her from seeing anything clearly. She didn't know which choice would lead her out of the cold and the brambles.

When she squinted along the paths she saw one seemed to lighten, the other to darken. It seemed obvious she should choose the path with glimmers of light, yet something in her heart whispered that it was a trap. Maybe the other darker path was also a trap.

What should she do?

She felt a familiar sense of miserable helplessness. One path led to the wailing beast. One path led into darkness. She didn't know which was the right way, she didn't even know how to find out. She stood stock still as snow began falling. Gradually it buried her, still standing at the fork in the road.

***

She woke feeling sweaty and strange feelings going up and down her legs. She remembered the cold and the little devils and shuddered at the dream, so she climbed out of bed doing her best not to disturb the Danish lady-in-waiting who was still asleep. She put her fur-lined gown on because the air was sharp and knelt to say her prayers and do

neither of them had the resources they would need to bribe enough MPs to let it happen. Nor was she a peasant to just move to the next county and change her name and never see her husband again. She was neither rich enough nor poor enough for a separation. Staying at King James's Court in Edinburgh was the best she could do. And in any case, she had never felt that she could just tear apart her marriage which was founded of God and intended to be lifelong.

She changed into her hunting habit and left her Court clothes hanging on the wall. She looked well in it and its forest green wool matched at least one of Robin's dizzying array of ridiculously fashionable and expensive doublets. Elizabeth had always insisted on her own horse and had often hunted on it. Chasing a deer with her husband's surname around her and the cries and horn calls going up was one of the few times when she felt let out of the gaol that was her marriage. She had hunted less as Sir Henry grew less and less able to follow the hunt and for the last couple of years she had worn her hunting habit mainly to travel in. She had three kirtles and a gown at Widdrington and plenty of linen so she didn't need to pack a bag except for one spare shift and a cap. The journey would only take two days with a break at the inn at Berwick.

All of them sat in the hall, the old refectory of the monks with Roger sitting at the head of their mess. He had said grace in a flat voice and added the Our Father, then fell silent. They shared a mess of bacon pottage with oatmeal and another of salt beef stew, with bread and cheese and then the luxury of an apple for dessert. Hers was wrinkled but still sound, probably from the very back of the provisions shelf. The small ale was sweet and good as well.

She tried a couple of times to get Roger talking but failed. Never mind. His father was on his deathbed, after all.

How would Young Henry take the news of his father's death? She knew he wouldn't be as happy as she was, unfortunately. He would surely be sad. He had had good times with his father as a boy, learning to shoot a bow, learning the basics of swordplay.

However that had ended after he had stood between her and his father when he was only 14 and a bony beanpole with no breadth at all, and faced him down too. Sir Henry had never forgiven his defiance.

She smiled again. Against all the odds Young Henry had turned into such a fine man, such a good man. Somehow his father's total unpredictability and sudden rages hadn't ruined him the way you might expect. It was a pity Young Henry had left for Caerlaverock the day before; she must remind Roger to send him a message about his father, if he hadn't done it already.

There was Roger, now waiting for her in the stableyard, the other Widdringtons already mounted and chatting quietly. They gave her a couple of odd looks, probably because she was still smiling slightly at the thought of freedom. She straightened her face, felt her cap and beaver hat to make sure she was decent, went to his stirrup and reminded him about telling Young Henry.

He gave an odd little nervous grin and told her that a messenger had already been sent direct from Widdrington, so she hurried to the mounting block and mounted to her new sidesaddle. It wasn't worn in yet and was a little uncomfortable still. She settled herself with her leg round the hook and clucked to Mouse who snorted and started forwards reluctantly, kicking a little.

She watched as Roger climbed aboard his horse – Young Henry would have made a steed leap – and found his stirrups. Rat was in place at the end of the line of remounts. Including Roger there were four men and herself and a drover for the packponies. Well, with luck they wouldn't meet anyone like Geordie Burn on the way south. She looked around for anything out of place or missing, couldn't see anything and nodded to Roger who lifted his cap to her. They rode out of Holyrood House and headed for the Great North Road.

WEDNESDAY 28TH FEBRUARY 1593

Two days' travel later, in the evening, she arrived at Widdrington with Roger and the four men who had escorted her all the way from Edinburgh.

She dismounted, feeling very tired and unusually melancholy, mainly because her courses had come on halfway down the Great North Road, that being the most inconvenient moment they could choose, and she had had to improvise with her spare shift.

"Roger," she said, "I'm not feeling very well. I think I'll go straight to bed in the chapel so I don't disturb your father. I'll go to his bedside in the morning."

He lifted his eyebrows and said, "Very well, ma'am, I'll... er... go to him myself."

She saw strange horses in the stables and there had been a lot of new horses on the infield on the way in as well – a couple of very handsome geldings, one of them a large animal that seemed to be unwell. She couldn't see the grooms who were usually running about. Still it was well after sunset and they were probably all in bed and she didn't feel up to finding out what was going on.

Ah, there was Sam Affleck, Sam the Man they called him, and so she handed the reins to him, He was looking very shifty. Had he been doing deals for reived hobbies, she wondered?

Actually she didn't care, because her belly was hurting and she felt exhausted. She walked alone into the barnekin and went up the spiral stairs to the chapel that had been turned into a spare bedroom cum armoury. She undressed herself without the help of her tiring woman who seemed to have disappeared, knelt to pray for Sir Henry's soul and Robin's safety, and fell into the half-testered bed.

THURSDAY 1ST MARCH 1593, WIDDRINGTON

She woke as the sun rose and at first simply stayed where she was, looking up at the arched ceiling and the fragments of paint on the walls. Could it really be true that her husband was dying? Did he really want to reconcile with her?

She couldn't believe it. Perhaps Roger was stretching the truth, or perhaps the apoplexy had taken the knowledge of words from him. She had heard of that happening with very choleric men, which her husband certainly was.

She didn't actually want to go and see him on his deathbed and pretend regret or grief. She had no regrets. She had done her level best to be a good wife to him and if God was calling him to Judgement, that was God's decision. She had a good jointure of £500 per annum thanks to Lord Hunsdon who had arranged the marriage, which she had no doubt she would be able to live on. After a decent pause, she could allow Robin to make suit to her and perhaps marry...

She stopped herself thinking in that direction, because she simply couldn't imagine it. She couldn't imagine that the man who was her husband would actually die. It's as if her mind balked like a horse at a fence.

I might as well get up and get the unpleasantness over with, she thought, so she got up, made the bed, and dressed herself in her hunting habit again, without even the help of a mirror. Then she went out into the barnekin which was still full of strange horses, and paused to frown at the strangers on the walls looking down at her, then went to the stableyard to greet Mouse and Rat as she usually did when she could.

Suddenly there was a shout, and a flurry of boots. A party of men marched into the stableyard. At first she thought they might be a raiding party... But no, for there was her husband in the middle of them, looking very pleased with himself.

Just for a moment the world rocked around her. But he was dying, he had had an apoplexy...

No such thing, came an imperious voice inside her, in fact you have been tricked.

Sir Henry was red-faced as usual, with his lips pushed upwards in a highly satisfied expression. Beside him was Lord Spynie, looking highly satisfied as well and another man, a minister by his long black silk gown. The other men weren't Widdringtons, they looked like they were from Edinburgh and no doubt were Spynie's hangers-on and henchmen.

Had Roger Widdrington lied to her then? But why? And where was he?

She caught herself and stopped staring in confusion.

She immediately curtseyed to her husband and his lordship, as was right and proper. She stayed on one knee when he didn't acknowledge her. He nodded at the Minister who produced a paper that he read over her in a brass tone of accusation.

It took her halfway through the reading before she caught up with what was happening and stood up. Her own husband, with the help of the Minister, was indicting her on a charge of...

Witchcraft? To wit, that she had enchanted his privy member, causing it to fail, and put a curse of gout on him so he had gravel in his bladder.

She almost laughed out of sheer bewilderment and because the whole thing was so ridiculous. Of course, there were witches who did such things, but she wasn't a witch. She was a good Protestant woman and considerably more inclined to pray than Sir Henry. She had never done any scrying or charms, unless you counted normal country charms like hanging wormwood branches over the dairy windows to keep the faery folk away. She most certainly had never taken any lovers as she was now accused of doing, nor flown to meet Sir Robert Carey on a broomstick, though, by God, if she only knew how, she would do it now.

Her escape from Geordie Burn was now due to a spell; her bringing draughts and possets to people in the villages who were ill, was magic; she had even glamoured the Queen herself.

And the thing got less and less funny and more and more frightening as she looked at hard-faced men who wanted to put her down.

She was so outraged she stood up straight in complete silence and when the catalogue of idiocy was coming to an end she said nothing until finally the Minister, whoever he was, ended with an exhortation to admit her crimes of witchcraft, confess her sins and perhaps save her soul from Hell where her lover the Devil waited for her.

"How d'ye plead, woman?" said Sir Henry, grimly.

She was furious and humiliated but she did not speak at once. The silence drew out until some of the men at the back started shifting around.

Finally, she said, in a voice which trembled, damn it, because she was so angry, "I am not guilty of any and all charges, Sir Henry Widdrington, my lawful husband. I am not a witch, I have never been a witch and I am a good Protestant woman. I have done my best to serve you as a good wife should. How dare you accuse me? How dare you, you and your Court friend and his pet Minister? Your gout comes from God to punish you for your ill treatment of me. I have done my best: I have nursed you when you were ill and run your estate for you as best I can while you gallivant after that revolting creature Lord Spynie. As for Sir Robert Carey, I have been a good honest wife to you and never have I taken any lover, especially not Sir Robert."

Now he slapped her, quite hard, but she had held in so many words over the years it was a dark thrill to speak them now. "Shut up!" he said.

"By God and His Son, Jesus Christ, who was also arrested unjustly, I am no witch and I will swear it on the Bible..."

He hit her again and her nose started to bleed.

Suddenly she was held by strong men who had come up behind her. Her wrists were gripped and tied behind her and the Minister came towards her with a little smile on his face. He was holding some kind of harness or frame. Her head was held still by her hair, her hat knocked off, and she tried to fight, brought her knee up, hampered by her heavy skirt. A thing made of sharp metal was forced into her mouth and fastened there by straps and a metal bar.

"There," said the Minister, rubbing his crotch, "you will not be able to make any incantations and the bridle will teach you some humility."

She tried to speak and found the words came out as meaningless noise. The straps and metal bar were cutting into her face, holding her head tightly. It was a scold's bridle. Her own husband had put a scold's bridle on her.

The metal bit had a foul bitter taste of iron and she drew her lips and tongue back from it as far as she could. They grabbed her by the bridle itself and her shoulders, pushed her through the castleyard where there was a whirling of faces – she recognised some of them, there was John's wife, Amelia, looking shocked, Young Hutchin Graham with his mouth open like a handsome codfish – then she was shoved through the gate into the stable yard again and round to the place where the jakes and the dungheap was and a couple of woodstores. They pushed her into a woodstore. They slammed the door and locked it and she could hear her husband and Lord Spynie congratulating each other. Then they left her there, shaking, in the dark, the alien metal still invading her mouth so she couldn't close her teeth or lips. Her hands were still behind her, still tied tightly.

Her knees were trembling so that she thought she might fall. She tried kicking the door, but hurt her toes, tried rubbing the scold's bridle off her face but it was on too tight.

She had to sit down so she sat on a pile of cut wood. How long she sat there, she didn't know. She was still furious but gradually the sustaining anger faded and bled and drained away, leaving her feeling hollow and terrified.

Maybe she dozed off. She came to in an even greater darkness when somebody scratched on the door. For a moment she couldn't think where she was or what had happened.

"Missus," came Young Hutchin's voice, "Missus, are ye there?"

She tried to say something but it came out as "Yaya ya."

"Gimme some token to show the Courtier."

She had nothing... Or no, she did, she had something, but could she get it off her hand? She strained her fingers to reach it, pulled and pulled with her numb fingers, but thank the Lord, the old handfasting ring from her mother wasn't tight on her and she got it off. Damn it, she'd dropped it!

She took a deep breath and another one to calm herself although her heart was thundering again. Very carefully she sat down on the floor next to the door, felt about with her tied hands for the ring... Stone flags, bits of wood, insects, odd little balls of dung, a pillbug that escaped, metal... But not the ring. Yes it was, it had split when she dropped it. She couldn't tell which half it was, the man's half with the diamond, or the woman's half.

Never mind, she had it in her fist now. "Uh-in!" she said, frightened he had given up and gone away.

"Ay missus," his voice was low but there was something steady in it.

The door was high off the floor so it wouldn't stick in the damp. She pushed the ring to the gap, pushed again, sweating hard now, drips going down around the straps, she found a long splint of wood, pushed the ring further and further...

"Ay, I got yer ring missus..."

"Ur Obet Ca'ey"

"Ay missus, Ah'll tek it tae the Courtier, dinna fash yerself."

She heard him stand and then didn't hear him leave because he must have taken his clogs off.

She leaned against the door with no energy to get up, longing and longing for Robin to come and make it all better again, longing to feel his arms around her. She dozed off and was woken by a shouting and tumult over by the stables, Hutchin's voice raised in excuse and then swearing and then the thudding sound of someone being hit and the other voices of Jamie's Jock, Wattie and Barney, the other stable boys, all in a confused medley of shouting. Then a scuffling sound and another door shutting.

Then the measured sound of boots coming towards her.

"We have taken your messenger to your lover," said the witchfinder, "Young Hutchin Graham, yes? He's in the tool cellar." Elizabeth's eyes opened and the ghostly arms of Robin holding her flicked into non-existence. Sir Robert would not be coming.

The minister gave a dry little chuckle. "Dinna be concerned," he said. "We have already written to your lover ourselves. I'm looking forward tae meeting him."

The tread of boots went away, and Elizabeth's heart sank as she realised that they were planning to indict Robin for witchcraft too. Would they lure him to Widdrington to rescue her and trap him somehow? Men could be witches too – hadn't the second Earl of Bothwell got into serious trouble with accusations that he had been trying to cast a spell on King James in North Berwick of all places. He had got away with it, but most of the other people accused with him had hanged. She couldn't remember the details.

She couldn't even pray properly to God because her mouth was full of metal. She couldn't with her hands behind her, and she needed to piss desperately.

Jesu, she was exhausted. She leaned her back against the door and forced herself upright, scrabbled with hands that felt like sausages to pull up her riding kirtle and petticoats and her shift and stood with her legs wide to pee. Then she remembered that she had her courses and so there was a pad of rags there and she let go with some difficulty and pissed into that. Some dripped down her leg. It was disgusting. She let her skirts and petticoat drop, sat down squishily on the ground and just like that found tears coming out of her eyes and dripping down her face, over the straps and metal of the scold's bridle.

She let them fall, not caring that her face would go blotchy and her eyes swell. What did it matter? She couldn't even hope that Robin would come and help her because if he came, he would be accused of witchcraft too.

FRIDAY 2ND MARCH 1593, WIDDRINGTON

Jane woke up in the dairymaids' chamber before dawn. She always slept very well and particularly well after she had spent a day to go and see her mother which she had done the day before. She stared in shock to see one of the other maids, a skinny young scrap of a thing, sitting hunched up in a corner and crying into her apron.

Jane sat up and swung her legs down, leaving Marjorie and Ann who she shared the bed with still snoring. "What's wrong, Little May?"

"I'm frightened."

Was it thunderstorms and pigs still or was it something else?

"Why?"

"I'm afeared of witches and the missus is a witch and what will become of me?"

Jane got out of bed, resisted the impulse to slap the girl, pulled on her kirtle and her boots, went to her and held her heaving shoulders. "Whit are ye talking about, the missus isnae a witch?"

The girl started crying harder. "She come in the day afore yesterday and yesterday they came and arrested her and the Minister read a paper saying she was a witch and Sir Henry says she is and pit her in the woodstore all day and... and... Young Hutchin tried to steal the minister's horse to get to Carlisle and... and..."

Jane was utterly shocked. It always took her a full day to see her mother because her family's bastle was about twelve miles away from Widdrington. She usually left after milking her cows before dawn and came back long after sunset to milk them again. She had missed the whole thing.

"I never heard such blather," said Jane at last, pulling up the laces of her kirtle tight and tying them. "Why would Lady Widdrington need to send a messenger to Carlisle if she's a witch, eh?" This silenced Little May. Jane put her cap on and tied it at the back. "Ye say she's in the woodstore?"

"Ay and she canna talk cos the Minister put a thing on her that stops her tongue..."

"Jesu. Where's Young Hutchin?"

"In the castle cellars."

Jane looked at Little May with new appreciation. She was so small and generally annoying, but she must have been hiding and listening hard yesterday while Jane was away.

Jane nodded. "Ay, thank ee," she said, with a strange feeling in her heart, as if it was bigger than she realised and was ready for something. "Now Little May, I'd say ye should go home to yer mam, if you're that frightened, d'ye think?"

Little May nodded vigorously and picked up her blanket and pillow, folded the blanket tidily, blew her nose in her apron. "Can ye take me? It's ainly three miles but I'm scared to go on my own."

"I've got my kine to milk and ye should be washing the dairy floor, let's get some work done, eh?"

Jane went down the stepladder into the dairy yard which was small and only had a few looseboxes for cows in calf and sickening for something. Little May crept after her. Most of the milch kine were kept out on infield pasture - unless the bells were ringing round the country in warning of a raid, at which time it was her job to go out and help the men bring the cattle in. She had had to do it three times and had found the confusion and the shouting terrifying. It had been the hardest thing she had ever done, to keep her countenance with the bells ringing and fire on a distant hilltop and the men running around shouting, and then she had had to catch Fireweed, the lead cow who trusted her, and put a halter on her while she tossed her head and then run with her back to the castle with the other kine thundering behind.

She picked up two buckets and went to the castle yard for water, wandered near the woodshed but she saw there was a man standing there to guard the door. It was best not to go near Lady Widdrington although she longed to do something to help her. But a charge of witchcraft is catching, especially if you're a woman.

So she turned away and went to her few milch kine who were lowing urgently to be milked and milked them all as fast as she could. Then there was a commotion of the bell being rung in the daytime which was so unusual, everybody ran to the castle yard to see what was happening.

***

They had cleared all the hurdles for fencing the kine and the sheep when there was a raid, so the castle yard was open and there were two chairs brought from the parlour for Lord Spynie and Sir Henry to sit in. Spynie's henchmen were everywhere and they were setting up the hurdles to separate the people watching from the cleared area. Jane stood to one side and stared and wondered what was going on.

Then she saw a tall man in a long black robe march into the middle of the yard and a woman was brought out in front of him with her hands tied behind her. There was something on her face and she had lost her hat but not her cap and Jane suddenly recognised her as Lady Widdrington. She was squinting and blinking in the dull daylight and finally she shut her eyes and just stood there. She looked desperate and alone. Jane scowled and folded her arms and stared, and Little May crept up behind her with her thumb in her mouth and stood scowling like her.

Spynie's men cut Lady Widdrington's hands free and then shockingly pounced on her and pulled off her kirtle over her head. They did it clumsily and Lady Widdrington struggled to stop them and they cut the laces and stabbed their fingers on the pins but finally it came off and there she was standing in the view of everybody, in only her stays and petticoat. They cut the laces on her stays and pulled it off her, while Sir Henry and Lord Spynie sniggered at her. They cut the ties of her overpetticoat and bumroll and her underpetticoat so they all dropped to the ground and there she was in her shift and nothing else.

Jane had never seen anything so horrible in her life. Lady Widdrington was red in the face for shame at being stripped in public like that. Then Amelia Widdrington, came out and unlaced her riding boots very slowly, ungartered and pulled off her knitted woollen stockings so she was bare-legged and barefoot and then Amelia put her hand up to take Lady Widdrington's cap but Lady Widdrington slapped it away.

She took off her cap herself and dropped it behind her and stood there in her shift which had bloodstains on it, her red hair piled on her head.

Jane felt twisted inside with embarrassment for Lady Widdrington. How could she bear to stand there in just her shift, it was awful, and she had her courses? "Why is there blood?" came Little May's tremulous voice and Jane whispered, "It's her monthlies." She looked around at the crowd and saw that most of the women were looking away and some of the men as well. Some of the young lads were puzzled though and muttering to each other, the idiots.

Amelia Widdrington picked up all the clothes scattered around, bundled them together and went into the castle with them. While she did that, the Minister walked up to Lady Widdrington, and started pulling the pins out of her hair so it fell down, bright and carroty.

And Sir Henry laughed his approval, with one swollen gouty foot up on a table, Lord Spynie drinking and giggling by his side.

"Behold the witch!" said the Minister. People were looking at her and muttering to each other. "Behold the witch!" he said again since this was seemingly not a good enough response. "Behold the witch, Elizabeth Widdrington."

More muttering. At the edges of the crowd some of the women were moving away. Jane looked around her. Would Lady Widdrington's people try and help her?

"See the manifest signs of her guilt," he shouted, "She has taken Satan as her lover and she kisses him on the bum, the blood proves it. The blood is a sign of her guilt for we have made no investigations on her body, and a sign of her defiance, for when she bleeds in the dark of the Moon, a witch is at her strongest."

Jane looked at the man with contempt. Did he think that your courses came when you wanted them, did he think they were like piss?

He brought out a new set of manacles and locked them on Lady Widdrington's wrists where they hung, shiny.

"Now, Elizabeth," said the Minister and got a pungent look from her which should have told him that he had no right to use her Christian name, none at all. "I invite you to confess your witchcraft openly and cleanly in front of this company, now, in the sight of God. Tell us your confederates, tell us the spells you use and tell us your familiar and how you worship Satan."

She was staring at him and doing nothing. Jane thought that was brave of her because she herself would be curled up on the ground with embarrassment and shame. Though why should she feel shame? Lady Widdrington had been stripped by the men, she hadn't taken her clothes off herself.

The Minister went up to her and unlocked the little padlock on the side of the scold's bridle, took it off.

"Confess your guilt," he said to her coaxingly, "and it will go easier with you."

She stood up straight and braced her shoulders. "I am not a witch!" she shouted, ringing through the courtyard, "You should be ashamed of yourself, husband, for what you are doing. I am a good Protestant and if anyone is a witch, it is Lord Spynie over there..."

Lindsay slapped her and nearly knocked her down, Spynie's men grabbed her and the Minister put the scold's bridle on her again.

"Alas," he tutted, "She remains obdurate and will not confess her evil."

Lord Spynie was laughing elaborately, but Sir Henry was scowling as if he had expected her to confess. Do you know your wife so little? Jane thought.

Then they brought out Toad, his hair all on end and his face bruised and bewildered.

Jamie's Jock, one of the stable lads, stepped forward proudly and denounced him as a witch.

"Ay, I seen him," said Jamie's Jock, "many times, he can get horses to stay still and calm, he whispers the horse word to them and they let him do anything he likes wi' 'em which is sorcery, in't it? And there's a cat that he gives scraps to, lives in the stable..."

"His familiar?"

"Whut?"

"A devil disguised as an animal that does his bidding."

"Ay well, she disnae do his bidding, she's a cat, he does her bidding..." There was a fake-sounding guffaw from Lord Spynie and some titters from the people.

"An animal that is his favourite," said Lindsay grimly.

"Ay, and he's got funny eyes and he canna talk properly and he's stupid..."

"All diagnostic of demonic persuasions, my lord."

And so Lindsay called on three of Spynie's thugs and they hit Toad while Lindsay asked the questions.

"Your name is Toad, yes?"

"Y...yesh sir."

"And you serve the Devil, Satan?"

"Who?"

"The Devil. In Hell. You serve him?"

"N... no, sir, I sherve Sir Henry Widdrington, him over there."

The fists struck him in the face and the body and he started crying. "You serve the Devil, yes? When you magic a horse, the Devil helps you to do it, it is a curse from Hell. So you serve the Devil, yes?"

"No, Sir Henry's my master, sir..."

"But you have another master, the Devil, do you not?"

"What?"

More fists. "You serve the Devil, do you not?"

Hunched over and crying bitterly, Toad choked out, "I dunno, maybe sir, if ye say, maybe."

"Good. You serve the Devil because the witch taught you to do so."

"What?"

"You serve the Devil because the witch taught you to."

"Who?"

"The witch. Her. Lady Widdrington."

"Lady Widrinton?"

"Yes. Lady Widdrington is a witch and she taught you to serve the Devil?"

"She did?"

"Yes, and you kissed the Devil's arse and..."

"Sir, what's a witch?"

More fists.

"Do not make a game of me, Toad," said Lindsay coldly, "Do not pretend innocence. You are deep dyed in sin, you will be hanged and you will go to Hell where you will burn in agony for all eternity because you were beguiled by the woman as many better men than you have been beguiled. Only confess your sin to me and you will not go to Hell."

Toad's eyes bugged. "I dinna ken," he wailed, "I dinna ken what's a witch... I dinna ken..."

Elizabeth was looking round the yard for Sam the Man, rumoured to be poor Toad's father, and didn't see him. She almost called out for someone to go fetch him, but the bridle reminded her not to speak. It told her she was helpless here and that she should not hope for Robin to come and rescue her because that would mean his death as well.

This entire performance was for her benefit, she knew, she was being pressured to confess to save Toad. But it seemed to her an utterly false trail because if she confessed to being a witch when she was not a witch, she would betray Christ and herself and Toad would still suffer. But if she didn't confess then Toad would also suffer.

There was no way out, there was no escape. Toad was beaten unconscious and Lindsay started rating Spynie's men for clumsiness. It seemed unconsciousness was not in his plan. Toad was carried into the wine cellar and locked in, they would run out of cellars at this rate.

Lindsay was close to her, she could smell him, as sour as the King of Scotland, he was.

"Will you confess?" he hissed at her.

She looked at him considering. She might have said to him if the branks hadn't been pressing her tongue down: if I confess to being a witch, then you will hang me, after you have tortured me to find out my friends and accomplices. If I do not confess, then you will torture me anyway. Nothing I do will have any effect on what you do, as you have demonstrated. So now nothing you do will have any effect on what I do for as long as I can bear the torture.

She looked away from him and into the middle distance, staring at one of the windows of the hall, recently glazed with good glass at considerable expense. It was something she did when Sir Henry was berating her. Lindsay asked her to confess, ordered her to confess, shouted at her to confess, struck her face, and she ignored him. It seemed he hurt his hand on the scold's bridle so he stopped slapping her and she continued to ignore him.

He gave another mighty sermon on witches and the devil and her womanish evil and obstinacy. All the people in the courtyard shrank into themselves a little. A few listened carefully and nodded, most seemed bewildered. Nobody even tried to defend her. At the back she could see Jane, the dairymaid, with her hands over her mouth and her eyes staring hard and she didn't blame her for not saying anything, but still... It made her feel sad.

When Lady Widdrington had been taken away and locked in the provisions cellar, Jane stood in deep thought for a while and Little May squatted at her feet, sucking her thumb and clinging to her blanket like a much younger child. Finally Jane went in the other direction, to the castle, which was open and talked to the gate guard. Little May trotted after her.

"Fat Malky," she said to him, "I'm to turn the cheeses."

"Ay? In ye go then." He made a big play of gesturing her through as if she was a lady which she thought was silly. "Oh... dinna talk to Young Hutchin, he's in the tool store, the second cellar."

"Ah wouldna lower meself," she said. "what's he done then?"

"Tried to steal Minister Lindsay's horse, that's all."

She rolled her eyes and shook her head. Of course he did, she thought irritably, it wouldna occur to him to get out of the barnekin first and then find a horse to steal, now would it?

She went into the cheese store to which she had a key and started turning the cheeses, every other one, explaining to Little May how to do it. Then she left the maid to carry on struggling the big wheels around and went along the narrow smelly dark passage to the second cellar. She had no keys to the other cellars, especially not the wine cellar, just the cheese store, but she scratched at the door.

"Young Hutchin," she whispered, watching the passage for the shadow of a man coming or for Little May. She could still hear the cheeses being moved.

"Ay." Young Hutchin's voice was muffled, and angry and he sounded as if his nose was stuffed up.

"Did ye have anything to show Sir Robert?"

"Ay, my lady's ring."

"Good. Have ye still got it?"

"Ay, I put it in my mouth, nearly swallowed it twice."

"Gi' it to me."

"Why? Ye canna take it anywhere..."

"Ah can."

"Nah, ye're a maid, ye canna go all the way tae Carlisle."

She didn't have time to argue, the sun was high and she had a lot to do before it got dark. "I'll give it to a man who said he'll take it," she lied, "I think he's a Graham at the horn, working for Spynie and he's angry wi' them."

"A' right then. Get his name, find oot where he comes from and tell him I'll find a way tae thank him. Tell me when he's gone."

"Ay," said Jane, "Ah will."

There was a rustle and a scrape and something bright was pushed under the door. Jane picked up the ring and kissed it. She felt her heart large and brilliant inside herself because she loved Lady Widdrington and she knew that she was only a dairymaid, but she was Jane, she would do this impossible thing for her ladyship as if she was a knight in a story and Lady Widdrington was a damsel in distress.

She couldn't possibly wear the ring because someone would accuse her of stealing it, so she put the ring into her inner stays pocket, where she had a couple of shillings wrapped in leather so as not to chink, to her dowry. She didn't see how she could use the money though, since anywhere she tried to spend it, men would ask awkward questions. Boys her age often carried messages, especially the smaller lighter ones who could go faster. Maids never ventured anywhere, they stayed where they were unless they got kidnapped for ransom in which case they were always blamed for it.

Jane went back to turning the cheeses, thinking how she could do it. Little May was unwontedly silent and helped her with the larger ones. She couldn't get on a carrier's cart, they would want to know why a maid had no companion and they would think she had run away, which in a way was right. Also no doubt some young chancer would try to get her to bed and she couldn't be bothered with it, besides she was a virgin and planned to remain so. All young men were the enemy that way. Even Young Hutchin was. She couldn't even walk in the day time because someone would ask questions and there would be trouble. She sighed. She certainly couldn't run where anybody could see her.

She had to run and she had to run at night when no one would see her once she had gone past her parents' farm, and she had to hope she didn't meet any reivers either. Jesu. So. She needed a leather bottle for ale and she needed some kind of excuse in advance so she could get well away with nobody the wiser.

"Where's yer family, Little May?" she asked.

"Ye go down the Great North Road and ye watch out for a pollarded ash wi' white stones around it and you turn down the lane and ye're there." whispered Little May, "Lady Widdrington wilna come and get me, will she?"

"God save us, of course she won't."

"She might. I'm afeared of her."

Jane could have shaken the child but stopped herself. Little May was frightened of everything, as far as she could tell, which must be very tiring. Jane's own family's bastle was on the Great North Road as well, although twelve miles not three miles away, and there were two sons and a string of daughters nobody could keep track of, older than her and earning their own living as outdoor dairymaids and such. She would say to the Mistress of the Dairy that she was taking Little May home and she had heard a rumour about her own mam being sick and she wanted to make sure she was all right and she would be back late that evening. She thought briefly about taking a horse when she got to the farm, but they needed all the horses when raids came, she wasn't a lady and she didn't know how to ride – though how could it be so difficult if silly lads could do it?

She sent Little May back to the dairy to ask Missus Widdrington if there was any mopping to do. Then she picked up one of the cheeses that had spoiled with blue mould and cut a large lump off it, wrapped it in a cloth and put it in her petticoat pocket. Then she went to the buttery and got a leather bottle filled with small ale that she stoppered tightly and stuffed down the front of her stays.

She went to Miss Widdrington, the Dairy Mistress, who was a harassed forty year old spinster, unbelievably ancient, and told the tale about Little May. The Dairy Mistress actually thanked her for taking Little May home because she was such a nuisance with all the things she was afraid of, but could she take the cows out to the infield first since everything was so far behind.

So Jane went to the cowsheds, found the ones that were in calf and then got Fireweed, the lead cow, an imperious old lady, and led her so the other kine followed as always. Fireweed lowed and sniffed her suspiciously. It was true she was excited and nervous. Had any maid done the journey she was planning before? She didn't think so. A maid couldn't be a knight or even a squire. She had wished she could disguise herself as a boy, but no one would ever believe that since her breasts were so large. But she didn't mind not being delicate and pretty. She was strong and her face was square; she would be like Lady Widdrington when she was taken by Geordie Burn, a story that had grown in the telling; she would be brave and sensible and she would do it.

Little May was trotting after her, clutching her blanket to her breast, her face creased with worry as she looked over her shoulder.

They went to the dairy postern gate and were stopped by one of Spynie's men standing there.

"What are ye doing?" he asked rudely.

"We are taking the kine out to the infield and then I'm taking Little May home to her family," said Jane, outraged that he should presume to ask. Could he not see the kine lined up behind them? Could he not hear them lowing impatiently? She gestured at them.

He didn't like something about Jane, perhaps because he was one of the ones who had beaten Toad up.

"Well bide there..."

"Oh no," burst out Little May, her eyes staring, "Oh no, Lady Widdrington will catch us, she will, and she'll turn us into a toad and I'm so frightened..." And she burst into tears and squealed and cried and the man looked over his shoulder in case anyone should blame him for the noise and the snot, and he waved them on quickly. Jane trotted with Fireweed, followed by the ten cows who were hungry for the grass in the pasture, what there was of it and Little May trotted still gulping and hiccupping behind her, occasionally looking over her shoulder.

Once the kine were into the infield, which needed resting really, they went on down the Great North Road, walking fast and trotting sometimes. It turned out that every fifth tree had white stones around it, but Little May knew which was the right tree and guided Jane to her home. It was a small cottage with half walls of stone and the rest wattle and daub and thatch on the top and marks of burning on the stone from a big raid a couple of years ago. Little May's mam had died in the cottage, trying to rescue the littlest babby and failing.

Little May rushed up to a girl who was feeding chickens in the yard and grabbed her and started telling her how Lady Widdrington had turned into a witch and how she was frightened. Jane waited for a gap in the explanation and told Little May's big sister why she had brought Little May home and was thanked and offered a drink of ale which she accepted gladly. Then she said she had to head for her own family farm, and left as the sun started westering.

She kilted her kirtle up into her belt as she always did when she ran home, made sure her knitting needles and wool were in her needle case on her belt and she had her eating knife, got onto the path that led south to the Great North Road and started off slowly.

SUNDAY 4TH MARCH 1593, CARLISLE

Nicholas Stephenson was his real name but he called himself Nick Smithson as his nom de guerre since he was indeed the younger son of a smith, from a village near Hereford. He had been full of enthusiasm when he had followed his lord, the Earl of Essex on the biggest adventure of his life to the French wars.

Now only two years later, he felt ten years older and looked back on the excitable young fool he had been with a sort of wonder at how completely naïve and idiotic the boy was. Along with the other soldiers of the troop and the old Spaniard, he had come back to England after the Earl had just left them there, abandoned them in hostile France, clearly not giving a farthing for their lives, nor indeed a penny of pay either.

He had loathed the business near Oxford, although he had robbed travellers with the rest of them. They had found a place to live in the wrecked monastery, burnt fifty years earlier because the monks had rebelled when they were told to leave. Don Jeronimo, the old Spanish tercio, had terrified and intrigued him and he had listened to his tall tales and found him laudanum in Oxford for his pain.

Their lives had settled to something not quite as awful as being wandering upright men and then they had beaten up another traveller and that one had been Sergeant Dodd. Sergeant Dodd had somehow broken out and taken over the troop. He had got rid of Captain

Leigh, killed Jones and Peter Sheffield, challenged them all to stop him becoming their captain. Nobody had taken the challenge except Mr Arden who promptly died of it. The hard-faced incomprehensible northerner had told them his right name and promised them a way of living as soldiers in Carlisle. The remains of the troop had chosen Nick to give Sergeant Dodd their answer and he had felt sick with fear as he carried his eating knife on his palms over to Dodd and offered it to him on bended knee, as the custom was in the Netherlands and France. But afterwards there was a feeling of relief, a feeling of lightness. Did they now really have a captain who could do the job?

Nobody had liked the way he made them clean and sharpen their swords, although Nick Stephenson, the smith's son, could see the sense in that. And they had walked to Oxford to meet Sir Robert Carey, who was Dodd's captain, and found they had a long way to walk to Carlisle, although at least they had food to eat as they tramped their way north.

In the few months since then, Nick had learned how to understand the northerners quite well, and was starting to pick up the accent: he had learned much better marksmanship with a gun and bow; he had started learning Cumbrian wrestling; got a lot better at riding although he still preferred his feet and had begun to seriously admire Carey after the incident at Dick of Dryhope's tower.

He climbed the narrow spiral stairs in the dark to the top of the Queen Mary Tower to give Sir Robert a message, expecting him to be in bed by then. But he found him sitting in the dark, staring into space and a pile of letters in front of him.

"Sir?" he asked, wondering at it. Carey was a lover of mornings and would be taking his men out on patrol the next night. He normally tried to stock up on sleep the night before a patrol. Carey didn't seem to hear. "Sir!"

"Er... yes, Smithson."

"Message for you, sir, from my Lord Scrope."

Nick came into the office, nearly tripped on a half-grown hunting dog lying directly in his path. Jack yelped and moved for him, trotted over to where Carey sat, pushed his nose into Carey's crotch and let out a worried little whine. Carey fondled his ears absent-mindedly.

Was he drunk?

"Shall I fetch a candle for you, sir?" The one on the desk had burned down.

"No. Would you despatch these letters for me?" They were all neatly folded and sealed. "These must go tonight by special messenger, one to Mr Anricks in Keswick or wherever he is now, possibly Bristol, the other to my father in London."

"Yes sir." There was something odd about the way the man spoke, as if his teeth were clenched and the words had to fight their way out.

"I'm going to visit Sergeant Dodd in Gilsland and I won't be back in time to take the patrol so Acting Sergeant Andy Nixon will take it.

"Yes sir," That had been the arrangement while Carey had been busy in Keswick. Nick wanted to ask what was wrong, what had happened, but felt nervous of doing it. Why?

Jack suddenly barked and growled but Carey tapped his nose in warning and stood up. Nick instinctively backed up a few steps and then realised why as Carey turned his face and the glow from the fire caught it. Even with so little light, Nick could see that he was white with rage, his whole body was stiff with it.

"Sir, what's happened?"

Carey paused and then said, "My Lady Widdrington is in... she is in danger. I am planning to rescue her in whatever way I can."

Carey's hopeless love for Elizabeth Widdrington was notorious among the garrison where the book on whether he had had her yet was approaching a hundred notional pounds, although those who had actually met the lady when she was in Carlisle or Dumfries, bet against.

"I'm sorry to hear that, sir," said Nick, taking the pile of letters in his hands. "Is there anything we can do to help?"

Carey stopped on the landing and looked assessingly at him. "Who? The men of the castle guard?"

"No sir, I was thinking of us, Hieronimo's troop." That was what they called themselves now, since none of them had any respect at all for their erstwhile Captain Leigh or that able but sad drunk, John Arden. It was also perverse to call themselves after a dead Spanish nobleman who hadn't even been the captain, but there were good reasons for it and Nick liked the exotic ring of the name.

For a moment, Carey looked as if he was about to give Nick a curt no, but then he paused and thought.

"There might be," he said slowly. "Would you be willing to come to the East March?"

"When, sir?"

"As soon as you can."

"Leave Carlisle?"

"Yes. I have... I have business with the East March Deputy Warden, Sir Henry Widdrington. Some soldiers might be a very good idea."

Nick felt a little winded because essentially Sir Robert was asking Hieronimo's troop to desert and help him with his personal business. He paused. Then he said, although he wasn't entirely sure why, "I'll do it sir, and I'll ask the others if they want to come with me. I think we could leave tomorrow night, or possibly earlier."

"Do what you can," said the Courtier, "I'd appreciate it."

Suddenly he extended his hand and Nick shook it. Then the Courtier turned away. "I'm for Gilsland. I'll be rousting Sergeant Dodd out of bed, so wish me luck."

Nick grinned. Sergeant Dodd was famously ill-tempered immediately on waking, and dangerous to boot. "Good luck sir, we'll see you near Widdrington."

Carey nodded and clattered down the stairs, followed by the dog. Nick paused and looked at the letters in his hands, paused again because he had glimpsed the last one and it was addressed to Lord Scrope. That one wasn't sealed because the Warden was in the Warden's Lodgings. On impulse he took a spill from the glowing charcoals in the fireplace, lit a watch candle and as the light brightened, sat and squinted to read the hurried Italic. He had learned to read as a boy at a dame school, kept by an old nun, the first in his family to learn.

It was Carey's letter of resignation from the Deputyship.

"Jesu," he whispered because that told him far more than he had realised about what Carey was planning. His first impulse was to burn it, but then he thought again and slid the refolded letter under a heap of fodder and horse-coper bills. Then he stood, conscientiously covered the fire, and clattered down the stairs himself in the new boots he had just bought himself with his pay.

SUNDAY 4TH MARCH 1593, CARLISLE

He came into the hall at almost a run. The other seven men of Heronimo's Troop were organising their pallets and blankets in their usual space near the fire, which was already curfewed. Nick saw that East had set up his pallet for him. True, there was a bunkhouse for the men of the guard, with a tiny cubbyhole for the Sergeant, currently slept in by Andy Nixon and his wife, but those beds were all taken, some of them twice, many of them by inheritance, and nobody fancied tripling up.

He beckoned them into a corner where there was a bench which he sat on. There he put the proposition to them: that Carey's woman was in some kind of danger; that Carey was riding to Gilsland to find Dodd who was only part-recovered from a near death-wound that would have killed anyone less stubborn, and that there would probably be some kind of fighting with the Widdringtons. And that he personally would be going to the East March to see if he could help Carey in some way.

He didn't mention that Dodd had promised them food they could mostly eat and a place to sleep that didn't leak and that Carey had kept that promise. He didn't mention that since they had got to Carlisle in October they had actually been paid - money, not tickets - by Carey personally. And that this had happened twice, the second time allegedly with Carey's winnings from playing primero with the courtiers at King James's Court, the first two times they had ever been paid anything at all for soldiering in more than two years of doing it.

They looked at each other, the remnants of fifty strong young men from the Earl of Essex's lands on the Marches of Wales. Even Clockface was nodding slowly.

"Will there be pay?" asked Garron, ever practical.

"Probably not," said Nick.

Everybody nodded solemnly again. Nobody really expected to be paid for something like this, except perhaps in loot.

"Well, where's Widdrington?" asked Falls Off His Horse Perkins.

"East March, about halfway to Berwick up the Great North Road," said East, who often knew that kind of thing.

That gave Nick an idea. He asked around and found nobody had any paper for a letter and then asked for a volunteer to ride to the other half of Hieronimo's Troop in Berwick garrison, where they had been sent to serve under Carey's brother, John Carey. He was to ask them if they wanted to join in and if so to meet them outside Widdrington in two days' time or anywhere else they thought good. Tarrant volunteered for it since he was a better rider and his brother Skelly was at Berwick.

Everybody nodded again in approval. The other eight men of their troop had been sent to Berwick because Mr John Carey, Chamberlain of Berwick, was always short of men and it couldn't be helped, but it would be nice to see them all again.

Nick tried to sleep on his lumpy palliass but found his head was boiling with ideas. The men needed weapons – each now had a plain metal helmet and either a buffcoat or an ancient jack, often with old blood stains on it and a mended hole. They had lances from the armoury and daggers, some of them had swords including Nick who had acquired his from John Arden's corpse. Nobody had any firearms although there were sound ones straight from the Tower of London now in the armoury. However nobody had a key to the armoury obviously, although Acting Sergeant Nixon did.

Was it worth asking him? Nick wondered and decided that it was, because Andy deserved to know what Hieronimo's Troop was up to.

SUN 4TH MARCH 1593, GILSLAND

Carey rode the sixteen miles to Gilsland in a couple of hours thanks to the Reivers' Moon that poked its head out of the clouds every so often and the road which had been mended again on his insistence.

Carey did his best not to let his imagination run wild over the information Jane Fenwick had given him after her extraordinary journey. It made his blood run cold that Elizabeth had been accused of witchcraft by her own husband, who was the Deputy Warden of the East March which he ruled in Lord Hunsdon's absence. And he had Lord Spynie's men to back him, maybe fifty of them.

Of course, Carey had written to his father, begging him to come north and exert some authority, but he didn't know when his father would get the letter or if he would do anything about it in time. He couldn't stop himself thinking about the scold's bridle which stopped Elizabeth speaking and he also couldn't stop himself thinking about how he could best kill Lord Spynie, which tended to get over-elaborate.

Sometimes as he rode, he looked at Elizabeth's ring, the woman's hand part of it, which was shining on his left little finger. He had forgotten his gloves in his hurry to leave Carlisle. Obviously he must get her out, get her free of Sir Henry and ideally kill Sir Henry as well, but he wasn't at all sure how it could be done. His heart kept coming up with simple solutions and his logical mind kept telling his heart that those solutions would put Elizabeth in more danger and probably lead to her hanging.

For a start there was the legal position. He hadn't been able to talk to Richard Bell before he left, but he thought he now understood the peculiarities of the March law at least better than he had. Sir Henry Widdrington, as Deputy Warden, was the chief magistrate in the East March, just as Carey theoretically was the chief magistrate in the West March. In fact, the other Deputy Warden, Sir Richard Lowther kept a very tight grip on the law courts and let Carey have none at all of the profits from fines and confiscations. But anyway, Carey's theoretical jurisdiction was in the West March of course. He had no official authority in the East March.

According to Marcher Law, a Warden or Deputy Warden as an officer of the Crown, could accuse, arraign and find guilty a raider simply on his say-so. The phrase was "of his own knowing." Sir Henry could say that a person had done the crime and Sir Henry knew he had, so he could be hanged. Carey had always thought that such justice was rough but necessary for the greater good of the Border, but now...

It was unheard of that a Deputy Warden should accuse his own wife of such a crime as witchcraft, but since he had, as far as Carey could work it out, he could also declare of his own knowing that she was a witch and hang her. It would be legal according to the Leges Marchiorum.

The law couldn't really help him. He had not only written to his father, he had also written to King James of Scotland, begging him to help, but he knew it was very unlikely that the hunting-mad monarch would pay any attention to business until he had finished his hunt.

That left force. He thought it might be the only answer but he was struggling to find some other answer, to get her out by guile, because when you started a fight, you never knew how it would end and he was convinced that Sir Henry would simply string Elizabeth up rather than lose her, especially to him.

His stomach was clenched in a hard knot under his breastbone with rage and fear of what Sir Henry, Lord Spynie and his tame witchfinder would do to Elizabeth.

That scold's bridle... He had heard of such things, never seen one. Once he might have laughed at the thought that in the last resort a man could use one to get his wife to shut up. He wasn't laughing now. Whenever his thoughts fell over that rock, they started to fight each other until all he could do was pray incoherently for Elizabeth.

He was riding alongside the Giant's Wall now, not slowing very much as he covered the last couple of miles to Dodd's tower. Gilsland was a point where many reivers' roads entered England from Scotland – and admittedly Scotland from England. He slowed his horse as he came in sight of the sleeping barnekin with only smoke going up from the baker's oven. It kept puzzling him that the alarm bells weren't sounding from Carlisle cathedral and spreading ripples of clangour out to warn the Border of incoming raiders. He felt it should be but tonight all was quiet, perhaps because the moon was bright, and everyone had been so busy the week before that they were tired and taking a break from cattle-rustling.

He clattered over the drawbridge, found the main gate locked as it should be at this time of night and tried the equally locked postern gate. Hammering on it with his fist relieved a tiny bit of the tension in him and he almost thumped the large gentle-faced man in the chest when he opened it with a sword in his hand.

"Where's the raid, Deputy?"

"Big Clem Pringle," said Carey in a rush and then got a hold of himself. "Is the Sergeant there, I need to speak to him urgently."

"Ay," said Big Clem, "Is it wardenry business?"

"Not exactly," admitted Carey, "but it is very urgent."

"Ay, well, where are yer men... Good God, man, ye're all alone, are ye wood?"

"Er..."

"Ye havena even got Jack with ye, and he's the softest lymer I've ever known. Richie Graham o' Brackenhill has offered fifteen pound English for yer heid, ye do realise?"

"Yes I do," said Carey, "but I don't have time to worry about that now. Where is Dodd?"

"In bed wi' his wife, what do ye expect...?"

"I'll wake Janet... er... Mrs Dodd," said Carey, slipping into the barnekin. "Then she can wake Dodd."

Big Clem shook his head and went back to his watch. Carey went up the ladder to the first floor, stepped over a large number of Armstrongs dossing down on the rushes in the hall, ran up the spiral stairs and nearly got stabbed in the face by Janet in her shift. He reared his head back just in time and turned, the dagger scraped across the stones in a shower of sparks.

She recognised him a fraction of a second later and put her weapon down.

"What the Devil are ye doing here, Courtier. It's hours before dawn."

"I'm very sorry Mrs Dodd but I desperately need your husband's advice."

"Why?" She pushed his doublet front and he backed down the stairs to a passing place set into the wall where they could stand and talk and didn't have to stand so near each other which was troubling to Carey, if not to Janet.

He explained as quickly as he could and as soon as he finished, he heard Janet say "Jesus Christ" deep in her throat.

"Ye ken he's still not a well man," she said, "the ride out to the Tarras Moss the day afore yesterday tired him out."

"I know Mrs Dodd, but..."

"Ay, ye can waken him then, but be careful..."

Not entirely happy with this, Carey tiptoed up the stairs and into the Dodds' chief bedroom, saw nobody in the bed and froze when he felt a loaded crossbow nudge him in the kidneys.

Lifting his hands, he turned and saw Dodd with an actual shy grin on his face as he took out the bolt and released the string.

"Naething wakes me faster than a man tiptoeing on the stairs," said Dodd.

"Of course," Carey said, letting his breath out, "I'm sorry, Sergeant, I should have gone on hammering and shouting and then I could have surprised ye in yer bed."

"Ay," said Dodd, going purposefully to a table with a flask and two horn cups on it. "Though I dinna sleep so well as I did."

"Does your back still pain you?"

"Now and again," Dodd admitted, pouring whishke be into the cups and giving Carey one. "Whit is it? Ye'll never tell me ye've changed yer mind and ye want me tae help ye plan a rough wedding for that married woman o' yourn."

"Yes," said Carey, a little surprised. "How do you know?"

"Och, no bells so it's not a Border matter. Ye're on yer ain and in yer jack and helmet and it's so late it's early. So it's bloody obvious. Either that or ye've killed somebody in a duel, probably Lowther, and ye need to get tae the Netherlands."

Carey grunted. Normally he would have laughed.

Dodd gestured at a stool by the bed and Carey sat while Dodd lay back down on the pillows and sipped the booze.

Carey looked at the canny face with the perpetual grim expression and started to explain. Within minutes Dodd was sitting up again and his mouth turning down further and further. When Carey finished, he was silent for a minute.

"Whit are ye gaunae do about it?" he asked curiously.

Carey explained some of his ideas and Dodd groaned. "Och, Jesus," he said, "ye're going at it sae complicated, why not just turn up wi' a noose round yer neck and surrender and be done wi' it."

"You remember Widdrington Castle, don't you, Sergeant? Would you say it was an easy nut to crack?"

"Ay, but if ye can but get into the barnekin..."

"It'll be locked up tight. And it would be very easy for Sir Henry to hang her before we get anywhere at all. And Lord Spynie's there with his men."

"Ay," said Dodd, "That's a problem."

"We have to get her out first. And of course, they know that." Carey sighed.

"Umm... is Young Henry Widdrington hereabouts?"

"I think he's still at the King's court,"

"And have ye called out yer affinity? Ah think ye could raise about fifty men or more if ye set yer mind to it, or a hundred wi' Jock o'th'Peartree."

"I've written to my father and King James..."

"Who gives a toss for them?"

"Well my father is still the actual Warden of the East March, even if he's not in the north very often nowadays."

Dodd grunted.

"And ye know," said Carey, "I'll raid Widdrington for sure, burn it down around Sir Henry's ugly ears, but not before I've gotten Lady Widdrington away from there."

Dodd couldn't believe what he was hearing – was the Courtier finally talking sense?

"Whit about the Queen?"

"What about her? If I marry Lady Widdrington she'll be furious with me anyway. I'll probably end in the Tower if she catches me."

"And yer office?"

"I left a letter of resignation for Scrope. Whatever I do, it will be as my own man not as a Deputy Warden."

"Ay," said Dodd thinking that was a pity. "And whit will ye do after Widdrington is in ashes?"

"And Sir Henry kicking from his own castle gate?"

"Ay."

"I'll be at the horn in England for sure, so I'll leave."

"Where will ye go? The Low Countries?"

"No, Sergeant, I'll go to the King of Scotland. I'm sure he'll find a use for me at his Court and Elizabeth is already in favour with his Queen. Although she'll be... Well, neither Scottish monarch has Her Majesty of England's romantical notions of their courtiers never wedding."

Dodd tapped his horn cup on the table. "Ay," he said, "But ye canna do aught until ye've broken the woman free, alive and unhanged."

"Precisely."

"Ay."

They were both silent. Carey broached almost timidly the only good idea he had had. Dodd listened to it, his mouth turning down, sourer and longer until finally Dodd asked conversationally, "Are ye wood?"

"I know it's not the best of my ideas but..."

"Ah mean, d'ye want tae end up hangit beside her?"

"Well no but..."

"And ye canna disguise as a pedlar again, they all know that trick."

"I know," sighed Carey.

MONDAY 5TH MARCH 1593, GILSLAND

Dodd was up early for him and digging his smart London suit out of the clothes chest and putting it on with Janet's help. They had had a massive argument over whether Dodd should ride to Widdrington that day and another one about the way he was refusing to share all his plans with her. She suggested bribing everybody.

Dodd shook his head. "Wilna stop Sir Henry hanging her. Also Lord Spynie is there with his pet witchfinder and a troop of fifty and he wants revenge on the Courtier."

"But you canna ride all that way, Henry, your back might bleed again..."

"Phooey! Ah'm no' made o' rose petals, woman."

Janet took breath to speak and then stopped herself. She recognised the expression on Dodd's face, and she had admittedly never once argued him out of anything while he was wearing it.

She tried a new tack, planning furiously. "Ay, well," she said pointedly, "at least I've got a babe to remember ye by if it lives and ye dinna."

He suddenly grinned at her, like summer lightening, and he caught her to him and kissed her and she held him tight, smelling his musk, feeling his heartbeat, and he was going, he was leaving her. As men did. The men went into battle, the women stayed behind, it was the way of the world and a good reason for not loving your husband too much, especially on the Border. But.

It was too late for her. The deed was done.

For a moment she just stood there, feeling the heft of him, the way his fever had wasted his flesh terribly but the solidity was slowly coming back. She pushed him away and turned him, lifted his doublet but she had forgotten about the waistcoat holding up his fashionable canion hose.

"Can I at least check the scar, Henry?"

For a moment, she thought he might refuse, but he unbuttoned the waistcoat and shrugged his shoulders out of the armholes so she could lift his shirt.

His poor back... There was an ugly scar there, gnarled and purple, but no part of it was red nor smelled bad, no part of it was hot, it was slowly turning into just a scar. Very gently she kissed it better and then pulled his shirt down again.

"Ah ken it's much better," said Dodd, "it disnae even itch."

"Does it still catch ye when ye ride?"

"Sometimes," he admitted reluctantly, "but I think that's the scar pulling."

"Mebbe ye could rub some butter or goosefat into it, just to soften it."

"Hmf."

"And Henry, will ye please take it... I don't know... just a little bit more gently, eh? Just a bit?"

Dodd took a breath and then his face relaxed and his shy smile peeped out again. Two in one morning? Wonders will never cease!

"Ay," he said, "Ah will."

Carey had got up before dawn and gone down the stairs from the little guest chamber next to their bedroom. They found him in the first floor hall where the porridge was and he was tipping salt into a bowl of oats with his knife blade. He didn't look as if he had slept well, he had circles under his eyes, but he tipped his hat to Janet's curtsey and Dodd's salute.

Sitting opposite him was Mrs Hogg, the midwife who had come to help Ellen when her babe came too soon, in the autumn. She was looking tired as well.

Janet went to her at once and greeted her, "Mrs Hogg, I'm pleased to see ye, but my babby's by far not ready yet." Mrs Hogg was eating her porridge.

"I came to Goody Pringle so I thocht I'd see ye as well, Missus Dodd, while I was here."

"Ay, but surely..."

"Get yer porridge first."

Janet had had no courses since before Christmas and had felt sick in the mornings until recently. She thought she could feel a hard lump right down in her stomach, though not very big, and wondered was that it, was that the babby?

Suddenly Dodd pulled her aside. He felt in his shirt and pulled out the little leather bag of his amulet hanging round his neck, that Janet had bought for him from Mrs Hogg. "Ah want another one of those."

"Why? One's enough to do the job."

"Ay, it's kept me lucky, I think, so I want one for the Courtier. Tae make him luckier, ye follow."

"Jesu," said Janet, "is yer plan that bad?"

"Nay," said Dodd, looking offended. "It's as good as we can get it, considering... Well anyway, a bit of good luck wouldna hurt."

Janet shook her head and went to Mrs Hogg and asked her for an amulet for the Courtier and Mrs Hogg looked dubious. "D'ye think he'd wear it?"

Janet shrugged so Mrs Hogg put her hand in her bag and brought out several tiny leather bags. "No, they're no good."

"Why not?"

"Sir Robert disna need protection in childbed," she said drily. She delved again and found a larger one. "Here ye are, Missus, it's for luck in battle and St Michael's protection against evil."

"Perfect," said Janet.

"Now can we go tae yer bedroom. Ah want to feel yer belly."

Janet gave the amulet to her husband. "Luck in battle, protection from evil." He gave it back.

"I want ye to slip it in his doublet pocket when he's not looking and never tell him," said Dodd. "Now I'd best be going so I dinna need to hurry to Widdringon."

"Is the Courtier not going with ye?" She was annoyed with her husband – how the devil did he think she could do that, she wasn't a pick pocket. Or did he suspect... No, he'd be far different if he did.

"Not yet," said Dodd, "he's got some things he needs to do first."

"Like?"

"Never ye mind," said Dodd pompously, "the fewer people know the better."

Janet nearly asked him if he thought Sir Henry had spies in their own tower but left it because that was never the way to get anything out of her husband. And it wasn't impossible that he did, although it wasn't very likely.

Dodd took three spare Armstrong cousins of hers, Tiddler, Nuts and Benny Armstrong, to go with him to Widdrington and Janet kissed him lovingly and wished him Godspeed. Then she went upstairs with Mrs Hogg to let her feel her belly and then persuaded the midwife to take a rest in their guest bedroom because she was looking so tired. She pottered around and finally found the Courtier's impressive pair of dags, so she dropped the amulet into the bag for wads and cleaners. Then she got Shilling from the stables on the ground floor of the tower, found another one of her cousins, a young lad called Ekie Armstrong, told him to tack up Shilling and a hobby for himself and come with her to Carlisle since she had a mind to go there. Only an hour after Dodd had left, they went through the west gate onto the Carlisle road, to see if she could find Jane Fenwick the dairymaid.

MON 5 MAR 1593, CARLISLE

By the time they clattered in through Carlisle's east gate it was after noon. She called in on Mrs Kate Nixon on the way to get the latest news, but thereafter headed straight to Bessie's on the grounds that Jane might be staying there – definitely not in Carlisle Castle which was nearly all men now that Lady Scrope had gone south, and most unsuitable.

She found Bessie's Wife in the common room and a group of men sitting at a side table whom she recognised as the Earl of Essex's men. Acting Sergeant Andy Nixon was sitting there too as his wife, Kate, had suspected he would be, and they were all abstemiously drinking small ale.

They looked the way men looked when they were planning a raid, so she marched straight over to them and coughed.

The young man with the thin brown moustache and goatee and the very bright blue eyes looked up at her. She couldn't recall his right name but he was sitting at the head of the table, not Andy.

"Ay, good day tae ye, goodmen," she said politely, "Are ye the Earl of Essex's men?"

The young man exchanged looks with Andy. "In a manner of speaking," he said, "although we prefer to call ourselves Hieronimo's Troop."

"Ay, Mrs Dodd," said Andy, looking at her shrewdly. "Have ye seen the Courtier?"

"I have indeed. He rousted Sergeant Dodd out of bed last night and Sergeant Dodd headed east this morning. I expect Sir Robert will be leaving Gilsland today although I dinna ken where he's headed."

"Not Widdrington?"

She shook her head. "I dinna think so. Though he'll be heading there eventually, I'd put money on it. In fact the whole of Gilsland."

There was another exchange of looks. "We're waiting for Jane the dairymaid to come," explained the young man.

"And ye are?"

"My right name is Nick Stephenson, at your service, Mrs Dodd," he said, "though I've called myself Nick Smithson for so long, that's what everybody calls me. I suppose you could say that I'm in charge of Hieronimo's Troop if anyone is, under Sergeant Dodd, of course."

"Ay? Ye were the pack of broken men that Dodd brung north to soldier at Carlisle."

"We were," said Stephenson, flushing slightly. "However, we are now part of Sir Robert's establishment."

He spoke nicely, with a little lilt from somewhere down south on the Welsh marches.

"Ahah," said Janet and sat herself down on a stool at a corner of the table. "So that's why ye look like men plotting a raid. Ye are plotting a raid."

Stephenson smiled. "A raid on..."

"Widdrington village at least, possibly the Castle. And it's a fine idea once Sir Robert gets his woman out of the Castle. Until then..."

As every kidnapping showed, until then you were helpless.

"My idea was to make it look like a normal raid, so they wouldn't cut her throat, they'd defend themselves," said Stephenson, "that's why we're waiting for Jane. I want to find out what's at Widdrington and where everything is."

Janet looked hard at him. That was a surprise. He didn't look a day older than twenty, but that was a very good idea.

"And would you help us by sitting with the maid, Mrs Dodd," he asked, "so she won't feel too nervous."

Good God, where had this one come from? Every time he opened his mouth, he made sense.

"Gladly," she said, waving at Bessie's Wife to bring her something to drink. Bessie's Wife pointed and she found a pint jack already in front of her.

Bessie's Wife turned and smiled at Bessie herself who came into the common room with a girl by her side, a broad square-faced girl in a cap and a woad-dyed kirtle stained back and front with sweat and rain, where the dye had run. She was limping, looked very tired and had bandages on her feet and a pair of slippers.

Andy Nixon and Nick Stephenson were on their feet, as if Lord Scrope had come into the room, so all the rest of the men stood too.

Janet was getting to her feet as well and her jaw dropped as she realised that they were standing for the milkmaid.

"Goody Fenwick," said Stephenson respectfully and Janet's jaw dropped again. You didn't call a mere milkmaid "goodwife" or by her surname, you called her by her Christian name at best. She was nobbut a maid.

On the other hand, the maid had run at least 80 miles in a couple of nights which wouldn't be easy to do on a horse. Janet stood for her as well.

Jane looked about at them blankly and it was only when Bessie whispered in her ear that she coloured and smiled a shy smile.

Bessie helped her sit down on the bench to Stephenson's right and seeing Janet was there to keep the decencies, went off for another tray of beer. Jane sat and took her pint and drank half of it down.

They were all seated, staring curiously at Jane Fenwick, and Stephenson opened his mouth to speak, shut it again and coughed. Janet decided to help him out while she wondered if he was still a virgin: after two years as a soldier in the Netherlands, probably not physically but mentally, yes, definitely.

"Goody," she began and Jane flushed again and looked down.

"Aren't ye Missus Dodd?"

"Ay."

"Could ye... er... call me Jane? I'm not used to being a goodwife yet."

Janet smiled at this modesty. "I think ye've earned the right to be called a goodwife," said Janet judiciously, "but ye can stay as Jane if ye like."

"I only ran a long way," she said, into her apron. "Widdrington to Carlisle, ay, it is a long way, I dinna ken how far..."

"Seventy miles as the crow flies, I think," said Stephenson, "Much more if you go by the Great North Road and the Giants Road."

"Ay, that's the way I went, I didna want tae get lost on the Border."

"When did you leave Widdrington?"

"Afternoon on Friday, after I took the cows to the infield wi' Little May. I took Little May to her family and then I ran on. I often run to see me mam and she lives about twelve miles away and then I run back, I only take a day and I can milk ma cows i'the morning before I leave and milk 'em in the evening when I get back. Maist of them are in calf now." She looked down again. "I fed me chickens at ours, I miss 'em."

"And ye just kept going after ye'd seen yer mam?" asked Janet.

"Ay, I took Little May home because she was afeared Lady Widdrington would get her, the silly maid, then I ran home and fed the chickens and me Mam gave me an early dinner and I took a nap and then when the rain came down I started running alongside the road, heading south, and then it cleared up when it got dark and so I could see the Haywain and the North Star at me back, and I went around Newcastle until I found the Giant's Wall and I followed that with the North Star on my right. I had to hide from raiders once, I was right scared but they didna see me. And when the sun come up, I hid under a haystack and slept out the daylight until night. When I woke, I drank my ale and I ate me cheese and I went along the Giant's Road in the night and it took me longer because I had to hide from more reivers. I hid some of the Sunday in a sheepfold and then I thought I might be near Carlisle so I walked and I borrowed a cow from a field and led it along and I ran when it was willing and I went on until I found the road going to the Bridge and saw the fortress in the distance.

"My feet were hurting bad by then so I led the cow in at the evening and naebody noticed and I got to Bessie's which I'd heard about and I told Mrs Bessie what I'd done and when she saw me feet she believed me and so she took me into the castle to see the Cour.... Sir Robert and tell him what had happened to my Lady Widdrington."

A dispatch carrier riding post could have bettered it, but nobody else.

"What has happened to Lady Widdrington?" Janet asked.

Jane scowled and her square hands fisted. "It's a wickedness and a shame, so it is," she said. "I hate that fancy Lord Spynie, ay, and I hate Sir Henry worse. They've brung in some man called Lindsay that calls hisself a witchfinder and they've locked her in the woodshed with that thing on her face that stops her speaking so she canna curse them, they say, because they're saying she's a witch and she enchanted Sir Henry's... er... his... ye ken..." She gestured.

"His yard?" said Janet helpfully and Jane blushed beetroot.

"Ay, and they say she gave him the gout too and it's WRONG!"

"Well there are witches..." said Andy Nixon doubtfully.

"Ay, there are, but Lady Widdrington isnae a witch, no, never, she's a good Christian woman and a sight better than the maist of them. That's how I kept going, Ah wis thinking all the time of her having that thing on her face and how it would hurt and every time another blister popped, I'd think of her in the woodshed and I want to get her out of there and kill that witchfinder and Sir Henry and Lord Spynie and I don't care if I burn for it, so there!"

By the time she finished she was shouting with both fists rammed on the table and she was standing. She sat down suddenly and breathed hard.

Stephenson nodded slowly. "How do you know she's not a witch?"

Jane rounded on him and looked ready to hit him, so Janet put her hand on the girl's arm to stay her.

"I know because she says her prayers night and morning and never once has she done anything like scrying or making charms, and she even stopped us saying "Heavy Maria, grass a plenty" to the cows to help them calve, just a little charm like that."

"What would you say to us raiding Widdrington and bringing off the cows and the horses?"

"Well, go easy on the cows so you don't bring 'em on to calve, but ay, if ye kill the witchfinder and Sir Henry and..."

"We'll do our best."

"Ah'd say, go tae it and how can I help?"

Stephenson started unrolling a piece of paper. "I want a plan of the castle and village and a map of the area," he said.

"Whit's that?" asked Jane, frowning at the paper.

"Er... it's like..."

"Ay, it's like as if ye were a bird and flew over Widdrington and looked down and saw everything all laid out as if ye were looking at it from a hill only better," explained Janet who had heard of this way of picturing the countryside from the Sergeant.

"Oh."

Stephenson produced another piece of paper from his belt pouch and spread it out. It was slightly smeared and had beer stains on it, but there was a name that Janet read as Caerlisle and a square for the castle and English street and Scotch street and the Eden bridge and the Giant's Wall crawling across it like a a worm.

Jane looked at it carefully as Stephenson told her what the things were and then she nodded.

"Ay, I see."

"I needed it at first because I wasn't born here," said Stephenson, "although I've learned the lie of the land by now. Certainly, around Carlisle."

"Och," said Jane, still staring at it, "so ye want tae ken where everything is and what's the best way in, wi'out having to go there and look."

"Yes. So to start with, when you stand in the barnekin at Widdrington castle and look straight at the North Star, what's on your right."

"On my right is the sea, on my left is the Great North Road going straight tae Berwick and then tae Edinburgh."

It took a long time with Stephenson painstakingly drawing the answers to his careful questions and rubbing the blacklead off the paper with a bit of bread when Jane misremembered.

At last it was done: a plot of the land around Widdrington as far as Jane knew it and a detailed plan of the village with its church and tithe barn and the fortress with its yards and stables and dairy. The postern gates were all kept locked at night as they should be though the Dairy Mistress had a key to one that led directly into the dairy yard, so the maids could use it to bring the milch cows in when the bells were ringing. Stephenson took a special note of that. Jane had finished all her salt beef stew and cleaned the bowl with bread.

Andy Nixon was staring perplexedly at the plan of the castle. "It looks awfy strong," he said.

"What's the Courtier doing?" asked Falls Off His Horse Perkins.

"I have no idea," said Stephenson. "I don't even know where he is. Do you know, Mrs Dodd?"

Janet shook her head. "Nae dout he's long left Gilsland but I dinna ken where he's going."

"Well, Ah have tae go back to Widdrington," said Jane definitively. "I've my chickens to feed and once the cows have calved they'll need me in the dairy and I want tae know how my lady fares."

"Wouldn't you rather stay here?" asked Janet.

Jane shook her head firmly. "I miss my ain country."

Leamus the Irish kern who had been sitting one man down from Janet, leaning back with his eyes half-shut and completely silent, suddenly sat forward, taking a breath to speak. Then he stopped himself.

Stephenson looked at him shrewdly. "What do you think, Leamus?"

"We need someone inside the castle who won't be suspected, sorr," he said. "Why not this ... this brave hard-running King's Messenger of a maid?"

Janet frowned. She didn't like the sound of it. "Because it's not suitable."

"Why?" asked Stephenson.

"Because if she's caught, she might be accused of witchcraft herself."

Jane scowled at that, "Ah'm no witch..."

"Nor is Lady Widdrington."

There was a moment of silence. "I just want tae get back to my chickens and Buttercup and Tansy and Thistle and Fireweed... and see if my lady is all right," said Jane stubbornly.

"She should have a woman with her for the journey at least," said Janet. "She canna run all night again."

"Well, Mrs Dodd, would you be willing to accompany us?"

Janet was so surprised at this request that she sat and stared at Stephenson for a full minute. And then she thought that at least she would know what her still only half-recovered husband was up to at Widdrington and be a lot closer to him than Gilsland if he should need help. It almost felt like blasphemy to her to think that way, but if she had been with him up on the Scottish moors on that black winter's night, he might not have got a crossbow bolt in his back.

"Ay," she said slowly, "I'd be willing to do that although it won't be easy to spare the time as there's the spring plowing to finish and the sowing to get on with and... but ay, I'll do it."

"And what do you think the Sergeant would do if he was here?"

"He'd want more men."

"We're hoping for the other half of our troop to join us from Berwick if they can."

Janet dismissed them with her shoulder. "I mean, he'd want as many right reivers as he could get. Like my ain Armstrong cousins for a start and maybe some Dodds, and Johnstones if they can spare the men fra the fight with the Maxwells, and Bells..."

"Could he get the Grahams?" asked Andy Nixon. "The Courtier tellt me once, right here in this room in fact, that Jock o'th'Peartree Graham said he'd come out for him after the business at Netherby Tower."

"Did he so?" said Janet, surprised but not shocked.

Andy shrugged. "The thing at Netherby happened before I joined the castle guard, I was still a rent collector then, but when he told me, the Courtier didn't sound like he was just boasting."

There was another silence while everyone contemplated the possibility of the Grahams getting involved in their raid.

"Is Young Hutchin Graham a relative?" asked Jane.

"Ay," said Janet, "Jock o'th'Peartree's his uncle."

"Well Sir Henry pit him in the tool cellar for trying to steal the witchfinder's horse to carry Lady Widdrington's ring to the Courtier. My lady gave him the ring first but he couldna carry it being locked up in the cellar and I got it from him and I told him I'd get a man to carry it, but there wasn't anybody so I did it."

"Ay," said Andy with a scowl, "That'd fetch out Jock o'th'Peartree and maybe Wattie too and perhaps even Ritchie of Brackenhill. They dinna like their kin to be locked up."

"Tell me, Jane," said Janet, "D'ye think Sir Henry is wood?"

"Ay, he is," she said with certainty, "he's all eaten up inside wi' rage and gout and... Lord Spynie is so fine and handsome and he's a rotten, spiteful man but the one I'm afeared of is the witchfinder. He's all bald, he hasna even eyebrows and... he's cold. Everything he says sounds so reasonable until ye listen again." Jane gave a little shudder. "He gave us all a sermon about witches, about how they have chosen evil and they kiss the Devil on his arse and they might be men but women are more tempted by him because we're weak and foolish and they do charms and raise the dead and they fly about on broomsticks and I nearly asked him..."

"What?"

"Well if Lady Widdrington is a witch, why didn't she just fly away on her broomstick when Sir Henry was going to take her prisoner?"

Leamus smiled and Clockface nodded wisely. “I’ve always wondered about that.”

“He’d say the Devil betrayed her and serve her right,” said Bessie as she came back with the ordinary for all of them. “The likes o’ him have allus got an answer that puts the woman in the wrong.”

FRIDAY 2ND MARCH 1593, WIDDRINGTON

Toad was crying again and Lady Widdrington could do nothing about it. She was exhausted and dizzy with hunger and thirst, her mouth was full of blisters from the scold's bridle and she was freezing cold because she was in her shift.

They wanted her to confess to witchcraft. The only time the scold's bridle came off was when they were harassing her to confess and since she wouldn't do that, it stayed on. Her shift was disgusting, it made her skin crawl to wear it.

At first she had simply been dazzled by the daylight, after a full day in darkness.

And then she had been outraged, appalled. Never in her worst nightmares had she imagined even Sir Henry could do something so ugly. Never ever had she been in front of her serving men and maids in just her smock, though it covered her from neck to ankles. It was horrible. And it was all she could do not to fight them, which she knew was what they wanted so they could make more of a spectacle of it. It was all she could do to keep her head up and not hide away although she knew her face was flushing red with the shame of it. The worst was when they snatched her married woman's cap away, leaving her bareheaded so everyone could see her awful red carroty hair.

And Sir Henry had laughed his approval, with one swollen gouty foot up on a table, Lord Spynie drinking and giggling by his side.

The bloodstains from her courses which had leaked from her pad was another sign of witchcraft, according to the witchfinder. Did he really not know that women bled with the moon if their man couldn't plant a babe in them? He seemed to think that it was voluntary and under her control and that she was bleeding on purpose to defy him. She supposed that all women hid their courses as much as they could and women with able husbands had few of them anyway, being often with child. Still, she wondered at him being so ignorant – had he never been married, never spoken to a sister? Perhaps not.

At least her hands were in front of her, not tied behind, which eased the cramps in her shoulders, although the new shiny manacles hung heavy on her wrist bones.

She was in the provisions cellar now, the one with the barrels of salt meat and fish in it, nearly all of it pickled by her. They took two of the barrels out at the same time and joked about how she would rot all the rest of them. And then they had locked the manacles to a new staple in the wall so that although she could lie down, she couldn't move very far away and certainly not reach the barrels and boxes. Poor Toad was now in the wine cellar and also manacled and, God give me strength, he had woken up again and was still crying.

If she had been able to talk, she might have been able to get him to stop crying, but she couldn't. All she could think was that she couldn't sleep with Toad crying and she wished he would go away and shut up and stop.

She thought that Young Hutchin was still in the small cubbyhole of a cellar used for brooms and mops and buckets. She was worried about him because he had gone very quiet. She tried calling to him despite the bridle, making stupid noises like "Yushin" and "yarigh'"

At last she got a response. "Ay missus," came a weary answer, "Ah'm a'right." So at least he was still alive, that was something, she supposed.

She curled up on the floor where there was some straw. They had given her a Bible so she could better repent of her sins but had obviously not thought it through or not cared that there was no light to read by. Still it made an inadequate pillow and she could take some comfort through the thought of the Word of God at least being with her.

Although she was not happy with God. In fact, she was furious with Him. She had done her level best to be a good and obedient wife to Sir Henry and he had repaid her with abuse and cruelty, topped and crowned by this outrageous attempt to arraign her for witchcraft.

She knew he had been put up to it by Lord Spynie, for he would never have thought of it for himself. Spynie wasn't that bright either and had clearly got the suggestion from his sinister follower, the witchfinder.

She knew her husband was besotted by Lord Spynie who could do no wrong in his eyes. She knew that Lord Spynie wanted vengeance for the way she had protected Robin when he got himself into trouble at Dumfries in the summer, and the way she had protected the young Lord Hume in the autumn, causing the King to be estranged from his erstwhile minion. It didn't surprise her in retrospect that Spynie had manoeuvred to bring a charge of witchcraft against her. She supposed the witchfinder needed business too.

What surprised her was that God had let it happen. That surprised her. That enraged her. She had done her best, prayed morning and night, tried her hardest to forgive her husband for his cruelty, tried her best to be a good Christian woman. And it had been hard, so hard. And after all that effort, all the tears she had shed, the anger she had suppressed until her stomach soured with it and she couldn't eat, this... THIS was how God treated her? She had been tricked into leaving King James's Court where she was happy. She was sleeping on the floor of a cellar in nothing but a disgustingly dirty shift. She couldn't sleep because a poor innocent of a man had been beaten up and bullied to try and get a confession out of him to accuse her. Do You hear that, God, she shouted in her mind. Do You hear poor Toad crying because he doesn't understand what's happening?

She would probably hang for it at best in the end, if she didn't burn for petty treason, because a charge of witchcraft was not easy to disprove and Sir Henry was the magistrate.

And worse was on its way. She knew she was bait. They would be writing to Robin to challenge him to come to Widdrington, to put his head in a noose. And knowing Robin, he would do exactly that.

She clenched her fists as the rage and tears rose up in her again, rage and tears that God ignored, didn't care about, so what good did they do? A letter would go to Robin or probably already had, and he would have no idea what was happening.

And then he would gallop to Widdrington, probably ride post on his own because Sergeant Dodd wasn't fully healed yet and Spynie's men would take him and he would be accused of witchcraft as well. Bothwell had got away with it, but Carey would not and they would both hang.

The tears had beaten the rage again. She was so helpless. She wished she was a witch so she could curse Spynie and Lindsay, ay, and her husband. Tears rolled out of her eyes, snot from her nose, dribble from her mouth where the metal bit stopped her from closing her lips. Finally she got to sleep.

***

She woke hearing somebody scratching at the cellar door. She had been dreaming that she was warm in her own bed and Robin was a warm comforting shape beside her. She tried to say "Who is it?" and hurt her tongue on the rough metal.

"It's Sam, my lady." She heard his gruff voice through the door, but it didn't sound blurred or drunk which was unusual.

"Toa'?" she asked.

Sam started to sob heartbrokenly, which annoyed Elizabeth. Why hadn't he protected Toad better? At least he could have been there.

"Where... were you?" she asked carefully.

The sobbing got worse and she rolled her eyes.

"Ah... wis drunk, my lady, I wis in me little room, and drunk asleep."

For God's sake.

"Ah canna get to him, I have nae keys, Ah canna help him, he's not saying aught."

"Cryin... be'ore."

"Och God, Ah heard what they did... I canna bear it."

What could she say to that? Nothing. He had to bear it.

"The Widdringtons sent me, the cousins in the castle and the women. They wantae ask you, my lady, what are they tae do? There's more of Spynie's men than there are of them and they're afeared."

"Fi'."

"Ah dinna think they will, maist of the right fighting men are in Edinburgh wi' Young Henry and the rest are loyal to the old man."

If Robin was on his way, what would help him most?

"Lea'. Go."

"Ye say they should leave Sir Henry and the castle."

"Ay. E'in'urgh."

And tell young Henry why they left, thought Elizabeth but didn't have the energy or the spit to say.

After he comes back from Caerlaverock, of course. Whenever that is.

The planning of her arrest had been well done, that was sure. She supposed that the Maxwell had been told to keep Young Henry as busy as he could with hunting and suchlike before giving him the wolfhounds. She sighed and crushed the urge to weep again.

"Ay missus," he said, "I wilna go meself, but that's good advice. Thank 'ee."

Elizabeth grunted. She didn't know how many men Lord Spynie had brought but whittling down Sir Henry's manpower might distract him from her perhaps – and no doubt she would get the blame anyway. It was quite refreshing to be guilty as charged on this point,

SUNDAY MARCH 4TH 1593, WIDDRINGTON

I cannot believe this is happening, thought Elizabeth as she stood shivering outside the church. At least Tim, her husband's valet, had insisted she should have a fresh shift for the occasion, since the one she had been wearing was so filthy with blood. That was something she supposed. The new one would be marked pretty soon, though her courses had stopped.

She was still wearing the scold's bridle and was getting used to not being able to answer stupid male comments. Instead she had developed a stony stare which did seem to abash some of them.

One of Spynie's men came up to her with a candle and tried to get her to hold it, but she simply let it fall as often as he put it in her hands. After about five times it broke. Another man came up behind her with a piece of paper on which had been written the words "witch and adulteress" and pinned it to her shift.

She was supposed to do penance for her adultery with Robin, which as she hadn't committed adultery with him was going to be hard to do. I don't know what they want me to do about the witch part, she thought distantly as she watched all the people from the village going into the little church, turned from wood to stone a hundred years before, and small for the prosperous place the village was now, with the traffic from the Great North Road and the cabbages and potherbs the peasants grew to send to Berwick market.

A few people turned to look at her but most ignored her or even looked away frowning. Nobody dared to protest to Sir Henry or Lord Spynie. Minister Lindsay would give the sermon and Elizabeth had the feeling that it would be on the well-worn subject of witches and witchcraft. There was a hungry looking young curate who had about three parishes to see to on a Sunday and had his hobby tied up by the gate, ready to ride off after the service was finished. He gave her a deeply anxious look as he came by, pulling his plain linen surplice out of his bag.

She practised her hard stare on him, and he speeded up.

Then two thugs from Edinburgh grabbed her shoulders and pushed her into the church to stand at the back next to the font. Sir Henry came limping up to her.

"Why will ye not hold the candle?" he demanded of her.

She didn't bother to answer since she couldn't, went with the slaps and dropped the new candle he tried to give her. She couldn't do penance for something she hadn't done. She seriously wished she had now, but she hadn't and that was that.

In the end Lord Spynie came up and put the candle in a holder near to her. She stared into space and wished to feel warm and wished to go to sleep without a thing in her mouth and wished she had never come back to Widdrington and wished Sir Henry was dead... No, she shouldn't wish that. Actually she wished all three of them were dead, Spynie and Lindsay as well, and if she had been a witch she would have cursed them very happily. Fortunately, or perhaps unfortunately, she wasn't a witch.

For which she struggled to give thanks.

The reading told the story of Saul going to visit the witch of Endor, a fine and spooky tale. If she were a witch she would call up the shade of Sir Henry's first wife and see what story she had to tell. There had been whispers from Young Henry when he was a boy about his mother, who had died when he was only young, shortly after Roger's birth. Elizabeth had assumed it was of childbed fever but now suspected it wasn't. She knew the poor woman had been badly treated because after she died, Sir Henry had not been able to convince any of the local families to give him a second wife, and so he had appealed to Lord Hunsdon who had found a suitable wife for him as far away from the Border as possible, among Lady Hunsdon's Cornish relatives: to wit, herself, Elizabeth Trevannion that was.

There went Lindsay, up to the pulpit which was carved with angels and stern evangelists, a rather beautiful thing. He started easily, making the congregation laugh, and then drew attention to Elizabeth, standing at the back of the church in her shift, next to the candle, bare-headed and humiliated.

She felt the brunt of all the eyes as if it was a blow, but stiffened her back and stared at Lindsay, only. That was all she could do, stare at him.

Lindsay was helpfully telling her what she should confess to: adultery with many men, chiefly Robin, of course, and witchcraft against Sir Henry, and sleeping with Satan and kissing his bare bum and a great deal else that she would have called revolting pornography if it hadn't been in a sermon.

She noticed a stir among the women standing at the back as the lewdness continued, and three mothers left with their children dragging behind trying to hear what Lindsay was saying. A sturdy husband with a brood of five spoke to his wife and then all of them marched out, the wife scowling at Lindsay and holding her hands over her youngest child's ears – that was Goody Affleck, who wasn't even a friend of Elizabeth's.

Elizabeth had a strong urge to giggle at it, because some of the lewdness was really idiotic, but she kept her countenance and stared at Lindsay.

He came striding down the aisle to her, with people standing in the nave making way for him, stood near her and started haranguing her.

She didn't listen to it but kept staring at him straight in the eyes, since it seemed to make him uncomfortable so he avoided her glance. He wanted her to confess to her adultery and her witchcraft, did he? She was sure he did want that, but she didn't think she would do it just because he was shouting at her.

Suddenly he produced a little key, unlocked the branks and took it off. He seemed to think that she would be encouraged to speak by that. Well it was nice not to have the metal in her mouth for the moment, but she knew perfectly well he would be putting it back sooner or later. Also the ulcers and blisters on her tongue and lips made it hard for her to speak clearly.

She stood and stared at him and let the shouting and hissing roll over her, thinking of Jesus Christ and how he had to take the mockery of the Roman soldiers, saying 'hail Caesar' to him and the crown of thorns and the cloak of purple.

He struck her a few times but she was getting used to it and now had a trick of moving with the blow so it hurt less.

Finally he put the branks back on and tightened it a notch which hurt a lot, the metal bit was deeper in her mouth. She sighed and continued to stare at him.

And then it was over and Lindsay marching up to the pulpit again. There was a buzz of talk among the people, some of the men scowling, some of the woman frowning. The buzz got louder as the service ended, the curate having to shout the final blessing above it.

Sir Henry and Lord Spynie processed out ahead of the curate, Lindsay came last and Elizabeth was shoved out after him to stand in the graveyard where everyone could see her in her shift.

Her back was aching from standing for so long, her face was aching and burning from being slapped, her bare feet were cold and her calves cramping. She did her best to stand up straight under the weight of it all.

She stood there and all three of them were shouting at her to confess now, it seemed Lindsay hoped that sheer volume would do it.

Some of the people suddenly began to gather round her, she recognised the bailiff and the blacksmith, the owners of the two inns, the alewives who supplied them, some of the local farmers and horse smugglers, a merchant who had his warehouse in Berwick. Over in the distance there were some children playing tag and ignoring what was going on.

Well she couldn't help it if some people believed what Lindsay was saying about her, so she carried on staring at Lindsay. Her husband was now a rather unhealthy colour of puce from the shouting.

There was a scattered crackle of clapping, and then more and more people took up the clapping and then there was a beat in it, quite slow, clap... clap... clap... clap... getting louder and louder as more people joined in.

The merchant pushed her backwards quite gently and she stumbled, found herself supported by one of the alewives and that was when she realised that the slow clap was for Sir Henry, Lord Spynie and Lindsay. It wasn't for her at all. It was for them. The people were standing round Sir Henry and Lord Spynie, not her, slow-clapping them. The two alewives held her elbows and moved her back, one of the blacksmiths stood in front of her.

Now Lord Spynie's men realised what was happening and tried to shove into the crowd. She was moved carefully back. The mercenaries found it hard because suddenly there was a wall of people round her. Instead Spynie's men surrounded Sir Henry, Lord Spynie and Lindsay and drew their swords to bring them back to the castle.

The clapping broke up. The two groups of people stared at each other, Sir Henry purple with anger at this defiance from his peasants, Spynie looking supercilious and a little frightened, the witchfinder blank-faced.

Suddenly Lindsay broke out of the circle of men, strode over to the children and caught two of them by the hands and dragged them back to stand next to Lord Spynie. The two little boys squirmed and tried to free themselves of his grip and two of the women gasped and screamed.

Spynie was smiling now, the witchfinder again looking pleased with himself. It was very obvious what the deal would be.

Just for a second Elizabeth found herself bargaining with God over the children and then she stopped.

"I need some new page boys," shouted Lord Spynie, "Or you could give the witch back to us."

"She has cast a spell on you to free her," explained Lindsay in his sonorous voice. "This is all a foolish waste of time."

The alewives had let go of her arms and so Elizabeth forced her knees straight and walked out into the gap between Lord Spynie's men and the villagers. She couldn't speak but she gestured at the two boys. Their mothers followed after her. The boys were frantically twisting their arms, trying to escape from the witchfinder's iron grip.

A couple of Lord Spynie's henchmen were coming to meet her and she waved her arms together and shouted "Un, un." One boy put his face down and bit Lindsay on the hand, the other stamped his foot on

Lindsay's boot; both of them ran to their mothers who swept them up and backed off.

Elizabeth looked at the distance between her and the villagers and her and the henchmen. Perhaps she could beat them into the crowd of villagers but then the swords would be out and she didn't give much for even the blacksmith's chances. Some of the villagers were leaning forward ready to fight, others were leaning back, some creeping away from the back.

Elizabeth had tears in her eyes because the villagers had done more than she could ever have expected. She supposed that Borderers, even those who lived in the (fairly) peaceful East March, would be less easily cowed than people from further south. But it was no good: she would not put Spynie's henchmen into a pitched battle with the villagers because the henchmen would win.

Somebody grabbed hold of the scold's bridle and dragged her back to the castle, surrounded by the nervous swords of Spynie's henchmen while the people followed shouting that Lady Widdrington isna a witch and can ye grab aholt of her, Jock... Until the henchmen were running at the double up to the castle and thundering across the bridge to the gate and it suddenly occurred to her that now it was too late.

She almost collapsed at that thought, and they brought her roughly into the castleyard and then took her into the kitchen passage and half-carried her down the stairs, into the provisions cellar where two more barrels of salt pork had been taken out.

They locked her to the staple again and left her there and she was gasping for breath suddenly and sick with anger.

Monday 5th March 1593, Widdrington

Sam had brought her some food the night before, bread and cheese, but her mouth was too painful to eat it and besides she hated dribbling food and having to suck it off the metal bit. She drank the ale though it had been attacked by the vinegar fly and was sour. At least her stomach had stopped rumbling.

She was standing and stamping her feet that were cold and numb and singing the tune of a lewd weaving song when the door unlocked and there stood Lindsay with a candle lantern. His usual assistants were there, four ugly-looking men, including one with a nasty scar down his face. Lindsay gestured and two of them came forward and grabbed her, the other unlocked the manacles and started marching her out of the door.

Were they going to hang her now? She felt her whole body go cold at the thought, her stomach coiled in on itself. Well she couldn't ask anyone.

Sir Henry's chair with arms was sitting in the middle of the yard and they took her over to it, made her sit down and then tied her arms and legs to it so she couldn't move at all. It was the first time she had ever sat in Sir Henry's chair. She was frightened, she couldn't help it, and she held her breath and then let it all out at once. It was terrible to be so helpless, so isolated. There were a few people standing around but most of them were Spynie's henchmen; there were many fewer

Widdringtons than there had been. Then Lindsay advanced on her waving a thin spike with an elaborate top to it.

"The witch has often kissed the Devil and suckled him on special nipples that can be anywhere on her body – we can know which blemish they are because they are numb and feel no pain. So. I shall test her with this pricket."

He pressed the spike on one of her freckles on her upper arm and she flinched and said "Ow!" He nodded and tried another place and that hurt too. Then he tried a third place and he had a cocky little smile on his face and there was no pain, nothing.

Was it possible that she had such numb places on her? Elizabeth scowled – it was impossible that she could have some kind of superstitious nipple for the Devil to suck on. Therefore there was trickery here. She watched his fingers carefully as he spiked another part of her – not hard enough to bleed much, just enough to hurt. Yes, his fingers weren't over the top part when the spike didn't hurt and they were when it did hurt.

A stroke of genius came to her. Every time he touched her with the pricket, whether it hurt or not, she shouted for pain and after a while he was scowling and jabbing harder and drawing blood on her nice clean shift.

At last he gave over and she was hustled back to the cellar. He looked furious and well he might, for she now understood that he knew she wasn't a witch at all. Otherwise why would he have to trick her into showing places on her body that were numb, where the Devil suckled, by the trickery of his prickets? If such things existed, he would find them without trickery, would he not?

But when Scarface started to lock the manacles to the staple again, Lindsay gestured for him to stop. He manacled her arms behind her instead of in front and then made her kneel before him. He passed a rope around behind her knees. He knotted another rope around her ankles and passed the rope around the chain so that she was stuck with her wrists behind her pulled down to her ankles. And then he knotted her knees together and passed the rope around her neck so that she was forced to curl over into a ball and stay there.

"Do not presume to make a game of me," he hissed in her ear, "do not think you can fool me, witch."

She was finding it hard to breathe, tied in a ball the way she was, with the rope around her neck and the branks still on her face. Her knees and lower legs were already going numb from being knelt on.

He waited patiently for a while, as she writhed and wriggled and grunted and tried to find a comfortable position. There was none.

"Confess your sin, confess your witchcraft, your unhonesty with Sir Robert and the Devil, and I will release you from these bonds."

She wanted to look him in the face and snarl at him since she couldn't talk, but the rope was tight enough around her neck that she could only look down and a little to the side and her breath was already coming short.

"Only nod your head for me, Elizabeth, and I will release you."

She shook her head as hard as she could and so he left her there, tied in a ball, locked the door.

She was half-conscious when he came back, in the dark, she didn't know what time it was, just that she couldn't breathe properly, her chest was too constricted and her breasts were in the way. Her legs were completely numb. Sometimes she would try raising her head and that would tighten the noose round her neck until she was gasping and unable to think straight.

She knew it was him from the ugly smell, sour and rancid, with the lantern in the darkness, although he didn't speak and he was behind her. She felt his hands on her, roughly touching her, scrubbing his hands over her bum and her back and poking in his fingers painfully at her cunny. At least she still had her shift on. His breathing came loud and short while she could only take sips of air a little at a time.

There was a sound, of lacing being unlaced and then a rhythmic noise that went on for a minute or two and then he gave a soft gasp and a shower of warm liquid spurted over her back, and quickly turned cold. She still couldn't breathe, she was dizzy from it.

"Confess!" he hissed at her and her wrists hurt and her ankles and her knees and her neck and her back... oh God, her back hurt most of all and she couldn't even remember what it was he wanted her to confess.

She grunted at him like an animal and he tipped her over on her side and although she could breathe a little better she still couldn't move and her back was breaking. And now the blood was returning to her legs and agonising pins and needles starting to burn through her calves and feet.

What had the liquid been? The rhythmic sound? She was too stupid from lack of air to think it out and now she was on her side her arm was going to sleep. She tried to wriggle a little and then something broke inside her. She struggled and fought and tried to untie the knots with fingers like sausages; her lack of breath was the worst. She knew she was dying.

Please God, don't let him leave me like this all night.

But he did.

TUESDAY 6TH MARCH 1593, WIDDRINGTON

She was unconscious from sheer exhaustion and lack of air when he came in the morning. He shook her, released her neck from the rope pulling her head to her knees and then released the rope holding her wrists to her ankles behind her, shook her again. The arm she had been lying on had gone completely dead, she couldn't move and knew she had pissed herself. The world went in and out and she tried to escape from him, get away from him and he kept shaking her and slapping her face and she could not be bothered with it, she had nothing to say to him and no strength to say it with. So she left again and let the world slide away.

The next thing was, the branks was off, she was lying on her poor abused back, pins and needles were raging down her arm. Astonishingly, he was lifting her head and giving her ale. She turned her head and spat, it was horribly sour. She wanted nothing from him.

Yet he seemed worried, as if he hadn't expected this result of his torture, as if he was alarmed that she was so close to death. Why was that? What did he care? Was it so important that she hang or burn for him? Why? What was he saying? "Come on, come on, wake up!"

Eventually her curiosity about this strange matter got the better of her and she came back from somewhere else. She managed to gulp some ale in a totally dry throat, gulped again, gulped some more and dribbled a little because of her poor lips. She finished the whole lot.

Somehow she was still at a distance from herself, as if she had stood up and removed herself from the sufferings of her body. Why is it important to Lindsay that I don't die yet, she wondered.

He went out of the cellar again and locked the door, and she lay in the darkness enjoying her ability to breathe, enjoying the feeling of air going into her chest and leaving it, unobstructed. It was delightful and she had never noticed before: it tasted like wine in her body and her head, better than wine, something that sparkled inside her. The scold's bridle being off her face was pure bliss.

After a while she sat up, found that the manacles were back on her poor bruised wrists but at least they were in front of her, though still attached to the staple. There was nothing left to drink and she was thirsty again. In the Lickingstone Cell in Carlisle, it was said that prisoners had to lick the rock where the water dripped, but this cellar was weather tight and dry. So she lay down, luxuriously on her straight back and dozed off.

The noise of the door woke her and she looked up into Lindsay's carved face. Behind him were five men she couldn't rightly make out, one much shorter than the others. Lindsay put his lantern on a barrel with two panes open so there was plenty of light from the mirror at the back. Right at the back was a skinny man in a black gown who might have been the curate from the church.

The shorter man was staring at her in terror and she suddenly recognised Toad, with his sparse beard and ugly face and squinty eyes. His face was badly bruised and his nose had been broken, he stumbled as they marched him in.

"Now then Toad," said Lindsay with great satisfaction, "tell the witch what you finally told me."

Toad looked panicky. "I c...canna remember," he stuttered, "what did ye shay, shir?"

Lindsay rolled his eyes and his jaw clenched. “You must stop playing the fool with me,” he said, “I know you are deep dyed in sin and that you have fornicated with the witch on many occasions...”

“Sorry sir, whatsh fornicated?”

“The act of darkness, Toad, the act of lewdness, the act and sign of wickedness.”

“Oh. But...”

“Tell her what you told me?”

“What did I tell you, sir?”

“How many times you have fornicated with the witch and the acts of wickedness you performed on each other and...”

“Did I?” Lindsay raised his fist and Toad cowered. “Shorry sir, sorry, I did the act of darkness with the witch...”

“Very good, which was...”

“I dunno, sir.”

“Fellatio and buggery, Toad, I have told you at least a hundred times.”

“Fargery and botio and bugging...”

This time Lindsay did hit him and he cowered away again. “I’m sorry, I’m sorry, I didn’t mean to be bad, but I’m not good at words. I’m good at horses, not words.”

It was a long sentence and not mushy. Elizabeth narrowed her eyes and looked at Toad carefully. There was no sign of cunning or knowledge there, but...

“Start again. Say it after me.”

“Yesh sir.”

“You did the act of lewdness with the witch...”

“You did the act of lewdness with the witch...”

“Not me, Toad, you. You did it.”

“Not me, Toad, you. You did it.”

It looked as if Lindsay was having a job to keep hold of his temper. "Very well, you numbskull, you halfwit..."

"You numbskull... you halfwit..."

"STOP COPYING ME!"

"Yesh sir."

"So. Once more. I did the act of lewdness with the witch..."

"Did you, sir?"

Lindsay struck out at Toad backhanded, and Toad cowered again. "Shorry sir, shorry," he shouted.

Elizabeth had a terrible urge to giggle although the situation was very far from funny, it was nerves and tension and lack of food and... Well Lindsay had done an act of lewdness with her, or on her, hadn't he? If he had done what she thought he had while she was trussed up in a ball, it was certainly lewd, wasn't it?

She lay on the ground with her back still hurting, just grateful to be straight again and able to breathe. She waited for Lindsay to get a grip on himself.

"All right, Toad," he snarled, "show me what you did with the witch."

Toad stopped and wrinkled his brow. "But I dunno, sir," he said.

"The... the act of fornication?"

"What's that?"

One of Spynie's men who was holding Toad, sighed deep in his throat and said, "What horses do, ye numpty, a stallion and a mare."

Toad turned to him and he had his mouth open and his brow was wrinkled again. "A stallion and a mare in season?"

"Ay," said the man, while the one on the other side of Toad said "Fer chrissakes,"

"Oh."

There was a pause into which Lindsay interjected, "Ye know ye want to fornicate with her, Toad, I see it in ye, that's what ye can show me."

"But... but Lady Widrinton isna in season."

"What does that matter, Toad, imitate the actions of a stallion."

"But sir..."

"What is it now?"

"Ah dinna ken how?"

Lindsay drew up his body and stiffened his neck. "Toad, listen to me. If ye do not, immediately, fornicate with the witch, I will hang you tomorrow."

"What sir?"

"I. Will. Hang. You."

"Oh."

Toad looked from Elizabeth to Lindsay, to Elizabeth and back to Lindsay. "A'right sir, if ye must."

There was silence and then Lindsay stalked out of the cellar, followed by the Scotsmen and the curate who seemed to be shaking, the door was locked. Elizabeth heard Lindsay's boots walking away, but not the henchmen's boots, so she concluded that they were supposed to wait until Toad did the deed of lewdness and then come in and witness it. At least there was the candle still burning in the dark lantern, providing light for the witnesses, so that was better than the constant darkness and cold.

She looked at Toad who was sitting down carefully on the floor and putting his face in his hands. Oh God, please don't let him start crying again, please.

He sniffled a couple of times and then a couple of times more. Damn it!

She took a deep breath and let it out slowly, breathed in, slow out. Was it really so terrible if Toad fornicated with her? Why should he hang for her virtue, came the nasty question from somewhere deep inside, after all, she wasn't a virgin. She had heard that some women liked the marital act and sought it out in other men, but she had never understood what the point of it was, apart from making babies. In the early days of their marriage, Sir Henry had just scooped up her smock and climbed on top and then there was a rather painful pushing and rubbing inside which got easier sometimes, and then he would gasp or cry out a woman's name, Margaret, and there would be wet and that was it. She was quite relieved when those occasions became fewer and fewer until they had stopped a few years ago.

Robin had a strange effect on her, that was true; she felt desperate for his arms around her, she even enjoyed kissing him. He had taught her how to do this strange thing when he was staying with them, waiting for the word to come from the Scottish Court that it was safe to venture into Scotland and give the King the official news of his mother's execution. She had become addicted to his kisses and the way her whole body seemed to light up at them. But the word never came and when he had finally mounted up and ridden away with his remount and packpony, she had spent a great deal of time in the wet larder with onions and meat pickles where no one could suspect her tears. Some of the barrels of pickle from that time were still there. She knew he had wanted to commit adultery with her, but she didn't see the point of it, to be frank.

Lindsay had forgotten to put the branks back on her when he stalked out – he must have been upset. Well that was something happy anyway.

"Don't cry, Toad," she said, hating the way her voice sounded, hoarse and cracked and breathless and mushy.

"Yer hurtin, m'lady."

"Well so are you. I'm sorry you got mixed up in this."

There was a confused silence. "But m'lady," said Toad, "yer hurtin, it makes me sad."

"Never mind. I don't mind if you fornicate with me Toad, if it saves you from hanging. I don't think it will, mind, but..."

"No m'lady, My dad told me, if she dunt say yes, ye can't do it with her."

"Well that's very chivalrous of you but..."

"Never, never."

"Well..."

"Nevernevernever!"

"But Lindsay might hang you."

Toad put his head in his hands again and then lifted his head slowly. "He will," he said bleakly, "He'sh already decided. To make you 'fraid."

Then he started to cry again. "Oh Toad," she found herself saying and heaved herself up on one elbow to the chink of metal links, "don't cry." She could just reach him, maybe she shouldn't touch him? But she leaned towards him as far as she could, touched his leg and he took her hand, gripped hard. He was crying so desperately, she couldn't make out what he was saying,

"No Hell, nono no..."

"What?"

"I'm feared of goin' to Hell, Ah don' want to go... go to Hell," said Toad brokenheartedly, "for helping horshes, I don' want..."

She sat up properly and forced some authority into her voice. "Do not believe Lindsay," she said. "You helped horses because you are a good man and you did it out of kindness. Never believe that bastard's lies, Toad. You will not go to Hell, you are not a witch any more than I am. If Lindsay hangs you, you will go straight to Heaven, do you hear me, because you are good and kind. Jesus was good and kind and look what the Romans did to Him and He forgave them. You are good and kind and if Lindsay hangs you, you will go to Heaven and be with God forever."

The sniffling stopped. "I will?"

"Yes," said Elizabeth, firmly suppressing all doubts and any cruel notions of predestination. "I know you will." She didn't add that he was an innocent and there was a special place for him in Heaven, but she thought that. Jesu, the wickedness and cruelty of Lindsay.

"Sure, m'lady?"

"Yes."

Suddenly he was smiling and, yes, giggling a bit behind his hand. "Will there be horses in Heaven?"

She had no idea. "Well..."

"Horshes are my friends, m'lady. And ponies. And donkeys."

Horses often had such hard lives. "Yes," she said firmly, "Lots of them."

He laughed again and made a little crowing noise behind his hand again. "And there's no sharp bits or bridles or saddles or spurs or ropes or whips and there'sh lotsh of meadows and streams and salt licks and it'll be beautiful, m'lady."

"Yes," she said. "It will."

TUESDAY 6TH MARCH 1593, WIDDRINGTON

A little later, Lindsay reappeared with Scarface and his mate, and hauled Toad out of the cellar. He came back a minute or two later and they grabbed her and shoved her along. The weather was getting colder, not warmer for spring; the cold cobbles of the castle yard struck upwards through her bare legs and feet and she shivered in the wind.

As soon as she emerged blinking in the dull daylight she saw the noose hanging from the gate and her heart dropped. She had known with her head that Lindsay would probably hang Toad because he could, but her heart had hoped that he wouldn't. Well that was a lesson for her.

Sir Henry, Lord Spynie and Lindsay himself were sitting at the parlour table, covered with a nice white table cloth she had embroidered herself with subtle white flowers. You couldn't actually see the flowers well in grey daylight, candlelight showed them much better...

Toad was already standing at an angle to the table, his hands bound behind him, his head hunched between his shoulders and his little eyes blinking.

Rage was starting to burn inside her; not red rage, cold white rage, consuming her scruples and her worries until inside her there was a vast open space full of it. Where had it come from?

Sir Henry was looking distracted and confused, Spynie very smart in his cutwork leather jerkin over a red brocade doublet, Lindsay stone-faced as always.

There were a few of her people there, the ones who had no relatives anywhere near like Sam and the Dairy Mistress, with the rest of the people standing around being Spynie's henchmen and wearing his livery. She was glad to see that most of the people who could, had left the castle.

Spynie made some kind of joke to Sir Henry who smiled mechanically.

Once she had been made to stand facing Toad, Lindsay stood up with awful solemnity and paced slowly round the table to loom over Toad.

"Tell Sir Henry what you told me."

"Shorry shir, what?"

Lindsay reached for patience and Elizabeth saw a flicker go across Toad's face, as if he was settling himself and preparing to do battle. Surely not? But although he was clearly an innocent, he wasn't as want-witted as he appeared to be.

"About fornicating with the witch, Toad," said Lindsay through his teeth.

"Oh. With Lady Widrinton?" He pointed. "Her?" He was speaking slowly and scowling with concentration

"Yes, Toad."

"Doing what stallions do to a mare in season?"

"Yes Toad."

"When you left me in the cellar with Lady Widrinton?"

"Ah..."

"I din't, sir. I'm shorry. My dad told me, if she dun't say yes, you can't do it with her. Never nevernever."

"Don't lie to me, Toad, you did the act of lewdness with..."

"She said I could if I wanted so you wouldn't hang me, but I din't."

"You're lying..."

"I was feared of going to Hell, but now I know I'm going to Heaven."

"Toad..."

"So if you'll be happy when you've hanged me, you can hang me. I don't want you to go on hurting and itching. I want to go to Heaven, me, and see all the horses there."

It was obvious that Lindsay had no idea what to say next and Elizabeth again had to fight down the crazy urge to giggle.

Toad looked around at the unsympathetic faces of Spynie's men. "If I canna help horses when they're hurtin', I don't want to go on living," he said quietly. "Sho ye'd best get on wi' it, eh?"

And he turned and walked under the noose.

There was complete silence.

The rage inside Elizabeth was practically lifting her up onto her tiptoes. She took a deep breath and shouted, "My life for his!"

Lindsay spun and stared at her and she stared right back, hard stare, thinking to herself, now let's see what you do? Is this even about me or are you up to something else?

For a second, perhaps two, she balanced there on the knife edge of uncertainty, of chance. She was fairly sure, but not certain. Perhaps he would take her at her word, and she would be choking for twenty minutes on the end of the rope there, dangling down over the gate. There was something desperate and sweet about the moment and for all her bruises and sickness she felt a kind of joy and a kind of wild glee at the same time, looking at the castle and the women and the chickens exploring from the dairy yard because someone had forgotten to shut the gate and the grey sky crossed at just this moment by a flock of birds, so beautiful, it was all so beautiful. Her heart felt it was bursting with happiness, as if it had broken out of a carapace like a caterpillar and was itself a glorious butterfly, a thing of life and splendour and magic.

"Taken, taken!" came Sir Henry's shout, there he was on his feet, bobbing about, a very nasty smile under his moustache.

But it's not up to you, is it? she thought, smiling at him very sweetly. And if they do take my offer, well, it's not so bad, I can't have Robin and I can at least respectably leave Sir Henry by dying and Toad is a good man who deserves not to hang.

It was very strange. She felt as if entire worlds were hanging on what would happen next, as if this was an important moment for kingdoms, not just people. So she smiled again at Sir Henry and curtseyed to him.

"Thank you, my lord," she said, and the smile dropped off his face. Was he upset to realise that she would rather die than stay his wife?

Spynie was up, looking very alarmed and bustling over to Lindsay who stood like a stone market cross, staring at her. Spynie whispered, Lindsay tilted his head, and coughed.

"Fetch the branks," he ordered, "Silence the witch and her lies."

Nobody else said a word as one of the younger of Spynie's men ran for the castle. He slowed down almost at once, looking over his shoulder, clearly dying of curiosity to know what would happen next.

Then Lindsay stalked over to where Toad was standing next to the noose, looking quite happy and relaxed now.

"Sir Henry," he shouted, "your verdict on this witch."

"No, not him," Sir Henry shouted back, "Hang my wife!"

Lindsay's lips twisted with rage. "No, Sir Henry, not until she confesses. Your verdict?"

"Has he confessed to witchcraft?"

"You can say of your own knowing that he is a witch," said Lindsay, "We discussed this."

Sir Henry looked rather thwarted which was always a bad sign, but she was delighted to find that she didn't care. If he beat her which he probably would, at least she would know that was better than being tied up in a ball all night.

"Pah!" he said, "Toad's quite useful..."

"But he is a witch."

"Oh very well. I declare of my own knowing that Toad is a witch."

Immediately Lindsay put the noose over Toad's head, tightened it under his ear and then gestured to the men in the little room between the gatetowers, over the gate itself. They could hear the windlass operating.

"I forgive you all like Jeshus!" Toad shouted quickly and up he went, choking and struggling.

Somebody broke from the back of the crowd, it was Sam the Man. He ran over, jumped and caught Toad's legs and dangled there to make him strangle faster, and someone else came from another little knot of people, and then another man until there were two men dangling from Sam's feet who was dangling from Toad's feet. Toad's face was purple but otherwise not much changed because his tongue had always been too big for his mouth. Finally he stopped moving.

***

Toad was still and the people helping him die had dropped down. Sam the Man was crying hard desperate tears like stones coming from his eyes, not water. The lad arrived, carrying the scold's bridle and a funny look on his face, half defiant, half frightened. Lindsay grabbed it off him and slammed it on Elizabeth's face, almost knocking her front teeth out with the bit.

"Where's the padlock?" Lindsay snarled at the boy.

"Ah dinna ken, sir," he said, "is it not there?" His speech had the softness of a Highlander although he was dressed in Lord Spynie's livery.

"It is not. Where is it?"

"Perhaps it fell off while I was carrying it. Shall I look for it, sir?" Lindsay cuffed the boy round the ears, and the boy stepped backwards and put his hand to his sword.

Lindsay chose not to see this, only turned and said, "Never mind, I can use a piece of wire."

It took a while, but eventually someone produced a bit of wire which was twisted around the place where the padlock went. As Scarface and his friend pushed Elizabeth into the cellar again, nobody said anything, but they were a tiny bit gentler to her.

Sam scratched on the door about an hour later.

"I'm for Edinburgh," he said without preamble, "I'll find Young Henry and bring him here."

"Goo'" she slurred to him. "Caer'av'ock. He 'ent to Caer'ave'ock."

"Do you mean he's gone to the Maxwell? Why?"

"'olfhou'ds. Dogs."

"Ah, I see. Be patient, milady, help is coming."

"So shorry abou' Toa'."

He was silent for a minute and she wondered if he would be offended. Surely he was what rumour painted him, Toad's father?

"Ay," he said in a soft dry voice, "Ay, an' there was me thinkin' Toad was nobbut a ninny and good fer nothing save gentling horses, and getting bitter about it and thinking on about other fathers that had real brave sons that they could talk to and drink wi' and such."

There was nothing anyone could say about that.

"Go wi' God, Sham," she managed as she heard him turn and leave.

Monday 5th March and Tuesday 6th March 1593, Berwick

Carey had sixty-odd miles to cover between Gilsland and Berwick and would have done it in one day if one of his horses hadn't thrown a shoe near the old Roman wall. He found a blacksmith and stayed the night at the post inn at Lariston and paid full price for a revolting bean pottage well over the hill and producing bubbles. The pottage or possibly the worse ale gave him a nasty flux that next day had him hopping off his horse to untruss every five miles thereafter, delaying him so he got to Berwick after the city gates had shut.

He finally found a place to stay at a tiny alehouse on the Greens that would let him doss down in the common room with an ancient blanket and his saddle for a pillow. His horses went into the tiny backyard stable where they shared with an ancient donkey. He had to get up every hour of the night to visit the revolting jakes in the backyard, and of course the cockerel challenged him loudly every time he went out.

So possibly he was not at his best when he went to visit John Carey, an older brother of his who was in his early forties and even more pompous than George the eldest and Lord Hunsdon's heir for the baronetcy. It was a matter of great satisfaction to Sir Robert that he had been knighted in the field by the Earl of Essex two years before, while John was still plain mister.

Mr Carey was not in the Castle, he found, but on the other side of Berwick in the Ness, where there was an old Carmelite nunnery that had been taken over by the garrison, complete with a large paddock and stables, brewhouses and bakery, and some waste ground. Around it mushroomed small cottages and even the kind of huts soldiers built in the Netherlands.

It took him a while to find his brother, currently the Chamberlain of Berwick, which meant that he was effectively the Governor in his father's absence. He had an office in one of the old nunnery's rooms and a well-built townhouse with a large garden squashed in beside the lane leading to the nunnery's door, with its obsolete barred iron grill and complex of rooms within.

"I beg your pardon?" John said incredulously when Carey had finished explaining what he wanted his brother to do. "I am not sure I have understood you. Are you actually telling me that you want me to give you the Garrison Horse, to wit eighty-eight men, their mounts and remounts, plus one of the lighter guns, for an undisclosed... adventure for which you do not intend to pay them?"

"Why not?" asked Carey belligerently, feeling his guts starting to roil again. "Ye lent them to Sir John Forster at least three times last year for exactly the same purpose?"

"Sir John Forster is Warden of the Middle March and had need of them."

"I have need of them..."

"Why?"

"I can't tell you, it's secret."

"Rubbish."

"And I'm the Deputy Warden of the West..."

"Not according to Lowther, you aren't..."

"I received Her Majesty's Warrant and her thanks..."

"What's that got to do with anything," roared Mr John, "you can't just borrow eighty men to gallivant around the country..."

Carey took a deep breath and blew it out slowly. "If I tell you, will you lend me the men?"

"I don't know. It depends on what your purpose is, Robin. I can't just hand Her Majesty's Garrison to just anybody who turns up and demands..." Carey managed not to grind his teeth at being called Robin by his pompous fool of an elder brother. Two could play at that game.

"I'm your brother, Johnnie, remember?"

"Well then tell me."

"Lady Widdrington has been accused of witchcraft by her bastard of a husband, Sir Henry and..."

"I'm surprised at you, Robin," said John busily putting away papers from his remarkably tidy desk, "Sir Henry is effectively the Warden of this March, along with me, while Father is in London and just because you've been lusting after his wife since your first clapped eyes on her doesn't mean you can... Jesus God, you're not planning a raid on Widdrington?"

"No," shouted Carey, "But Lady Widdrington is not a witch..."

"Well she very well might be a witch and in any case I cannot possibly lend you any men if there's a chance you might use them to commit March Treason against the Deputy Warden. I'm surprised at you for even asking me. Honestly, Robin, you never have any money, why on earth don't you just settle down and ask Father to find you a nice merchant's daughter with a large dowry rather than dangling after a woman who is a witch and who has no doubt found a much better-funded lover than you..."

That was when Carey punched him and Mr John punched back, after which there was an unseemly brawl which ended by Carey being thrown out of the Palace by four grinning garrison soldiers.

He landed rather hard in the mud of Palace Green, picked himself up, grabbed his morion off the patch of grass where it had landed, paused with his hand on his swordhilt and then paused again. He supposed his father would be upset with him if he ran his nitwit of an elder brother through his ample gut, richly though he deserved it. He sighed, coughed, felt his own guts give subterranean warning of a new eruption and sagged. He visited the soldiers' jakes which was a thoroughly unpleasant experience and wished fervently he hadn't eaten the pottage two nights before.

He wandered through the wynds and vennels of Berwick which he knew so well, up Hidegate and into Hide Hill. Maybe he should go to the Castle?

Maybe they wouldn't let him in.

So he wandered to Marygate at the junction with Soutergate and saw the large two and three storey houses built there. Who did he know in Berwick now? After all, he hadn't been back in many many years – for good and sufficient reasons – and the boys he had known would be men of course, if they had been spared.

He realised he was staring at the decoration on a particularly fine house, clearly owned by a prosperous merchant. Yet the new gilding and painting of the crossbeams was rather unusual: white roses-of-the-field on black beams was a bit close to his father's coat of arms. Most people used Tudor roses in compliment to the Queen and coloured them pink and white.

He went to the street door of the house, hesitated, lifted his hand to knock, hesitated and then knocked.

The door was opened by a young girl who looked blankly at him. Carey was wondering who the blonde curls bouncing out from under her biggin cap reminded him of.

"Is the master of the house within?" he asked.

"No, he's deid a year gone," said the child matter of factly. "D'ye want the Missus?"

"Ay, thank ee."

She turned and roared up the stairs, "Mam! MAM! There's a gentleman at the door..."

"Wait a minute..." came a voice from the first floor.

Carey cocked his head. There was something about that voice, something from a long time ago, something...

She came down the stairs in a very respectable grey wool kirtle and a dark cramoisie gown, a falling band at her throat, her cap still struggling with her blonde curls, her blue eyes as merry as ever and when she saw him she put her head on one side and frowned as if she knew him as well, but in a different shape. But he knew her, oh yes, for she had changed less than he had, hardly at all and she was still, for all the twenty years lying between now and the last time he had seen her, a spectacularly pretty woman.

"Cicely!" he said, and then bowed as extravagantly as he could, "Cicely Swanders as I live and breathe!"

She flushed nicely and he heard the silver bells of her laughter again. "Sir, you have the advantage of me although..."

He took his morion off and shook out his hair and then laughing himself, he crouched down to the height of the twelve year old boy he had been when he last saw her. He suspected it was more the way he did that than what he did because she shouted "Rob! Robin Carey!"and immediately hugged him.

The child was goggling at them and Cicely let go at once and coughed with embarrassment, dropped a neat curtsey and pushed her cap straight.

"Well," she said, "well, what a wonderful surprise, Rob, where have you been, what have you been doing? Did you get knighted, I heard that you were..? Oh and I'm keeping you on the doorstep like a stranger, come in, come in... Now you can take your jack off as well, Robin, surely..."

He did and had to leave it on a clothes chest since there was no jack-stand in the place. He put his morion on top where it looked like some kind of skulking shellfish. He had his green velvet arming doublet underneath, which was not very respectable, and his leather fighting breeches and his muddy boots.She led him across the hall and into the parlour where there was a plate cup-board, locked up, and a dining table and chairs and a small fire in the grate and all was as polished and neat as a pin. There were elaborate painted cloths on the walls and a tapestry showing a King and a beggar maid from a story.

She dusted off the master's chair with arms, made him sit down, hurried through the small hall to the kitchen and Carey could hear her talking to someone who presumably was the cook.

The child was still there watching Carey suspiciously. Carey smiled at her. "How old are ye, maiden?" he asked her, falling into the comforting rhythms of Berwick.

"Ah'm seven years old."

"Is the lady of the house your mother?"

The child nodded.

"Well, when I first met your mother, I was only a year older than you are now."

"Oh. Do ye know Uncle Danny?"

"Er... I did," said Carey cautiously, wondering what tale Cicely had been telling about her bastard eldest son. "We were close in age."

"Ye've a lot the look of him," said the maiden, very considering. "Except your hair's dark red. And his is black."

"Ah, yes." Carey thought it would be better if he didn't say that that was because they both had the same father, Lord Hunsdon. "And what's your name?"

"Madeleine. It's like Maudlin but French."

She continued to stare at him and then when he smiled at her, raised her eyes to heaven like a mother of ten, and turned to go to the kitchen at the back.

Cicely came through followed by a girl carrying a tray with a plate of wafers and a promising-looking flagon. Cicely went to her cup-board, unlocked it and brought out two very nice silver goblets, left the doors open so Carey could see the silver platters and bowls and two more goblets.

"Will you stay for dinner?" she asked, "We eat quite early once the boys come home from school and it won't be what you're used to..."

"I think it will probably be a good sight better than the stuff I ate the night before last which gave me a flux. My guts are still in an uproar."

Cicely's brow wrinkled slightly. "Oh dear," she said, "I think I may have some fennel water – Mary, will you go up to my still room and see if you can find it?"

"I'm sure I don't need to take physic..." He changed his mind. "But for you, I will." He had long ago discovered that if a woman wanted to give you medicine, it was hopeless to resist, more tactful to take it and wise to claim a miracle cure afterwards.

Cicely poured some of the wine which smelled of sloes, being the usual gutrot the merchants sold in the north, for triple the price of decent wine down south. He sighed, smiled and toasted Cicely.

"How did you find me?" she asked, "Did you know I'm now the Widow Hall?"

"No. I saw the decoration on your house and wondered who was using my father's coat-of-arms."

"Ah. Yes. That was in the way of putting bread on the waters, Robin. I was hoping that your father might come back to Berwick one day and notice it and then perhaps I might see him again."

Mary came hurrying back with an ominous dark glass bottle and a large spoon and sure enough, Cicely dosed him with three spoonfuls as she had when he was a boy. The taste was strongly aniseed but not too terrible. Perhaps his guts even quieted a little.

Once Mary had hurried back to the kitchens, Carey tilted his head. "Father married you off to..."

"Timothy Hall, draper and merchant. It was a very good marriage, never think my lord was casting me off, only he was going south and he said I must be respectable and he settled money in trust for Valentine and he paid a huge dowry for me so I have a good jointure now. But I still miss him, especially now I am a widow."

By God, thought Carey, as he often had before, how the devil does the old buzzard still draw the women to him like that? Look at Emilia Bassano down in London.

Her entrancing laugh reminded him of his worship of her when he was a boy and he saw she was blushing. "My nature is warm enough that being without a man is... well, it's hard for me. So the end and cross-beams of my house sport their roses-of-the-field and at the back there are hearts and turtle doves."

He couldn't help it. He looked at her as she was and certainly she was older than him by about twelve or fourteen years, and certainly older than forty but... He had always liked older women and she was still so easy on the eyes. If you wanted to be poetical about it, you could say that when he had first known her, she had been like the apple blossom and now she was like the fragrant ripe apple itself. And everybody he knew - except his father - kept telling him to marry money.

He pulled his thoughts back from going down that alley: what was wrong with him? Elizabeth needed him desperately, needed him to help her defeat a very dangerous charge, and he was thinking of another woman.

Just wondering, said the ugly part of him that had raised this. Nothing more.

Cicely put her goblet down and turned to him: her kirtle and gown were appropriate to her station, but her cap couldn't cope with her curls and her body was only a little stouter than the days when she had been so young and slim. Carey had thought that his old childish love for her was dead and buried, a rose bush with no blossoms, but now he realised that the rosebuds were sprouting again. God damn it.

"So what brings you to Berwick after all this time, Robin?" she asked. "We heard you were Deputy Warden in Carlisle and about Dick of Dryhope's Tower, but not much else."

Carey told a couple of funny stories about chasing reivers over the Tarras Moss to avoid answering the question and then decided to tell the truth. What did he stand to lose by telling it or gain by not telling it? He explained about Lady Widdrington and his desperate need for men and then he explained about his stupid pompous brother...

"You didn't ask him, did you?" said Cicely frowning.

"I had to if I wanted to borrow some of the Garrison as Sir John Forster does regularly."

"Yes but he's hand in glove with Sir Henry Widdrington and Sir Richard Lowther and some of the reivers as well, like the Scotts and the Kerrs. So I heard. My late husband was always complaining about him. Everybody on the town council hates his guts."

"I'm not surprised."

"Hmm. Are you sure Lady Widdrington isn't a witch?"

He did his best to be patient. After all that would have been his first question about any woman whom he didn't know who was facing such an accusation. "Yes, I am."

"Poor lady, then," said Cicely tactfully.

"Sir Henry has put a scold's bridle on her."

Cicely winced. "How horrible. But how will you rescue her, Robin? The Widdringtons are a strong surname, which is why Sir Henry is Deputy Warden."

"I don't know. But if I'm to get her out of Widdrington castle, I'll need men and I only have about eight or maybe sixteen at the moment."

"Couldn't you use the Carlisle Guard?"

Carey shook his head. "I don't want to strip the West March of men, even if it weren't far beyond my office to use them so and I've resigned it anyway. The Maxwells and Johnstones are feuding again and the Elliots and Armstrongs and Grahams... well, it's a mess. I thought that with Berwick being less busy and a little nearer to Widdrington, John might... It was a mistake. I've no chance of getting reinforcements now."

She put her head on one side and narrowed her eyes. "Hm. I think we need to talk to Socrates – that's my eldest son. A lot of the officer's sons are at Aristotle Knowsley's school in the old chantry. Soldier's sons usually go to the knitting school."

And Carey looked at her and felt the familiar sensation of bubbles going up and down inside him which he had first felt when he was eight and met with Cicely who was just Danny's mother then and not at all respectable. Back then he had had to look up at her.

The last time he had felt those bubbles so strongly was when he bowed in 1587 to Sir Henry Widdrington's pale severe young wife, Elizabeth. And yes, when he saw Signora Bonnetti at the Maxwell's dance and Emilia Bassano in London and even with Janet... How he had puzzled over those peculiar woman-connected feelings of happiness and excitement when he was a boy.

TUESDAY 6TH MARCH 1593, BERWICK

Carey had an idea for something that might help and Cicely brought some of her facepaints down from her bedroom and tried them out on his face. She had an old pot of woad and some kohl for her eyelashes and they played with the paints for an hour but when Carey looked in the mirror he knew it wouldn't do. What worked in a playhouse would not work in real life. He put the pots back on the table and shook his head, then wiped his face off with rosewater. His sister hiding that damage from Jock last summer was a different matter.

Then they spent the rest of the time reminiscing about Carey's days at Berwick. He started telling about some of his adventures since, on embassies to France and Scotland with Sir Francis Walsingham and his service at Queen Elizabeth's Court until Cicely was pealing with laughter and begging him to stop about Lord Burghley wearing an inkpot on his head after a particularly difficult audience with the Queen. Even Madeleine was smiling, although she was still staring disapprovingly at Carey when she remembered.

At last there was a sound of running footsteps and a crash of the kitchen door from the backyard and a small whirlwind arrived, with no cap, his blond curls on end and his collar falling off and the distinct mark of somebody's small fist on his chin. Behind him came another boy who Carey thought must be a friend, dark haired, dark eyed, and shutting the door carefully after him. He took his cap off very properly and bowed to Cicely and Carey. He punched the other boy in the ribs as he started to go through to the kitchen.

"Hey Tom," he hissed at the whirlwind, "Pay yer respects to Mam's guest!"

"Whit? Oh. Ah." Tom reached for his head, found that his cap was missing. "Jesu, where did it go this time?"

"It probably fell off during your fistfight with Hugh," said the other boy prosily, "Why don't you go and look for it cos that's the third one this month."

"Damn it!"

"Tom! Don't swear!" said Cicely sternly but he was already out of the door at the run, heading back the way he had come.

The dark-haired boy came forward, bowed tidily and said, "Pleased to make your acquaintance, sir, my name is Socrates Hall and I am Mrs Hall's eldest son and insofar as my still small stature and want of years allows, the man of this house."

Carey held out his hand and shook. "I am an old friend of your mother's, Master Hall. I first knew her when I was about your age."

An extremely suspicious look crossed Socrates Hall's face. "Ah, then you know Uncle Danny?"

"I last saw him in the summer when he was very helpful to me and I was able to recompense him with a good suit of clothes, but since then I haven't seen him."

"Oh, that's where he got the duds, is it?" said Socrates Hall, "I did wonder. He told me he was bound for the Netherlands and took ship from Maison Dieu quay and tipped me a shilling. And the others too."

"That is what uncles are for," said Carey wisely, "I'm an uncle more times than I am able to count and visiting my nieces and nephews always nearly beggars me."

Cicely giggled like a girl and then straightened her face. "Darling Socrates, will you go and tell Mr Barley that dinner will be delayed a few minutes, until Tom turns up again." The boy nodded seriously and went along the kitchen passage to the kitchen.

Madeleine and the serving maid came in and started to lay the table with a good linen tablecloth and napkins and trenchers of wood and horn cups for the children, silver plate from the cupboard for Cicely and himself.

She stood up and led the way to the kitchen yard which had the normal jakes in the corner and a large number of chickens trotting around and raised beds which had been dug but not yet planted.

"Remember the chickens in my old cottage?" she said, scooping up an elderly hen. "This is the great great-granddaughter and I'm too soft to kill her for the pot even if she isn't really laying eggs any more."

"Socrates Hall?" asked Carey with a slightly wry expression.

"Mr Hall was one for the new learning and after he met Mr Knowsley – his name is Aristotle – nothing would do but for his first son to be called Socrates. It's a bit of a mouthful."

"Nobody calls him Socky?"

"Not twice. That's the only time he fights, when somebody calls him something he disapproves of."

"Ah."

"At least Mr Hall thought better of calling my other son Euripides." Her eyes danced and Carey couldn't help laughing.

The whirlwind arrived again, skidding into the yard from the wynd and kicking a bit of stone into one of the raised beds. "Now Tom," said Cicely, "Here is Sir Robert Carey, please do your duty to him."

The whirlwind took off a boy's cap that was so full of mud it squelched, dropped it, picked it up, said "Pleasedtaemeetcha, sir," and then to his mother, "What's fer dinner?"

His mother grabbed him, hauled him inside while rating him in a fierce whisper for putting such a muddy cap on his head and getting it so muddy in the first place.

Carey was left at a loose end in the yard after he had shut the wynd gate that Tom had forgotten about, before the chickens started exploring.

Socrates Hall was standing there, looking at Carey with the same suspicious expression as his sister and Carey wondered what to say to him.

"Who was Tom fighting," he asked at last, "somebody called Hugh?"

"Ay," said Socrates, "Hugh Collingwood, he's the best fighter in the school."

"I wonder if he's any relation to a person I knew many years ago, with the same name."

"Well Hugh's the son of the Sergeant at Arms of the Garrison Horse. I dunno what his dad's Christian name is."

"Hm. Could be? Is there anything special about Hugh Collingwood?"

"Well, he's already got big shoulders and he's a nice lad but he's a devil in a fight. That's why Tom keeps fighting him, they're best friends."

"Ay, sounds like the boy I knew. Well, well."

Madeleine came out and announced that dinner was ready in strangled tones. Carey went in, followed by Socrates and didn't miss the look exchanged by Socrates and his sister.

Carey had considerable difficulty not bursting into laughter during dinner which was only one remove and had a salt pork stew and a dried pea soup and some sausage and bread with no butter, some elderly cheese and a large dish of fresh scurvy grass and new dandelion leaves which Cicely insisted everybody had to eat, yes, including you, Rob... er... Sir Robert.

He dutifully chewed some, washed the bitter taste out with some more terrible wine and considered that even the East March would probably get seriously hungry by June. The West March, which was poorer and found it harder to import food, was already in a bad state, as demonstrated by the way everybody was so busy raiding, fighting and killing each other.

Tom was sitting on his mother's left, Madeleine opposite him. Socrates was at the foot of the table while Carey himself had the head of the table and said grace at the beginning.

Tom had a terrible time sitting still, his hair was still soaked with water and standing up straight. There had obviously been a titanic struggle between mother and son in which she had succeeded in forcing him to change his shirt. He was eating ravenously and said nothing. Socrates gave a little lecture about amusing Latin poets and Madeleine sat there rolling her eyes every time one of her brothers said or did something embarrassing.

Carey ate as much as he could and then asked if the boys would be returning to school and if they were, could he see the school. Cicely tried to get him to take her late husband's robe to keep him from the nasty March wind, which he refused, but he did take the man's sober and unfashionable beaver hat which was slightly too large for him but at least kept him decent without putting his jack and morion on again.

Five minutes later he was casually kicking a pebble back and forth with Tom while Socrates told him an interminable tale about the walls and the amount they cost to build which his father had told him and was not that a terrible waste of money since Berwick had never had to stand attack since the Queen came to the throne?

"No," said Carey, "ye see, because Berwick stands here, it means attacks and raids from Scotland know they must get past, which they generally don't fancy trying, and so they must go a longer way around and thus Northumberland is rarely troubled now. It's like wearing a jack: it's heavy and slows you down, but men see it and whereas they might try to rob you if you weren't wearing it, generally they won't try once they've seen it unless there are plenty of them."

"Oh."

"Have you got a jack?" asked Tom.

"Yes," said Carey, "It's in the hall."

"Oh sir, could I see it?"

"Of course you can, after school, although it's not as interesting as plate."

"What does it weigh?"

"About fifty pounds. You probably couldn't lift it."

"And you've got tilting plate too?"

"Yes," Carey answered, leaving out that it was in pawn in London. "that weighs eighty pounds."

"Have you tilted in front of the Queen?"

"Of course I have, many times. Although not last summer because I was in Carlisle and probably not next summer because... well, anyway, I doubt it." He also left out that if he had married Elizabeth by then, he would be out of favour with the Queen, and if he hadn't married Elizabeth, he would likely be dead.

They came to the old chantry chapel which was being used as the school, where about twenty boys were streaming in through the door. A tall man with a good beard was standing at the door in his scholar's gown, lightly cuffing boys who hadn't stopped fighting.

"Tom," Carey said, "Could you bring Hugh Collingwood to me?"

Tom grinned and sprinted over to a group of students who were playing dice round the side of the chapel where the schoolmaster couldn't see them. He brought back a lad who had such a look of Carey's old friend, it was quite strange to see.

Hugh Collingwood pulled off his cap and made his courtesy which Carey acknowledged with a nod.

"Tell me, Hugh," he said, "What is your father's name?"

"Same as me, sir, Hugh Collingwood."

Carey grinned. "Born and bred in Berwick?"

"Yes sir."

"Started in the Castle stables?"

Hugh exchanged looks with Tom. "Yes sir?"

"Where is he now?"

"He's out on patrol. He's the Sergeant-at-Arms of the Garrison Horse."

"Exactly what I would have expected. Hugh, I want you to take a message to your father when he comes back. Tell him Robin Hood is back in town. Oh, is the Old Castle inn still in business?"

"Yes sir."

"Tell him that Robin Hood will buy him a quart of ale at the Old Castle Inn around sunset today."

"I'm to say, Robin Hood is back in town and will buy him a quart of ale at the Old Castle inn. At sunset."

"That's right. Don't forget now, he won't want tae miss his ale."

Hugh squinted at him. "Are ye really Robin Hood?"

"No lad, that was a game we played when we were your size."

Both Hugh and Tom looked deeply sceptical about the idea that Carey had ever been their size but politely said nothing and ran in to their lessons.

Carey had to go back to the little alehouse on the Greens to rescue his horses. The man charged him a lot for fodder and neither animal had been groomed, but he sighed and paid up and led them to Cicely's townhouse. There was one excellent argument for taking a servant with him, even when he was in a hurry. He took them into the backyard which was overrun with chickens, and found a harassed young woman who agreed to give them food and water.

After he had closed the gate carefully on two more adventurous chickens, he stood and thought a while. There was still some feeling of nostalgia in him that wondered what Berwick Castle looked like now. So he walked along Marygate to the Westward Gate, crossed the removeable wooden bridge over the moat and continued along Castlegate, ambling along in the weak sunlight and blustery wind of March.

He came to the Breakneck steps which looked steeper than he remembered and climbed up them, finding them longer than he remembered as well, thinking how he had run up and down them thousands of times and barely noticed they were there.

***

The postern gate from the Steps was open and two men above it on the wall. Carey put his hand up to the man, but they waved him in, being busy in conversation.

Eyebrows up, Carey went into the large castleyard and looked about. There were hobbies there in pens and some looseboxes, but no sign of soldiers or officers. He couldn't see any more sentries on the walls either.

The Castle itself was no longer there, though you could see some of the stone-picked walls still standing. All of it had seen better times: some of the towers had lumps of stone at their bases where the walls were crumbling. The two entire walls nearest to the wall of the Greens were actually mere tumbled heaps of rock that were being methodically quarried for the best stones.

No doubt it was in tribute to the peacableness of the King of Scotland, but even so Carey didn't like what he was seeing. If the Chamberlain of Berwick was allowing the Castle to be stripped and wasn't even using it as a convenient look out post for raids from Scotland – well, what was he doing?

He had intended to talk to some of the Garrison soldiers, perhaps even find some of the Garrison horsemen that weren't on patrol. Instead he wandered around, lost in thought. For the first time since he had heard what had happened to her, Elizabeth wasn't at the front of his mind, only as a nagging bass note of worry.

There was a loud shout, and Carey saw an old man walking fast towards him from the stableyard. It was the way the man walked and the vinegary expression on his face that told him who this was, not the lined face nor the white hair.

Carey stood still, doing his best not to grin inanely at the man he hadn't recognised at first.

"Yes, you, sir! What the devil are you doing in here, sir, this is the Queen's property...?"

Carey resisted the temptation to tease the old man, which was an idea straight from the ten year old boy hiding inside him, and decided against saluting him as well.

"Mr James Heron," he said, "I am delighted to see you looking so well. I own I only came in to have a look around my boyish haunts and I will straightaway depart."

He started to walk to the Breakneck steps, counted three under his breath and was rewarded by Heron saying in a strained voice, "Your voice and something about you is familiar although I am not sure what – forgive me, sir, my eyesight does not improve with age."

"Perhaps I should be wearing a muddy statute cap, or be triumphantly leading a reived cow and..."

"Good God Almighty. Is it Rob Carey?"

"Ay, Mr Heron, it is. Although I have to tell you that I am now Sir Robert..."

"Ay, I had heard about that... Well well. Welladay." Mr Heron seemed a little breathless. "And of course, you are Deputy Warden in the West March."

"Yes," said Carey. "Could you take a quart of ale with me, Mr Heron? I'm sure I owe you at least that for all the trouble I caused you. I'm hoping to meet Hugh Collingwood at the Old Castle inn in a while – would you join me, perhaps?"

"One minute." The old man started hurrying back the way he had come and Carey went with him to a new cottage built against the wall near some new looseboxes next to the gun platform.

Mr Heron went in and collected a stick, a bundle of washing and some books and came out with something almost like a smile on his face.

When they got to the Breakneck steps, Carey offered his arm to the old man and was met by a haughty snort and a firmer grip on the stick – and in fact, Mr Heron seemed to go down the steps as fast as he ever had when Carey was a lad. "It's not the going down that's hard," said Mr Heron, "It's coming back up with a bellyful of ale that's the trouble."

"Why are ye still living at the Castle?" asked Carey, "Isn't it mostly empty now?"

"Ay, it is, but there are a few grooms there and some of the horses that can get up the steps and I can always walk along the connecting wall to the gate tower into the Greens if I don't fancy the Steps. It's more convenient for the horses to be in the Ness when they aren't on the Greens, not having to come up the steps. They are going to build a proper Palace there in the Ness any year now.

"Does my brother, the Chamberlain, ever visit the castle?"

Mr Heron produced a derisive snort. "Master Chamberlain Carey hasn't visited the castle in years or thought about it, except to sign permits for cash to any Tom, Dick or Harry to take stone to build their house. Tchah!" There was a long pause while they stepped over some broken stairs. "But I like it at the Castle. Your father gave me a pension, and that cottage and rights to it until my death and by God, I'll stay there as long as I choose."

And his face screwed up into the disapproving expression that Carey knew so well.

They came into the Greens, crossing the rough ground between the end of the Steps and Castlegate, crossed the road with its neat cottages on either side and went into the broad meadows where most of Berwick's garrison horses were kept. They took their time so that Mr Heron could tell Carey about the horses penned there. Carey admired the best of them, recognised several with the Arab breeding that told of their birth in Scotland at Falkland palace. Mr Heron also wanted to know about Sergeant Dodd's horse, Whitesock, now the hero of his own ballad, and how he saved his master and whether it was true or not.

And Carey somehow found himself telling Mr Heron about his love for Elizabeth and how her husband was trying to kill her with an accusation of witchcraft and how he didn't know what to do. It was strange – he didn't intend to confide in him, but there it was. And Mr

Heron leaned on his stick and listened, blinking at the horses cropping the old grass and the sweet new growth and at the other part of the meadow which was fenced off and lying fallow.

After Carey finished there was a long silence and finally Mr Heron said, "Ye came back to Berwick to get men to help ye?"

Carey was surprised. "Yes, I did."

"Ay, and yer brother told ye no."

"Kicked me out of the convent, in fact, but that was because I hit him."

Mr Heron tried to hide it but couldn't stop himself smiling wrily ."There's a thing about yer brother that very few men know."

"Which is?"

"Your brother John Carey takes money from Spain."

"He what?"

"He takes money from Spain. O'course he takes money fra the King of Scots too but that's normal. He takes money from cities in the Netherlands but that's normal as well. And he would take money from France if it wasn't such a mess, although he certainly takes money from the King of Navarre. Most of it is so he'll let their ships take shelter at Berwick from storms in the North Sea."

"But?"

"But he has regular payments that come through Antwerp, not Amsterdam nor the Hague."

"They could be from somewhere else."

"True they could. But last summer a man called Crichton came ashore at Maison Dieu quay, stayed a few days in the town, then got hisself arrested for saying Mass."

"Father Crichton!"

"Ye know him?"

"Yes, I do."

"A day later he was freed by order of the Chamberlain of Berwick and given a horse and he was ower the Border and intae Scotland like greased lightening."

"How did he get the horse?"

"It was one of the Garrison horses, Bugloss, out of Teazle by the Scotchman, and the bastard Jesuit never sent him home neither. I had to gae into Scotland to track him down and rescue him."

Now Carey understood why Mr Heron was angry about it. He tutted carefully.

"But that doesn't mean he's taking money..."

"Nay, but Crichton had some papers taken off him while he was under arrest and one o' them was a banker's order on a Scottish goldsmith for a thousand pounds English that was in John Carey's name to start with, and the bankers were the Medici."

"Jesus."

"Dinna swear, Rob, it disna help. When I went into Scotland to find Bugloss, I took that order to Edinburgh and a letter of authorisation from Master Chamberlain to the Scottish goldsmith and came back with the gold in my saddlebags." Mr Heron paused. "It were quite an adventure."

"But why did John let you see the banker's order?"

"He thinks I canna read. But I can. I learnt it so as I could read the sweet words of Christ in the Bible."

"So it was all coney-catching? John arrested the Jesuit to get the banker's order and the other papers were forgeries?"

"Seems like it."

Carey was silent for a moment. "Thank ye very much for telling me this, Mr Heron..."

"Ay. There's more."

Carey waited.

"Ye didna ask where I found Bugloss. He was wi' Lord Spynie's horses at Edinburgh."

"This was last summer?"

"Ay, July."

"Tell me, did you know that there were two serious attempts at assassinating the King of Scots at Christmas, which a friend of mine and I were only able to foil by the Grace of God?"

"I heard some rumours. That's why I'm telling ye this. The same thing happened in February this year. Yer man comes off a boat at Maison Dieu quay, gets arrested, interrogated by yer brother. Surprise, surprise, he's let go and off he gallops tae Scotland with a verra nice tall black horse between his legs, by the name of Beaumont from the Garrison herds..."

"A son of Beauregard?"

"Nay, lad, Beauregard's long dead, one o' his sons, Beaujoie, and the best horse I've seen for a long time... Out of Violet, in fact."

"Did he have a banker's order too?"

"I didn't take it, but the lad who took it showed it to me and that wis for another thousand pounds English but drawn on a man called Thomas the Merchant Henderson, of Carlisle."

"I know him."

"Ay, I thought ye might. It was an Antwerp bank this time."

"February this year?"

"Ay. That one wisna a Jesuit, so far as I could tell, but he wis completely bald."

Carey thought he recalled sharing a bedroom with a bald man recently but couldn't place the memory. He thought for a while. "Mr Heron, can I ask ye to keep this secret while I decide what to do about it?"

"Ah wis thinking they should know about it in London, who's that man wi' all the spies – Sir Francis Walsingham?"

"He died a couple of years ago. Now the man to tell is Lord Burghley's son, Sir Robert Cecil. I agree, but I don't want to accuse my own brother of treason unless he is in fact a traitor, even though he chucked me out of the Nunnery."

"Ay, I'll do that. For a day or two. Nae longer."

"Jesu. John's not even a Catholic, he's just bloody greedy."

Mr Heron snorted. "How would I find Sir Robert Cecil, any road?"

"If you're willing to make the trip, Mr Heron, I could give you two letters to show to... er... certain people that will get you into Cecil's office. I'm afraid I'm not in funds at the moment but..."

"Nae matter. I've the money to dae it and naething more to spend it on and I'd like to take a ride to London. Ah've niver been there and I'm curious."

"But... er..." Carey couldn't think how to phrase 'but aren't you a bit old?' more tactfully.

Mr Heron heard what he wasn't saying and twisted his face into something like a cross between a smile and a scowl. "I'm nobbut seventy, me, and while me knees is something chronic, me hips is fine and I can still ride all day and all night if I want."

Carey was silent because he was thinking. When he had heard that John was taking large sums of cash from Spain, his first thought had been to blackmail the bastard over it and get some serious co-operation. But now he was reconsidering. If he blackmailed his brother, he might get the men he needed, but he would endanger Mr Heron and possibly himself – and he would also be wasting a very nice intelligence coup with Cecil. Sir Francis would have left John Carey in place and watched all his correspondence and thus found out about it every time the King of Spain sent assassins to Scotland. Which he would certainly continue to do until James, Elizabeth's only realistic heir, could provide the country with his own heir, a son.

So which would it be? Use the wonderful gift of intelligence from Mr Heron to force his brother to help him rescue Elizabeth – or send Mr Heron south with the letters to get him in to see Cecil. Then he would have to keep his mouth shut about John's greed and treason.

Damn it.

They walked to the small southwestern gate under the gun emplacement. There were sentries there who actually bothered to ask their business and had hidden their tobacco pipes as well, probably in honour of Mr Heron. They headed straight for Marygate where the Old Castle Inn squatted between two taller houses, looking dishevelled and suspicious with its old thatch and battered red shutters.

As they came into the common room there was a shout from a broad man at the bar. "By God,"shouted Hugh Collingwood, "It's Robin Hood!"

Andy and Archie, once the dogboys, cheered. They immediately put their heads together and started singing, "Oh I must to the greenwood go, alone a banished man," quite as badly as they sang it when they were boys. Carey grinned because they were suddenly grown up but still smelled pungently of dog. Cuddy was already going bald, there were Sam Dixon, David Trotter, Jonathan Gray. The bar was full of young men that looked familiar in a strange way and turned out to be the boys they vaguely resembled, as if they were their own fathers

Carey came forward and found himself embraced by all of them which made him feel strange and happy and melancholy at the same time. Mr Heron was already on a settle by the fire, scowling, and Carey resignedly started a tab.

Between the quarts, Hugh Collingwood asked Carey, "What brings ye here, Rob?"

Carey hesitated and then he told him the full story of Elizabeth Widdrington and why he was there. He took it up to being thrown out of the Palace by his brother, left Cicely out of it entirely, and finished by saying, "I wish I could tell ye I have a wonderful plan, but I haven't."

"That's not the Robin Hood that I knew," said Hugh, shaking his head.

"I know. I came in hopes of borrowing the Garrison Horse..."

Hugh laughed shortly. "The official strength is eighty-eight men, horses and remounts."

"But?"

"More like sixty men at best."

"Faggots?"

"All the captains have some, but I've tried to keep them down to two each. Nay, it's your bloody brother, Rob. He hires them out to anybody that asks and so we lose a few each time."

"Ye could argue he's keeping the men sharp..."

Hugh looked steadily at him. Carey sighed and nodded. "I should ha' realised," he said. "So I've got some men of my own which is maybe enough for a night attack if we're very lucky, but..."

"Well, I've got troubles of my own. My son told ye I was out on patrol, ay?"

"Ay."

"We go every few days or so. And while I was out we found the tracks of a company of horse, some of them shod, at least fifty men, come due south fra the direction of Edinburgh, down through the Merse and intae the English East March, ower the Cheviots intae the Middle March and along Coquetdale. But there wasn't any burning and naebody had had cattle nor horses reived. What d'ye make of that?"

Carey thought for a moment and then he realised. "They must be Lord Spynie's men."

"What? Isn't he King James's catamite?"

"He was. He's in cahoots with Sir Henry Widdrington to try Lady Widdrington for witchcraft."

"He is?"

"Ay. He hates me, for good reason and he hates Lady Widdrington for good reason as well. And I've heard he's staying at Widdrington from a good source."

"But he's Scottish. Whit's he doin' in England?"

"Helping Sir Henry judiciously kill his wife."

"He shouldna be ower the Border, leave alone sixty odd miles intae the Middle March."

"I agree."

"And the Chamberlain wouldna help ye?"

Carey shook his head. Hugh sat back and took a pull of his ale. "Ah dinna like it," he pronounced. "What's tae stop him hitting Alnick or Norham Castle or Bamburgh - or us - on his way back?"

Carey almost explained that Spynie was a courtier and a coward and would probably not dare, but then thought better of it. "Well, nothing," he said, "if he dares to do it."

Hugh took another pull of his ale. "A'right Rob, ye've got yer wish. I'll supply thirty horsemen of the Berwick Garrison and possibly another thirty footsoldiers to see Lord Spynie safely off the premises, as it were. I'd offer ye the Earl of Essex's men, but they went off yesterday on some business of their own."

"Ah," said Carey, feeling a little more hopeful. Sixteen men was much better than eight and it sounded as if Tarrant had persuaded the other half of Hieronimo's Troop.

"The only thing is, I can't do it now, I have tae wait until the Chamberlain rides over to Sir John Forster to talk tae him, which he does regular as clockwork. Then I'll turn 'em out for ye." He finished his beer and Carey nodded at the potboy to bring some more. "We'll escort Spynie and his men north again for the avoidance of alarm among the good folk of the Middle and East March."

Carey smiled, felt his guts relax a little. You couldn't say fairer than that and it sounded as if he would have a very nice force of men as soon as his brother left town. However, not now. Now he was looking at Hieronimo's full troop and that was it. And of course, he still didn't know if Dodd would manage to get into Widdrington.

The evening was long and liquid, they tried a barrel of new beer and finished it and sang, of course. Carey discovered again that he was terrible at shove-groat and listened as different people bemoaned the state of the Castle and the Garrison to him – as if he could do something about the loathesome John - and Cuddy and Hugh asked him about the fighting in France which he explained at length and in detail with bits of pork pie as artillery and trenches.

In the end mine host asked pointedly if they didn't have no homes to go to, they drank a toast to the memory of Thomas Fenwick and then Mr Heron announced that he would be staying at the inn rather than climb the unlit Breakneck steps which had after all been named that for a reason.

Hugh walked back to his house beyond Marygate and Carey went with him, his belly full of beer and ale, but relatively sober because he hadn't drunk any spirits except a brandywine by accident towards the end. They tramped through the darkness, swaying slightly and diverging occasionally and laughing often.

"I'm told that your son is the best fighter in Mr Rowsley's school," Carey said.

"Ay? I think he is." Hugh suddenly went silent and took a quick gasping breath as if he had tripped on something or stepped on a sharp stone.

"I didn't even know ye were married?"

"I was," said Hugh very softly. "She died last year of plague, along with our daughter."

"Oh. I'm right sorry, Hugh."

"Ay, so'm I. But at least Young Hugh got better and he won't get plague again. It was the worst year of my life, 1592."

Carey couldn't think of anything to say. It was such a common tale and yet plague hit every person it touched with the finality of a lightning bolt. "Was the deathrate high last year?"

"Nay, just a normal year wi' a few plague deaths, but Kat was one of them and little Beth was another."

Carey nodded, hearing the mortal sadness in Hugh's voice. They walked on in silence and then Carey saw the smart house decorated with carved roses of the field and a candle burning in the window and he looked at it and he thought, can I trust myself to sleep in Cicely's house and know that she's on the other side of the wall and not... explore to find out if she might...?

There was immediate uproar inside him. A small devil was sniggering and rubbing his hands and a voice, very possibly of his guardian angel, was telling him off and wagging his finger.

He could have asked Hugh for a bed for the night and for certain got something better than the alehouse in the Greens the previous night. He could have gone to another inn or even stayed at the Old Castle with Mr Heron. He nearly started to ask Hugh and then noticed that Hugh was looking at him with interest.

"Do ye know Widow Hall, then?" he asked.

"I certainly knew her as Mrs Swanders," Carey said. "She's Danny's mother."

Hugh smiled and dropped a hand on Carey's shoulder. "Sleep well, Robin Hood," he said. "I'll be at the Ness tomorrow, writing reports and arguing over feed bills. Surprise me wi' your astonishing plan to smuggle yerself intae Widdrington inside a deerskin, eh?"

Carey laughed and shook his head at him. He turned to Widow Hall's house, found a note attached to the knocker which told him to look for the key where it always was and try not to wake the children.

He found it tucked into a flowerpot on one of the windowsills, tried the yard door, tried the front door and it worked. Tutting at such lack of security, he went in and found that a bed had been set up for him in the small hall, on a couple of long settles next to the wall, with a palliass and sheets and blankets. He took his boots off with difficulty, stripped down to his shirt, folded his arming doublet and hose. He knelt swaying, said the Our Father in a gabble and then climbed into bed.

WEDNESDAY 7TH MARCH 1593, BERWICK

He woke after one second of sleep and found broad daylight flooding the parlour and Madeleine standing there staring at him. She turned and ran up the stairs, "Mam, mam, he's awake at last."

The headache wasn't terrible but he was feeling distinctly seedy. However he was very happy to see Cicely coming downstairs in her grey wool kirtle with a fresh shift just showing some embroidery and a neat cap. She smiled at him and went into the kitchen, brought a flagon of ale and two cups. Then she smiled with her eyebrows lifted at Madeleine who rolled her eyes again, dropped a curtsey and said in a loud voice, "Ay, I'm just going to play with Anna and Susan." She whisked out of the kitchen door, banging it behind her and the yard door afterwards.

"Mary is having the morning off, the boys are at school," said Cicely pouring the ale, "And Mr Barley doesn't come until ten o'clock anyway so we have a couple of hours." She sat down on a stool next to the bed, gave him one of the cups and drank some herself. "Well, Robin?"

He stared at her and knew exactly what was going on. Hadn't he done it himself many times? He thought back to his recent women: Emilia Bassano in London, Janet Dodd and of course the fascinating and outrageous Signora Emilia Bonnetti in Dumfries and Oxford. Here was a woman he had lusted after since he was a boy and he had left Berwick with no more than a kiss from her and now... Now, unless he was very much mistaken, here she was and she had organised everything so they wouldn't be disturbed and...

She leaned forward and kissed him gently on the lips then sat back and watched him. He sat up, polished off his ale and drank more. All it would take was one good hard kiss and a little work at her clothes, where he was an expert by the way, and then happiness and glory.

And dishonour.

Elizabeth was in peril of her life and suffering who knew what pains and discomforts and here he was, dallying. Here he was seriously considering swiving another woman and although they probably wouldn't be caught, still... How could he?

I am not a bloody monk, he thought, reaching for her cap and taking it off so he could admire her tumble of blonde curls. Elizabeth wouldn't expect me to resist this, would she? She's a sensible woman, she understands that I am a man and have a man's needs and I've wanted to tup Cicely Swanders since I was too young to know what it was that I really wanted. Why can't I...?

He could almost see Elizabeth standing there, watching him, her face expressionless.

This is ridiculous, snorted the little devil inside him. Women have to remain chaste and keep their honour, but men don't. Look how many women your father has had over the years and your mother is still perfectly happy with him.

It was true she had taken up piracy as a kind of pastime in her later years.

Elizabeth was still standing there, looking at him. He shut his eyes, but there she was inside his eyelids.

Remember the mine at Keswick, said something he assumed was the same interfering angel. Remember when you swore off all fornication if God would save you? Eh? He saved you, didn't He?

God will understand, Jesus is merciful.

Don't be stupid.

Maybe Sir Henry has already hanged her. Maybe...

Jesu, said another voice inside him, what's wrong with you, how can it be honourable to dally with another woman while Elizabeth needs you?

I can have Cicely and still rescue Elizabeth, he protested indignantly. Damn it...

But not with honour, said the voice flintily. Which matters more, your honour or your cock?

His eyes flicked open again and he looked straight at Cicely and she was as juicy and sweet as an apple, ripe and willing for the taking.

He sighed and then sighed again, tangled his fingers in her curly hair and she smiled and rubbed her face along his hand like a cat. So he sat forwards and kissed her on the mouth, considerably harder than she had done, telling himself he was kissing her goodbye. She stood up and caught his hand and he told himself that he would just look at her bedroom, nothing more, look, that was all. He followed her upstairs led by the hand, still really the boy he had been but now in the body of a man. That body had different ideas.

Her bedroom was the master bedroom, with a fine four-poster bed and well-embroidered curtains of peacocks and parrots, and the sun coming in through the diamond-paned windows to turn the blond wood into molten gold.

He was already wearing only his shirt and it was the work of a couple of seconds to pull it off and drop it on the rushmats. Then he kissed her again and she started undiving out of her kirtle. He moved smoothly to do the office of her tiring-woman, to help with the weight of the wool kirtle, and help untie the petticoats and untruss her out of her stays, all the complexity of a woman's armour. He thought of the French duchesse who had insisted on her own tiring woman instructing his nineteen-year-old self in how to undress a woman and make it fun for both of them. It took some time. Then he gently lifted her smock off so he could finally see her naked after twenty years of wondering. She wasn't as slim as she had been, since she had had five children, but he found her more enchanting for that she had given suck and there was no use pretending. The boy he had been and the man he was now combined to chase off both the angel and the devil.

She gave him a silver cup of wine and they drank from the two cups with entwined arms. And then she backed to sit between the curtains on the side of the bed and opened her arms to him, put her head on one side and then laughed in exactly the same way she had laughed when he first saw her at the age of eight and for the first time ever wondered why his heart was pounding and there were bubbles going up his insides.

That was happening again.

I'll handle this, said his body, and tipped her gently backwards onto the bed while the boy inside him watched and marvelled again at what bodies could do when they wanted.

At last he was lying on his face, breathing hard and full of the wonderful afterfeelings of joy. Cicely started talking to him with a warm tone of laughter in her voice. He knew he had made her happy, but what was it about women, why the devil did they always want to talk to him when all he wanted was to go to sleep? He managed a couple of grunts.

She eeled out from under him and he dozed off happily.

Suddenly she was dressed again and prodding him.

"Come on, Robin, wake up!"

"Urgh," he said and rolled on his back to show her what had sprouted up invitingly again and she giggled and prodded his belly.

"Up you get," she said, "everyone will be back soon."

"All I want is..." he said, expecting to say 'You' but finding it turned in midair into "...a way to change my hair."

"Your hair?"

"Yes." It had worked before, hadn't it? Everybody might be expecting a pedlar, but what about an old man? He looked at her shining curls and wondered if she had really outrun her age. "I need to get into Widdrington Castle somehow, quietly and out again."

"How will you do it?"

"I have no idea, but I think having white hair might help."

"Is that all?"

"Yes. I think facepaint is too obvious, but if my hair is white I think I could fool them for long enough."

"Oh Robin! Is this like the time ye went raiding for cattle?"

"Not at all. And that was a very successful raid, I'll have you know. I don't think I've been on a better one since."

She giggled. "Yes, but your father beat you black and blue."

Carey lifted his shoulders. "He had to. And so what? It was worth it."

She pushed his shirt into his arms.

"So will you do it?" he asked and she frowned.

"Are ye saying my hair is bleached?"

He looked hurt. "Never at all! I just thought you might have a gossip who knows how to do it and might lend you...er... whatever you need..."

She snorted. "Stay there," she told him severely as she trotted down the stairs.

He filled in the time by looking at the painted cloths on the wall: one of Susannah and the Elders, one of Samson and Delilah.

Well he hoped that wasn't a bad omen.

She came upstairs with his clothes, then with two buckets of water, went downstairs again and came back up again with a large jug of boiling hot water, a bowl and a razor. One more journey and she had a dish of what looked like wood ash and a pot full of something that smelled like ten day old urine.

She made him sit on the stool with the sheet round his bare shoulders. Then she made a paste with the wood ash and the stinky liquid in the pot and started rubbing and combing it into his hair. When he started to protest at the awful smell, she laughed at him and told him he was soft, this was how you turned your hair colour lighter.

"Yes, but what's in that pot?" he asked, breathing through his mouth. "It smells like ten day old piss."

"It's only eight days old, Robin, don't fuss so much."

"Ugh!"

Once his hair was entirely covered with the stuff, she wrapped it in a cloth, took a towel and the hot water and started to shave him, which she did quite expertly. He was used to doing it himself every few days, but he enjoyed leaning back and letting her pass the blade up his throat and feel the delicate spice of danger.

At last he could kneel by the bucket and dip his hair in the water and she scrubbed off the paste, paused to look at it.

"Now you look blond," she said and showed him in her hand mirror. More orange, Carey thought. "I have to do it again, I thought I would."

And off she went again with the disgusting paste which she mixed stronger this time so that his head fair swam with the pungent smell of old piss. At last she let him scrub his hair clean again in the second bucket and she trimmed it at the same time. He rubbed it dry with a linen towel.

She gave him the mirror again and he stared at a complete stranger with white hair streaked with yellow.

Not a complete stranger, but the different hair surely made him harder to recognise and if it was at night... Even better.

He stood up and started putting on his shirt and socks again, then his cannions and vest, and the doublet. She had already gone downstairs with the dish of paste and the pot of urine

He was pulling on his boots when there came a firm knock at the door. A double rap and then another one. Just for a moment Carey wondered if this was her husband... no, she was a widow thank God.

He heard her go to the door as all her servants were out of the house and open it herself.

"Oh, Mr Heron, is it? What can I do for ye?"

"Is Sir Robert Carey about? I've an urgent message for him."

Carey heard the imperious tone of his voice and trotted down the stairs, found his jack and morion and started putting them on. "One second, Mr Heron..."

"Ay, dinna take too long about it."

"Can I offer ye a drink of ale, Mr Heron?" asked Cicely politely.

"Nay, I'm sorry. And if the Chamberlain's soldiers come here, ye havena seen me nor Sir Robert, Missus Hall."

Carey came to the door, grabbed Cicely's shoulders and gave her a smacking kiss on the mouth while Mr Heron stared busily at the carved white roses above him.

Heron had two ponies behind him. Carey went through into the backyard, kicked the chickens out of the way and found and led his own horses out of the small stable in the yard.

Socrates was standing there, staring at him suspiciously. Carey went over and held out his hand.

"Master Hall, ye havena seen me," he said, "I left this morning," and he shook Socrates hand firmly.

"Ay, but what..."

He led the horses to the gate, opened it and found Mr Heron sprinting towards him with a crowd of morions and helmets coming after him. Mr Heron saw him, changed direction, and as he came up, Carey bent with his hands clasped in front of him and flipped the old man into the saddle on Sorrel. He made the steed leap onto Tundish, his other hobby with a roman nose, who promptly wasted time by crow-hopping in protest.

Carey was not in the mood for equine drama, whacked the nag hard and turned him to follow Mr Heron who was galloping down a narrow wynd across the street.

Through a dizzying maze of alleys, leaping one pig and a cat with kittens, through a gap between houses Carey would have sworn was too narrow for a horse, but wasn't, and out into some open ground.

"What?" asked Carey, coming up level with Mr Heron for the first time.

"A lad woke me up at the Old Castle Inn, he's one of the grooms in the Castle. Said the Chamberlain sent some men to find me at my cottage and they asked after ye as well. So I'm making maself scarce. I've got remounts waiting for us at the Bridge."

In a way, Carey was used to occasionally having to run for it out of a town. For instance, when he had left London in June of the previous year, there had been a few very tense moments involving bailiffs. But this was outrageous. Was bloody John his brother or wasn't he? He might have been ten years older but blood was supposed to be thicker than that.

They trotted over a few dead rats and a pile of vegetable peelings and ended up on Westerlane close to where it crossed Briggate and then they were out on the open ground near the entrance to the Berwick Bridge over the Tweed. Someone was waiting for them there, holding two horses and wearing a jack and morion. Carey tensed and then saw that it was Hugh Collingwood.

"Ay," said Mr Heron, coming past him again, "I rousted him out of his paperwork to help us get through the gate tower. Ye did me a favour, there, all those years ago. He's the best of the lot of ye, no mistake. Ho Sergeant!"

"Hugh," said Carey thoughtfully, "thank ee kindly for this. Can ye still come out for me after my appalling brother has gone to see Forster?"

"Ay," said Hugh, his round face hardening. "I dinna like to see Lord Spynie romping into the East and Middle March wi' his band of men."

"Do it when it seems good to you. Or if you hear my name."

"What? Robin Hood?"

"Or Sir Robert Carey."

"Ay, right enough. If I dinna see ye or hear from ye, I'll go to Widdrington anyway and tell the bloody Scots to get out o' my March."

Carey smiled.

They trotted onto the Bridge, and Carey looked at the bridge-tower slap in the middle of it, manned by four sentries. No help for it, they had to go through or ford the river which would mean swimming.

Would John have thought to secure the bridge-tower before he sent men to find Mr Heron? Maybe. Surely he wasn't that stupid?

Hugh chatted lightly to the sentries, no, there had been no orders, ay, they'd forget Mr Heron and Robin Hood, no doubt about it. He stayed with them, and Carey and Mr Heron went past and onto the second part of the bridge.

Both of them broke to a canter and then Mr Heron went to a gallop once they were in Spital and they got to the Great North Road in record time and headed south.

Swapping horses every few hours they reached a post inn around fifteen miles north of Widdrington, at which point Mr Heron produced an extremely valuable general warrant for the Queen's posts, of ancient vintage, so they could stay at the post house for free. In the common room sitting over oat pottage and ale with Mr Heron, Carey bought some sheets of paper at an exorbitant 2d a sheet and carefully drafted several letters.

"Is it true Sir Robert Cecil is a hunchback?" asked Mr Heron.

"Yes, it is, but I'm not sending you to him."

"Oh ay?"

"I'm sending you to my father, Lord Hunsdon, at Somerset House. He needs to know what John is up to first and then he can decide if he wants to share it with Cecil."

"He wilna."

"Probably not, no. But he will take it seriously and he will recognise you so you can give him more information than my letter can."

"Hmfm."

"It's better than going direct to Cecil."

There was a long silence while Mr Heron wore his normal expression of someone who is drinking vinegar at gunpoint. Then he sighed. "Ay," he said, "I suppose so."

Carey finished his letter in cypher, wrote another covering letter and folded both so that they were hard to open and fold again. "Your accusation is given a lot of backing by John's reaction. I've rarely seen such a guilty conscience. I wonder how much he's taken altogether. Hm."

"I'll give yer father yer duty, will I?"

"Yes. There's a verbal message. Sir, I told you in my earlier letter that Lady Widdrington, my cousin and your niece, has been baselessly accused of witchcraft by her husband Sir Henry acting with the Scottish Lord Spynie. I pray that you will come north in person and deal with them yourself. In the interim, I will be doing my best to rescue the lady."

Mr Heron's eyes gleamed and he repeated it three times. "Ay," he said, "that should get him moving. It's a pity he doesna spend more time in the north, yer father."

"I know, Mr Heron, but I think he feels his place is with the Queen."

"Hmf.

Next morning Carey bade him farewell and wondered if he would make it all the way to London and Somerset House. There was nothing more he could do about it anyway.

Wednesday 7th March 1593, Widdrington

Sir Henry stumped into the barnekin and looked around. A few of Spynie's henchmen was dotted around, the rest were in the hall. He was smiling grimly. On the Saturday he had had his secretary write a letter to Carey, telling him that he had Elizabeth under arrest for witchcraft. It also invited Carey to come to Widdrington, if he had the courage, to discuss the matter. The messenger had gone off that day, so the bastard should soon be galloping into Sir Henry's castle to save his strumpet and then he would be caught.

His younger son Roger was standing there, gripping his scholar's cap tightly and looking at him sideways. Well at least the lad had made himself useful for the first time in his life, by bringing his evil step-mother into Widdrington. Sir Henry smiled at the boy who flinched slightly.

"Sir," said the boy, "I should be going back to Cambridge."

"What?"

"I want to go back to Cambridge."

"Why?"

"I... er... I need to study, sir. I am not like you, a strong fighting man, nor like my brother Henry..."

"Who is a traitor to me,"

"Sir, I'm sorry, but... I... cannot..." Roger took a deep breath and swallowed hard a couple of times. "I... my Lady Widdrington has always been good to me..."

Sir Henry scowled and his fists closed. "She is a witch! She has been using black magic on me..."

"I d...don't know about black magic, sir, but she has been a good mother to me..."

"She's evil! She deserves to burn at the stake!"

"I didn't realise what you were p... planning when you asked me to tell her you were dying and now..."

"That's the first time you've ever been any use to me, you numbskull pipsqueak. Get out! Get out of my sight!"

As Sir Henry advanced on Roger with his fists up, the boy ran for the stables. Sir Henry would have chased him but found his bladder too painful to do it so he roared a few more curses at him.

He winced as his bladder complained again. He was finding it harder and harder to piss as Elizabeth's witchcraft took hold. He would stand there for ages, staring at a wall, dying to piss and then slowly a few drops would come, and then a few more and it would hurt more and more until he couldn't bear it any more and settled for the cupful that had come out. Sometimes he half emptied his bladder but he had forgotten what it felt like to have an empty bladder. It hurt all the time. Now he knew who had caused the trouble, his evil witch of a wife, it was all he could do not to beat her to death as she deserved.

He sighed and went to a favourite corner of the yard, unlaced and shook himself. A drop came and then another, a driblet, another driblet, pink with blood. He moaned high and desperately, another driblet, every single one hurting more.

For some reason, Spynie didn't want to hang Elizabeth yet, nor burn her for petty treason, for betraying her lord and master, her husband. He was waiting for something, him and his witchfinder were as thick as thieves. Why wait? It was clear as crystal to Sir Henry now that that woman was responsible for all his pain, all his gout and now this stoppage of his urine, it was all her fault, so why not hang her?

But Spynie would not have it so. He wanted Carey as well who had defied him last year in Dumfries and got him into trouble with the King and coney-catched him at Christmas to boot.

After a quarter of an hour trying to produce a few more driblets despite the horrible itching and burning in his bladder, Sir Henry heard four strange horses riding into the courtyard behind him. He spun with his hand to his sword hilt and saw a long lanky miserable-faced man at their head, not clad for business in his jack, but only in a tailor-made woollen doublet and hose. There was a respectable hat on his head not a helmet, and he had his sword at his side and a poniard as well.

Sir Henry narrowed his eyes. He had seen the man before at Edinburgh, one of Carey's affinity, in his jack. Oh yes, Sergeant Dodd. What the devil was he doing here?

Behind him were three open-faced carrot-headed freckled young thugs with a strong look of the Armstrongs, confirmed by the quilting of their jacks although it was an English diamond style. English Armstrongs, then probably, some of Will the Tod's numerous kin, not Kinmont Willie's from the other side of the Border.

He took his time lacing up again, wondering where Ekie and Sim Widdrington were, who should be coming forward to meet these newcomers.

Finally he started towards them. At last a Widdrington appeared, Jamie's Jock, the stable boy and a second cousin of his, who had denounced Toad a couple of days before, and quite rightly. He seemed a little hangdog and Sir Henry wondered why.

Jamie's Jock took Sergeant Dodd's horse and one of the others. The yard was full of young men walking their animals after him to the stableyard. Sergeant Dodd walked over to Sir Henry and tipped his hat to him. He was walking stiffly, as if he had taken a beating a week ago. Ah yes, hadn't he been wounded at Christmas or something?

"Sergeant Dodd, is it no'?" he said coldly.

"Ay."

That wasn't very helpful or polite. Where was the "sir"?

"So what brings ye to Widdrington Castle, Sergeant?"

The Sergeant looked away into space and his mouth turned down. "The Deputy Warden o' the West March, Sir Robert Carey, would like to arrange the duel that is to be between the twain of ye gentlemen, over yer foul slandering of Sir Robert in the matter of your wife, Lady Widdrington, and yer foul slandering and ill-treatment of your wife as well. He sent me to arrange it."

Sir Henry was instantly angry. Foul slander? It was nothing but the truth and quite mild at that, considering how long she had been bewitching him. Also he had completely forgotten about his challenge to the bastard at Christmastide. It seemed the bastard hadn't.

"Since Sir Robert is a young man and in his prime," droned Dodd mournfully, "and ye are an old man and in yer dotage, out of mercy and consideration for your years, he has chosen his weapons to be dags, being light enough to be held by you, one charge of powder and a ball of lead."

Sir Henry was gobbling slightly in fury. However a small scrap of common sense told him it would not be politic to draw his sword and run Dodd through, despite his insults.

"I am his Second, Sir Henry," said Dodd, "and he hopes you have given consideration to the position of your own Second. He will not accept a withdrawal of your challenge, nor any kind of apology from you nor offer of compensation, and he hopes ye can meet soon so he can have his satisfaction of you by blowing a hole through the place where yer guts would be if ye had them."

Sir Henry was breathing hard through his nose, his face and corrugated ears bright red. Never had he had such an insolent message brought to him. He actually couldn't move for rage.

Dodd was standing there quite calmly, his left shoulder pointed at Sir Henry, his arms crossed and his right hand close to his swordhilt, relaxed and poised to fight if he had to. The three young Armstrongs had returned from the stables and were backing Dodd properly, one at his shoulder, one behind and one... ah yes, one at the gate.

His bladder was burning again.

"I'll consider my answer," he said at last.

"Ay," said Dodd, looking around him.

It was proper to receive the Second hospitably and at least invite him to drink and eat. Usually he refused.

"May I offer you something to eat and drink." Sir Henry almost choked on the words.

To his shock, Dodd finally took off his hat and said, "Ay, that's kind of ye, Sir Henry. I'd like some ale, sir."

Sir Henry had never heard of a Second accepting the offer of hospitality.

"Och... ah..." he said, staring at the dour closed face. "Well, come to the parlour, Sergeant."

Dodd followed Sir Henry into the hall and up the spiral stairs to the small room called the parlour. It was morning, damn it. There should have been women sweeping and polishing, useless idiots that they were, and his wife should be there to greet his guest and bring them wine and wafers as a proper wife should. He stood with his fists on his hips and scowled at this further evidence of her dereliction of duty and almost bellowed for her until he remembered. She was in the cellar because she was a witch.

He harrumphed and stumped down the spiral stairs again to the kitchen where he found the cook and a lad he thought was called Bertram stirring pottage and slicing bread.

"Where is everybody?" he demanded. "Where are my lady's women?"

"Gone, sir," grunted the cook, not daring to look at him. Bertram was hunched over the bread, trying to be invisible. "Maist o' the women went home yesterday, and two more this morning. Many o' the men went with them to escort them."

"But why did the women leave?" asked Sir Henry, honestly puzzled.

"Ah dinna ken, sir," said the cook, "Maybe they was afeared o' being arrested and hanged as witches like Toad. So they went away, those that could."

Sir Henry blinked rapidly. Did they have guilty consciences, were they all witches, did he have a coven in his own castle? He would have to ask Lord Spynie what he thought about it, although at the moment my lord was out hunting.

"Bring some ale through to the parlour for Sergeant Dodd," he snapped and stamped back through the eerily empty castle. There should have been a couple of his cousins lolling about and chatting and then he'd shout at them to do something and they'd roll their eyes and eventually do it.

He didn't notice Roger creeping out of the stables on a horse, leading a couple of hobbies, riding across the barnekin and out of the gate, his spotty face wet with tears.

When he got to the parlour, Dodd was looking at the locked plate cupboard in a professional way and as he turned he made an odd face that may have been a smile.

"The ale's coming," grunted Sir Henry and went to his chair with the carved arms and back to sit down. He shifted restlessly because his bladder was burning again.

"Thank ee, sir," said Dodd. He coughed and said hesitantly, "Sir, I'm hoping ye know that the insulting language I used in the yard came from Sir Robert and not mesen."

"Ay?" said Sir Henry, slightly mollified.

"Ay. I offered to be Sir Robert's Second so I could come and talk tae ye."

"Oh?"

A long pause. Dodd looked at the window which also had proud glass in it.

"Sir Henry, I'm back serving the Courtier but that disna mean I've forgotten what he did at Dick of Dryhope's Tower when he let my blood enemies, the Elliots, go scot free. Nor I havenae forgiven him neither."

"Is that so?" Sir Henry was sitting up again.

"Ay," said Dodd, "He made me and my surname a laughing stock, so he did. And I willna stand for it."

Well this was looking promising, thought Sir Henry.

"Tell me Sergeant, has the bastard's get received a letter that made him angry?"

Sergeant Dodd looked blank and shook his head.

"Where is he?"

"At a posting inn, near Berwick."

"Well my messenger will probably find him soon. I'd like to know what he says."

"Ye want me to go back to him?"

"Ay. Ye can tell him I wisna here because I was hunting with Lord Spynie. How many men does he have?"

"Mebbe eight, from Carlisle."

Sir Henry chuckled to himself. Take on the Widdringtons with eight men? He didn't think so. He tried his best smile at Dodd. "Ye can meet Lord Spynie when ye come back."

Dodd paused a second. "Ay, I'd... er... like that, I didna get the chance while I was in Edinburgh."

"I'll introduce ye to Mr Lindsay as well, the Minister and witchfinder."

"Ay, well, thank 'ee sir, but I'd best be going then," said Dodd. "I'll not wait for my ale."

He stood up, made an adequate bow to Sir Henry, went out shouting to his Armstrongs. Sir Henry followed him out, rubbing his stomach and by the time he got to the courtyard, Dodd and his lads were in the saddle. Dodd doffed his hat to him gravely as he went out the gate.

WEDNESDAY 7TH MARCH 1593, WIDDRINGTON

Sir Henry went to bed that night after another exhausting session of trying to piss which had produced a few more driblets and nothing more. His whole lower belly was burning and aching, he felt hot and thirsty, his head was spinning, he thought he could hear his evil wife laughing at him. He glanced at the truckle bed where she usually slept and thought what a relief it would be to hang her.

Lord Spynie had saved him again and Sir Henry wished he could show his gratitude to the noble lord in some better way than just putting him up at Widdrington and laughing at his jokes. He had first seen Spynie about five years before while attending at the King's Court, when Spynie had been in the flowering of his beauty and in the fullest favour with the King. He had been a cleanly-built miraculously unspotted youth, still narrow shouldered but almost ethereally beautiful. In Sir Henry's opinion he had only grown more handsome as he aged into his twenties. Sometimes when he caught an unexpected glimpse of Lord Spynie, his heart would pound and he would almost be in tears at the beauty of the young man.

So yes, he loved Lord Spynie, but it was a pure love, completely non-carnal. They were friends as Jonathan and David had been and nothing more. He wanted to protect Lord Spynie. Sometimes he fantasised about how he and his surname would rescue the favourite from another surname and Lord Spynie would say thank you to him. That was all he wanted from him, and to be able to look at him and listen to him and be near him. At least Lord Spynie was willing to receive him at Court and was willing to talk to him.

He woke again and sighed, turned over. Every part of him felt sore, he had a backache and his skin smelled of piss again. He normally had no bedmate, not even a dog and especially not his wife. She tended to be a restless sleeper and often jogged or brushed his gouty foot which hurt. Of course he knew now she did it on purpose to hurt him. He had banished her to the truckle bed a couple of years ago for which she had had the insolence to thank him. His valet, Tom Widdrington, had been sleeping on a pallet for years but had been promoted to the truckle bed, now that Elizabeth's witchcraft had been discovered.

He turned over again, then got up and found the chamber pot under the bed. He sat over it because he was so tired, pointing at it, trying to piss. Nothing. Worse than nothing. When he strained, blood appeared.

He whined in his teeth. What would happen if he couldn't pee again? Would the piss find another exit? What?

He shook himself, tried again. Nothing.

He tried to get to sleep and dozed off to nightmares that he was in Hell, up to his waist in fire, burning, burning.

THURSDAY 8TH MARCH 1593, WIDDRINGTON

He woke into full sunlight, bathed in ill-smelling sweat and feeling a desperate urge to piss like a furnace.

"Aargh," he said involuntarily, sat up, grabbed the chamber pot and... nothing. Nothing. something spasmed deep inside him which felt like a knife in his privy member. The invisible knife twisted, probed and he screamed at the pain. He struck his own groin which made it hurt worse and heard his own voice wailing and screaming.

What was his witch of a wife doing to him? How was she putting a magic knife right into his privy member from below and digging upwards to the bladder which was swollen? He was frightened and he howled again.

Tim Widdrington was there, nervously fluttering his fingers at Sir Henry.

"What's wrong sir, will I get you some ale?"

"No, no, I can't piss... it hurts and I can't PISS!" he screamed at the stupid man.

"Wh... what should I do, sir?"

"Stop it! Stop the knife!"

"But I can see no knife..."

Sir Henry grabbed Tim by a handful of doublet and pulled him near. "It's a magic knife," he shouted, red and sweaty in the face. "My bloody wife is doing it, she's attacking me with witchcraft... aarrrgh!"

Still fluttering his fingers, Tim turned and ran out of the bedroom. Downstairs the dogs were all barking and howling while Sir Henry jacknifed into a ball on the bed as the magic knife probed and probed his bladder and he screamed and screamed.

"I'll kill her for this," he panted to the bed hangings, tears of pain running down his face with the sweat. "I'll hang her, I'll burn her... argh!"

There was a lot of shouting downstairs, Spynie's voice, oh thank God, he was back from his hunting trip, Anthony Lindsay's voice.

At last the door swung open and Spynie appeared, followed by Lindsay, and Elizabeth, held by two of Spynie's men. Through the watering of his eyes, Sir Henry saw that at least the witch looked satisfactorily frightened. Her disgusting red hair was tangled and hanging down, her smock was dirty, she smelled bad even to his nose which was part stunned by his own smell. And the scold's bridle had made her mouth swell and bleed so that it looked as if she had dined on blood.

"STOP IT!" screamed Sir Henry, "Stop hurting me, you're hurting me, you witch, stop hurting me!"

She tried to say something and he hit her across the face, hurting his hand on the bridle, hit her again.

"Stop it!" he screamed as a fresh knife started attacking his middle back.

He found his own knife and drew it, tried to stab the bitch and found that Spynie was in the way, caught his hand and easily twisted the knife out of his grip. Lindsay flinched back and Elizabeth went to both her knees. She had shut her eyes and clasped her manacled hands, waited in silence.

Sir Henry was panting, the heat from the furnace in his belly rolling up and down his body, the pain finding new angles to probe.

Suddenly the witchfinder unlocked the branks and took it off. Elizabeth moved her lips and jaw and looked like she was going to faint.

"Sirs," she said, her voice mushy and hard to understand. "I am not a witch and I am not the cause of your pain. I am only a weak and feeble woman and it is rank heresy to attribute powers to me which are only held by Almighty God. God is the cause of your pain, Sir Henry, because of your cruelty, injustice and unkindness to me, contrary to the oath you swore at our wedding."

He tried to hit her again but could only manage a feeble slap. He started to scream again with pain.

Lord Spynie was looking embarrassed and helpless. Anthony Lindsay was staring at Elizabeth as she still knelt in her soiled shift. She lifted her eyes and stared back, locked eyes with him as if she were bracing a sword against him.

"You could help him," said Lindsay thoughtfully to Elizabeth. "I have seen a surgeon do this thing. You pass a reed into the end of his privy member and clear a path for the piss to come out."

"I am no surgeon, sir. You had best find one quickly."

"You must do it now. It may go easier with you if you do."

"I am not a witch or I would already have flown away on my broomstick. This is God's justice on my unkind husband and who am I to argue with God."

"What do you want?"

"Drop all charges, clear my name."

"Let's see if you can help him first."

The witch shrugged, a gesture that obscurely worried him. "All is in God's hands," she said to him, her voice slurred by the effects of the branks. Damn it, why did she have to be a convinced and honest Protestant. It made his job so much more difficult.

Lord Spynie gestured to his men and they grabbed Sir Henry, and on Lindsay's instructions, lifted him onto the bed on his back with his feet in the air like a beetle, sobbing and wailing.

Sir Henry kept wailing and screaming hoarsely while they waited for the reeds to be cut from down by the river and brought up to the castle.

Tim Widdrington came into the room with a cup of laudanum, which Sir Henry drank and then complained about the taste. He joined Spynie's two henchmen in holding Sir Henry down.

Elizabeth had never even seen this operation done so all she could do was pray. She did so, with her head piously bowed and her manacled hands clasped, but internally she was rating God for His treatment of her. She stopped herself and said the most heart-breakingly faithful words in the Bible. "Not my will, but Thy will be done." It was mechanical, she didn't mean it, but it seemed to help a little.

She stood up as Jamie's Jock came trotting in with some reeds and held her wrists out. "Take these off," she said. Somebody had to run downstairs for the key and back up again. Then they were removed by Tim Widdrington, not looking at her. For a moment she wished for an apron but her shift was beyond help of lye or sunshine and it would do.

Her head was spinning, she was thirsty and hungry, her mouth was brutally sore and her hands were shaking. She took a deep breath, took the slenderest reed and started to feed it into her husband's limp cock. It was disgusting, the smell nearly overwhelmed her but the reed hit an obstruction that crackled almost at once.

Trying to ignore the renewed screaming and begging, she tried to ease the reed past the blockage. It wouldn't go. She took a deep frustrated breath and had an idea.

"Fetch me my eyebrow tweezers," she said to Tim and he stared at her blankly. "Take me over there," she said impatiently instead, pointing to the archway to the main bedroom where Lord Spynie and his poor little boyfriends were sleeping.

Finally Tim understood and took her elbow and took her into Lord Spynie's sleeping place, across and to her dresser. She saw that the idiot woman Amelia Widdrington had dropped her riding habit on a chest, petticoats and all and that her dressing table was covered by her gown. She lifted it up, found the tweezers immediately and then had a thought.

She looked at Tim who was staring anxiously over his shoulder at Sir Henry who was moaning and hitting himself again.

Of course she knew exactly where they were, her keys that she wore on her belt as chatelaine of the castle, in the middle of her spare caps. As quickly as she could with her hands shaking, she found the two she needed and took them off the ring, one, then the other.

Tim was looking back at her and she hid her hands under her gown, smiled. "They're here somewhere," and he looked back at Sir Henry.

Where in God's name could she hide them? She slid her hand in at the neck of her shift, put them in her armpit and gripped tight. Please God, she thought incoherently, feeling the cold metal under her arm. She kept her left elbow tightly by her side, lifted the tweezers and showed them to Tim.

They went back to the second bedroom where Sir Henry was, arching his back and moaning and trying to hit himself. Spynie's henchmen were laughing at him.

Suddenly Elizabeth was overwhelmed with pity for the ugly troll-like man in pain on the bed. She took a deep breath, bent over him, gripped his cock with her left hand, pulled back his foreskin and slid the tweezers down inside it, as gently as she could while he screamed and tried to hit her. She couldn't concentrate. "Hold him still!" she snapped and Scarface simply punched Sir Henry on the point of his jaw and knocked him out. Spynie's henchmen turned their faces away.

She could feel gravel with her tweezers. Slowly, sweating with tension, she pulled some of the pieces of stone out – who could say how stone got into a man's bladder, but it did. She had nowhere to put them so she dropped them on the floor. She did it until she could feel no more stones and there was a pink ooze coming out the end.

"Get a bucket," she ordered and Jamie's Jock sprinted down the stairs. More pink ooze. She picked up the reed again and slid it in slowly and gently while Sir Henry flinched and gasped but stayed unconscious.

Just in time Jamie's Jock dumped an empty bucket down beside her for the reed suddenly broke past more gravel. The ooze became a trickle, the trickle a flood and then suddenly piss was gushing through the reed as she drew it gently down so that a flood came. Some bits of gravel came out with the fish-smelling dark piss. The bucket was filled to the brim.

Sir Henry was silent. She wondered if she had killed him, which would lead to her burning for petty treason for sure.

He sighed and dropped deeper into unconsciousness.

Now! said a little voice inside her, now, run, get out of the castle. Run!

But how could she do that in her disgusting shift, barefoot, with no cap? It was a ridiculous idea. They'd ride her down in an hour. And she was exhausted.

Also Tim Widdrington was holding her elbow right elbow. Not the left, clamped to her side as it was.

"Ma'am, I'm sorry, I must put the manacles on again."

What did it matter? She let him do it, waited for the torture implement of the branks but he only pushed her down the narrow stairs to the kitchen and through to the cellar steps.

One of the scullion boys poked his head out and asked anxiously, "Whit was all the noise?"

"Sir Henry," said Tim, "Getting some justice."

Elizabeth stopped in her tracks. "If ye think that, let me go," she said urgently.

Tim hesitated and then shook his head. "I darena," he whispered, "I canna, I'm sorry."

"Do it, and come with me..."

He shook his head in panic. "Where should I go? I canna, my lady, I canna do it..."

Stupid stupid man. He pushed her into the next cellar, locked the manacles to the staple, locked the door quickly behind him. Jesu, so close...

"Then let Young Hutchin go!" she shouted at him angrily through the door. "Let the lad go, get him away from Lord Spynie at least."

There was a long silence and she heard his boots going up the stairs. No help there, then. She unclamped her left arm and squatted so she could drop the two keys on the floor where she could find them. One bounced and for a whole sweating minute she thought she had lost it and then she found it, thank God, still in range of the staple.

She picked the stitches out of the hem of her shift, managed to tear a long strip off it and wrapped both the keys up in it and knotted the cloth. Then she gulped, squatted and pushed them into what men called her citadel, leaving the long end hanging, like a pessary. Jesu, Jesu, it felt a little heavy but it was all right and didn't fall out.

There was a rattle of keys which terrified her, caught in the act. She stood up so fast that she felt dizzy.

"My lady?"

"Yes, Tim."

"He said no."

She took a deep breath in: Sir Henry's yard was now as clear of gravel as she could make it, and she had hoped he would let her go in return. It was a forlorn hope, for if Sir Henry had ever had a scrap of decency or justice in him, none of this would have happened. But it hadn't been for nothing and she now had her keys to the dairy's postern gate and the provisions cellar. All she needed now was the key for the manacles – or just a crowbar wielded by Robin, for instance and she could...

Elizabeth sat back against the wall. She felt... a little hopeful. Would she be able to find a way out of the manacles, open the cellar door, get up the stairs to the kitchen passage, go out into the dairy yard, and open the postern gate with her precious key? She would need some kind of clothes – maybe she could find something in the laundry yard?

She didn't know. But at least she had the keys and the branks wasn't in her mouth for the moment. The manacles bruised her wrists but it was the branks that stopped her sleeping properly. Despite the ulcers on her lips and tongue, shutting her mouth was an almost voluptuous pleasure.

She turned on her side with her arm under her head and fell into a deep sleep.

FRIDAY 9TH MARCH 1593, WIDDRINGTON

Sir Henry woke up after sleeping soundly through the night for the first time in weeks. His yard felt sore but his bladder felt… all right. He sat up and reached under the bed for the chamber pot – and pissed in it! It didn't even hurt much.

There. That was proof. That was clear and sure evidence that his bitch of a wife had used witchcraft on him. If she could take the spell off, then she must have put it on. His memory was very unclear about what had happened, but he could remember her arriving with Lord Spynie's men holding her, convincing them to take the branks off so she could recite charms and spells, even convincing them to take off the manacles. Then she… she… she had done terrible things to him which had hurt and there was a blank space and then at last there was the wonderful feeling of relief as he had pissed for the first time in days. They had taken her away again.

He called Tim Widdrington who was carrying a clean shirt for him and smiled to see him standing.

"Where's the witch?" he asked as he buttoned his doublet.

"Lady Widdrington is back in the cellar," said Tim.

"Did you put the branks back on her?" Sir Henry stopped. The scold's bridle was sitting on top of her gown on her dressing table.

"Well, sir, it had hurt her mouth and…"

Sir Henry cuffed his ears. "Ye fool," he shouted, "We have to keep her from speaking her charms. Go and put it on again!"

"But sir, she helped you..."

"If she can take a spell off, she can put it on again. Go and muzzle the witch again now, before she curses us all."

Tim picked up the branks and took it downstairs, his soft round face troubled. Sir Henry pulled his own boots on and went down to the hall where he found Lord Spynie eating fried sippets and venison kidneys for breakfast with the witchfinder.

"How are you, Sir Henry," asked Lord Spynie and as always, Sir Henry felt warmer just for having the sunlight of Lord Spynie's attention on him.

He sat down at the table and pulled one of the messes to him. He had always liked venison kidneys in mustard sauce, that dear Lord Spynie had so helpfully hunted while Sir Henry had been suffering the effects of his wife's magic.

Sir Henry grunted. "I'm better thanks to the witch taking her spell off me," he said. "We should hang her now and not wait for Carey to arrive. After all, she doesn't have to be alive to get him to come here, now does she?"

"Why are you so anxious to execute her, Sir Henry?" asked the witchfinder.

"To stop her cursing me again."

Lindsay shook his head. "That would be unwise. She has not confessed her witchcraft yet."

"What's that got to do with it?"

"I'm afraid ye know very little of the details of witchcraft, a subject I have studied since I was a young man," said Lindsay in his rich voice. "The witch's power comes from her pact with the Devil, and as long as that pact lasts, her power continues. Once she has confessed and shriven her soul, her pact is broken and her power destroyed. That's the only proper way of dealing with it. First, she must confess and then she must be executed whether by the noose or by burning, depending on her exact crimes, to be sure she doesn't remake the pact. She is damned for eternity anyway."

"Oh," said Sir Henry, "What do you think, my lord?"

Spynie gestured because his mouth was full of kidney. "I'm no expert on witchcraft," he said, "but it makes sense."

"So we have to get her to confess," said Sir Henry, "It shouldn't be too hard, she's only a woman."

"We must also be careful not to damage her too obviously," said Lindsay judiciously, "or the jury might start sympathising with her and refuse to find her guilty. After all there are still foolish naïve people who do not understand the full danger of witches. I have known even learned examining magistrates in Scotland find a very evident witch not guilty and then lecture me about the omnipotence of the Almighty." Sir Henry scowled. "Also she is a young woman and not ugly which will incline their phantasies to her."

Sir Henry made a face. "With her height and red hair?" he said, "I don't think so."

Lindsay smiled. "Some will incline more to her because of it, believe me."

Lord Spynie laughed. "A jury, eh? Well I may not know so much about witches, Mr Lindsay, but I do know more than you about March law. Or do you want to tell him, Sir Henry?"

Sir Henry smiled and bowed slightly. "Ye'll do it better, my lord."

Lord Spynie spent five minutes explaining the law of the Marches and the power it gave March officers to hang men of their own knowing. Now it was true that that was generally within ten days of a trod but Sir Henry had hanged plenty of men of his own knowing in the past when he caught reivers at home, and who could know better than him what his wife was.

Lindsay looked from one to the other. "And Carey? He's a Deputy Warden as well."

"Not in this jurisdiction," said Sir Henry and laughed.

"I meant, do you no longer want to hang both of them?"

Sir Henry scowled in puzzlement.

"There's no sign of him yet," said Lord Spynie, "and I do want him too, by God. Think of the fun we can have with the two of them? Getting confessions out of one by threatening the other, making one watch while we interrogate the other." He smiled. "Carey is the main reason for this… er… for our coming here to save you from witchcraft, Sir Henry. Lady Widdrington is small fry compared with him: she may be Lord Hunsdon's niece but Carey is his son."

"Hunsdon is also Warden of this March, no?" said Lindsay, seeing his complex but promising plan start to crumble.

"He always stays down in London with the Queen, raking in the fees that should go to me," said Sir Henry bitterly.

"I have men keeping an eye on the Great North Road already," said Lord Spynie, "in case he gets wind of what's happening here." The effort to win King James back to him might be ruined if Lord Hunsdon turned up.

"He won't," said Sir Henry, "he's not interested."

"He might."

Lindsay leaned forward. "And what about your eldest son, Sir Henry? Where is he?"

Sir Henry scowled again. "Oh my dutiful eldest son. He always takes his step-mother's part, always has."

"But where is he?"

"Probably somewhere north of Drumlanrig. I sent him off to ask the Maxwell for a couple of his Highland wolf hound puppies, they're wonderful hunting dogs ye know. But I could order him home if ye want."

"No, of course not," said Lord Spynie sharply.

"I would advise against it," said Lyndsay, more mellifluously. "After all, he might oppose you and would the Widdringtons follow him or you?"

"Me, of course, what are you talking about? The boy's a hulk and has more spots than a toad."

"I heard he won the dag shooting competition last month," said Lord Spynie teasingly, "and has half the wives in Edinburgh after him to marry their daughters."

"Hmf, well, he can bide there in Edinburgh if he likes it so much."

"Good idea," said Lyndsay, "although you might want to write to him to stay there with the dogs when he gets back from the Highlands."

"I could tell him his loving step-mother is a witch as well," offered Sir Henry.

Lord Spynie and Lindsay exchanged looks, Lindsay doing his best not to roll his eyes.

"Better not," said Lindsay brightly, "didn't ye say that he always takes his step-mother's part."

"Oh," Sir Henry looked down. "Well I'll write to him any road, tell him to stay where he is."

"A good idea, Sir Henry," murmured Lindsay.

FRIDAY 9TH MARCH 1593, WIDDRINGTON

Dodd hadn't bothered to go to find Carey in Berwick; he waited in one of the post inns on the Great North Road and then rode back – apart from anything else, his back still protested if he rode for more than a few hours a day.

Carey had given him a lot of money, so he could afford to stay at an inn, but he was worried. What he had it in mind to do was no less risky than a raid, perhaps a night-time raid, but it was slower and he was less sure of himself. In a night raid, he knew what to do, had done it many times. With this... He hadn't. It was new to him.

So it was with a very unaccustomed feeling of tension in his stomach that he rode into the Widdrington barnekin around noon with his lads behind him.

A couple of Spynie's bad lots turned up when he called and took the horses. Tiddler Armstrong went with them to the stables on Dodd's earlier instructions to make sure the horses were foddered properly or turned out to grass.

The Castle was open right enough although there were young men on guard by the old and rusty portcullis. There wasn't a drawbridge but a normal bridge over what remained of the moat, though the outer walls looked strong enough for what they had to do. They didn't have to withstand cannonfire, they didn't even have to stand siege. They just needed to keep off armed men on horseback and possibly Scottish rope ladders for a few hours until the Border could rise and strike back against the Scots.

There were men on the walls, though some of them looked drunk. It was adequate.

Dodd sniffed eloquently and went to find the lord and master of Widdrington. He found him in the tiny mews, shouting at the falconer over the body of a dead hawk, though Dodd had no idea what kind not being any sort of lord who went hawking.

Sir Henry stopped in mid-curse when Dodd sauntered in and leaned against the wall, watching. Lord Spynie came out of the mews after him.

"What do ye want?" Sir Henry snapped at Dodd.

"I'm Carey's Second," he said, "remember?"

"Oh ah."

"Sergeant Dodd of Gilsland."

"Och, are ye the Dodd who burnt..." began Sir Henry.

"The church? Ay. Do ye want tae hear what Carey did when he got the letter from ye?"

"Of course."

"Well he's in a taking about it, going on about how dishonourable ye are and how ye need killing to make the earth clean again."

"I?" said Sir Henry brushing his moustache, "I am not dishonourable. Dishonourable is tupping my bitch of a wife and helping her in her treasonous enchantment and cursing me. That's dishonourable."

"Ay welladay, he's not tellt me everything he's got planned but I ken one thing."

"What?"

"All in good time, Sir Henry. First he wants me to make sure ye havena strung her up already."

Sir Henry looked away. "I would have since it's no more than she deserves. But Mr Lindsay says and Lord Spynie concurs that she must first be brought to confess, then brought in front of the magistrate – myself in this instance – who will of course find her guilty and hang her. The confession breaks her power.

"Ay?" said Dodd with interest, "is that how ye do it? Wi' a confession?"

Sir Henry bustled out of the mews slapping his hawking glove on his other palm, explaining the whole thing to Dodd who nodded and said "Fancy!" and "Ye don't say" at intervals.

In the barnekin, Sir Henry hesitated. "I don't wish to see her, Sergeant," he said, "she's an evil devilish woman and very powerful. Even with the branks on her, she caused me to have a stoppage of urine which was painful and inconvenient."

"But it's better now?"

"Yes, she... ah... got rid of the gravel so I was able to piss."

"She did that? That was kind."

"No, Sergeant, it was nothing of the sort. It was a demonstration of her power to stop and let loose, that's all."

"Ah," said Dodd thinking that Sir Henry was crazy and that Lady Widdrington was definitely crazy – why had she helped him? There was a good risk that exactly what had happened would happen. And if she had let well enough alone, there was a good chance he would be dead by now, which would be a fine thing for all concerned.

"I'll get Mr Lindsay to accompany you," said Sir Henry and bustled into the hall where he found Lindsay at a trestle table near the fire, writing a letter. Mr Lindsay casually folded the letter and put it in his doublet pocket.

"This is Sergeant Dodd of Gilsland," said Sir Henry, "Could you show him the witch?"

Lindsay looked at Dodd and asked "Whose man are you?"

"I am Sir Robert Carey's Second for his duel with Sir Henry," said Dodd as friendly as he could, "Who are you?"

"Anthony Lindsay, at your service, Sergeant. I am a Minister of the Kirk and a witchfinder."

"Ay," said Dodd, showing his teeth, "Sir Robert wants a report on whether Lady Widdrington is still alive."

"The witch still lives because she hasn't confessed yet."

"So I heard."

"You want to see her?"

"Ay."

"Are ye not afraid," said Lindsay, "that she might curse you too?"

"No," said Dodd, "Isn't she wearing a scold's bridle?"

"That did not prevent her from cursing Sir Henry with a stoppage of urine," said Lindsay unctuously, "Somehow."

Or mebbe it wisnae her at all, but ye, Dodd thought but didn't say. He wasn't here to argue with the fools. He nodded. "Ay, well, I'm no' afeared of her because I've got an amulet, see."

Lindsay smiled pityingly at him. "A very weak defence and probably cursed by another witch as well. Remember she has made a pact with Satan and probably lain with him as well. Witches always do so."

"Hmf," said Dodd, "Well, all I want to know is whether she's still alive."

"She is."

"So you say. I wantae see her."

Mr Lindsay sighed, stood up, put the stopper in his ink bottle and his pens in his penner. He lit a candle from the fire and gestured to Dodd to go ahead of him, through to the kitchen and down the narrow stairs to the cellars.

In the narrow corridor two of the doors were shut. One was open, showing the wine barrels, the other was a small tool store, locked shut. The cheese store door was also locked.

Lindsay showed him to the one on the furthest left, where the salt beef and pork were kept from the smell.

"Who's in the other cellar?"

"It is one of the grooms, a Graham who tried to steal my horse."

"Oh."

Lindsay glared at the door with an odd expression of worry on his face. "This way," he said, brusquely and took Dodd to the other one. Lindsay had keys and the door creaked open. In the thick darkness, there were barrels and boxes all pushed down one end. At the other end there was a heap of filthy rags in the corner. It moved and sat up with a clink of manacles.

Dodd stood stock still and breathed out very carefully. He had admired Lady Widdrington as that rare thing, like Janet his wife, a completely sensible woman. Now her hair was in elf knots, her smock was filthy, her face was distorted by the scold's bridle and her mouth was red with blood. Bloody spittle dripped off her chin.

It was one of the hardest things he had ever had to do in his life, for her eyes were bright with hope once she had stopped squinting at the candlelight and could recognise him. He forced himself to stand still, forced himself to turn calmly to Lindsay and say,

"Ay, she looks more like a witch now than the last time I saw her."

"She must confess, it is essential," said Lindsay distantly.

"Ay, nae doot," said Dodd, his heart hammering. He wanted to tell her that Carey had got her ring, that he was planning to break her out. But how could he do that with the witchfinder standing there. How could he get it into the conversation for God's sake, without warning Lindsay?

He couldn't. He couldn't think of anything except that he would never tell Carey about what he had seen. God only knew what the Courtier might take it into his head to do if he saw her like this.

***

They had locked the door on Lady Widdringtoon and gone back to the hall. Dodd was thinking fast. He had seen a jug of ale in the corner of the cellar and a neat pile of turds as far from it as the manacles could reach. There was a small drain under the wall which was where the stink of piss was coming from. Lady Widdrington had stared at him as if she was drowning. Poor lady, poor poor lady.

Well at least she was still alive and unhanged. That was something.

Dodd followed Lindsay into the hall but didn't sit down with him. Instead he stood staring into the fire, his hand on his back where it felt stiff.

He wanted to ask Lindsay if he had ever arrested and accused a witch who turned out not to be guilty. He didn't ask. He thought he knew the answer to that and in any case, it wasn't why he was here.

The thing was exactly the same as when some pompous bastard like Lowther or Sir John Forster or indeed Sir Henry, declared of their own knowing that some man was a reiver and a March traitor and hanged him. Of course, often that was exactly what he was, but Dodd had seen occasions when the man was only an unlucky farmer or accused by someone who had a grudge against him. Carey very rarely used the power the Border laws gave him; in fact the only time Dodd could recall was at Dick of Dryhope's Tower.

A trial gave you a chance of arguing your way out, though it was slim. If there was no trial, then you were done for. But everything Lady

Widdrington did was seen as evidence that she was a witch, no matter how unlikely. How could ye fight against that?

"I wantae send a message to Sir Robert saying that I have seen Lady Widdrington alive."

Lindsay looked up and frowned. "I suppose you can," he said. "Would you like to dictate it to me?"

"Nay sir, I can write though slowly. If ye could gi' me a piece of paper and some pen and ink, I'll make shift."

Lindsay brought out a piece of paper, uncapped his bottle of ink and brought out a couple of pens. Dodd sat down and braced himself. He knew Lindsay would want to read it so he couldn't say where Lady Widdrington was – or could he? He knew that there were things you could use as invisible ink, like lemon or orange juice but somehow he didn't think there would be any oranges at Widdrington castle since Spynie's men would have eaten them by now if there were.

Was there milk? He got up, wandered through to the kitchen where there was a cook looking very harassed stirring some pottage over the fire. He went through to the dairy yard and into the dairy and found someone he assumed was Jane, busy cutting curds in bowl.

"Could I have a little cup of milk?" he asked. "To... er... ease my stomach."

Jane lifted her eyebrows, went to another bowl and ladled out some thin blueish milk into cup and gave it to him and he went back. Lindsay was reading a book and Dodd settled down again. He didn't like writing, always sweated over it, but he got on with it as slow as he could. When he finished he showed it to Lindsay, "Sir Robert, Lady Widdrington was alive when I saw her today, Sgt Henry Dodd." He put the date.

Suddenly there was the noise of many horses and men arriving in the yard and Dodd looked out of the window at the Scottish favourites' bunch of henchmen and hangers-on. He could throw any one of them a considerable way further than he would ever dream of trusting them, and Spynie as well.

He had seen Spynie in the distance at the King's Court in Edinburgh when they were hunting, but never spoken to him. The young German engineer had been the go between for himself and Spynie. He had heard Carey addressing him at full volume at the little inn at Dumfries, but again hadn't seen the favourite up close.

Lindsay got up, left his book behind by the fire, went out to greet Lord Spynie. Dodd picked up another pen, dipped it in the milk and wrote "provisions cellar" at the bottom of his letter. The milk soaked into the paper and took forever to dry until Dodd remembered the sand you could speed up drying with and sprinkled some.

It looked all right. At least you couldn't immediately see where the milk writing was. He hoped Carey would have the sense to check, but what could he do about that? So he folded up the letter and used some wax from a candle to seal it, wrote Sir Robert Carey in large letters on it.

Then he wandered out to the stableyard and found a stable boy, in fact the only one left. He was looking harassed as well. "I'll gi' ye a penny now to take this tae the Widdrington post inn and another penny when ye come back," he said to the boy who immediately took the letter and the penny and trotted out of the main gate with it.

Sir Henry had already gone out into the castle yard, smiling fondly at the young man in the fancy cutwork jerkin who was talking to him. Spynie was full of bonhomie and leaned forward to clap Sir Henry on the shoulder at which the old man beamed so much Dodd thought his face would split. Then the Scottish lord jumped down from his horse.

"Hey Mr Lindsay," he shouted and Lindsay bowed to him. "I had a message arrive while Ah wis oot hunting. The King is on his way!"

Dodd happened to be looking straight at Lindsay when he heard that. The witchfinder's eyes blazed with excitement, his skin flushed.

"Really?" he said, very calmly, after a short pause.

"Ay," said Spynie and laughed triumphantly. "He wants tae find out of Lady Widdrington is a witch or no' and he's coming here wi' only a few men to save oor supplies. So it's working, hey, int it? It's working."

"Indeed," said Lindsay with a quick glance at Dodd, who was good at staying poker faced. That glance was clearly meant to warn Spynie to be careful. However Spynie was too excited to notice.

"Ah niver thought it would, but it's working," crowed Spynie, bustling into the hall and clapping Lindsay on the shoulder. Behind him his henchmen were noisily coming in, boasting to each other, settling some bets, grabbing mugs of ale and spitting it out when they found it was sour.

What exactly is working, Dodd wondered, his ears almost turning backwards like a dog's as he tried to hear the whispered conversation between Lindsay and Spynie. There was a patronising expression sweeping across Lindsay's face and then it changed to a broad smile that never touched the eyes.

Spynie came up to him. "Ye're Sergeant Dodd, are ye no'?" he said loudly and Dodd realised he was drunk. "What are ye doing here, hey?"

Dodd managed a bow and took his hat off because the man was a lord after all. "Ay sir," he said levelly, "I've come as Sir Robert Carey's Second for his duel with Sir Henry."

Spynie sniggered. "Sir Henry will be looking for a champion..."

"Sir Robert has chosen dags as his weapons."

"Really?" There was another unseemly snigger. "I'll enjoy watching that."

"Perhaps it might be best to have the duel tomorrow before the King arrives?" said Dodd, just to see what might happen. Sure enough, Lindsay paled and whispered something to Spynie.

"We must wait for the King," said Lindsay sonorously, "He is a most respected expert on witchcraft. He will want to interrogate Lady Widdrington as well."

"Ay, that would be best," said Spynie with an uncertain frown as if he didn't know what was going on either. "Ay to be sure, the... ay."

"The duel will have to wait," said Lindsay directly to Dodd.

"Ah dinna care," said Dodd, "Whatever happens to Sir Henry, Sir Robert willna survive the duel."

Spynie turned and stared at him. "Qhat?"

"I said," Dodd was speaking through his teeth. "Sir Robert willna survive the duel. If I'm around any road."

And he waited to hear what Spynie would make of this, his breath coming a little short with tension.

Spynie gestured to Dodd to follow him and sat down on a bench in the awkward tentative way of someone whose laces are fashionably tight at the back. Dodd still had to move carefully but he stepped over the bench and sat down.

"What are ye saying, Sergeant?"

"I'm saying that I'm no' happy with the way he let the Elliots escape in last autumn and I've a mind to see it doesnae happen again," said Dodd coldly.

"But I understood you were still serving him."

"Ay, I am. And he asked me to be his Second and that's when I thought of it."

"To get your revenge," breathed Spynie, his eyes feverish.

"Ay," said Dodd and shut his jaw.

"We canna have the duel while the King is here."

"Why not?"

"He hates duels."

"Arrange it for tomorrow then."

Spynie shook his handsome head. "We canna risk it."

"Why not? D'ye not want Carey dead?"

Spynie tightened his lips. "If Sir Henry dies in the duel, then it would get… difficult."

"Why?"

"Well he's the magistrate," said Spynie confidentially. "Wi' him dead we might have to find someone else to arraign Lady Widdrington and that might be hard. Obviously Scrope willna do it and Sir John Forster certainly won't, he likes Lady Widdrington, Lowther probably not…"

"Lord Hunsdon?" asked Dodd because he could not believe what he was hearing. He had thought the point of the whole farrago was to arraign Lady Widdrington as a witch and lead Sir Robert into a trap which he had just made a lot snugger and harder to get out of. But from the sound of it, Lady Widdrington was just the means to another end and from what he had heard earlier, he rather thought it was bringing the King of Scots to Widdrington. But why?

"No, of course not," snapped Spynie, looking as if he wished he hadn't said as much as he had. "We'll keep Lady Widdrington here of course and when the King's gone home and me with him… Mr Lindsay will get her confession and Sir Henry will hang her."

Dodd blinked as Spynie turned away and shouted for more ale. He went out to see if the stable boy had come back, and there he was, clutching his statute cap and his paw out for the penny which Dodd gave him along with an extra penny to stay quiet.

Sir Henry came out looking for a serving man and grabbed the boy to carry an ale jug from the kitchen.

Yes, but why the Devil was Lindsay so excited about the King coming? It was easy to guess why Spynie was excited, he was plotting to get back into favour, although Dodd didn't see how he would do it. But what was Lindsay's interest? Maybe he was hoping to become King James's own personal witchfinder? Maybe. It was possible.

He shook his head, wondered if the letter would reach Carey, and turned his back to the fire again to warm the scar there.

TUESDAY 6TH MARCH 1593, NEAR WIDDRINGTON

Nick Stephenson was sitting in a village post inn, drinking terrible ale and playing chess with Leamus. There was the usual population in the commonroom, a group of three youths giggling over a probably obscene carving by one of them on the table, the town drunk arguing about sheep with the town idiot, players of shove-groat slapping the board and betting.

He spared a thought for Missus Dodd and Jane who were already in the second private room that Mrs Dodd had insisted on paying for, sharing a bed in a tiny room under the rafters. It was extremely unsuitable for the two women to come into the common room and the post inn didn't even have a parlour since women were not regular customers at all. However Jane was still tired and sore after her run and seemed quite glad to stay in the bedroom. Mrs Dodd had cornered the alewife and demanded some dried St John's wort for Jane's blisters. At that point he had retreated to the common room.

He and Leamus were alternating between styles – the original one with a Queen that moved like the King and you threw dice when two pieces of equal strength could take, or the new version from who knew where, with the puissant Queen who could cross the board and no dice throwing at all. They were deciding which game was better. Leamus had learnt the new version while he was fighting for Spain in the Low Countries.

"Do you speak Spanish?" asked Stephenson idly.

"Si, pero no muy bien," said Leamus, "Not well but enough to say where the enemy is and how it looks and understand their orders."

"So you're a Catholic?" Stephenson grabbed a vulnerable-looking bishop.

"In a manner of speaking," said Leamus with a slow smile, "I'm a Christian, sure, and no heathen. Which is why I'm telling ye that you might want to think about that move."

"Why?" asked Stephenson, scowling at the board.

"Might it be a trap, perhaps?"

Stephenson scowled harder and fingered his sparse goatee. He stared at the board.

"I told ye to look at it as blocks of power. The knight has his block here, the bishop his here, the castle..."

"And the Queen?"

"To be sure, the puissant Queen," said Leamus softly. "Here she is pent up in the corner waiting to be rescued so she may cross the board and rescue His Majesty."

"So if I take the bishop,,, Oh, the knight is free."

"Of course I could be leading ye into a worse trap, sorr. Ye shouldn't be trusting me."

Stephenson laughed. "You could," he said, grinning at the kern, "but what if I move this soldier there, eh?"

Leamus blinked at the board, blinked again and then smiled a slow and joyous smile. He leaned forward and flicked his king with his forefinger so that the piece rolled a little on the chessboard.

"Did you plan that?" he asked.

"No," Stephenson admitted, "but I'm starting to see what you mean about powers. Though how an Irish kern could know so much about chess..."

Leamus looked at Stephenson, his grey eyes suddenly hard. “You English talk about the Irish – the Wild Irish – as if we were like the savages of the New World.”

“I suppose we do. And it’s not true?”

“Some of it is true of some of us. But all men are not alike, are they?”

“No,” said Stephenson.

“We had Christianity before the English, taught to us by St Patrick as Rome fell and the sky went dark for a year. We kept it after all of England and Scotland had fallen to the pagans and we sent men to speak to the English and the Germans and the Arabs when we heard of them.” He drank some of the bad ale, swallowing with an effort. “But if you destroy enough... the English are like an oxplow in a meadow, up and down, turning the earth and the roots over, grubbing up the flowers and the grasses, naming as weeds whatever they don’t like... They have no respect for Our Lady, none for Saint Bride. And it seems we cannot unite before them.”

Stephenson sat back, nonplussed. Leamus finished his ale and shook his head.

“Do ye have a plan, sorr?”

“It was mostly to find Carey and fight for him if he needs it.”

“Why?”

“He’s a good captain. He’s paid us twice.”

“True,” said Leamus looking round the room. “But then where is he, pray tell?”

“I think he may have gone to Berwick,” said Nick uncertainly.

There was a small plump man in a good wool suit and linen falling band sitting drinking in a corner and looking very sad and sorry for himself. At the name of Carey he suddenly sat up and stared across the tables at them.

Leamus tilted his head gently and raised his eyebrows. Nick looked directly at the man, smiled and lifted his jack full of muddy ale to him, as if he knew him.

The man looked away quickly and licked his lips. Nick was about to go over and say hello when he seemed to come to some decision and walked across to their table.

"Goodmen," he said, "Do ye serve Sir Robert Carey?"

Nick lifted his own eyebrows slightly. "Possibly we do," he allowed.

"Is Sir Robert on his way?"

"Perhaps, perhaps not. He was talking about going to fight in the Netherlands."

"I serve… I served Sir Henry Widdrington as under-steward, but it was mainly my Lady Widdrington that I dealt with. Toby Hogg is my name."

Nick narrowed his eyes. "Ay?" he said.

"I have left his service, goodmen,"said Hogg. "I cannot abide what he is doing now, accusing his wife of witchcraft. The last straw was his hanging of poor Toad, an honest ninny who only loved horses. Would you be interested in some… er… intelligence?"

"We might be," said Nick, sounding bored.

Leamus scooted sideways along the bench, and then got up and went out restlessly to the courtyard. Clockface and Gorman were seeing to their borrowed hobbies. He went out by the main gate, made a quick circle around the inn and back into the common room.

Nick and Hogg were sitting with new quarts and Hogg was talking quickly.

"…on its way from Edinburgh, despatched by Lord Spynie. It's probably a day away now," he said. "Lord Spynie sent it with a full load of hay – you know that my lord has fifty horsemen with him?"

Nick said, "Really? That's a lot."

"Well the horses need fodder, so fair enough. But the witchfinder did the paperwork for the wagon and I've seen it and it's the strongest wagon he could find, what you'd use for coal or iron ore, not just hay. Why would he do that?"

"I don't know," said Nick, staring into his ale as if in search of fish.

"Because there's something under the hay, that's why," said Hogg, lifting an admonitory finger.

"Hm" said Nick, still looking bored. "very interesting. Where did you say the wagon is?"

"I'm not sure," said Hogg, "It's due to get here tomorrow afternoon."

"Thank you very much, Mr Hogg."

"Will you see to it that Sir Robert hears of it?"

"Indeed I will," said Nick with a flash of a charming smile.

Hogg finished his ale with a somehow self-righteous flourish and walked out of the common room. Leamus followed him out and came back a moment later, slid back in on the bench and picked up his ale. "Nobody with him," he whispered. "And he's staying here."

"It could be a trap," said Nick.

"It could," said Leamus, "But what if it isn't a trap?"

"What do you think is on the cart under the hay?"

Leamus grinned. "Gold? Guns?"

Nick contemplated this wonderful thought. "It's getting dark now," he said, "Would you go out early tomorrow and..."

"Sure," said the Irishman, "It would be a pleasure, so it would. The usual system?"

The men of Hieronimo's Troop had gotten quite good at taking wagons and carts full of booty while they were sitting around twiddling their thumbs just outside Oxford.

Nick smiled. "I think so," he said.

WEDNESDAY 7TH MARCH 1593, NEAR WIDDRINGTON

Leamus had already gone quietly into the night before dawn when Nick woke up and started pulling his boots on. All the men were crowded into one large room which had meant furious dicing for the bed and the truckle, three on the bed, two on the truckle and two on the ancient bundles of rushes on the floor. Nobody grumbled because it was a lot better than sleeping out on the road, though less cosy than the corner of Carlisle hall they had made their own. Nick had paid for two days in the room and stabling for the hobbies before he went to bed which had surprised and impressed mine host. All they had to do was wake up and get going on the road, but in twos, not altogether. A gang of seven young men moving in a group might worry a nosy official or even a nobleman on the road.

There were only six of them without Leamus and Tarrant who had gone to Berwick, but even so. They all had swords and two of them had lances. The last thing he needed was some sheriff rounding them up for being a gang of upright men, though that was exactly what they had been.

Nick and Falls off His Horse Perkins went first, since Falls had a mysterious talent which had often been useful before. They went sedately out the gate just as it was opened by a yawning scullion, got onto the Great North Road for Berwick and once they were out of sight of the inn, and on the road, Nick speeded up to a fast trot which also helped him wake up properly.

Falls was grinning slily at Nick. “Shall I…er…” he asked.

“If you would,” said Nick gravely. He was staring ahead into the dawnlight, still grey and indistinct, looking for the right kind and size of copse. The road stretched straight ahead, quite well-made with Roman stones patched with cobbles and the occasional flagstone. It was one of the busiest roads in the country which was why it was so good.

They kept on as the road slowly filled up with occasional peasants going to their outfields. A messenger on a posthorse thundered down the road towards them, so Nick and Falls got off the higher part of the road as the messenger galloped past, waving his hat and shouting at the shepherd with a small flock who was filling up the road. Beyond that was a powerful woman pulling a cart full of winter cabbages and a squawking baby in swaddling clothes hanging from the front which the messenger swerved past still shouting.

Nick got back into his stride again and finally as the sun rose behind the clouds could make out a scarecrow figure running lightly down the road towards him. Leamus arrived with his boots around his neck and a hunting dog grin on his long face. He turned about and fell into step alongside.

“Well?” asked Nick.

“Two men driving,” said Leamus, “one young, one old.”

“Escort?”

“None.”

“Are you sure?”

“I am, sorr, I checked. I started behind them from the inn where they spent the night and there is neither hide nor hair of any soldiers or interference at all.”

Nick answered Leamus's grin with one of his own. "Are you sure it's Spynie's cart?"

"No other carts on the road between there and here. It's the only one, full of hay and with four horses pulling it."

"Four?"

"Sure, sorr, the four of them would eat the cart bare in the five days from Edinburgh, they must be paying for fodder on top of the cart and the men."

Well that was idiocy – it stood to reason there was something else on the cart.

"I want a good place for an ambush about halfway to the next post inn,"

They found a nice place that had been coppiced about six years before so it was good and thick though the leaves weren't out yet. The deerfences had been taken away now the ash shoots were thick enough to fend for themselves.That didn't matter because there was a wall alongside as well which was tumbling down. Nick was certain that they weren't the first and wouldn't be the last to use the place for nefarious purposes.

They trotted past, the three of them, until they came to a place where the road bent smoothly northwest. Nick and Leamus stopped there while Falls Off His Horse Perkins continued up the road, running quite quickly because the sun was out and he wanted to come at the cart from behind. There were plentiful crowds of folk by then, mostly farmers going to their fields and some people even heading for Berwick, three men on horseback, a gaggle of women walking together and chatting.

Another messenger galloped past in the opposite direction, this one not shouting so much.

Nick sat down on a stone scratched with spiky incomprehensible letters. There was a man in a cloak carved there as well. He fished out a couple of penny loaves he had saved from supper and gave one to Leamus, who squatted down next to him.

He didn't plan to eat the penny loaf – it was a bit stale but more importantly he had the itchy internal feeling of impending action which always killed his appetite stone dead. He drank some ale from his pottle which was shoved down the front of his doublet, but only enough to wet his whistle because the ale was still bad. Leamus disapproved of the ale at least as much but still drank some.

The road cleared as the sun rose higher and actually broke through the clouds a couple of times. Nick made the penny loaf last at least half an hour, mostly by breaking it up into crumbs and watching the hedge sparrows and various tomtits pecking them up and arguing and fighting with each other. Leamus watched the birds as well, making no comment but not wasting any of his penny loaf, that was sure. At last in the distance there came a sound of singing by someone with a strong voice. Nick stayed sitting and ignored the cart that rumbled past him with Falls Off His Horse Perkins standing behind the bench, warbling Scarborough Fair or something similar. He met Leamus's eyes, knowing that his eyes would have the same sparkle. The road wasn't nearly as busy as it had been earlier.

He stood up and trotted after the cart, with Leamus at his shoulder. They caught the back posts and swung themselves up onto the back of it, moved quickly forwards crawling on the hay until they were behind Falls whose singing was getting louder. The younger of the drivers was singing the chorus now.

Gorman and East, with their lances, came out of the copse, jumped the wall and ran round the back of the cart to approach it from the rear, Clockface and Garron did the same on the nearside of the cart.

The young man who wasn't driving spotted Clockface and Garron, stood up and aimed a caliver at them. Nick leaped forward and coshed him on the back of the head so he went down half stunned and Leamus put his knife to the man's neck and shhhed him like a baby.

The driver touched up the horses and then reined them in violently as Gorman's lance pressed against his chest. Nick grabbed him and rolled him off the cart where East turned him on his face expertly and tied his wrists together. Leamus had already shoved the young man, now without his caliver, onto the ground by the cart where Clockface tied him up.

Nick climbed over the back of the bench and took the reins, rescued the whip from falling off and set the horses moving again. Meanwhile Gorman and East, Clockface and Garron were carrying the two unfortunate drivers into the copse, bumping them a bit as they heaved them over the wall.

Falls was still singing lustily and had gone to Who's the Fool Now? Nick continued peacefully driving the four horses, the rear two of whom had their ears right back. He chucked and talked to them, keeping his voice low and finally the ears relaxed.

Leamus trotted up and gave Nick the thumbs up, then ran on ahead to look for trouble between them and the post inn. Gorman brought a bundle of clothes and boots to the back of the wagon and tucked them into the hay. Falls had switched to a filthy Dutch song which they all knew and Clockface took up the chorus a bit flat, Garron and East sang along as they swung along behind the cart while Gorman hummed all on one note. Even Nick sang along with the chorus. The carthorses continued their steady plodding down the Great North Road to Widdrington.

WEDNESDAY 7TH MARCH 1593, POST-INN NEAR WIDDRINGTON, MORNING

Janet woke up early and lay on the bed next to Jane's quietly sleeping body, working out where she was and how she had got here.

The journey from Gilsland to the post inn ten miles north of Widdrington had been swift, thanks to the horses and the fact that they didn't have a cart to pull like they had when she, Mrs Ridley and her lads had gone to Edinburgh. The world was different for young men, she thought, completely different – although she recalled her grandam telling her stories of how she herself had gone on pilgrimage in the days before the Old Religion died, with the Guild of the Blessed Virgin, ten sturdy women on an adventure and only one man with them as the chaplain.

She sat up and went to look out the window. The hobbies were being fed and watered, she saw, and lined up to go out to the inn's pasture nearby. She had been more tired by the journey than she expected and wondered why until she remembered the babby. She kept forgetting that she was pregnant at last and should probably rest more, despite the Sergeant's nagging.

She pulled on her kirtle, tied her laces and put on her shoes and her cap and went down the rickety stairs to find food, which she found at the hatch to the kitchen. The bread was made with red wheat and rye and there was cheese and a sausage as well, so she carried the trencher and two pint mugs of ale up the stairs and enjoyed her breakfast looking across at the courtyard and especially watching other people working hard instead of herself.

Jane was still asleep which Janet approved of – the girl had worked wonders and had every right to sleep. In fact, Janet thought a day or two in bed would do her a power of good and possibly herself as well.

However that depended on what the lads were up to. She got up, went down to the common room where she found the two Armstrong boys she had brought with her for extra protection, playing dice happily at one of the tables. Neither of them had seen Nick Stephenson and the other members of Hieronimo's Troop, so she went up the stairs to the small gallery and in at the door to the largest room. It was open and smelly of young men's armpits and feet, despite the fact that they had made both beds, pushed the truckle under the main one, and piled up the pallets in the corner, which rather surprised her. However there was no sign of any of them.

Rather annoyed, she went down and into the backyard where she found the alewife working to build the fire under her buck, ready to boil the wort while her daughter brought faggots of twigs out of the woodshed.

"Where are the lads, Goodwife? The ones sharing your best room?"

"Ah've not seen them since they went out before dawn this morning when I was fetching the cheese for breakfast."

"Did they say where they were going?"

"No, missus, they didn't, and I didn't ask."

Janet smiled at her. "Of course not," she said. "Would ye tell me if they come back?"

The woman grunted and Janet went back to the bedroom. She sat by the window and watched: she wasn't accustomed to sitting still but she thought she could get used to it. Jane could have a day in bed and so could she.

WEDNESDAY 7TH MARCH 1593, POST-INN NEAR WIDDRINGTON, EVENING

They were back in the common room at the post inn, they had eaten the ordinary and Nick had run out of money if you didn't count his prepayment for the room that night.. He was used to it but still he didn't like it and he particularly didn't like drinking the cheapest ale, which was definitely third wort and weaker than piss for certain, if piss wasn't what it was mainly made of. Most of the rest of the population were the same as the night before, only now the youths were giggling about some expedition and a white-haired old man in a worn jack was expounding about the battle of Zutphen or some such to the town drunk who was unconscious.

Nick was now feeling quite nervous after the triumph of the cart in the early afternoon. Where the devil was Carey? What were they supposed to do? He sipped the ale carefully because it had to last.

The white-haired old man got up and creaked his way to the bar for more ale and they could hear his Berwick tones complaining about the ale and his rheumatism. He picked up a wooden trencher of bread and cheese and came towards them, carrying it carefully and apologising when he bumped into the three men at the shove-groat. It was a better equipped post inn than most, being on the main thoroughfare of the Great North Road and having regular custom from messengers shuttling between Berwick and Newcastle, Carlisle and London.

He's coming straight for us, Stephenson thought, what's the old bugger want? However as he approached, something odd happened – the old man straightened up and lost his rheumatism. He put his bread and cheese down with a firm tap.

Leamus was already leaning back and grinning like a dog that has just caught a rabbit.

"Nicely done, sorr," he said.

"I think so," said the old man in Sir Robert's voice and Nick Stephenson sat bolt upright and laughed. He sat down with a twitch of his sword out of the way and a clatter of ironmongery – he had a plain dagger on the other side from his sword. His blue eyes were enjoying their reactions.

Stephenson could see now that he was nearer that the crows feet and lines around his mouth were drawn on.

"It's not too good close up," Stephenson said critically.

"I know," said Carey, "I had to do it myself with some charcoal and grease, but it only has to get me in the gate unspotted and as close as I can get to the woodshed where they're keeping her as quick as possible."

"How will you unlock the door?" asked Leamus.

"I won't, I'll use a doorknocker,"

"Oh?"

"Sovereign against skulking Papist priests or scurvy Puritan scribblers... It's a small battering ram. It'll be noisy so we'll need a lot of noise from you men in the barnekin to cover it."

Stephenson felt the thrill of excitement that he always felt at the prospect of action, a sort of bracing and sitting up of his guts. That feeling had been a good part of the reason why he had followed my Lord of Essex's call two years before, the feeling that life was passing him by and he didn't want to settle in as his father's third son and become somebody's serving man at a manor house, or a permanent journeyman smith or worse still, a day labourer. He didn't want to stay in the small town where he was born for the rest of his life because he thought he would go mad with boredom if he did.

Now, granted, soldiering for the Earl of Essex had been a disaster in stupid clownlike tangerine and white livery, but there had been a few night attacks and a couple of raids on fortresses or villages which told him that he liked not knowing what might happen next and could fight. He looked across at Leamus and saw his feeling mirrored there, a brightness, a stiffening.

He could hardly keep from grinning inanely at the Courtier who was currently gagging at the foul ale. Leamus was waiting. Nick beckoned Garron and Perkins out of the corner with the shove-groat board. Gorman was eating the ordinary, the last shreds of salt beef with some neeps and a brown sauce.

"Would you come with me, sir?" he said, having great difficulty keeping the excitement out of his voice.

Carey raised his eyebrows and followed them out of the common room and into the inn courtyard where the cart was just visible backed into the shelter of a lean-to. Clockface and East were squatting in front of it playing dice, waiting their turn in the common room.

Nick and his troop had been working hard on the cart ever since they had got back to the inn. The hay had been pitchforked off and piled into neat heaps; the planks from the false bottom stacked nearby. Underneath were long heavy wooden boxes. Nick had gone to the inn's blacksmith and borrowed a crowbar and opened up one of the shorter boxes. He had whistled to see the calivers daubed in grease and packed in straw, half a dozen of them.

Now he suddenly found himself tongue-tied so he just went over to the cart and peered over the board, pointed at the opened box. Carey followed him and looked.

He went very still. "Where in God's name...?"

Nick explained how Toby Hogg had spoken to them yestereve and they had gone out to grab the cart and its contents and... Carey had jumped up onto the cart and was examining one of the calivers, checking the underside, finding the maker's mark and nodding. He found the crowbar and cracked a longer box open, found the arquebuses.

"You're telling me Lord Spynie and his witchfinder sent these south? Into England? Secretly?"

"That's what Mr Hogg said."

"How many dozen?"

"Eight boxes, so four dozen."

Clockface was staring at Carey's head which was a sort of woolly white with yellow streaks. "What happened to your hair, sir?"

"Oh," said Carey, flushing slightly, "A friend of mine bleached it for me. I had a plan to... but never mind, it probably wouldn't have worked anyway. And now I have a much better plan thanks to your energy and initiative, gentlemen. This is wonderful. It's absolutely marvellous!"

"I thought you and I could drive it to Widdrington since they're expecting it and..."

"... fetch out Lady Widdrington. Precisely. Yes."

"What will ye do with the guns?" asked Falls Off His Horse Perkins.

Carey looked round at them, his eyes twinkling. "Oh, I think you should have them, don't you, gentlemen? After all, you stole them fair and square so now they're yours."

Nick laughed at that and the other men grinned. “We don’t need more than one each,” said Perkins, “Which means there will be thirty spare…”

“Which you can probably sell to my lord Scrope for a very reasonable amount once all this is over,” said Carey. “The arquebuses are matchlocks but at least some of the calivers are snaphaunces which is much better for night work. If all goes well tomorrow, there might be a hot trod by Spynie and his perverts which we might want to… er… interfere with.”

They looked at him expectantly. “We have to take all the guns out and store them here, then fill the boxes with rocks and nail them shut and forge the seals on them. And then we have to put the false bottom back and fork the hay back onto the wagon, ready for the morning. So we should get on with it.”

Leamus was sent back into the common room to get them some quarts of proper beer and not horse piss, while Carey himself took off his jack and worn velvet arming jacket and rolled his sleeves up.

THURSDAY 8TH MARCH 1593, WIDDRINGTON

Rory MacDonald was standing on the walkway above the gate, feeling uncomfortable in his lowland trews and Lord Spynie's livery, wishing he was anywhere except at Widdrington Castle. The minute he got back to Edinburgh, he would find himself a new lord, so he would, perhaps the Maxwell who looked like he might be a better bet for a chieftain. He had started off prepared to tolerate Lord Spynie, seeing as he paid quite generously when he paid and had been King James's favourite as well. He had seemed properly old-fashioned in the way he kept plenty of liverymen about him and rewarded them occasionally in gold or loot. That was how a lord should behave.

However when Rory started to realise what was really happening with Spynie's pages, he had been horrified. He had wanted to refuse to help with the young reiver they were still holding prisoner, but he had been frightened of the witchfinder and of Spynie's vicious temper and talent at finding ways to punish people who didn't do what he wanted. So he had done what he was told and had been sick to his stomach ever since. The argument went back and forth in his head: he should not have helped; he had to, he didn't have a choice; yes, and was that not cowardice? Of course, he had had a choice if he had been brave enough to take it. The excuses he had used, that Spynie was his lord, that he didn't know the youngster or his family, also tramped around his head like prisoners in a cell sounding lamer and more pathetic each time.

He had been innocent enough to think a lord wouldn't be ruled by his yard, the way some shepherds and cowherds were occasionally, mating with their animals which was disgusting and a sin. How much worse then, was Lord Spynie? Yet he was a lord which seemed to mean he could do whatever he liked.

And Rory had helped him to do it.

Rory pursed his lips as a new noise came to him from the Great North Road, peered over the battlements. He watched as it turned off the road and came towards the castle, a heavy-laden wagon, drawn by a rather extravagant four horses, driven by what looked like an old man and his son.

Minister Lindsay, the witchfinder, had told him the cart was expected today and what to do when it came. He had promised to be there but it seemed he was busy in the keep. Sir Henry was sick with something bad and and kept screaming and cursing so loudly it rang all over the barnekin.

Rory winced at the sounds. He had only seen Sir Henry's wife, the witch, in the distance and he felt very sorry for Sir Henry for marrying a witch in the first place and then getting cursed by her. The thought of the witch also made him feel cold and sick.

Rory trotted down the steps and lifted the bar, opened the gate. He sent Tomas the other gateguard, from somewhere foreign on the other side of the sea, to tell Minister Lindsay that the cart of hay had arrived. His Scots was better than Rory's, at least.

The old man in his hemp shirtsleeves and a greasy leather jerkin and blue statute cap, and his son in a worn woollen doublet, were arguing about something as they clopped to the gate. Rory listened hard, trying his best to make out the foreign language that was Scots. But it was worse than Scots, it was English from Berwick and they were going at it hammer and tongs.

"Ye're talking foolishness," growled the old man, "Ah'm telling ye that a horse with his natural hooves that God gave him will allus run better than a horse that's had his hooves trimmed and bloody iron bars nailed to them..."

"Mebbe on grass or heath," said the son, clearly struggling with his temper, "but I'm telling ye that I saw a shod horse beat an unshod one twice at Dryfe Sands and..."

"Pfooey," spat the old man, "that was fixed, that race..."

"Who are ye?" asked Rory carefully, trying not to laugh.

"Ma name's Robin Rose," said the old man, "he's John Rose, we're bringing the hay for Lord Spynie, all the way from Edinburgh."

"Ye're no' Scots," said Rory.

"No, we're not, thank God," said the old man, "The drivers wis taken sick yesterday but we've brung the hay in..."

The son was fishing in his doublet. "Here ye are," he said, "That's a paper wi' writing on it about the cart, they gave us that to show who we are."

"Bloody clerks," grumbled the old man, "bloody everywhere now."

Rory looked at the paper with ink on it in horror. Good God and Mary His Mother, did they think he could read? He was no clerk, that was sure. He took the paper, glanced at it and put it in his jack pocket.

"Ay, it's fine," he said in his best Edinburgh Scots, "take the cart to the yard, will ye? Yer horses go in the field if ye've a mind to stay the night..."

"We'll be taking the horses back to Berwick..." started the son.

"Nay lad," said his father, "we can stay here overnight if my Lord Spynie will have us, my lumbago is something chronic..."

"Ay, but Mam said I wis to bring ye back safely," said the son spiritedly, "soon as I could which disnae include getting drunk at my lord's expense..."

The old man started coughing violently. Rory waved them through grinning and shut the gate behind them, and the argument floated back to him about why the old man's wife wanted him back under her eye and how the boy could stuff that idea up his arse with the kettle.

The cart skreeled over to the backyard where the son got down and opened the wattle gate, closed it behind the cart. Rory could still hear the argument as they set about unhitching the horses.

Inside the back yard, Carey was purple-faced with the effort of not laughing while Nick went on at length and in detail about what a terrible drunk he was while he unhitched the horses. He had the inn's crowbar in a sack and he went to each woodshed and cracked open each door. Only one had a padlock, he opened it and went in, rummaged around.

He stopped as he came out, picked something off the ground and showed it to Nick: it was the other half of Elizabeth's handfasting ring, the male part. Carey put it into the jerkin pocket.

"She was here," he said, "Damn it, they must have moved her into the keep."

Nick took the crowbar and put it in the clothes bag. They moved around the backyard which was long and thin and divided by wattle fences.

There were footsteps coming quickly down the stairs to the kitchen. "We're going to get some ale at the buttery no matter what you think, boy, because my throat thinks a goat shat in it and that's tha'!" Carey rasped immediately.

"What am I supposed to tell Mam then when ye're under lock and key for fighting, eh? Eh?" Nick bellowed as the witchfinder came up behind Carey in his ominous gown and looked around.

"Where's the haywain?" he demanded impatiently.

"Eh?" said Carey, cupping his ear.

"Where is the cart?" shouted the witchfinder.

"Och nae need to bellow, A'm no' deaf, it's at the back of the yard and is this the way tae the buttery, sir?"

"Yes," snapped the witchfinder as he hurried off.

Carey and Nick trotted up the steps to the kitchen passage and down the steps to the cellars. Carey barged into the first one which was full of barrels of wine, ran to the other end where the wet larder was and found it was open and nobody there although there was a new staple in the wall and a pile of turds nearby.

"Jesus, where is she?" he hissed in frustration.

There was a new howling upstairs and shouts. Somebody ran down the stairs, ran back up.

Suddenly the middle door was being thumped and kicked, somebody shouting.

Nick had gone up the stairs to keep guard. Carey went over to the middle door and found it still had its key in it, opened the door and found a tow-headed boy with two black eyes and a fat lip standing there.

"Jesus," he said after a second. "Young Hutchin." He pulled the boy out of the broom store, found he was chained to a staple, broke the links with the crowbar. "Where's Lady Widdrington?"

"They took her upstairs to help Sir Henry I think."

"Damn it to hell." He closed and locked the door again, left the key where it was. Then they went up the stairs two at a time and found Nick standing there with a pottle of ale stuffed down the front of his doublet. Carey looked up the stairs to the hall and as he did, two of Spynie's men came downstairs, shouting at each other, ignoring them.

"They're all up there in the hall," said Carey, "Damn, damn, damn!"

Nick was looking askance at Young Hutchin. "He's coming with me," growled Carey.

They went down the stairs to the back yard and met the witchfinder coming back, looking very pleased with himself.

"Thank you, goodmen," said Minister Lindsay unexpectedly. "You did your job well."

He hasn't had time to look in the boxes, thought Carey, he's just checked they're there.

"Ay, where's our pay then?" he sniffed.

The witchfinder looked taken aback. Shrieking started again from upstairs.

"The second half," he explained. "We got the first half."

"Oh ah," said Lindsay. Out came a purse, it was opened and two Scotch shillings were put in Carey's outstretched hand, at which point he immediately started pulling on his statute cap and bowing and saying "Thank 'ee, thank 'ee sir,"

Nick could stand it no longer and tried to pull Carey away.The witchfinder hurried up the spiral stair again and Carey stood there, listening hard, his face in a rictus of fear and anger, his hand to his dagger.

Suddenly Nick understood. "It's a man's voice screaming," he whispered to Carey, "Not Lady Widdrington's."

At that they heard her voice, lifted in command. Carey moved to the spiral stairs, but Nick laid hands on him again.

"No," he said, "Most of Spynie's men are up there and Lord Spynie as well. You're a cartman, you have no reason to be upstairs whatever. We have to go."

"But..."

"We have to go now, sir. Now."

Surprisingly Young Hutchin moved past Carey.

"Well, I'm not waiting." That seemed to wake Carey up.

The four horses they had unhitched from the wagon were waiting outside the back yard gate, munching on haybags. They took them off as quick as they could, piled them up.

They started walking, leading the four horses towards the main gate where the young Highlander was standing. The second guard was up on the walkway. Nick had never in his life taken so long to walk anywhere, he could feel sweat dripping in rivers down his back. Young Hutchin was walking between the horses where he was hard to see, not saying anything.

Carey looked over his shoulder at the keep. "But..."

"Sir!"

Carey shook himself and his back bent, he started limping and his head was thrust forward and as they got closer to the gate his complaining about his lumbago got louder and louder.

"I never had any of this here trouble afore, it's terrible, that's what it is and getting worser and..."

Suddenly the young Highlander was looking at Young Hutchin and Hutchin was staring back at him with a look of horror printed on his multicoloured face.

Nick couldn't think of anything to say. Carey caught the look and scowled at the Highlander.

"Ay sir, my grandson's comin' wi' me. I'm not leavin' him here as a groom while that there Lord Spynie's about."

The young Highlander's lips parted, ready to shout. His face was red for some reason and Hutchin was staring at him fixedly.

Nick opened the gate as if nothing was happening, his heart pounding its way out of its chest.

"Ay," said the young man eventually, "Ay, ye're right."

"Thank 'ee, sir," said Carey. "What's yer name."

"Rory MacDonald."

"Thank 'ee, Mr MacDonald," Carey said with quiet dignity, "God bless ye."

They led the horses forward and Rory MacDonald reached out and pulled the gate closed again, put the bar across.

Nick, Carey and Young Hutchin kept walking the horses until they got to the Great North Road and then Carey blew all the air out of his body in a great sigh.

"Curse it to hell and back again. We have to do it all again."

They waited at the place where they had set the ambush and waited for half an hour. Nobody came from Widdrington. Carey shook his head and tutted. "God's death, they're bloody sloppy. I would have found the rocks by now and come looking for the lot of ye."

Very disappointed, Heronimus's troop put their their calivers and arquebuses on the horses' backs and went back to the post inn where Janet was waiting anxiously.

"Did ye get her?" she asked.

"No," said Carey, thin-lipped with frustration. "We couldn't find her because she was upstairs in the Keep doing something for her bloody husband. We couldn't risk hanging about."

Janet looked down and said nothing. "Ay," she said at last.

THURSDAY 8TH MARCH 1593, POST-INN NEAR WIDDRINGTON

Carey was struggling to eat the ordinary in a corner of the common room, while Young Hutchin stood staring into space. Carey's gut had turned to solid lead in his fear for Elizabeth and in the end he gave up and offered the dish – salt beef, sippets, bread – to Hutchin who stood over it awkwardly and threw it into his mouth with the bread. Once he'd started he seemed to realise how hungry he was and polished off the lot.

"They did this tae me at Widdrington, I'm niver going there again, the cowardly bastards," said Hutchin adenoidally, pointing at his face. "And that Lord Spynie... Ah hate him, I hate him so... I'll kill the bastard."

Carey could see tears in the lad's eyes, that his hands were shaking. Young Hutchin brought up a stool and sat down carefully. What had Lord Spynie done to Young Hutchin?

"Young Hutchin?" he asked.

"Can I have some bread, sir, I'm fair famished?"

Carey gestured open-handed at the bread and cheese and went over to the ale jug and poured a quart into his own jack. He found a horn cup on the shelf, brought it over, poured a good belt of the terrible brandywine and gave it into Hutchin's hand, who looked at it, sniffed, and swallowed all of it.

"Have it, I don't want it. But eat it slowly, your teeth might be loose. Dip the bread in the ale to soften it."

Young Hutchin grunted and did so. Three seconds later the bread and cheese had disappeared.

An inn-servant kicked the door open and brought in oatmeal pottage in a wooden bowl, with more bread and more ale. Then he stood there until Carey gave him a groat, English.

Once the man had shambled out, Carey turned back to Young Hutchin who was busily using the bread to shovel the pottage into his mouth. Carey fished in his belt pouch and found an old pewter spoon with a worn shield etched on it of three roses on a bar sinister. He handed it to Hutchin silently and Hutchin nodded his thanks.

After a while Hutchin asked, "I want a horse, sir. Would ye give me one so I dinna have to steal one?"

"Why?"

"I wantae ride tae Brackenhill and tell ma Uncle Ritchie that the Widdringtons slung me in jail."

Carey paused, thinking of the Border going up in flames from one end to the other and then he said, "Do ye think that's wise?"

Young Hutchin stopped eating and stared into space for a long time. "Ay," he said at last, "Uncle Ritchie might think it's funny."

Carey would have given a lot to be able to say convincingly that Ritchie Graham of Brackenhill, headman of the Grahams, reiver, blackmailer, biggest operator of protection rackets in the West March, prolific counterfeiter, would never find such a thing funny. But he couldn't.

He stopped pacing and sat down again opposite Young Hutchin. "I don't know if he will or not but I say ye shouldna tell another soul."

The rage had gone down to a steady simmer, stewing in the pit of his belly.

"Whit about Uncle Jock o' th' Peartree?"

Carey couldn't answer.

"Uncle Jock's a right reiver and he'll come oot for me. Just fer the mischief and because the Widdringtons banged me up in the cellar for so long. He willna like that."

"D'ye really think he'll come out for ye?"

Hutchin blinked at the wall and shook his head. "Nay," he answered, "Naebody will give a toss for it, will they? A few bruises." His voice was cold as snow.

Carey took him to the dormitory over the stables where the stableboys slept and gave the Head Lad a penny to let Hutchin sleep there. At the steps up to the loft, Young Hutch stopped. "Ah need a knife, sir," he said, his blue eyes suddenly anxious. "They took my knife off me at Widdrington and I… I dinna think I could sleep wi' out a knife."

Carey still had the old driver's dagger which was perfectly workmanlike. He found it and brought it out. "Wait a few days before you ride for your Uncle Jock's place."

"Ay," said Young Hutchin grimly, "I'll wait a day at least." Carey gave him the knife and he turned and ducked his head to get into the dormitory where three other boys slept. They looked at him assessingly as he strapped the dagger on but when he glared at them, they avoided his gaze.

Carey sighed and went back to the last bedroom that was left in the inn.

FRIDAY 9TH MARCH 1593, WIDDRINGTON

The witchfinder finished his breakfast first and left the hall, heading for the rear courtyard, where the jakes was and the woodsheds. He was looking for the cart he had managed to get Spynie to order to follow him south which had arrived the day before, driven by the old fool and his argumentative son. The two had taken their horses with them but had left the cart as instructed. He had ordered that to happen as well because the last thing Widdrington Castle needed was more horses eating their heads off. He and Spynie could use the cart for their return, although with luck, that return would be delayed.

He tried not to think of his itching sore skin, but he found his mind returning to his sins of concupiscence. Or rather the sin the witch had tempted him into, damn her soul. What was it about witches? Why did he always get aroused every time he thought of them, and their pricket-marked skins and their wide eyes above the branks, their fear? It wasn't fair, he was only made of flesh and blood, he couldn't...

He had sinned the sin of onanism as well. How had she brought him to do it? There he was interrogating her and encouraging her to give up her confession by binding her into a ball and he had become aroused. He had left the cellar and tried to control his arousal, but nothing would do but for him to come back later and... and... sin again.

It was humiliating and it was all her fault.

He paced into the back yard and found the big heavy wagon, half sheltered in the biggest shed. As per his orders they had only half-emptied it and put the hay into one of the haylofts. He climbed up onto the bench and then sighed because he hadn't thought it through. Of course the hay would irritate his inflamed skin. He tried to offer up the pain and irritation to Jesus and stepped into the bed of the wagon. One minute of digging and he had found a box of calivers.

He had to lean out of the wagon and call to the only groom left, that he should bring a crowbar. While the boy dallied over finding it and bringing it, he dug up another box of calivers and a long box of arquebuses. There would be eight boxes in all, containing half a dozen weapons each. And there should be gunpowder and shot as well in barrels. He had checked them the day before, counted the boxes but not opened them.

With those firearms he would become a power in the land after he had succeeded in his mission. When it was done, from Widdrington he would move to Berwick with Spynie's men, where the fat Chamberlain was in the pocket of Spain. A trifle of blackmail, a little more gold and Berwick would be his and the Garrison as well and he would open the port to the ships waiting in the Spanish Netherlands for his word.

And then... glory. His glory, and the glory of the Spanish Duke.

The boy came back with the crowbar and Lindsay started cracking the caliver box open. The nails gave quickly and there... there...

It was impossible. What could have happened?

He quickly levered the arquebus box open. The same. And another box. More stones.

He was panting and sweating. He slumped onto the driver's bench and stared at the boxes in horror. The weapons had... disappeared. The weapons that were an essential part of his long complex plan and had cost him nearly all the gold he had brought with him to Scotland, they had somehow turned into rocks.

How... Could it be the witch? Could she have done it? Or maybe her paramour, Sir Robert Carey?

He kept on thinking. The wagon had arrived while he was busy with Sir Henry, very much against his will. Who had admitted it? He didn't know but he could probably find out who had been on the gate yesterday morning. He had made a quick inspection to be sure that the boxes were there... and then he had paid the two drivers, the old man in his dotage and the bright-looking lad. He had been busy upstairs again when they left.

Who had taken his weapons?

He should ask Lord Spynie... but no, he couldn't. Lord Spynie didn't know that Lindsay had arranged for the haywain he had ordered south to also contain four dozen firearms. Lindsay hadn't felt it necessary to give him that information for good and sufficient reasons. Those reasons still held good.

Sweet Jesu. What could he do now?

FRIDAY 9TH MARCH 1593, WIDDRINGTON

Lord Spynie finished his breakfast and left the hall through the kitchen door, to go down to the cellars. He thought he would go down to the broom store and have a little chat with the young reiver, whatever his name was. Anyway, he had been in the dark for many days now and might be grateful for a lantern.

Spynie collected a lantern from the entrance to the hall, lit it and trotted whistling down the stairs and went to the door of the broom store. The key was still sticking out of the lock so Spynie turned it and then had to turn it again as it had been unlocked to start with.

That made him uneasy and when he opened the door he found... nothing. No tow headed lad blinking in the light, not even a corpse. Just a broken chain still attached to the staple and a pile of turds in the corner.

Sheer indignation made him stand and stare for more than a minute. Who had stolen his prisoner, damn it? Who had dared to balk him of his prey?

Was it the witch? Had she done it? Was this powerful magic like her ability to give Sir Henry gravel in his bladder and take off the charm as well?

He looked at the chain and he rather thought it had been broken by a plain and ordinary crowbar. And it was true that he had left the key in the lock so the young reiver could be fed and watered without the need to bother him for the key.

He turned and stamped his way upstairs, scowling mightily and out to the hall again. He found his Sergeant-at-Arms who was playing dice with a couple of sycophants and winning. He walked up and waited for the man to stand and pull at his statute cap and then said up close and very quietly,

"Sergeant Knox, where is that young reiver we captured?"

"Young Hutchin Graham?"

"Ay, whatever his name is."

"In the cellar, sir," said the man, frowning.

"Come wi' me."

Sergeant Knox and his friend stood at the door to the cellar and looked at each other.

"Ah," said Sergeant Knox, looking anywhere but at Lord Spynie.

"Who was on the gate?"

"Oh that was the Highlander, sir, Rory MacDonald."

"Fetch him for me. Now."

He stood in the hall, staring at congealed platefulls of kidney and half empty pewter mugs and cups of ale. Shouldn't there be servants coming to clear it all away?

Sergeant Knox came back and there was no rawboned young Highlander with him.

"Well?"

"We can't find him, sir. He's nowhere in the castle."

"Did he take a horse?"

"No, I don't think so for I saw him yesterday afternoon when he came off watch. He went out to play football with a few of the lads and I think that was the last anybody saw of him."

Spynie was fuming and furious but there was nothing he could do. "Send ten men out after him. Find the boy's footprints and find McDonald's footprints, track them both. Bring them both back to me."

He suddenly understood what had happened. The young Highlander had stolen the boy away. He sat down on a bench and tapped his fingers impatiently. "Go on, off with you."

"Ay sir," said Sergeant Knox, exchanging another look with his friend.

"And don't tell Minister Lindsay or Sir Henry."

"Ay sir."

FRIDAY 9TH MARCH 1593, WIDDRINGTON

Elizabeth was sitting in the dark trying to focus her mind on higher things than her body which was so tired and cold, so dirty, so uncomfortable and hungry. The manacles chaining her to the wall were making holes in her wrists and they tired her. She had lost hope that Robin had got her ring and she was actually considering saying that she was a witch so that the idiot men who had locked her up would hang her and put an end to the stupidity.

But no, she couldn't. That would be tantamount to saying that she wasn't what she was, which was a follower of Christ, a Christian. She still was, despite the way God was treating her. In a manner of speaking, she couldn't help it.

Ever since she had read the Gospels for herself when she was a despairing young wife, not understanding why her husband was so cruel to her, she had taken hope from the Man in those pages. She had taken hope even if it was an illusion or even a heresy, that the stories of the Son of God could comfort her. She loved Jesus's firm kindness but also His honesty when He said He had come to bring a sword. And He had.

And He had let them crucify Him when he could have cursed the Romans and made them wither like the figtree with no fruit. It was strange that that story was so misinterpreted. Jesus had known He would likely be arrested and He had gone off alone and found a fig tree that was barren, that had no baby fruit on its branches. Whenever she ate a dried fig she thought of the story.

In three of the Gospels, it said that Jesus had cursed the tree and it had withered. The tree was giving no fruit so the farmer would take no loss by it, he would probably be coming to cut it down and burn it anyway. And Jesus had brought out His marvellous power to heal and somehow turned it inside out, reversed it.

He was a young man still, only thirty-three. He must have wondered if He could fight back. He wasn't short of courage as He showed when He cleaned the Temple of moneylenders. So He went off to find out if a fight was possible – and it was.

And He had snapped at the disciples for following Him and seeing what He could do with His Godly power. That told her more: it told her that He hadn't been sure He could do it and now He knew He could, He was troubled, not triumphant.

Then when He was arrested, He had not used any of it. He had even healed the ear of the High Priest's servant that Peter cut off. He had let them bind Him, flog Him, crucify Him when He didn't have to. He could have cursed the soldiers sent to arrest Him, He could have likely destroyed a legion with that power of cursing, made Himself literally the King of Israel.

Because He was a man as well as God, He had wanted to fight. Because He was God as well as man, He had the power but didn't use it, allowed the Romans to torture Him to death. That steadfastness, that willingness to risk everything on following God's will, it took her breath away. And it was all part of God's plan, so Jesus could go through the Gate of Death and open it for all mankind.

It was a strange romance, but still it thrilled her, and she had read it often enough that she could picture Palestine as a kind of warmer and drier England, with London as Jerusalem and the Borders for Galilee.

She was no healer; she had no power to curse despite Sir Henry's certainty. She wondered what she would do with that power if she did have it? Would she be able to resist the temptation to use it to destroy Sir Henry and Spynie and the witchfinder? She didn't think she could resist it and so she was grateful she wasn't a witch.

She could not say that she was something she was not. She could not say that she had a power to use like Christ's when she didn't. She certainly couldn't say that she was a worshipper of the Devil when she was a follower of Christ.

She sighed and spat some gunk out of her mouth. They were going to hang her, whatever she said because they had already made up their minds that she was a witch, certainly her husband had. She regretted clearing the gravel from his member, of course she did, but it had been worth a try. In fact, although she had done it at Lindsay's bidding, at the time she couldn't help pitying Sir Henry, in his pain and desperation. She supposed that made her a soft fool.

And anyway, it hadn't worked. Sir Henry had simply concluded she was taking off a spell she had put on. There was no way she could prove that she wasn't.

She felt through the darkness for the jug of ale and managed to drink some although she couldn't help spilling some of it on her smock and it tasted of metal and stung the sores in her mouth. She had tried untwisting the wire holding the branks on but hadn't been able to take it off.

Sergeant Dodd had looked at her with pity, she thought, but then he had done nothing about her state. She hadn't heard anything from him. At least her belly had stopped demanding food so uselessly, that was a good thing since she couldn't eat anything round the scold's bridle anyway.

There was a clatter and a scrape and the door swung open. She wondered what time it was, whether this was Scarface again with some more ale for her...

It wasn't, it was that foul creature Lindsay the witchfinder. He came in, carrying a dark lantern, on his own. He came in shutting, but not locking the door. He had the key and it was her husband's key, she recognised it. He put the dark lantern on a barrel with one pane open so that the candle shone out and made her eyes dazzle and water. Then he stepped towards her, a strange little smile playing around his lips.

Unconsciously she shrank away. There was no woman here to keep her company and be a witness. She was alone in the cellar with the shadowy barrels of salt beef and pickles and Lindsay was coming towards her, that nasty little smile on his face, expecting no trouble, expecting she would be cowed and obedient and his yard sticking up and making a bulge in his crotch.

FRIDAY 9TH MARCH 1593, POST-INN NEAR WIDDRINGTON

Carey woke before dawn and came down to the common room which was empty of all except the alewife who was eating bread and cheese with her daughter. He had not been able to sleep well, because he had been running and rerunning the short time they had spent at Widdrington, trying to see where he had messed up. Only he hadn't. It had been simply bad luck that Elizabeth was busy at the top of the Keep at the time he came to get her.

If only there was some way to tell her when he would come, some way to get a message to her by magic, tell her to be ready for him. He thought about pigeons which he knew that Dr Nunez used for important messages – hadn't the news that the Armada had left Lisbon come to him by pigeon from his nephew? That's what he needed, although he didn't think Elizabeth could actually catch a pigeon when she was chained up in a cellar.

Everything hinged on Sir Henry. If he hanged Elizabeth then there would be tutting in London but everybody would believe the charge of witchcraft, nobody would listen to him because they knew he loved her. His father would be furious about his niece by marriage, but the fact was no one would really care except Lord Hunsdon and even if his father came north and dismissed Sir Henry from his Deputy Wardenship, which would be hard for even him to do with Sir Henry's connections, Elizabeth would still be dead.

The only reason why Sir Henry hadn't hanged Elizabeth already was presumably because he wanted to hang Carey too, no doubt on the same charge of witchcraft. Hence the impudent and poorly composed letter which had caught up with Carey the day before, saying something about the charge of witchcraft and insinuating that he, Carey, was a coward and saying that Elizabeth had confessed her adultery with him.

That letter was designed – clumsily – to push him into coming to Widdrington to try and rescue Elizabeth which he wanted to do with all his heart but... Thanks to Jane he knew what the real situation was, that Spynie was there and with a large troop of men. And that changed everything.

It was like when he was at Goldscope mine in Keswick, intending to go down the ladder after Hochstetter. His body had refused to do what he wanted. And then his brain had caught up and explained how, thanks to Hochstetter knowing the mine a great deal better than him, he would be a fool to follow his heart. His heart had wanted to go down the ladder, and also to disprove that he was afraid of the dark, which he was. And his heart had been wrong.

This was the same. His heart wanted to charge into battle and save Elizabeth like somebody in a song. But his brain and his body knew that only cunning and planning could save her.

If it was true that Elizabeth had confessed to adultery with him, that meant they had broken her, somehow.

Carey went out restlessly into the courtyard and paced around, trying to get a grip on himself, trying to stop the feeling of sickness and emptiness in his stomach at the terrible not-knowing what was happening to Elizabeth. She was a strong woman but everybody had limits...

And that took him back to another cellar, the cellar at Dumfries, dark as pitch, the dazzle of the lantern, the smell of rot from the poor German, the desperate pain in his own fingers, the pinniwinks tightening and him retching from the pain...

The memory was so strong, he felt ghost pains in his fingers, until his eyes cleared and he saw the boy standing in front of him and asking if he wis Sir Robert Carey?

"Yes," he said and the boy carefully fished a letter out of his jerkin. "Sergeant Dodd said I could get a penny from ye, sir."

Trying to hide the fact that his hands were shaking, Carey found his purse in his belt pouch and fumbled a groat out of it. "There," he said and the child looked quite joyful. Solemnly he handed over the letter and then ran off before Carey could change his mind.

He stood holding it for a moment, his heart still pounding from the memory. Spynie changed everything. He wasn't afraid of Lord Spynie at Court where the King could intervene but he was afraid of Lord Spynie out on his own with his corrupt and dangerous gang of henchmen. The witch-finder, Lindsay, was an unknown quantity but it stood to reason he would hardly help Elizabeth, would he?

He was afraid. In fact, that was what had made it so hard for him to sleep. Now he thought about it, he thought that he had dreamed of Dumfries, that he was back in the cellar, and Lord Spynie was putting the thumbscrews on him again. It had all come back, summoned by the men in Spynie's livery, the knowledge that the ex-favourite was upstairs in the Keep... He had thought he had succeeded in forgetting the Dumfries cellar, when all he had done was bury it. The darkness. The sad faltering mushy speech of Hans Schmidt, the fake gunsmith, Lord Spynie and Sir Henry overcoming him and the agony in his broken fingers...

Was that why the darkness of the Keswick mine had frightened him so? Maybe.

The strange thing was that he didn't really remember the pain itself, just him trying to puke from it, an enormous overwhelming monstrous thing in his body.

Fear seemed to have been growing inside him where he couldn't see it, like some kind of canker: fear for Elizabeth, fear for himself. When he looked back at the man he had been before Dumfries, that man seemed a stranger to him. For the first time, he realised that Lord Spynie and Sir Henry between them had changed something vital inside him. He wasn't sure what it was either.

Had they made him into a coward?

He felt paralysed with indecision, more uncertain than he ever had in his life before. Elizabeth was in terrible danger, was actually being tortured at least by being forced to wear a scold's bridle, never mind what else might have been happening to her. And he had done nothing about it.

He had made love to Cicely.

For a full minute he burned red with shame at the thought. Was that why he hadn't been able to find Elizabeth when he had miraculously gotten inside Widdrington castle? Was it? Was God punishing Elizabeth for his own sin?

No, he couldn't believe that. God was merciful and just and fully capable of punishing Carey for his fornication, but He wouldn't take it out on Elizabeth?

Would He?

He closed his eyes and took a deep breath, another one. It didn't help. Every plan he could come up with was just another weak pawky thing that would dissolve in pieces and end with him getting hanged and what was infinitely worse, Elizabeth getting hanged or burnt.

"My life for hers," he whispered, but he knew that would be a totally wasted sacrifice. In fact that was what Sir Henry's stupid letter was supposed to push him into offering. If he gave himself up to Sir Henry, at best he would be hanged and Elizabeth would be exactly where she was now. Or hanged. Or burnt.

Or was that his new-found cowardice speaking?

Carey gave a little grunt, as if somebody had punched him in the gut. The fear for himself, the terror for Elizabeth were still there, settled in the pit of his stomach. The rest of him was full of whirling confusion.

He looked down at his hand and found he was still holding the letter, painfully addressed to Sir Rbt Carey in Dodd's appalling handwriting. Dodd?

It was extraordinary. Just the thought of the man somehow steadied him, although Dodd had been very much too busy in his teens to learn to write a fair hand.

He opened the letter and read that Elizabeth was alive and unharmed apart from the branks. That eased the sickness a bit.

He would show Sir Henry and Lord Spynie that he was no coward.

FRIDAY 9TH MARCH 1593, POST-INN NEAR WIDDRINGTON

Janet came downstairs from the tiny room she was sharing with Jane in the post inn where Hieronimo's Troop were staying, about seven miles from Widdrington. Jane had gone to her work in the dairy at the castle, very early in the morning so she could take the cows out, with a tale of having been sick of a fever at her mam's. The Mistress of the Dairy had a key to the postern gate so the cows in milch could go out and get some spring grass on the infield and Jane and Janet were trying to concoct a plan to get the key away from her although she guarded it zealously. Jane had a story for why she wasn't living-in any more – she had said she was staying at her godparents' farm and running in from there because the other dairymaids had all gone home and she didn't like sleeping alone and indeed it wasn't at all suitable that she should do so with Widdrington full of Lord Spynie's men. At least the Dairy Mistress agreed with that.

Janet got her morning small ale and some bread and cheese and sat down at an empty table. She felt uncomfortable without a woman with her and wished she had thought to bring Mrs Ridley. She had stopped feeling sick in the mornings the week before and the child inside was a lump low down in her stomach. She had ridden astride as always to get there and felt fine and healthy, almost worryingly healthy, although she had a lot of wind.

The rather bright young man called Nick Stephenson was piling oatmeal into his mouth and the Irish kern with his plait down his back had finished his and was sitting there whistling softly under his breath. She didn't like sitting at table with strangers and she was annoyed with all of them for not telling her about the raid the day before, although Dodd never told her about a raid in advance either. And men were always secretive about a raid that had failed, although it hadn't failed that badly since none of them were hurt or locked up. However Lady Widdrington was not with them although Carey seemed to have accidentally freed Young Hutchin Graham.

She decided not to say anything about it. Instead she asked, "Where did the Courtier find someone with enough lye and ten day old piss to bleach his hair? There won't be any players here until the summer, if then. Where has he been since he left Carlisle?"

Stephenson and Leamus looked at each other. "We don't know," said Stephenson.

Janet managed not to roll her eyes. "Well we can't stay here forever, it's costing tenpence a day."

Leamus nodded.

Janet sighed. Why were men such idiots? And why was Carey, an especially highly-bred and highly-strung idiot, making a mystery out of where he had been?

"Well, we can't take Widdrington by assault with fewer than fifty men but we could run a nice little night raid with what we have, if we could get intae the castle," she said thoughtfully. Both of the young men looked at her in alarm but she continued. She was an Armstrong, damn it, a great-granddaughter of the famous Johnnie Armstrong that was hanged by the King of Scotland. "Spynie has about fifty men in the place, according to Jane, but they're often drunk. It's a pity because the maist o' the Widdringtons have gone home to their farms and villages, so if it weren't for Lord Spynie we could likely do it."

"How do you know?"

That time Janet did roll her eyes.

"Where is the King's Messenger now?" asked Leamus pointedly.

"Eh?"

"Jane."

"Why do you call her that?"

"Because there were certain women of the Irish King's household who knew how to run for a long time, far far longer than men, and would carry the King's Messages for him. They were better and more tireless than horses."

Janet had never heard such a strange story.

"Could Jane get the keys to the postern gate and the cellar?"

"She said she'd try, but last night she said that Minister Lindsay has all Sir Henry's keys and keeps them on his belt and it's hard to steal a key that is always being used."

Stephenson smiled and looked oddly boyish. "Well if she could find a way to press both sides of the key into some wax, I could likely make a key from it, if I could find a forge, some tools, and some bronze."

Janet stared at him. "Could you really?"

"Yes," said Stephenson, "although it's a while since I did anything fancier than cast bullets and mend gunlocks. I have some tools as well, but they're more for opening latches and bolts from the wrong side. I don't have anything to open a lock."

"How would you do it?" asked Janet suspiciously.

"Well, if Jane could get two good impressions of the key, both sides, I'd make a clay blank from it. Then I'd make a wax mould from the blank and cast the bronze into it and with a bit of filing, I'd have the twin of the key."

Janet thought about this for a time. "That's clever. How long would it take?"

"With the run of a good forge, perhaps a day or two? I could find the blacksmith and ask him."

"We need the key to the postern gate and the key to the cellar where she is," said Janet, "but the trouble is, Jane's an outside worker, she's in the dairy not the Castle.Talking of keys… I'll bet that nobody has thought of Lady Widdrington's keys… Hm." Her face brightened.

"What are you thinking, Mrs Dodd?"

"I'm thinking I should go and visit my husband," she said with a smile. "I want to find out what he's up to anyway."

"There's danger to you, missus," said Leamus softly.

"Oh? Why?"

"Lindsay may accuse you of witchcraft as well."

"Hmf."

"Remember the charge is like pitch, it sticks to anyone it touches."

She nodded at him. "I'll keep it in mind. But I'm for Widdrington. I'll take my cousins with me or the Sergeant will be fit to be tied."

FRIDAY 9TH MARCH 1593, WIDDRINGTON

Elizabeth had scrambled to her feet and flattened her back against the wall, staring at Lindsay. Her heart was pounding uncomfortably, and her knees were shaking. She had not forgotten what had happened with the Burns, nor Lindsay's strange behaviour when he was torturing her. At least I'm not a virgin, she thought, but Oh God, how will I keep it from Robin and what will he think of me when he finds out and...

Lindsay licked his lips and unlaced his codpiece. There it was, in the shadows, reared up and peeking out like a pink snake. His was bigger than Sir Henry's, it really did look like a snake – or a mushroom, like stinkrod. She had always thought it a remarkably unattractive part of a man's anatomy. At least she hadn't had to look at it last time. She took a grip on the chains of her manacles and stared, she didn't know that her lips had drawn back into a feral snarl. Once she might have tried to talk to him, argue him out of it, but she couldn't speak, they had taken words from her. But not her voice.

Something guttural and ugly was coming out of her mouth, a kind of wailing, wordless shouting, like an animal, a wolf, a cat. She was trying to shout "No, no!" but it came out as "O, O!"

"Listen witch," hissed Lindsay, "Ah'm offering ye a kindness. Lie with me now and none o' this nonsense and I'll give ye a fair wee bairn and ye can plead yer belly to the noose..."

You unutterable scum, she thought, you'll have me commit adultery as well as everything else I'm accused of, a fig for you! And she found her fist forming the shape of the gesture, since she couldn't say what she thought.

Besides she had been forced before, although that had been by her rightful husband so it wasn't rape. God help her, no other would she admit to her citadel save Robin. And then she remembered what she had put in there. It made her gasp, since she had got used to the feeling of heaviness and managed to forget it. But under no circumstances could she allow Lindsay to rape her.

So she loudened her wailing shout, clenched her fists, wailed and screamed.

"Shut up you stupid bitch, someone might hear ye; come along, easy now, there's a good girl..."

"Arrow, aoowaow!" shouted Lady Widdrington like a lovelorn tomcat, back to the wall.

"Mr Lindsay, what are ye doing?" It was Tim, her husband's valet de chamber, standing in the door holding a clout of cloth as if he'd forgotten he had it.

"Go away," said Lindsay, "I am interrogating this witch."

"Ye are no' Mr Lindsay, unless ye're interrogating her with yer prick," said Tim, outrage in every line of him, "That's Sir Henry's wife ye're trying to rape..."

"She's a witch, she's the paramour of Satan..."

"So ye say, Mr Linsday, but why is she defying ye as a good wife should?"

"She is staying faithful to Satan not her rightful husband."

Tim drew his dagger. "That's a foul lie," he shouted, "and you are a whited sepulchre. I'm no' a right fighting man but I'll stop ye if I can…" He started prodding the air with his knife and actually advanced on Lindsay.

Elizabeth had stopped shouting because her voice was tired and she wished she could burrow backwards into the wall and get away from the fight and that she wouldn't have to watch Tim be killed. And then she heard a savage roar and her husband limped in, and swung his sword at Lindsay, let the weapon travel round and turned it back in the upswing. Lindsay ducked, dodged and ran out of the door between them in a half bent-over scampering run.

Sir Henry stopped dead when he saw Elizabeth, her fists up. He paused as if he saw something he didn't expect, but then he lowered his sword and his face hardened.

"Was the bitch selling herself to Lindsay?"

"She was not, Sir Henry," said Tim, panting and outraged. "She was defending her honour as she should."

"Hah! Defending herself from Lindsay perhaps, but would she defend herself from Carey? She would not!"

And Sir Henry sheathed his weapon and stalked out of the cellar, followed after a pause by Tim. She heard the lock turn and looked at the light from the lantern on the barrel, miraculously not knocked over. Elizabeth was exhausted again and found her legs wouldn't support her any more. Although at least Sir Henry's jealousy was consistent. He couldn't swive her but nor could any other man.

Would it make Sir Henry less trusting of Lindsay's opinion on witches and herself? Probably not. It was too convenient to Sir Henry's limited intelligence that Elizabeth should be a witch; otherwise he would have to ask why God had afflicted him in his privy member and that he would never do.

She put her head on her knees, felt the cold metal of the manacles press against her stomach and let herself tremble like a chased deer until it had faded out. Lindsay would be back and the next time he would be prepared to shut her up properly.

She heard shouting upstairs, could not be bothered to wonder what was causing it.

Ah well, at least poor Tim had defended her. She would never have thought he would have it in him, he was a timid man, quite tall but not well built and with a tendency to cough when he ran, preferring books and beautiful fabrics to gambling and drinking like most of the Widdringtons.

At last she stopped trembling. She found the ale jug which still had a little ale in it and finished it and then a sudden spate of rage lanced through her and she threw it at the wall. She heard the dull thud as the leather jug bounced and fell to the floor well beyond her reach.

Why was Lindsay playing for time, why wasn't he torturing her? She would probably give in and confess. Why was he being so careful? What was he waiting for?

So she curled up on the stoneflagged floor, the cold striking through her from the floor and the stone wall behind her, and she thought.

She could feel something there as if part of her already knew but that part wasn't telling the rest of her. She was bait in a trap then. But bait in a trap for what? Or perhaps for whom?

Who would be attracted to Widdrington by an accusation against her of witchcraft? Apart from Robin? Most people would be repelled, not attracted, they would want nothing to do with her, would get as far away as they could.

Then the thought came to her.

Except the King. King James VI of Scotland. He believed himself to be an expert on witches and witchcraft, often lecturing people at Court when they joked about the second Earl of Bothwell and the witches of North Berwick. It's no laughing matter, he would say, wagging his forefinger, witches have betrayed Jesus to swear allegiance to Satan... Was it possible? Was Lord Spynie trying to lure the King to Widdrington? But why? What was the point of it?

FRIDAY 9TH MARCH 1593, BERWICK

The King of Scotland was incognito which he always enjoyed, just as he was when he was stalking deer in the Highlands. He was wearing a gentleman's plain woollen doublet and hose, a white falling band and quite a fashionable beaver hat. The doublet was well padded, of course, and had fine chainmail in the lining. He had ten men with him plus supplies on pack ponies. His horses were good – none as spectacular as Whitey, his marvellous grey Arab, but good enough. The only clue that he was the King was the Coronation ring on his hand.

He was plain Mr James Stewart – Scotland was full of them thanks to the activities of all of his ancestors that had lived long enough to sow their seed. As he rode on the rickety bridge between Scotland and Berwick, he felt that he was on holiday. His Sergeant-at-Arms had the papers to get him through the gate of Berwick as plain Mr Stewart, visiting his cousins at Widdrington.

FRIDAY 9TH MARCH 1593, WIDDRINGTON

Lord Spynie trotted into the main bedroom in Widdrington castle, stripping off his gloves and muttering to himself. Lindsay had somehow managed to convince Sir Henry that he was lusting after Lady Widdrington too and Sir Henry was now in a foul mood and had tried to kill him, according to Tim.

Lindsay of course denied everything, said that he had only been interrogating the witch when she started making those peculiar noises, probably with the help of Satan. He had certainly not been untrussed before her, certainly not, the idea, he was completely celibate as any true Minister was.

That sounded a mite papistical, now didn't it? And Lord Spynie didn't believe a word of what Lindsay was saying. He was quite sure that Lindsay had been clumsily trying to seduce Lady Widdrington and had only failed because he was the witchfinder and the author of Lady Widdrington's misfortune. Spynie didn't find her at all attractive, but then he had never in his life lusted after a woman, On that count he was chaste.

Boys, of course, he often lusted after, and he thought sadly about the reiver boy that had got away somehow. What was his name? Harry? The boy wasn't as pretty as he had been in the summer and Lord Spynie decided that he was already tired of him. So it didn't matter that he had somehow escaped, probably by the witch's magic.

Oddly, that thought calmed him a little, made him feel a little more peaceful, a little more safe.

But the fact was that he could never feel truly peaceful until he had the favour and the love of King James back again. He still loved him with all his heart, felt bereft when they were apart, felt happy when he was near. And there was another important fact. Sooner or later he would run out of money and not be able to afford so many henchmen and then, then he would no longer be even a little bit safe.

One of the two boys he had brought along, Robbie, carefully carried a silver cup of ale to him. All the wine in the place was gone, of course, and this ale was pretty poor stuff, third or fourth wort.

"Go and find me something to eat," he said irritably. The boy trotted off, his brow furrowed for some reason. Once alone, Lord Spynie checked behind the tapestries and the crewelwork bed curtains, under the bed. There was no one in the room with him.

He went to the bed and lifted the mattress. There was a small flat wooden box lying on the bedstrings.

He picked it up and opened it.

There it was, the wax doll Lindsay had sold him for twenty pounds Scots, guaranteeing that it wasn't witchcraft, no, indeed, because Spynie's motives were pure. It was simply a Hermetic use of the natural properties of like things, *as above, so below*, that was all. Lindsay had explained it all to him in his rotund way and Spynie had been quite reassured. Sometimes he did find himself wondering about that: could it be true? But he usually managed to stifle such thoughts aborning, because after all he had tried to get back into the King's favour by every method he could think of and nothing had worked and he had to get back the King's favour somehow, didn't he? What else was left to him?

The wax doll was dressed in a scrap of linen that came from a filthy shirt worn by the King, that Spynie had laid hands on after the

King was sick on it. Over that was a crude coat of brocade, cut from a doublet of the King's. The hair on the doll came from the King and although the doll's face didn't look much like James's canny shut expression, you could imagine it did, you really could.

He lifted the doll and snuffed it like a dog. A smell of wax and the penetrating cheesy smell of the King's unwashed body, it brought tears of remembrance to his eyes. Why on earth had the King cared so much that Spynie had slightly ill-treated the Deputy Warden of the West March? Why had he sent Spynie from his presence? It wasn't fair and it was all the fault of Lady Widdrington.

But now it didn't matter. Soon the King would be his again. That boy Robert Kerr who was being groomed by his Border reiver relatives to take over as James's mignon as soon as the King deemed him old enough – he'd be out on his ear. Soon Spynie would be sleeping in the King's high bed, curled into James's stomach, safe at last.

He put the doll carefully back into the box, rearranged the vines of convolvulus binding him, the sprigs of rosemary to remind him, dried rose petals for love. Then he put the lid back on and put the box on the bedstrings again.

Spynie looked around, at Lady Widdrington's riding habit in a bundle on the floor, her black velvet gown draped across her dressing table, all higgeldypiggeldy, just as Spynie's men had taken it off her and the woman had brought it up here.

Spynie frowned and wondered for the first time, where her women were? Where were the servants? It was disgraceful the witch's clothes were still lying there, that's what it was. He stalked out of the master bedroom, kicked Lindsay's truckle bed and his untidy pile of bags as he went. Lindsay was stupid to risk fatally offending Sir Henry for the sake of a woman, never mind a witch.

FRIDAY 9TH MARCH 1593, POST-INN NEAR WIDDRINGTON

With nothing to do that day except worry about Elizabeth, Carey had got on Sorrel and ridden a wide slow circle around Widdrington village and its castle. He had opened and glanced again at Dodd's letter, refolded it and put it in his doublet pocket. He never went above a canter for the whole trip.

Had he turned into a coward? He rather thought he had. So. Was he going to wait around even longer, dithering, in fear of trying anything else in case Sir Henry killed Elizabeth.

And Sir Henry was going to do it at some point, wasn't he? Sooner or later, he would hang his wife. The only thing Carey could do to try to prevent it was take action.

But I don't have enough men.

So what? asked one of the voices inside him, something more steady than most of them. Do it with the men you've got.

He rode back to the Star Inn and put his horse in the stables, thinking hard. All right. Eight, no, seven men. It has to be a night attack and we have to get into the castle courtyard quietly. Either we need the keys or... or we need rope ladders. Dodd has to make the ladders fast on the inside, that or open a postern gate for us.

Dodd is on the inside. I have to find a way to tell him. How can I do it?

Carey found Dodd's message which was crumpled from living in his doublet pocket and smelling faintly of sour milk... He stopped, sniffed it again. Then he took the letter into the common room, held it near a candle and found Dodd's writing in milk coming clear. As far as he could make out, it said "provijuns sellar".

He almost crowed and some of the tension in him reduced. At least he now knew for sure where Lady Widdrington was, in the cellars of the keep. If he could trust Dodd, if she wasn't moved. Just because she had been alive today, didn't mean she would be alive tomorrow.

He took Dodd's letter, crossed out his message and wrote on the back with a piece of graphite from his belt pouch, folded it carefully and sealed it with his one remaining ring, the one the Queen had given him. Yes, but who would take it? Not a pigeon, that was sure.

There was a lot of noise coming from the common room so he went in and found Nick Stephenson shaking another man's hand, whose face he vaguely remembered – what was the name, Tarrant?

Eight more men were crowding around Heronimus's troop, some embracing each other. The common room was overwhelmed by bodies in old jerkins and canions, with the occasional tatter of filthy tangerine and white livery. Clearly John didn't believe in paying his troops the way Carey did.

Nick spotted him and brought him into the throng. "Sir," he said, "here are our old friends from France, back from Berwick with Tarrant, come to help us out."

A couple of them pulled their statute caps. Not one of them had more than a knife on his belt and a veney stick. Carey knew he was being assessed, he even heard one of them mutter, "Well, he don't look much like the Chamberlain..."

Carey suppressed the instant irritation caused by hearing of his brother and drew Nick Stephenson aside. "What do you think? We can give them a caliver each and still have plenty to sell to Scrope," he said.

Nick grinned and called for silence. Eventually he got it. "Would any of you like a new caliver?"

Several of the men laughed and one said, "Ay, and a couple of cannon too."

Carey went up the stairs and the men formed a queue, still laughing at the idea. The laughs went to silence when the first two of them, Tarrant and his brother, came back down with gleaming new weapons. The arquebuses were under the main bed, Carey got the calivers out from under the pallet and handed them to each man as he came up.

"You can keep the weapon, we've got plenty," he told each one of them. "Just come with me on a night raid to Widdrington castle."

Most looked surprised at being paid before the fighting. One or two nodded seriously. "Ay, sir, Tarrant explained about Lady Widdrington, sir. I've bet my pay you'll have her."

Carey did his best not to look too disapproving. "Thank you... er... what's your name?"

"Longdown, sir. Mike Longdown."

"Thank you, Goodman Longdown."

When he had finished, he came back down and went into the kitchen where he found the innkeeper and his wife staring at each other. The innkeeper scowled at him.

"Did ye ken that that boy who'd been beaten up, stole two hobbies and rode off at noon today."

Carey sighed. "No, I didn't."

"Ay, well, that's what he did. Offered to help in the stables, took two horses out to the infield and disappeared over the hill. Wi' both of them."

Carey shook his head.

"Master Innkeeper," he said very politely, "may I have a word?"

"My name is Onslowe," said the man. "All I want to know from you, sir, is who will pay for those two hobbies? And where and who are you and your ruffians attacking?"

"Not Berwick and not you," said Carey. "And if any one of my ruffians, as you call them, is anything less than polite to you, your women folk, your servants or anyone in the village, pray tell me at once and I will flog him personally."

"Hmf."

"My name is Sir Robert Carey, I am the Deputy Warden of the West March, here on a private matter between another gentleman and myself."

"Oh?"

"I am going to ask a favour of you, Mr Onslowe. If you decide not to grant it, I and my ruffians will leave this inn today and not come back."

"Ahuh."

"The favour is, that you allow all sixteen of my men to stay here, give them food and drink..."

"Ay, but who are ye attacking?"

Carey paused for only a second before he said definitively, "Widdrington Castle."

"Sir Henry Widdrington?"

"I told you," said the alewife sourly to her husband.

"Yes. You may not be aware of this, but my Lord Spynie, from Scotland is also there with fifty Scots backing them."

"What?!" The innkeeper was scowling heavily.

"You may wonder what he's doing so far south and so far over the Border into England, to which I can only say that I would like to know that myself."

"Where did ye get the guns?"

"Lord Spynie sent them south from Edinburgh under a load of hay, and we stole them."

Silence. This close to the Border there was a lot of history around and many grudges, mostly against the Scots. Carey took a deep breath and then pulled the ruby ring from the Queen off his thumb, with his initials carved into it.

"This is my last ring," he said. "It is, as you can see, ruby and gold. All the rest are in Carlisle, hocked to a man named Thomas the Merchant Hetherington. It was given to me by the Queen herself, as her thanks for my handling of a delicate matter, and it has never been off my hand before now." It had of course, that ring had had an exciting life, but it made a better story so.

He put the ring down gently. "Here it is as my security that I will pay you for all your disbursements, including the hobbies, when we leave."

How would he do it? He had no idea. Maybe he could find a card game somewhere. Oh well, the ring by itself was worth a great deal more than sixteen men could eat and drink and a couple of hobbies.

Mr Onslowe stared at the ring. His wife came and snatched it up, put it in the pocket of her stays. "Thank you, Sir Robert," she said. "You are welcome to this inn. Is there anything we can do to help you."

"Do you have anywhere we could do some target shooting with calivers?"

They looked at each other. "Well, perhaps the second pasture, it's fallow at the moment and there's an earth bank at one end. Will that do?" said Mrs Onslowe.

"Excellent. Many thanks."

He went back into the common room and called all the men together, interrupted a ferocious game of shove-groat, and told them they could come with him and learn to shoot. There was actually a cheer and they all went out to the second pasture in a group, the men eagerly talking and making bets on how good they were with guns.

He was glad to see that all of them knew one end of a caliver from the other, all of them had some notion of how to load and fire and nobody got shot accidentally.

"Ay sir, Sergeant Collingwood has been teaching us when he has time, though we're not in the horse, only the foot soldiers," explained Longdown.

"That sounds like him,"

At the end he supervised them cleaning out their guns and led them back to the inn as the sun went down. The bank was full of holes although they had only been using quarter charges and everybody was happy, although the badgers who lived there had come out at the run and galloped over the fields to the sound of firing by anyone who could reload fast enough. No badger was hurt by it.

In the common room the village idiot, the village drunk and the three youngsters were nowhere to be seen which was a good thing since the reunited Heronimo's troop took every table and stool in the place and nearly lifted the roof off with their noise.

Carey sat with his back to the wall and surveyed them for a while. None was as skinny and desperate as they had been last autumn and most of them were talking happily. Leamus came and sat at the table and Nick Stephenson joined them.

"What's the plan, sorr?" asked Leamus. "Are we going tonight?"

He grimaced and rubbed his face. "I want to. God knows, the quicker she's out of there the better, but..."

"But?"

"We need somebody to let us in, somebody to open the dairy postern gate for us."

"Do ye have anyone on the inside?"

"Yes, Sergeant Dodd went there a day or two ago and sent me a letter to say that Lady Widdrington is still alive. It's too late to send him a message tonight, the Castle will already be shut up tight. He says that my lady is in the provisions cellar but he won't know to open the postern for us. It has to be tomorrow night."

"How did ye get him in?"

Carey smiled faintly. "Dodd is my Second for the duel that I have pending with Sir Henry."

Leamus's eyebrows went up. "Diasmarieduit," he said. "When are ye planning to meet?"

"I'm not," snorted Carey. "Sir Henry will certainly have a large bunch of Spynie's outgrown bumboys waiting to grab me and hang me and I don't fancy it." He paused as Tarrant and his brother started up the incomprehensible Dutch song and all the rest of them joined in, especially Falls Off His Horse Perkins with his particularly fine and resonant voice. "I'd like to give them a night to rest anyway, since they've just come south from Berwick."

He wasn't sure that was the right decision. It would be possible to go that same night, but something was holding him back. Maybe he was turning into a coward, but still, he wanted to do some practising to find out which of the several plans he was thinking about might possibly work. And of course he needed to alert Dodd to the attack.

The only thing he didn't know was how to get the letter back to Dodd without any of Spynie's men seeing it. Young Hutchin was no longer available to take it and in any case he wouldn't have asked the boy to go back to that place.

Then he heard the sound of hobnail boots running up to the inn and glimpsed Jane greeting Janet on the stairs as she came in. Could she? Maybe? She was only a maid but she was clearly very determined.

SATURDAY 10TH MARCH 1593, POST-INN NEAR WIDDRINGTON

Carey went to bed in his clothes, only taking his boots off, knowing that he would sleep lightly and wake early. He slept very badly indeed, thinking hard about how to achieve the perfect night attack against a castle garrisoned by fifty thugs, with only sixteen men of his own. He pictured it one way, and another way, his heart keeping up a steady pounding through the night. At around three am, he rolled out of the bed and crept down the stairs to the yard, lit a lantern, found Sorrel his favourite hobby and got him tacked up and fed as quickly as he could.

Out in the yard, he could just see a shape with a white cap, washing her face at the horse trough.

"Is it Goody Fenwick?" he asked cautiously.

"Ay, what?" she had her hand to her knife, which he approved of. He lifted his hands.

"It's Sir Robert..."

"Ay, I know ye of course. What d'ye want?"

"Could ye take a message to Sergeant Dodd at Widdrington?"

"Is this to get Lady Widdrington out?"

"Er... yes. Of course."

He could see her teeth in the starlight as she smiled grimly. "Ay," she said. "Tell it to me."

He pulled the folded letter out of his doublet. "I want you to give this to Sergeant Dodd and nobody else. He's nearly as tall as me, he's a bit thin because he was ill a few months ago, and he's got a miserable face that looks like a wet Sunday."

She took the paper, put it under her stays and said, "I need to go now."

"Can I give ye a lift on my horse? Ye could ride pillion."

"Och. I've never done that."

"In front of me or behind me, I don't mind. It's easier if you go in front of me."

"Um..." There was that fierce grin again. "Ay, a'right!"

He moved Sorrel over to the mounting block and mounted, instructed her to pull up her skirts and sit sideways in front of him, lift her leg right over the horse's neck and settle herself.

Sorrel snorted in disapproval and Carey patted him. "I'll have to hold ye tight."

"A'right!"

He went slowly to start with, then went to a heavy canter which was all Sorrel could manage with the two of them, for Jane was not a lightly-built lass. He stopped the horse a couple of miles from Widdrington and helped her lift her leg and slide down.

"It's more ladylike if you ride pillion behind me," he admitted.

"Pfui. Ah'm no lady," she said with a toss of her head. "That's about all I can take of riding, I think. Thank ee kindly, Sir Robert, I'll see you tonight."

"Oh, I don't think ye should..."

But she was off, her hobnailed boots thudding and crunching on the turf and the road.

SATURDAY 10TH MARCH 1593, WIDDRINGTON

Sergeant Dodd was in the stables, making friends with the horses, mostly hobbies but at least three of them came from the King's famous stud at Falkland palace with Arab blood for their height and the shortness of their back. One was a lovely black creature with the Berwick garrison brand on him, recovering from some injury in his mouth.

There was still some fodder left, though it was getting low in the hungry time of year, before there was good pasture on the infield, when everyone got low on fodder and low on people's food as well. Your joints creaked and sometimes your gums bled then, though scurvy grass helped, anything green really.

There wasn't a lot of food of any kind left at Widdrington since Spynie's men had eaten it all, but Dodd had some salt and was letting the beautiful black gelding lick it off his palm. He was thinking quite seriously about how he could steal the nag and not get caught, since he was bored and nervous and had to while away the day, and it annoyed him that Lord Spynie or Minister Lindsay had such a nice horse.

He saw a girl walk into the yard and look around. She looked like a dairymaid or a laundress, she had a sweaty white cap on her head and she was clearly looking for somebody. Then she saw Dodd and her square face lit up.

She came over and dropped a curtsey and asked, "Are ye Sergeant Dodd, master? Ye look miserable and grim but I seen ye smiling at the horses."

"I am Sergeant Dodd, ay."

"Message for ye, master."

He looked around for the messengerboy and then saw she was holding a letter out to him herself, so he took it. It was on the other side of his own message, with the milk writing clear and brown on it. The new italic was the Courtier's and it had rubbed a bit so some of the message was missing, but it was clear enough. The Courtier would attack Widdrington with what he had at midnight that night.

By the time he finished reading the letter the dairymaid had gone, probably into the dairy yard. And there it was, he was stuck with it. He had to find the key to one of the posterns, ideally the dairy gate.

Robbie was trotting past with some bread and cheese on a pewter plate.

"Robbie, are ye taking that to Lord Spynie?"

The boy stopped and knuckled his forehead shyly to Dodd. "Ay sir, he wants it in his bedchamber."

"I saw him go out and down to the orchard not a minute past," said Dodd helpfully which was actually true.

Robbie sighed like an old Edinburgh wifey and turned to go down to the orchard as well.

"Hey, where's Jimmy?"

"Och, he's not well, he's just gone to bed wi' a flux," said Robbie. "He's allus getting fluxes."

"Poor lad," said Dodd doing his best to sound sympathetic which didn't come easy to him at all. Robbie gave him a fishy look and he coughed and ambled across the yard. From the butts at the end of the orchard came the occasional sound of gunfire as Sir Henry practised his marksmanship in case the duel with Carey happened.

Dodd ambled slowly in and up the stairs to the hall. He needed to find those keys and he also wanted to know more about Lindsay who was sharing the master bedroom with Lord Spynie and his two boys and a young man-at-arms who slept the night across the threshold. He paused at the big Hall fire to burn the twice-used paper, then went up the spiral stair that went to the bedrooms. Once up on the third floor, above the hall and the parlour, he found the door to the main bedroom. It was half open and inside it was full of the sour smell of dirty linen but it was the main bedroom right enough – Sir Henry's four poster was empty with the crewel-worked curtains of peacocks and flowers, the truckle pushed against the wall. Where was Jimmy?

There was a groan from the garderobe in the corner, let into the wall so that the shit could fall into the moat. Dodd stepped softly on the old rushes and squatted by Lindsay's bags under the truckle bed. One bag was full of shirts, a book called *Malleus Maleficarum*, whatever that meant, full of pictures of wicked witches stealing men's yards. Could they really do that? Under it at the bottom was a bag of herbs, a large pot of ill-smelling ointment and a small bottle of something oily that smelled revoltingly bitter.

The other bag had a waistcoat in it and another book. Neither bag had the keys in it. The book was *Institutes* by Calvin, which Dodd flipped through idly. Then he stopped and looked closer.

At the back of all the foreign writing were some tightly folded pages and when he took them out and opened them, he found table after table of letters with numbers in columns.

He blinked at them and folded them up again, put them back. Then he straightened up and put everything else back and heard a noise from the garderobe of someone hopping down from the seat.

Instinctively he scrambled under the bed, where there was a mummified mouse with its legs bitten off, a lot of dust and a box that must have fallen down between the bedropes because it was lying with its lid off.

The boy came shambling out of the corner with the garderobe, his bare legs stumbling under his shirt, sighing and oh-godding like anyone with the flux, just soprano. He climbed into the four poster bed. Dodd could hear him wriggling and rolling over and then he was silent.

He waited. Very stealthily he moved to one side of the bed ready to come out nearest the door. He heard the boy roll over and sigh. He looked at the box, picked it up and found a thing on the floor, a wax doll wrapped in leaves. He scooped it up and put it back in the box, put the lid on. Well that was witchcraft right enough, making a puppet of some poor soul to harm him by proxy. At least the doll didn't have a pin through it.

He waited, patiently as if in ambush, for the boy to go to sleep. Soprano snoring started but Dodd wasn't convinced by it, waited longer until the boy rolled over and groaned and got up and shambled to the garderobe again. As soon as he'd pulled the curtain across, Dodd slid out from under the bed and almost trotted to the door.

He wondered about the code sheet, painstakingly copied by someone in Italic – unusual looking Italic too. So Lindsay was a spy as well as a witchfinder, but where was he from? There was a large choice even in Scotland: England, Spain, France, even Ireland or the Netherlands. And what was he after? Had he given Spynie the wax doll or had that been there for a while, was it Sir Henry's doll or Lady Widdrington's?

He trotted downstairs again, his mouth pulled down sourly. Maybe he would give this whole business up and go home to Gilsland and his wife, concentrate on his own lands and his own borders. What if Lady Widdrington was in fact a witch? What if Carey got them all killed?

There was a commotion in the barnekin and as Dodd came out of the door to the outer hall, he stopped dead because he thought he was dreaming or woodwild.

Was that Janet sitting astride Shilling with her kirtle kilted and only two of her cousins with her? Not that the lads weren't welcome, but...

Janet? With the babby inside of her? In the same place as Lord Spynie's men who looked as brutal a bunch of bastards as he had ever clapped eyes on? What?

At Widdrington which the Courtier was planning to attack tonight? Jesu!

He strode forward and took Shilling's bridle. Shilling nickered to him and shoved his nose into Dodd's chest, delving for carrots.

"Wife!" he said to Janet severely, who smiled radiantly at him, lifted her leg over the saddle pommel and slid down like a lad, showing off. As she landed she managed a neat curtsey to him.

"Ay," she said, "I ken ye werena looking to see me, but I thocht I'd come and make sure ye werena doing aught to hurt yer back again."

"But the babby!" he hissed at her.

"Och, I'm feeling fine," she said, "much better than last month when I felt so sick. And naething's showing yet. So I thocht I'd come and see how ye were."

Mouth tightly compressed, Dodd led Shilling to the stableyard. All the looseboxes were full of Spynie's horses and he knew that the infield was crowded with Sir Henry's horses, but he moved four hobbies out of one box and snuck them in beside other hobbies, and put Shilling in and the Armstrongs' hobbies too. At least Janet hadn't brought remounts, the silly woman. Now he would have to protect her and there was witchcraft in the place and who knew whose it was?

She came with him, followed by the youngest Armstrong cousin, and Dodd had to stop her bringing in a heavy bucket of water to give the horses.

"Will ye be careful!" he snarled at her under his breath.

"Och Henry," she murmured to him, "ye'd have me all wrapped up in lambswool, tapping my fingers at Gilsland if ye had your wish."

"Ay, and why not?" he growled back, "Look what happened to yer cousin."

"The babby had something wrong with him, he'd taken the Devil's Spear."

"Ye should be careful, yer not a young woman any more!"

"Och Henry," she laughed, "D'ye not know better than to say something like that?" She couldn't help it, she reached up and kissed his ear.

"And there's witchcraft here," said Dodd gloomily, after he had secretively caught her shoulders and kissed her back on the mouth. "D'ye ken what I found in the master bedroom a moment ago, under the bed? I found a wax doll wearing brocade, so I did!"

"Did ye now?" said Janet, "Where did it come from?"

"How would I know?"

"Was it dusty?"

"No."

"Hmf," said Janet as she went in and started trotting up the stairs to the hall in a way that made Dodd want to shout at her again. "D'ye have yer own room?"

"Ay, I'm not dossing down in the hall, I'm in the old chapel the ither side of the hall, up the other stair."

"I'll ask Cuddy to take my bags up there."

"But... but ye're no' planning to stay?"

"I am," said Janet, "Where else should I stay but with mine ain husband? D'ye want me to go to a post inn, there's one about seven miles north and one ten miles south..."

"But... one o' Spynie's pages is sick with a flux."

"Poor lad, I'll pay him a visit."

She would tell him later where Hieronimo's Troop was and where she had been staying and all that. She heard Dodd growl inarticulately and told herself not to tease Henry. Though it was funny how he had suddenly become so protective of her. Of his child really, and fair enough, you couldn't fault him for that.

"But it's all full of swords and shields and lances and guns..."

"Is it now. Well, that will make a change," she said and Dodd blinked and finally heard her tone of voice, stopped. "Come on, Henry," she said, "Where have you ever seen a tower with an old chapel upstairs that the place wasn't used as an armoury? Eh?"

"Ye'll be looking at swords and calivers. It might hurt the babby."

"All the better if the child takes something from it, maybe he'll be a fine fighter like yerself," said Janet, on the basis that flattery rarely worked with Henry but was worth trying. "Anyway, I canna go home yet because I should wait and rest a bit."

"Ye see! Ye're feeling tired!"

"I'm not, but I should probably rest."

They were at the door of the master bedroom and Janet looked around her with interest and marched in where Spynie's poor page was trekking back from the stinking garderobe, white-faced and hobbling like an old man.

"Well well," she said to him sympathetically, "Ah heard ye wis ill and so ye are." She sniffed the air, went to look behind the curtain at the garderobe and shuddered.

"Husband, will ye ask Cuddy to come up here with two buckets of water and some vinegar... Is there any mild ale in the place?"

"That's probably the only drink Spynie's men haven't drunk dry."

"Will ye fetch some? I'd go get it myself, but..."

"How much d'ye want?"

"A quart jack and a horn cup."

"Ay," said Dodd and trotted down the stairs. She looked after him, liking how smart he was in his tailormade woollen doublet and hose and his beaver hat. Then she helped the boy into the bed and tucked him up.

"Ah feel awfu' dizzy, missus," whispered the boy.

"Ay, ye need some ale," said Janet, "now shut yer eyes."

"Will ye stay?"

"A little while. Go to sleep."

She waited until his eyes had drooped shut and then she went quickly to the dressing table and picked up Lady Widdrington's gown and kirtle and hung them both on hooks on the wall. She saw the belt, picked it up with the purse and knife on it. Lady Widdrington had come straight from Court but when she was here she would have... Where were they? Janet tidied the table, looked under it, then saw a pile of white linen caps and there, coiled like an adder in the middle of them, was another plain brown belt with the keys on it.Managing not to cheer in an unseemly way, she took them off the belt, wrapped them in a kerchief and put them in the pocket of her petticoat.

"Missus, could ye tell me a story?"

She went back to the boy in the bed and smoothed his hair away from his forehead which was very hot. Just in case she gently checked his forehead for the cobbled feeling of smallpox, his armpits for lumps of plague. Nothing, so it was probably just a flux but even so, you could die of that too.

"I'll sing ye 'Tam Lin,'" she said and started the song at once. Dodd came back with a jack of ale and a pewter cup, followed by Spynie complaining that Janet was in his bedchamber.

"My lord, did ye ken yer page has a flux?" she asked coldly.

"Ay, he's ill, but..."

"D'ye want him tae die?"

"Well, no, I..."

"Because he will die if he has the flux and nothing to drink."

"Maybe he needs to be bled?"

Janet rolled her eyes. "By all means spend good gold on a doctor, though ye'll need to send to Berwick for one, ye'll find nae such thing round here. But I've found that a flux will usually get better by itself if ye stay in bed and drink as much small ale as ye can." Her voice was tart.

"Oh."

Dodd put the jack full of ale on a chest and Janet poured a cup of it and helped Jimmy to sit up and drink it and then another cup and another. "Is that better now?" she asked and Jimmy nodded and shut his eyes.

"D'ye want me to send a lad for a doctor?" asked Dodd who was enjoying the expression on Spynie's face.

"No, no," said Spynie, staring at Janet like a mouse at a cat.

Janet was now straightening up the room, removing a tray, half a dozen pewter goblets, a couple of drinking jacks, full of stale small ale, and two horn cups. There was a nest of dirty napkins and shirts, the ends of a couple of large pork pies and a sausage.

Janet favoured Spynie with a particularly brilliant smile as she left the chamber carrying the things she had found, including the linen under her arm, headed down the stairs.

"That's yer wife?" said Spynie. "Did ye ever think of beating her to teach her better manners?"

Dodd regarded this specimen of impertinence for a minute. He made no move at all against Spynie, who still shrank back slightly.

"I ha' never felt I needed to, my lord," he remarked neutrally, and trotted down the stairs.

At least Janet was happy. He found her in the room he was using. She was still singing Tam Lin as she moved around the tiny old chapel with the arched place on the wall and the stars on the floor tiles. She was busily stacking arrows in neat piles, putting swords on their racks, and calivers on their stands, helmets on the top of jackstands, bent to hang up some old mailshirts that were lying on the floor. Dodd found himself moving to pick them up first so she wouldn't try to lift fifty pounds of metal. Suddenly, miraculously, there was more space. She blinked at the bed with its old coverlet, took off her shoes and got in.

"Would ye mind if I had a nap, Henry?" she asked and Dodd came to her anxiously, felt her forehead. She giggled and fended him off.

"Are ye all right?" he asked, instantly terrified that there was something wrong. "Do ye need the midwife?"

"No, I'm fine," she said. He caught her hand and she pulled him down and then sat up in bed to kiss him on the cheek. "Where is the bag I brought." Dodd pointed to it lying on the floor with her old kirtle peeking out of it. She kissed him again. "I'm no' a flower that a puff of wind might snap."

"Ay but..."

"I'll sleep an hour or so and then I'll take a look at the kitchen and see what's left of Lady Widdrington's stores – not much, I'd say. Is the baker still baking?"

"Ay, but he's near run out of flour."

"Of course he has. Widdrington isna Holyrood House, is it? And Sir Henry is too besotted with Lord Spynie to see how he's wasting is lands and supplies with no wife to see to them. Mark my word, there's a hungry summer in store here or else the Widdringtons will all be out reiving."

Dodd nodded. "I wis thinking just that."

"Oh, and by the way, the Courtier's planning a night attack wi' Hieronimo's troop. Sixteen men. Tonight at midnight."

Dodd stared at her. "How the hell d'ye ken that?"

"The Courtier tellt me this morning hisself. That's why he let me come here, so I could make sure ye know because he didna trust Jane to deliver his message."

"Well, she did. So ye can go back again and get oot o' the way of the attack."

Which was why Janet decided not to tell Henry that she had Lady Widdrington's keys. She could tell him later. "I think I'll nap a while first," she said.

"Are ye sure ye're well?"

"Husband," said Janet, "I've niver been wi' child before though I'm sure I will be again, but I feel better than I've felt since January."

She put her hands protectively over the small lump in her stomach.

"Have ye felt him kick yet?" asked Dodd, staring at it.

"I've felt some flutterings but I think it's still too early. And I'm eating a lot."

"Will I get ye some food?"

"That would be kind," said Janet with another one of those radiant smiles. Never in her entire married life had Dodd fetched and carried for her and offered to bring her food, although he had brought her stolen apples when they were courting. She was liking it. "Ah wis just thinking I could maybe eat some bread and cheese though I suppose there's no butter. Or some pickles. I'd love some pickled onions if ye can find any."

SATURDAY 10TH MARCH 1593, WIDDRINGTON

Janet woke up to the sound of many shod horses coming into the stable yard. She got up and tried to squint out one of the chapel's arrowslits but couldn't see anything. So she pinned her cap on again, put on her shoes and trotted down the narrow spiral staircase and into the hall. There she saw Lord Spynie with an excited smile on his face heading out the door and down to the yard. Sir Henry limped behind him with his lumpy gargoyle face twisted into a thing that might also have been a smile if it wasn't for the plain jealousy under it. She started to move to the kitchen but then saw Antony Lindsay coming from there in a hurry and wondered what the Devil he was up to and there on the stair was one of Spynie's men acting as sentry, damn it.

Someone shouted, "Who are they?"

Lindsay answered, "The King of Scotland."

Oh really? She had heard gossip while she was in Edinburgh that the King was an expert on witchcraft – was that why he was here?

She could see one man in a brocade doublet that she assumed was the King and his ten men as they dismounted and there was Sir Henry hurrying through to the stable yard behind some and coming back with a sulky looking youth.

There were eleven horses and ten pack ponies laden with supplies which was very thoughtful. One of the men in jacks was ordering the others around and after a pause the thing got organised.

If there was a single full barrel of ale anywhere in the Castle she would be very surprised so she was delighted to see that the two last ponies had barrels strapped to their backs. Clearly normal huswifery had stopped dead when Elizabeth was arrested and none of the idiotic men prancing around the Castle had thought anything was wrong.

The King had thought. She liked him despite his stink and liked him more for the fact he had brought supplies.

However this was a major problem for Carey's plan. She was wondering how she could tell the Courtier that the King was here with more men. She felt a hand caress her back and turned smiling to see Dodd there, looking grumpy and miserable as usual.

"Who are they?"

"The King of Scotland and his men," she said, "Come to see how Lady Widdrington turned into a notable witch."

Dodd immediately turned and went back into the hall where the five Armstrongs, his and Janet's, were dossing down in a corner although at the moment they were playing their interminable games of dice for thousands of sheep and cattle apiece.

Dodd spoke to Cuddy, Janet's second cousin and about sixteen. The lad stopped looking bored and got up. He left the hall by the stairs and ducked down to the ground floor stalls which were full of hobbies. He came out with one of the hobbies and led him to the main gate where one of the King's men, already posted, turned him back.

"Damn," swore Janet, ducked back into the hall, went through the passage to the kitchen out into the dairy yard where two cows were standing munching hay and Jane was busy washing some wide bowls at the well.

Janet went up to her. "We need to get word to Mr Stephenson," she said, "King James is here with ten men. We can't follow the plan at all."

"Cuddy's supposed to take messages."

"He's just been turned back at the gate."

Jane's busy hands paused. "Ay," she said, "but where is Mr Stephenson?"

"He'll be moving the men of Hieronimo's Troop here after it gets dark."

"But I don't have the key to the postern gate."

"I have it," said Janet triumphantly, "And no need to make a copy, I have Lady Widdrington's own keys."

Jane nodded seriously. "Ay," she said, "I could run to Mr Stephenson..."

"Good God, child, I wouldna ask ye to run at night to any soldiers! Cuddy will do it."

"I'm glad," said Jane flushing, "I wouldn't want tae leave Lady Widdrington here, she needs me."

Janet nodded and went straight to the ground floor of the castle where Cuddy was feeding the ponies there, including Dodd's famous horse Whitesock, hero of the ballad.

She broke the news that he would be going anyway, and on foot, and arranged to meet him when it was full dark.

She went up to the hall again, poked her head round the door and found the hall crowded with men, with the King's men disposed, not around the one in the brocade doublet, but one of the ones in plain wool, with a dingy face and wary eyes and quite short legs.

Lindsay was standing in front of that man like a boy reciting a lesson, speaking fluently in Latin, bowing every so often. Janet squinted at the one in the plain wool doublet and decided that yes, it was indeed King James. The King asked Lindsay sharp questions in Latin.

Next the King called upon Sir Henry to explain in English why he had taken the extraordinary step of arresting his own wife as a witch. Sir Henry explained with passion why Lady Widdrington must be a witch, born of Cornish witches, who had enchanted his privy member so it wouldn't work and stopped up the piss in his body, so he was in agony.

"You seem recovered," said the King seriously, "How did that happen?"

"The evil woman used a torture instrument to pull the gravel out and a reed as well..." Every man there winced, and several crossed their legs. "...so the blockage cleared and my piss came out."

"She cured you of the stoppage of urine," said the King, "Did she say any charms?"

"Oh yes, she was muttering charms the whole time."

"And then ye were able to piss?"

"Ay, though it hurt bad at first. So she must have cast a spell on me, that's proof, that is."

"Hm," said the King.

"There ye see," said Sir Henry to Dodd who was sitting on a bench listening to this. "She's as guilty as sin."

"Could she not have been doing ye a favour?" asked Dodd in an interested voice.

Sir Henry glowered at him.

"It's not a kindness to remove a spell you have set," said Lindsay smoothly. "It is a demonstration of power."

"Hm." King James looked sideways at him. "I'm puzzled though, Minister Lindsay. Lady Widdrington was at my Court only a couple of weeks ago and my Queen rates her very highly. She refuses to believe that she has turned into a witch. She even wanted to ride here with me to clear milady's name."

"Why are you surprised that a witch enchants whomever she needs to so that she can do her evil work?"

"So she was already a witch when she came to my Court?"

"Of course. She has been casting spells of gout and impotence on Sir Henry since she was married to him."

"Not exactly..." interrupted Sir Henry but was ignored.

King James looked at Lindsay without saying anything. "Minister Lindsay," he said at last, "I hardly think I could have nourished such a viper in my bosom without even suspecting."

Lindsay smiled patronisingly. "You did not have me there to help you detect her evil."

King James's eyebrows went up.

"Indeed?" he said, "Well, I wish to interrogate Lady Widdrington myself..."

"Certainly, your highness..."

"Mr Stewart, please, as I am incognito."

"Mr Stewart. I will have to be present to be sure she doesn't try to attack you."

"Bring her up here."

"With respect, Your High... Mr Stewart, she should be interrogated in the cellar where we are holding her to be sure that she doesn't defile this hall."

"Oh?"

"And we need to wait a little. We need to pray to God for his protection over us and... er... in Catholic lands they would say a rosary to be sure of the protection of the Blessed Virgin as well..."

"I'll have no such superstitious nonsense in my presence, the Kirk would have a collective fit," said the King tartly, "But perhaps ye could entertain us with a sermon on witchcraft and its manifest delusions and treasons against God, eh, Minister Lindsay?"

Lindsay flushed and Janet saw his jaw clench. He seemed quite put out by the suggestion which was very odd for a Scottish minister. "I... I need a little time to gather my thoughts, Your... Mr Stewart."

"Take all the time ye want," said James with a large gesture. "My Lord Spynie, will ye have your henchmen bring us the pack marked with red and we'll have ourselves some brandywine to keep us going until supper. Meanwhile, Michael, will ye go and see what ye can dish up for us in the kitchen, eh?"

Dodd came out with Michael and found Janet just outside the door. She grabbed her husband. "Can ye follow Lindsay," she said to him, "I'm pushing Cuddy out the postern gate to warn Mr Stephenson."

"Ay," said Dodd, "There's summat not right wi' that witchfinder."

"Hmf," said Janet.

Saturday 10th March 1593, Widdrington

Elizabeth was lying on her back in the cellar, watching the walls of the world become the finest gauze, so that the stones of the cellar that had imprisoned her became like hanging curtains at a playhouse and they moved in the wind to give glimpses of Heaven.

She was very very hot and her mouth was utterly dry like leather. Her sight had suddenly got much better: she could see the empty barrels and the ones with salt herring and ancient salt beef in; she could even see a barrel of pickles she had quite forgotten, hidden at the back in an alcove. They all gathered together and turned into short dwarves who drank together and argued over which was better, to be filled with herring or pickles or beef, and came to the unsurprising conclusion that ale or wine was a much better and more respectable filling.

That's odd, a small part of her thought, barrels don't normally converse. Well never mind, thought the rest of her, at least they're getting on nicely and not fighting.

What had happened to make the walls of the world dissolve? That man she feared, Lindsay, had been in the cellar, his lantern lit and dazzling her. She had been suffering from terrible thirst because no one had brought her anything to drink since she had forgotten when.

He had brought in a pewter flagon and a clean cup and left them where she could reach them. She had been on her feet, tense and afraid of another attempt to force her, but Lindsay had avoided her eyes and left the place, locking the door behind him.

She had taken the spiced brandywine he brought her and drunk it down since she was so desperate, though it was sickly with sugar and cloves and had brandy in it. She thought she knew why he wanted her drunk, but she had a hard head.

So she was surprised when she did start to feel drunk, but then as her body became hot and her heart thundered like a drum in its cage of bones, she knew something else was happening, something connected with the bitterness of the wine but not with the wine.

Had there been something else in the wine?

She saw herself giving a packet of dried and ground nightshade berries to Robin last summer, before he went off to try and scout Netherby Castle in disguise as a pedlar.

She could see herself at the inn, telling the scruffy-looking Robin that the berries would make him feel very ill and give him a high fever so he looked as if he had plague but that he would recover. He hadn't had a chance to use it to escape from the tower and she thought that the packet must have stayed in the pedlar's pack he had been carrying.

Very ill. She knew she had a raging fever. Her body was also filling up with rage that seemed to have no point.

She struggled to think straight. Why had Lindsay poisoned her, when he could just hang or burn her?

The pounding of her heartdrum got louder and louder and suddenly she was floating in the air above the dirty red-haired woman who was rolling and jacknifing, trying to scrape something ugly off her face. She felt quite sorry for the woman who was so helpless, as she swam absentmindedly for one of the holes in the wall to Heaven that had appeared so conveniently.

On the other side was a pleasant looking parlour, like one of Queen Elizabeth's chambers, hung with blue silk and yellow oak panels, and there was a window which overlooked rolling hills.

She looked out of the window and saw herds of horses, galloping past, shaking their heads and a young man running with them and laughing. He looked like Toad but like a happy Toad, she thought. The horses came to him and stood around him and he petted them and gave them apples and then he changed. He changed his shape and became a sturdy brown centaur who ran and bucked with the other horses. She felt cheered to think that there were indeed horses in Heaven as she had told him.

She saw two people coming in. One was a stout middle aged woman in a white veil of the last century, not a linen cap, and the other was a tall dark strong young man, with long hair like a courtier, and a beard. He was wearing a white brocade doublet trimmed with scarlet braid that had an oddly uneasy look to it, as if it was a snake that was trying to escape.

She curtseyed deeply to them and stayed down on her knees as she would to the Queen. She knew them for the King and Queen Mother of this land. She could see the terrible scars on the King's wrists and more scars around his forehead where the thorns had pressed in.

The Queen Mother smiled and came forward to raise and embrace her, and compared with Elizabeth she was quite short which made her feel awkward again.

"My dear," she said, and Elizabeth remembered her from previous furious conversations with her, "You are so brave."

Elizabeth shook her head and heard herself say, "What am I to do? What else can I do?"

The Queen Mother waved her hand at the window and the view changed to a sombre palace in a hot desert and a skinny unhappy old

King locked in one luxurious chamber, whence came a spider web that went everywhere, to the Holy Roman Empire, the Papacy, France, the Netherlands, England... The King himself was utterly tangled in it. One thread travelled across the sea to Scotland.

Other visions followed which she could never remember afterwards although she could remember the room and the King and the Queen Mother.

Something grave was happening, something deadly, against the King of Scots. She saw through the window all the consequences: Scotland descending into chaos; England descending into chaos; marching soldiers everywhere, spearing pigs and children, burning barns...

And there was Robin, his face marked by sorrow, in a dirty doublet in a boozing ken in the Netherlands, drinking.

"Jesu!" she said and then blushed. "I'm sorry."

"My dear, don't apologise. Only think on this."

She saw herself tied to a stake and the faggots and gunpowder being piled up around her. Everyone was howling and shouting at her with hatred and throwing mud and stones. She could see her face marked with bewilderment and sorrow and, yes, guilt.

She saw Robin wearily climbing a scaffold, an older Robin, his face blurred by drink, his shirt badly darned when he took his worn doublet off. He knelt and prayed, put his hands forward and his head was chopped off.

She winced to see it, turned to the King standing by her. "My life for his," she said without hesitation.

The King of Heaven smiled. "You don't understand," he said in a rich deep voice, "This is Sir Robert after your death from any cause. You can't offer your life for his since if you die, he believes that his life is ruined and so he will die too before he can do the things he came to do."

"We all owe God a life," she said to him tartly, "He giveth and He receiveth. Even you, Your Majesty."

He laughed and said, "Not exactly." Then he gestured for her to sit down at the parlour table, covered with a Turkey rug of wondrous complexity, sparkling with diamonds, covered with spirals and sea-horse tails packed into something rhythmic and wonderful.

She gasped at its beauty. Silver goblets of wine and silver plates of wafers appeared as though brought by invisible servants. At the door stood the King's bodyguard, a fair man with a sword at his waist and lilies on his blue silk surcoat and the shadows of wings on his shoulders.

They conversed at venture about things philosophical and deep and she had never enjoyed a conversation more because so many things became clear to her. It was as if the world was immensely and beautifully complicated, but at its core, there was one word, one idea, that generated everything in it. She looked at the core, at the word, and couldn't believe it was that simple and tried to puzzle it out.

At last she stood up and said, "I must go."

"I know," said the King.

"What should I do?"

He lifted his scarred hands. "What seems to you best, Elizabeth, Lady Widdrington. That is all anyone can do. It's all I could do myself – do you think I knew what would happen after they arrested me, after I was crucified? Why do you think I shouted at God in accusation, that He had abandoned me? I thought He had."

"But He hadn't?"

"No, of course not."

"But, Your Majesty, you are God as well as Man."

He took her hand in his, she felt the carpenter's callouses. "So are you," He said. "So are all of you, every one."

"Lindsay? Lord Spynie? Sir Henry?"

"Them too. All of you. Why do you think you suffer so greatly when you do evil, as Sir Henry does?"

She took her hand back. "I know you said, 'Don't ye know that ye are gods!' But I don't know what it means."

"What I said."

She shook her head, baffled. "Thank you for the wine and the wafers," she said politely, "I really must go now."

She stepped forward onto the Turkey rug which had grown enormous and her foot found a particular spiral and she fell and fell.

***

She fell straight into her absurd body and all the lovely clarity was gone because it was a Hell of fire and fury and confusion and there were lights that dazzled her and somebody standing near the door who smelled bad and someone else right next to her who smelled bad as well, though different and dusty as well.

She glimpsed the bald head and knew it was Lindsay who was next to her, too close. Oh God, he had his hands on her breasts, he was kneading them like cows' udders, muttering to her in Latin. She tried to shout at him, tell him to get off her, but the scold's bridle was in her bleeding mouth and her throat was so dry she could only make a croaking sound.

"Have ye used her so ill she canna speak?" That was King James's reproachful voice over by the wall. Right. She knew what to do but was horrified and appalled at the idea.

It was against everything she had ever been taught, everything that any woman was allowed to do, all the endless rules that hemmed her in as they hemmed all women in.

And where had keeping the rules gotten her? Locked in a cellar on a charge of witchcraft, that's where.

And hadn't Jesus Christ himself said, "Don't ye know that ye are gods"?

There was a strange fury rising up in the heat and it carried power and strength with it. It dug deep and married with the rage that had lived secretly in her heart over the years of her marriage, for the way she had been treated; for the injustice and stupidity and cruelty of Sir Henry; the casual cruelty of Lord Spynie; and the revolting lickerishness and lust and cruelty of Lindsay.

God, how she hated them all, the witchfinder above the rest. His head was close to hers, he was sweating, excited.

He was whispering to her in Latin and then in English. "Attack him," he said, "and all shall be well with you, he is the cause of your misery, you want to kill him, so you do..."

"You are the cause of my misery," she tried to say but it came out as meaningless noise that rose and rose until she was shrieking. Lindsay let her sit up, he was smiling triumphantly. He pointed commandingly at her, pointed at the man over by the other wall, like setting on a guard dog. He wanted her to kill the King for him, did he? Her heart was roaring and pounding, her body felt light and filled with anger and rage but she had always liked King James.

Lindsay the witch-finder however...

She put her chained hands together, clasped them tight, and smashed the manacles across Lindsay's smiling face, smashed them back again. He fell back, got up staggering, blood from his nose and marks on his face. She rolled away from him, was brought up short by the chain, stumbled to her feet, snarling like a she-wolf. Lindsay had his knife in his hand, and it seemed to smoke from the point. He slashed with it and she dodged faster than she could have thought possible, her body somehow knowing its business when she herself did not. She kicked out and he backed again, looked from her to the King.

Suddenly he stabbed at the King who screamed and leaped out of the way like a startled deer, deep into the shadows of the cellar. A hand reached out from the corner and knocked over the lantern and everything went dark – although she could still see.

She pulled on the chain, wrenched on it and somehow the staple pulled out of the wall. Blood appeared on her wrists.

She was so full of fire and fury, her rage was gigantic, bigger than the world, rage with Sir Henry, with Lindsay, with Lord Spynie, with all men. She knew her strength must be immense to be able to do something like that, and so she went after Lindsay boldly as he groped for the King in the darkness. His fumbling made her laugh wildly. She caught up with him because he was intent on his prey, she crossed her wrists, wrapped the chain round Lindsay's neck and jerked her hands apart as far as they would go and he gurgled and stood up and tried to stab backwards and she avoided him easily.

She held him with her immense strength, her heat and fury, her righteous rage at all the men who thought she was nothing at all, not even a person. He made animal choking noises and she jerked the chains apart more, feeling happy and joyful.

King James was fumbling about in the dark, trying to find his way to the door and going deeper into the cellar in his panic, she heard him knock over the barrel of cucumbers of uncertain age. There was a strong smell of vinegar and pickles.

Lindsay was still fighting her, she jerked the chains playfully and held them and at last she felt him give and go heavy. Yet she was so strong, she could hold him up and she knew his head was lolling. She dropped him, and stamped her foot on his neck. She stamped again with her bare heel. She stood on him and stamped the serpent into the ground until he gurgled.

Then she looked for the King and there was his shape on all fours, trying to escape by the drain she had been pissing in, and that was so funny she laughed again.

King James scrambled away from the pickles. "By God, she's got a demon," he was muttering through his teeth, "Oh Jesus Jesus Jesus..."

Did she have a demon? She didn't think so, but maybe she did. She was panting like a dog, her head was fit to burst, she could still feel the fury and heat running through her and there was a sound of howling echoing in the walls.

She went over towards the King, wanting to help him, but he shrank away from her.

Suddenly she saw that handsome King of Heaven standing there and smiling, so she fell to her knees.

"He'p me, ma'eshty!" she said through the branks.

King James was panting too, he was hiding behind another barrel which had lost its label.

"Demon!" she shouted at the King of Heaven, but He had blown away like smoke.

"Do you want me to command the demon from you?" asked King James in a voice that tried not to quaver.

She wanted to explain that she had been talking to Jesus, not him, but that was too complicated and hard to say, and maybe he could do something about the horrible strength still flooding her.

"Yess!" And she shouted again and beat at the branks with her fists.

She heard a scuffling, King James was upright, coming forward with his hand raised trembling above his head, his greasy palm forward.

Now his voice came clear and certain. "Foul fiend! In the name of Jesus Christ, who cured the demoniacs and raised the dead, I bid you be gone from this woman! Begone! Begone!"

She sat down suddenly as sleep came reaching hungrily for her. Maybe it was a demon. She keeled over sideways and the last thing she felt was the King kneeling beside her and gently fumbling with the scold's bridle, finally using his little eating knife to unwind and cut the wire on the lock. He took it off and threw it away from her and she felt him stroking her sweaty hair.

"Sleep now," he said softly. "Ye're free."

SATURDAY 10TH MARCH 1593, WIDDRINGTON

Janet was trying every key on Lady Widdrington's bunch of them and none of them fitted the dairy postern gate. She started again at the other end, her hands trembling. What would they do without the key? She heard footsteps, gestured wildly to Cuddy to hide and put the keys back in her petticoat pocket just in time as the Dairy Mistress came round the corner of the dairy.

"I thought I heard someone at the gate?" said the woman.

"Ay, so did I," said Janet, her heart thudding, "d'ye have a key?"

She did, on a smaller bunch of keys hanging at her belt, and Janet was just about to pounce on her and wrestle it away from her, when two of the King's men came round the corner from the castle and stood there watching. The Dairy Mistress unbarred and opened the gate and peered through it, then grunted and locked and barred it again.

"Some bloody lad looking for his sweetheart," she said dismissively and went back into the dairy again, followed by the King's men. Jane was finishing up inside and Janet paced past the brewing sheds, wondering what the devil she could do now. Why wasn't the key on the ring? Had the idiot men actually thought about it and taken the important keys off? Damn it! How would she get word to Carey not to attack? Nobody could get out of the castle except through the front gate and the King's men weren't drunk like Lord Spynie's.

She was planning another attempt on the Dairy Mistress when she heard it, a strange sound, like a dog howling only deeper.

It kept on, eldritch sounding, a wolf howl with words, perhaps like a banshee. Janet tracked the sound to the castle itself, in at the ground floor where the steps went up above the door to the first floor hall. The animals in there, a crowded bunch of hobbies and kine, were alarmed at the noise too and shifting and snorting in protest.

Janet ran up the steps, though the noise had stopped, found the hall where Lord Spynie and his men were all drunk and playing stupid games of throwing knives and the like, up the spiral stair to the bedrooms, through the master bedroom where the two boys were sleeping in the truckle bed and no one else there, under the arch and into the smaller room where Sir Henry was standing over the chamber pot with his yard out and sweat pouring down his face. He smelled of piss too.

She stopped dead and turned away, to save his modesty. He hadn't seen her, he shook himself and got a couple of drops of blood and started wailing and howling again and so she had found the source of the noise.

"What are ye doing?" she asked, but he didn't answer - only shook his head like a horse at a fly. "Can I help ye..."

"I can't piss!" he screamed, "I can't piss! She's blocked me again... The bitch! Go get her. She's got to take the spell off me again."

Janet backed up with her eyebrows raised and a flinty expression on her face.

"Yer wife is in the cellar," she reminded him severely, "where you put her, in fact. And Minister Lindsay and the King went down to interrogate her less than an hour ago."

"Get her here!" The howling began again. "My bladder's going to burst."

"Hmf," said Janet and heroically did not say that she hoped it would because it wasn't her place to say such a thing. So she stood by the arch as Sir Henry started punching his own groin. "Maybe yer good friend Lord Spynie can help ye?" she said to him with poisonous sweetness.

And just at that moment, who should arrive but his lordship, with two henchmen behind him.

"What's making that noise… Och God." His narrow face always had a slightly furtive expression and when he saw Sir Henry's trouble, that face said furtively but as plain as day, the old man is ill and smelly and I'm so busy.

Sir Henry saw it too and paused, looking struck to the heart. "My lord," he whispered humbly, "will ye help me please?"

"Whit d'ye want me to do?"

"Try using a reed or something to clear the…"

Disgust was followed by hauteur on Spynie's face. "No, indeed, I am no barber surgeon."

Sir Henry turned to Janet. "Somebody must… awoww!" he panted, "You, Goody Dodd, please..?"

Janet backed up more. "What, dig around in your yard to pull out stones? I will do nae such thing, Sir Henry. How dare ye? I dinna ken how to do it and forbye even if I did, I wouldna do it for you. I dinna want tae be accused of witchcraft as well."

She curtseyed to both of them and trotted down the stairs, out to the yard. On impulse she went to the dairy again where Jane was outside, squeezing cloths out and hanging them up on the hedges behind the dairy yard, probably gooseberry and raspberry, not blackberry, Janet thought.

"Jane," she said, "Sir Henry's piss is blocked again…"

"Ay?" said Jane, "Is that the howling?"

"Ay, and I think ye should come wi' me now and sleep in the old chapel wi' me and my husband. It'll be safer..."

Suddenly two of Spynie's uglier bruisers burst into the yard, barged past Janet, ran to Jane and grabbed her by the elbows. She snatched her arm back and lifted a fist. "Get off, ye bastard!" she shouted.

Janet stepped between the other man and Jane and shoved him back. "Stay away from the maid," she roared, "What are ye at?!"

"My lord wants her to help Sir Henry..."

Janet was filled with contempt. "Why does he not ask one of ye to clear the man's prick, eh? Ye'd know as much about it as a milkmaid, I'd say. Why's it got to be the maid that does it?"

The younger one with the patchy beard looked at the floor as more screams filtered from the castle. "Sir Henry does need help," he said helplessly.

"Then mebbe he should have thought of that before he called his ain good wife a witch so she's in the cellar now, if she's not dead."

"Both of ye come," said the older one, drawing his sword.

Janet set her jaw and grabbed Jane's hand. "Come on," she said to her.

Janet deliberately took her time crossing the castle yard, and once the older one had gone up the steps to the hall, she lifted her head and pitched her voice to carry: "Henry Dodd!" she bellowed, "Henry! Help!"

The younger one flinched and hurried her up the steps, and up the spiral stair again, paused to let two more young thugs hurry down. Janet used the time to whisper to Jane, "If it comes tae fighting, run. If ye canna run, get in close as ye can and hit him as hard as ye can." Jane nodded once, her lips firm, determination on her homely square face. By God, thought Janet with affection, she should ha' been a man, there's few dairymaids in this situation than wouldna be greeting with fear,

They went up again, followed by swords shining dangerously in the hands of frightened men.

At the top of the stairs she met Lord Spynie who scowled at her.

"What's she doing here? I told ye, I want another woman..." shouted Lord Spynie, hard to hear against the howling coming from the bed.

"Ye fool," shouted Janet thoroughly roused now, "D'ye think I'd let a maid go among ye and yer bullyboys and catamites on her ain? Did ye?"

Jane's face had changed to horrified pity as she looked at the man writhing on the bed. Lord Spynie said, "We only want her to help unblock Sir Henry by clearing his yard of the stones," he stammered, "Nothing else."

"Good God, that's revolting."

"Lady Widdrington did it last time," said the younger man.

She rounded on him. "And look where she is now!"

"We won't..."

"So ye say!"

"I wouldn't mind doing it," said Jane unexpectedly, "only I'm feared because I dinna ken how and he might die and then ye'll blame me and say I'm a witch..."

Sir Henry was now screaming and pleading now and talking to somebody he called "Mam."

"We won't," said Spynie unconvincingly.

"That's not good enough," said Janet, "Put it in writing."

Spynie had a look of panic on his face. "My secretary isn't here..."

Janet shrugged and held Jane's hand more tightly, listening hard past the screaming.

Sir Henry was now banging his head on the bed and clawing at himself.

Janet turned her back on him and made sure Jane turned away too. It was too ugly a sight for a maid.

Then she heard the crash and shouting downstairs that she had been waiting for. There was a clash of weapons, a scream, a thunderous sound of boots on the stair that came closer, the thud of fists on flesh, somebody fell down the stairs, more yelling and swordplay.

Janet caught Jane's other hand and pushed her against the wall, turned to stand between her and the fighting men who were grabbing their swords, because she knew what those sounds meant.

Then Jane put her arms around Janet, turned and lifted her bodily about so she was the one next to the wall. Jane's broad back was now between her and the fighting.

"What..."

"Missus Dodd," hissed Jane ferociously over her shoulder, "Ye've got a babby!"

She had forgotten all about it in the hurry, but she let Jane take the outer place with her knife in her hand and her jaw clenched.

"Ay but it's..." said Janet smiling lovingly.

Sergeant Dodd erupted into the room with his sword and his eating knife in his hands, kicking the lout who was trying to stop him clear across the room where he crashed head first against the bed and collapsed.

"... my husband," she finished.

Dodd strode over, saw the way they were standing and put himself between Spynie's men and them, with his sword and knife en garde and the grim look he always wore when he was killing.

"Who..." he asked, a little breathlessly, "is bothering my wife and her woman?"

Spynie had his mouth open and hadn't even drawn yet.

"Sergeant Dodd," he said with a ghastly smile, "we were only asking if Goody... er... Mrs Dodd or the dairymaid could try to help Sir Henry who is as ye see..."

Dodd glanced at the man on the bed who was jacknifing and crying with pain, turned on Janet and Jane.

"Are ye willing?" he asked.

"No, I am not!" snapped Janet. "If I try anything to help him and succeed or fail they'll say we're witches." She held Jane's hand tightly. "And I dinna think ye should even ask a maid to do such a thing, my lord. For God's sake, where's yer decency!"

Lord Spynie's face was a picture. It went through frustration, annoyance and then selfish relief.

He shrugged and walked out of the room, went down the stairs and his men followed him, two of them dragging the man Dodd had kicked and who was still googly-eyed. Like a procession they all went down the stairs, leaving Dodd, Janet and Jane in the chamber.

Janet glanced at the man writhing and whimpering in exhausted agony on the bed. Her face went flinty.

"Help me," he whispered.

"God have mercy on ye," she said coldly to Sir Henry. "Ye've no friends left."

Then she followed Jane and her husband down the stairs, feeling something like wind in her lower stomach, wondered what it was and then stopped and smiled. It was the baby. It was kicking. God be praised!

SATURDAY 10TH MARCH 1593, WIDDRINGTON

King James had given up trying to light the lantern because although he did have a tinderbox, all his life he had had somebody else deal with mundane things like lighting fires and he wasn't at all practised at it and his hands were still trembling. Lady Widdrington was unconscious and he had pushed her against the wall so he wouldn't trip on her. Lindsay's corpse he had kicked across the floor so he was under one of the empty shelves.

At least Lady Widdrington was definitely still alive. She was warm and breathing though completely still. Lindsay was surrounded by the smell of death which was the same as shit, his knife was still in his hand. James didn't want to go near it, he was sure it was poisoned and he had a horror of blades.

And there was a horrible howling noise coming from somewhere above, something like an animal, maybe a dog – except that occasional words mixed in said it was human or maybe another demon.

James stood in the dark, unable to move. His heart was slowing but he was still trembling like an aspen. Somewhere slightly sideways of his body, the part of his brain that loved reading, that loved writing books on important subjects, it was talking to him. He tried to listen.

It said methodically: Lindsay was an assassin, clearly, and the whole accusation of Lady Widdrington as a witch was a ruse designed to attract me here and so kill me. The plan was to have the woman attack me and Lindsay would stab me in the confusion and that would then be blamed on the woman.

The thoughts made him shudder again. He put his folded hands against his chest and hunched his shoulders forwards. And Spynie was part of it, he thought next, though it hurt terribly to think so of someone he had loved. Somewhere inside him was weeping at that thought, that Spynie could have done it.

Surely Spynie hadn't realised what Lindsay was? He's not very bright, thought another, more forgiving part of him. The trembling was getting worse and his knees felt soft. He needed a drink. God, how he needed a drink. Was there anything...?

He could leave the cellar and order someone to bring him brandy-wine, sure. But he didn't want to do that while that demonic howling was going on. He didn't know if Lindsay had assistants either. He didn't know what to do and the trembling was getting worse. He desperately wanted to hide somewhere, preferably under a bed.

He closed his eyes, no difference in the darkness between open and shut eyelids and also of course, no bed. Then he thought he remembered glimpsing a flagon near the staple in the wall that Lady Widdrington had been chained to. He felt his way along the wall, found the staple which was bent off the wall. He felt around carefully, bent and scrabbling in the pitch darkness, careful to avoid Lady Widdrington who was breathing deeply. There it was. A flagon and from the smell there was still some spiced wine in it, thank God.

He upended the flagon, swallowed the bittersweet booze which reminded him of something and waited to calm down.

Now he felt surprisingly light-headed, and hot and thirsty... What was happening?

He fell against the wall, sat down suddenly with his back against it. The stone walls of the cellar were starting to move and lift and past them he could see a much larger Edinburgh castle, a giant's castle, and there was a giant woman there, with blonde curls under her cap, wearing a kirtle of dark blue velvet and a small pearly ruff and a jewelled belt around her slender waist. He was looking up at her adoringly, lifting his arms to her. She laughed and picked him up and cuddled him on her hip. He poked his fingers at the glittering things hanging round her neck, shining in the sunlight.

"Maman," he said, lisping, "Maman, je vous aime!"

"C'est certain," she said, "et jc t'aime toi meme, mon petit."

French flooded him like a warm bath of words, sweet as an apple. She danced with him in the sunlight and she laughed as he laughed and she spun round and once again and the spinning became a golden wheel and she was pinned to the wheel but still laughing as it carried her round and round.

"Why?" he shouted in Scots, "Why did ye leave me, why did ye betray me, you mermaid queen, you false bitch..."

The laughter went on until he shouted "Stop!" and then it speeded up and became ugly and suddenly the whole world broke apart into shards of golden glass with her beautiful smiling face on every one and James tried to pick up the glass and hug it to him but it cut him and hurt him. He was weeping, trying to pick up the glass and then suddenly there was a tap on his back.

There she was again, only this time wearing a blood red bodice and petticoat and she had a golden wig on and a little dog hiding at her feet among her skirts and there was a red line across her throat where the axe had passed five years before.

She wasn't a giant any more, although she was still quite tall.

"Jamie," she said in French, "I never wanted to leave you but I lost the battle and had to flee. I love you. You are a good King and a brave wise man. I am very proud of you."

And she kissed him gently on the cheeks and then dissolved into the blackness of the cellar and the sound of his own crying.

Eventually the tears stopped and he blew his nose with his fingers, wiped his sleeve across his eyes. He felt... he felt lighter. And not so frightened. Had it been his mother's ghost? Maybe, but what she said...

It made him feel stronger. A better man. She loved him and was proud of him. Even if she was a wicked woman, a wicked woman who had killed his father Lord Darnley, or at least winked at the true killer, the Earl of Bothwell, and then married him... Buchanan had taught him to hate her, told him she never loved him because she was evil, told him he was much better off without her.

Buchanan had beaten him black and blue to get the sin he had inherited from her out of him. Buchanan had hurt him worse than beating, again and again. He had obediently tried to forget her as best he could but...

She loved him and she was proud of him. Even from a mermaid queen, that was something, surely? Surely?

James tipped his head against the wall which he was already sitting against. He sighed a long sigh. He would stay where he was for a while and sleep. He needed to sleep. The howling was still going on, Spynie wasn't there, he had no energy left to get up and call for help and it was peaceful in the cellar now Lindsay was dead and the woman asleep.

As good a place to hide as any, he thought.

SATURDAY 10TH MARCH 1593, MIDNIGHT, OUTSIDE WIDDRINGTON

It was a pity that Sir Henry was an active lord of his castle, Carey thought as he crawled between two tussocks of grass and found another small stream he had to crawl through. They were close to the North Sea and the country was sodden after the winter and the snow melting. He didn't know if Dodd would be able to do as he promised but in case he couldn't, Carey had what the pursuivants called a door-knocker being brought up behind him by Garron and East. Helpfully it was starting to rain.

Leamus was ahead, eeling through the rough grass on his elbows. Above them they could just see the deeper dark of the walls of Widdrington castle, with occasional dim watchlights showing. It wasn't a big castle, not very much bigger than a pele tower and nowhere near the size of Carlisle or Berwick for that matter – but the walls were thick enough to keep them out if things went wrong. Of course, a couple of cannon from Berwick with powder and shot and a couple of gunners too and they would be through them easily. But he didn't think his brother, the Chamberlain, would have been any more willing to lend them to him than the Garrison Horse. Possibly less. In fact, he could picture John's face and John's double chin quivering at the idea which almost made him laugh.

They were crawling towards the Castle in the dark, their faces striped with soot and their swords and guns muffled with rags. Carey was wearing an old helmet with the padding falling out because his morion was such a giveaway. It was probably populated by lice but he had to hide his bleached white hair somehow.

He had sixteen men because the whole of Heronimo's troop was with him, the eight men who had been sent to Berwick by his father were willing to fight for him as well once Tarrant had talked to them. He was touched by that as he hadn't rated them as soldiers and certainly hadn't expected loyalty. And he rather liked Nick Smithson, their de facto leader – no, his name was actually Stephenson, wasn't it? – who was a steady and rather bright young man, who was brisk and useful in a fight and able to think for himself. He wouldn't have the calivers for the men without Nick's taking of the cart, after all.

He was pondering whether he could get back the eight men sent to Berwick by swapping men of the Garrison who wanted a change but thought that wouldn't work. Besides, why would anyone want to swap Carlisle for Berwick and his pompous older brother?

They had come to the small moat – it wasn't deep but it was wet and muddy and they had to hope that the leeches hadn't woken up yet. The rain hissed softly on the surface.

Carey looked over his shoulder. The men were well spread out with bushes tied to their backs so they would look more like the scrub pasture they were crawling through. Garron and East also had the door-knocker on the grass between them in case the Dodds failed him and Stephenson's mysterious tools too, and they had to go loud. They were sliding it along and not even complaining about it. Nick Stephenson was over to his left, Clockface to his right, Falls off His Horse Perkins, Gorman, Tarrant and after him, the eight he didn't know so well apart from Mike Longdown, impossible to see in the darkness. And Leamus ahead, scouting of course.

They went through the moat because although there was a bridge, it was made of hardwood and would echo with their footsteps, as it was supposed to do.

The freezing muddy water soaked into his fighting breeches and the lower part of his jack, making them heavy and chafing. He waded slowly and climbed out amongst a few rushes to the mound. There above them was the postern gate, big enough to let one cow through at a time.

Sir Henry had ordered it cut into the wall a few years before so he wouldn't be disturbed by the lowing when the cows went out the main gate – at night you had to keep the cows in calf in the barnekin during the raiding season or someone would for certain try to raid them. The barnekin was choked with horses at the moment from all the people staying there and Carey was hoping that would help him. He knew most of the kine were out on the infield with the less valuable hobbies which was a risk in itself.

He had heard nothing from Dodd since his letter, knew nothing of what was going on, nothing. Perhaps Dodd had been taken prisoner by Sir Henry and Lord Spynie? Jesu, he hoped not. Or had Dodd betrayed him? It wouldn't be the first time, after all. He had promised to try to find a way to open the dairy postern gate, failing which there were Nick Stephenson's tools, failing which there was the door-knocker. He really hoped he wouldn't have to use the door-knocker, despite all of Tarrant and Stephenson's labour which had gone into giving a heavy bolt of wood an iron shoe and iron handles.

They had spent most of the day memorising the sketch map of Widdrington castle and practising variations on what they would do and Carey had boiled all his plans down to the simplest essence of a night attack that he could. The villagers had found the proceedings hilarious and one bold lad had asked were they players, and Carey had told him a long and complex tale about how they were practising for a play to be shown before the Chamberlain of Berwick.

There it was. Carey climbed squelchily to his feet and trotted as softly as he could up the mound. Behind him came the lads with the doorknocker, and all the rest of them. Hoping against hope, his heart beating fast, the feeling of gambling for high stakes drawing his lips back in a fighting grin, he lifted the latch and pulled.

The postern gate opened.

Joy burst through him briefly before his stomach tightened again at the thought of the ticklish job that was next. He turned and beckoned everybody else. Nick arrived first. Leamus was grinning like a wolf and unplaiting his hair, while he held the gate open with his foot. Once everyone was in, he closed it very softly.

They were in the small dairy yard with the long low stone building that was the dairy up against the walls of the castle ahead and right. Directly ahead was the door to the kitchen, shut and certainly bolted on the inside. To their left was another small gate that went straight into the main castle yard, by the woodsheds.

Perkins and Clockface went to that gate and Stephenson went and tried to open it. It was locked, but he had a claw hammer in a tool bag, and briskly removed the nails holding the hinges on the door. Perkins and Clockface slipped through the narrow gap.

Meanwhile Carey trotted towards the dairy door that Jane had described and found that although there was no lock, there were no hinges visible and the door was bolted from inside.

He pointed at Stephenson who came up close with a long tool, flat with a hook on it, jiggled it carefully through the gap between the door and the stone wall. That took at least a hundred years because after the first bolt slid back, there turned out to be another high up.

Carey kept watch while Stephenson stood on Gorman's back to jiggle the top bolt back. He couldn't believe that no one had spotted them yet – what were Spynie's men doing for their livery? If they had been his men, he would have flogged them for negligence.

Stephenson was squatting by the door, feeling with his tool, a look of concentration on his face and then a grin and a thumbs up.

He opened the dairy door which led into the Castle kitchen, next to the hall.

They crept along the kitchen passage to the steps that led up into the hall, and down again to the cellars. Carey put his head into the kitchen. There was nobody at all in there, not even scullery boys. The brick oven in one corner was filled with tinder and timber, there was a curfew on the main fire.

They went down the stairs to the cellars, nobody was there either.

At the bottom of the stairs, in the passage, the one to the far left was unlocked, with empty wine barrels inside. Next to that was the cheese store, firmly locked. The little tool store next to it was shut but empty. Carey waited for Stephenson to bring up his tools, Garron and East to bring up the doorknocker. The provisions cellar on the right was where Elizabeth was.

He tried it gently, his heart hammering. The door moved, opened. Carey took the dark lantern Tarrant was carrying, strode into the cellar.

It was the right cellar but it was empty. A neat pile of turds, a stinking drain, a flagon abandoned on the floor, nameless lumps on the floor, one barrel had fallen over and disgorged pickled cucumbers in a corner...

Or not quite empty. Under the pantry shelves was a corpse dressed in black brocade, the corpse of a totally bald man. His face was mashed and dented and there were the marks of chainlinks around his neck although when Carey touched him, he thought the neck was broken. It felt like jelly.

Very swiftly, holding his breath against the smell, Carey searched the body, found a folded letter. He looked at it and it had the Papal seal on it, the text was in Latin and Spanish. He had no idea what it said but suspected it was a Plenary Indulgence. He found the knife still grasped in the bald man's hand, darkened at the tip. There was something odd under the man's clothes so he opened the doublet and the waistcoat, lifted the shirt and found a stinking hairshirt alive with lice bailing out.

Jesus Christ! A hair shirt? Only Catholic priests wore those things for penance!

And who had killed him? And where was Elizabeth?

Nearby were scuff marks where somebody else had sat on the floor. Carey picked up the flagon, sniffed inside. There was a nasty bitter smell that he recognised at once: was it poison? Belladonna and hemlock?

Where the Devil was Elizabeth? What had happened to her?

God damn it to hell, had he missed her again?

From above in the kitchen passage where he had left three men to keep watch came a shout, "A l'armes!" and the clash of weapons, a thud as a body hit the floor.

He ran out of the cellar and up the stairs, along the back passage where he found some of Hieronimo's Troop from Berwick standing over a body. Stephenson was behind him, Garron, East, Leamus. They went back through the dairy door, Carey opened the door to the main yard as far as it would go, looked out into the barnekin where Falls off his Horse and Clockface had been busy dismantling the hurdles that fenced the animals in. There was a chaos of wandering herds. He cupped his hands around his mouth and did a bad imitation of an owl's call. He heard someone answer, saw movement in the distance, but some men from the gate were coming purposefully towards them.

Understanding flowered inside him like a black rose. He had been coneycatched, he had been fooled. By Christ, he had been betrayed somehow, he didn't know how, but it was clear.

"Get out," he said to Stephenson as he went past, "Withdraw! It's a trap, they've moved the prisoners. Get everybody out!"

Stephenson nodded once and helped Garron and East throw the door-knocker at the nearest soldier, joined up with Clockface and Falls Off His Horse Perkins, shut the gate to the main yard and barred it. They sprinted to the postern gate around two puzzled and sleepily annoyed cows and the rest of the troop followed fast.

Leamus was holding the postern gate open with Stephenson standing there on the other side, with his sword out. One of Spynie's men thundered into him and Stephenson crossed swords, slashed once and Leamus squatted, reached out and hamstrung the man neatly. He was singing some kind of sad song in Irish as the last of the troop pelted past him into the night and he counted them, looked through two doorways at Carey. He raised his eyebrows and Carey shook his head, so he bowed, and Carey pelted up the stairs to the hall. From the arrow slit over the door Carey could see satisfying chaos breaking out in the yard as sleepy men tumbled out and ran around looking for enemies, some in their shirts. Pretty soon they had started fighting each other.

***

Leamus shut the postern gate neatly after him and put a plank across it, ran after the rest of troop.

"Where's Gorman?" asked Stephenson as they sprinted in a herd across the bridge and over the infield. "And the Courtier?"

"He got hit by a sword, Gorman," panted Falls Off His Horse.

"The Courtier?"

"I saw him heading up into the hall, sorr," said Leamus as he loped past.

***

Carey ran up the stairs two at a time, in at the door into the hall where Spynie's men were pouring out. He was shouting, "Sir Henry! My Lord Spynie!" as he went, and astonishingly he managed to cross the hall in the chaos. Maybe the white hair helped?

He ran up the north-eastern spiral stairs to the third floor, through the master bedroom which was empty, into the second bedroom where Sir Henry was lying on the bed breathing in an ugly way, as if he was sipping the air and it hurt to breathe.

Carey set the lantern on the chest, put his drawn sword at Sir Henry's neck.

"Where is Lady Widdrington?" he asked as the bloodshot eyes opened and stared at him.

"She'sh here," said Sir Henry in a slurred voice as if he were drunk. "She'sh staring at me."

There was an appalling smell coming from the bed, piss and a deeper note of rot, is if something was decaying fast inside the man.

Lady Widdrington was not in the room. Carey glanced out of the arrow slit into the barnekin where a very satisfying battle had broken out as Spynie's men and another group of men fought each other, and a Sergeant-at-Arms tried to get them to stop by bellowing at them. He even looked under the bed.

"She isn't here," he said, "What did you do with her? Did you hang her secretly, you rotting pile of shit, eh?"

"No, no, not yet, Lindsay said..." Sir Henry was staring anxiously at the far side of the room. "She's there, she's looking at me."

There was only a mirror, reflecting the room.

"She isn't," shouted Carey in a fury of frustration, "Tell me where she is or I'll cut your balls off one by one."

"Stop it!" shouted Sir Henry at the mirror, "Stop looking at me!"

Carey felt the man's forehead as he tried to raise his head and failed. It was furnace hot and dry. Sir Henry swiped feebly for him, then rolled and puked and that stank of piss as well.

Carey put up his sword. The man was delirious. It would have been so easy to kill him, but every chivalric bone in his body revolted at the thought of killing any man in his sickbed. Besides, why besmirch his honour when from the looks of him, Sir Henry would die soon anyway?

"Ye can leave him alone," said Lord Spynie's voice as he followed two of his men in. All three were aiming hunting crossbows at Carey. "He's dying anyway, I think his bladder burst."

"Good," said Carey, staying where he was. "I hope he's in a lot of pain too. Where is Lady Widdrington?"

"In the provisions cellar under the kitchen," sneered Lord Spynie, "Don't you even know that?"

"Oh?" said Carey, a pulse of hope following his bewilderment.

"Ay, His Highness the King of Scotland was interrogating her along with the witchfinder and..."

"What?" Just for a second, Carey doubted himself and wondered if he had mistaken the corpse and it was the King's. But it wasn't.

Sure, the witchfinder or Papist priest or whatever, he smelled bad but nothing like as bad as the King. So the King of Scotland had come to see the lady-in-waiting who had become a witch?

Carey started to laugh, completely devoid of humour. After all, the joke was on him.

Spynie whispered to one of his men, who turned and trotted out of the room. Then he came closer. He was nervous of Carey though; you could see the bow wavering.

Carey smiled at him, all his teeth showing. His first plan had been to take Lady Widdrington away with him with the help of Hieronimo's Troop, as quick and quiet as he could. His second plan if he couldn't find her or she was already hanged was to kill Sir Henry and Spynie and then do his best to get out. Now he assumed she was dead somewhere and Spynie was playing games with him.

Part of him felt the great yawning hole in his chest where his heart had just been ripped out, part of him felt strangely... free: it was the feeling he often got in a fight, when everything went slow and there were no rules to worry about. He was hollow and made of steel and gunpowder.

Sir Henry was at least moribund. Half done, only one more kill left and then they could do whatever they liked.

"Don't pity me, ye bitch!" shouted Sir Henry suddenly from the bed, "Don't ye dare pity me! Tell her not to pity me..."

Spynie glanced at the bed, no sorrow, just an annoyed wrinkle between the eyebrows.

A lad's feet were thundering up the stair, he burst in. "She's gone, my lord, gone and taken the King wi' her, maybe she's riding a broomstick, my lord, or..."

"What?" snapped Spynie, "What d'ye mean? Is she dead?"

The boy wiped his face, caught his breath. "No sir, ainly she's gone and ainly poor Minister Lindsay's body left behind."

"What d'ye know of this, Carey?"

Carey shrugged. "I think you're play-acting, I think ye're lying to me about Lady Widdrington, I think ye've hanged her and now ye wish ye hadn't and ye're too frightened to tell me." Come on, ye fucking pervert, he was thinking, just a little nearer, come on.

He was watching Spynie's knuckle tighten on the trigger of the crossbow. Just as it went white he dropped to the floor, rolled, came to his feet with his dagger in his hand, the sound of the released bow in his ears... But he only stabbed one of Spynie's men, Spynie was running for the door, there was a sproing as another crossbow loosed but somehow went into the beam just above his head. Then that man ran after Spynie and Carey felt himself grabbed from behind by someone who stank of piss, Sir Henry's face distorted with fever and rage, his fingers tightening around Carey's throat.

Carey elbowed backwards, half-turned and rammed Sir Henry into the wall, rammed again, loosened the grip. And then there was a crush of men around him, his sword was gone, somebody shouting from the door, "Take him alive!"

He punched a man in the face, knocked him down, took a blow on his shoulder, somebody knocked his helmet off, somebody else grabbed him round the body and a thing came to him from when he was a boy and he stepped back, lifted both his arms and elbowed whoever it was in the face, someone else had grabbed his feet and he tried to kick and then two men had his arms and he headbutted one but the other twisted his arm almost out of its socket and someone else buried the ball end of a dag in his stomach and he bent and tried to puke and they had him and he went to the ground in a pile of bodies.

He bit someone on the nose though, just before the lights went out. Everybody was panting for breath.

"Jesus Christ," said one of them nasally, "ye bastard!" and he got the toe of a boot in his chest and fell out of the world completely.

SATURDAY 10TH MARCH 1593, WIDDRINGTON, 10 PM

Elizabeth woke to the sound of a key in the lock, anxious muttering, more turning of the key, a thud, it turned again. There was a short snarl of "Bastard shit!" in a voice she recognised.

Sergeant Dodd was trying to get into her cellar. But he couldn't. Why not?

Because he didn't have the key. She had the key.

"Wai'" she said, urgently, "Wai', I go' i'."

"What? What are ye saying."

She shook her head, felt the top of it come off and float down somewhere. Angels were singing somewhere near, she knew that. Where had she hidden the keys? In her armpit? No?

Ah. Now she remembered. She squatted and felt herself, found the strip of cloth and pulled and after a brief struggle, it fell to the ground. Hah! There it was. What would Robin say? Habet? Only that would be wrong, wouldn't it, for some reason, habeo perhaps?

Very slowly she took the two keys, unwrapped the linen and carried them over to the door. She put the smaller one in the lock and turned it and the door opened and she looked out and saw two people at the end of the passage just about to go up the stairs.

A man and a woman, she knew that from their clothes. The man was holding a dark lantern with just a tiny splinter of flame showing. Yet the small light dazzled her eyes badly and she turned her face away. There had been… holes in reality, the walls of the world wafting like curtain. She had been dreaming, flying around, seeing things she couldn't have seen. She thought she had done something desperate with her chains, since her wrists were hurting and badly grazed and bruised. She couldn't remember what. When she put her hand up to feel her face, she found the branks wasn't there any more, although her sore mouth was crusty and like leather and she was desperately thirsty. There was still a smell of dirty man near her and another smell further away, of death.

She also couldn't think straight, she was exhausted, her head hurt and her eyes were streaming with tears.

She saw the man with the lantern approach her and she put her hand up to stop the light.

"Milady," he said, "ye had the keys? Have ye the dairy postern gate's key?"

She didn't want to speak, it hurt too much. She nodded seriously and held it up. Who was the woman behind him who was staring at her? By God, it was Janet Dodd. She could have hugged her if Janet's face hadn't been so printed with horror at the state of her.

"Janet," she said carefully, wincing with pain at the ulcers.

"Lady Widdrington?" And Janet dropped a curtsey and Elizabeth had the feeling that something that had put the world on its end and made it ugly ever since Lindsay had addressed her as plain Elizabeth, was now healed.

Dodd was standing in the middle of the cellar with the lantern raised high and its panel fully open. He was staring at the man sitting propped up with his back against the wall, snoring, his mouth open, his head tilted.

"Jesu," came Dodd's harsh mournful voice. "That's the King o' Scotland."

Janet squatted down next to him and took his wrist to feel for the pulse. "God be thanked," she said after a moment, "he's alive although his pulse is fast."

Elizabeth squinted at the man, was it really Sergeant Dodd? Her eyes were so dazzled she found she could only see a blur.

The snoring stopped, there was a snort and the King opened his eyes. Immediately he put his hand in front of him, fending off the small light from the lantern.

"Whit's wrong wi' my eyes?"

Janet looked around, found the flagon lying on its side, sniffed suspiciously. "I don't know, but there's a bitter oily smell." she said.

Elizabeth put her hands up to her face and covered her eyes. She couldn't bear the candlelight any more.

"Are ye dazzled?" asked Janet.

"Yesh," said Elizabeth, "I can't shee."

"Ay," said Dodd, "the Courtier got hisself poisoned while he was down south near Oxford and he said it was two or three days afore he could see right again."

"And who's this?" asked Janet, bumping her toes against Lindsay's corpse under the shelf.

"Och God, that's Minister Lindsay, the witchfinder," said Elizabeth, trying to crawl away from him, the chains on her wrists jinking, "keep him away from me."

"He's deid," said Janet, "deid and stiff. How did he die? His face is dark, his tongue is swollen and... ay... his neck is broken."

"It's coming back to me," said the King slowly. "Ay. He attacked me wi' ... wi' a knife and... I think I killed him. Yes, I did. I caught him from behind and strangled him."

Dodd and Janet exchanged looks, and Janet stared fixedly at Elizabeth's chains. "But..." she started.

"Ay, did ye so, Yer Majesty?" said Dodd, his voice full of fake admiration.

"As a matter of fact, I did," said the King complacently.

"Yes but…" Janet started again and there was a sudden movement of Dodd's boot and Janet hopped and grabbed her shin. "Damn it, husband…" Dodd glared at her. "Ah… er… ay, I see. Yes."

"Can ye stand up, Yer Majesty? Ye might feel very tired if you drank the stuff in the flagon, I'm thinking it was poisoned."

"Good God," said the King, "that's why it tasted familiar. Well Lindsay suddenly attacked me with a knife and I… I stopped him dead. Ye can see – is his knife still in his hand?"

"It is, Yer Majesty, will ye come this way."

Janet tried to help Elizabeth out the door. Suddenly, Elizabeth couldn't manage it, her feet were too far away and her knees trembled like willow twigs in a high gale. Not even Janet's sturdy shoulder was enough. She slumped down on the floor again.

Dodd came over, bent and picked her up easily enough and then he said "Whufff."

"Is your back hurting," asked Janet anxiously.

"I'm fine," said Dodd through his teeth.

"I'll carry her," said the King, standing up. "It's not long since ye had a crossbow bolt in yer back, did ye no'? That's an order now, Sergeant."

Dodd reluctantly put Elizabeth's feet down and she crumpled helplessly to the floor.

"I'm sorry," she said, "I can't…"

King James bent to her, braced and lifted. "Ay," he said, "Ah can put my wife in her bed when I want to, and ye're lighter." And he grinned a boy's grin.

"We'll go in the other cellar for the moment – Janet, have ye…"

"Ay, will ye carry her there, Your Majesty?"

"Certainly."

He puffed a bit but carried her down the passage to the storeroom where Hutchin had been kept, Dodd leading the way with the lantern. Dodd had a crowbar there to attack the lock on her manacles and once they came free, Janet chased the men out and shut the door. She turned to Elizabeth and found her in tears.

Janet clucked like a hen and came forward with her bundle. "Now my lady, I've brung ye my own old kirtle and a clean smock if ye'll..."

Elizabeth was already pulling her old smock off over her head and she threw it into a corner. "Thirshty," she said.

Janet was glad to avert her eyes from Elizabeth's body which was covered in bruises and sores and odd little round wounds up her arms. She found the pottle of ale at the bottom of the pack and handed it to Elizabeth who drank half of it down and sighed.

Then Janet brought her own clean smock and held it up and Elizabeth put her arms in and put it on, then Janet's oldest petticoat, and then a faded old kirtle that was much too short for Elizabeth as well as darned and stained and full of hay stalks from the last time Janet had worn it. Finally Janet tried to comb Elizabeth's red hair but it was too snarled in tangles and elflocks, so she gave up, wished for sheep shears which was about what you needed and she didn't have any on her. She twisted the whole mop up and pinned it with one of her own long pins and perched a cap on top.

Elizabeth sighed deeply. "At least I'm deshent now," she said. "Thank you, Mrs Dodd."

"Nae bother," said Janet, giving her a pair of old turnshoes which Elizabeth put on with an effort. "Everyone's asleep except for in the hall and they were singing."

They crept upstairs, listening to the blurred sound of drunken men still singing a sentimental song. Elizabeth managed the climb with only a few staggers, no one was there except a sentry at the end of the passage who now had a dent in his head and was snoring on the bottom step of the stairs. There was no one in the kitchen, not even scullery boys asleep by the fire.

"Where is everybody?" asked Elizabeth with a frown.

"Tell ye later," grunted Janet.

They went through the passage to the dairy yard, and found Jane waiting at the postern gate from the dairy yard, looking very anxious. She clasped her hands together when she saw Elizabeth still marked on her face by the straps of the branks. "Oh my lady!" and she hugged Elizabeth impulsively and Elizabeth smiled and hugged her back. When they drew apart, Elizabeth saw tears on her face.

"Who did you get to carry the ring, Jane?"

Jane looked at Janet and Dodd and swallowed. "Dinna be angry at me..."

"Jane carried the message herself in two days," said Dodd, "on foot."

"You did?" Jane nodded once. "But how could you go so fast?"

"I ran," said Jane simply, "Ye ken I like running."

"Good God," said Elizabeth horrified, "But..."

"Can we get on," hissed Dodd, "they willna sing forever."

Jane brought a hobby out of the cow byre with muffled hooves and Elizabeth stumbled to the postern gate and unlocked it with her key. Dodd took the hobby through the gate, followed by the King of Scots. He was still looking pale and seemed to be thinking hard. Elizabeth and Janet followed, and then Dodd went back, came out and shut the postern gate but did not lock it.

"Your Majesty," said Dodd, almost courtierlike thought Janet proudly, "would you like to ride?"

The King looked up. "Well yes, I would... er... perhaps I could take turns with Lady Widdrington, considering she is so weak."

"Oh no need, Your Majesty," said Elizabeth, "I can..."

Janet pushed her to the horse. "Get on," she hissed, "we havena time for this." Elizabeth allowed herself to be pushed onto the horse, put her legs in the stirrups and sighed, slumped in the saddle. She was more grateful than she could say that she didn't have to walk. It was hard enough to stay on a horse.

Another part of her head floated up and spun in the air, making her feel dizzy and strange. Part of her was shocked at her riding and the King of Scots walking. Another part said that if everyone was really a god, like Jesus had said, then it didn't matter that he was the King. He was letting her ride because she needed to. And another part of her wondered if he had really forced a demon inside her to leave? She wasn't sure, she was still confused, and she decided that she couldn't work it out and she wanted to sleep.

Dodd took the reins and went ahead, followed by the King, Janet came after the horse with a broom, brushing the footprints away. They walked down the mound and across the moat at the least muddy place where the King balked once and then philosophically continued, not wanting their steps to echo on the bridge. Janet lifted her skirts and waded across, Elizabeth stayed on the hobby which surged out of the water and nearly made her fall off.

They walked across the infield where the cows were disposed asleep on the ground, all pointing the same way and walked and walked across a fallow meadow full of young and juicy thistles and they walked. Luckily the land was quite flat and finally they came to one of the village's coppices that was mature enough not to have deer fences.

They rested there under the bushy trees. At least it wasn't raining yet. Dodd went investigating the little patch of woodland and he came back and forced them to go on further to a tiny charcoal burner's hut with a pallet in it and not much else. Elizabeth felt her knees go again and sat down on the floor which was a little padded with last year's bracken. She felt exhaustion climb up her body and grab her. She just toppled over. She was looking up at the King who had a surprising look of angry determination on his face and then her eyes shut. Somebody put something under her head and she fell asleep.

Behind them and unknown to Elizabeth or Dodd, Hieronimo's Troop were stealthily moving up from the south.

SUNDAY 11TH MARCH 1593, WIDDRINGTON

Carey woke up feeling cold, with a thundering headache and his hands somehow strained above his head and his wrists hurting.

A flood of water hit him like a wet fist and made him gasp and splutter: what the hell? He was standing on his toes, he shook his head which was ringing with whatever had put him out, he squinted his eyes open and looked straight into Lord Spynie's handsome face. Spynie was laughing at him and strutting to and fro.

A wind of terror swept through his body bearing the smell of a cellar in Dumfries and the thumbscrews. For a moment he almost lost his water as his guts congealed in absolute fear. His internal voices were let loose by that and hammered around his head shouting that he was a fool, he should have married Cicely, maybe he could bow to Spynie, say sorry to him...

The silent noise rose until it hit a fevered pitch of insanity and in the middle of it all one of the demons said casually, of course you know that Elizabeth is dead.

And his heart dropped and turned to stone and the whole world was ugly and pointless and he was alone, and nothing mattered any more. Spynie could kill him and welcome.

At that point, inside him, as he stood trembling in the hollow of despair, a still small voice said quietly, "Act brave. Pretend."

He breathed out and that hurt too. Then he forced himself to look about.

He was at the open gate of Widdrington castle, the traditional place to hang people. His hands were tied and a rope from his wrists went up through a murder hole where it was no doubt tied to something sturdy. It was hard to breathe properly.

He was also naked, not even a shirt on him and his skin staring with goosepimples. He felt ashamed to be naked in so public a place, although admittedly, it wasn't the first time. There were a lot of men standing around and he was facing into the barnekin where Spynie was standing with one hip cocked.

And yet now, inside him, something had congealed like a waterfall in a hard frost. He really didn't care that he was naked. Spynie had somehow managed to trick him, but he thought most of Hieronimo's Troop had got out which was something. Either Lady Widdrington was dead already which he thought the most likely option or she would be brought in soon. He looked around for her, looked everywhere. No Elizabeth. At the very least they would tell him they had her and start bargaining. He could act as if he was brave, even though he knew he wasn't really. He didn't have to tell anybody that.

So he forced his body to relax a little and studied Spynie. He was wearing his smart cutwork leather jerkin over a blood red doublet with a falling band and black tooled boots and a tall beaver hat, no helmet. No padding. All right, come close to me, ye pervert, come close.

Spynie stopped strutting and smiled at Carey, took a long whip from one of his men.

Oh for God's sake, Carey thought, do ye think ye can scare me with your little whip?

Spynie made a negligent movement and the end of his whip flicked a bit of skin off Carey's shoulder, then another bit of skin off his buttocks. Unfortunately, it seemed Spynie had practised with the whip, and being the pervert he was, he had studied it well. Then the whole length of the whip struck Carey around the middle where the long scar from last summer was.

Carey gasped but more with the shock of the blow than pain. There was a certain amount of sniggering from Spynie's henchmen, enjoying the show. He kept his eyes on Spynie who was showing off now, prancing about and hitting him with the whip from a new angle every so often.

"Where's the witch," he sang out, "where's your trull, Lady Widdrington, where have you got her, eh?" Crack went the whip. "Tell me or I'll really have some fun with ye." Crack across his groin and Carey grunted and reflexively pulled his knees up and got another crack on his arse. Not funny, despite the hilarity of Spynie's gutter sweepings and scum.

He was swinging gently from the gate, his arms protesting, spinning a little, his toes scraping the kerbstone which was a little higher than the flagstones. He put one foot down on it and steadied himself.

"Have yer fun," he growled, "ye're a God damned pervert my lord, with yer poor defenceless children and yer youths so slim and pretty and the King too back when ye were yerself slim and pretty enough to be his mignon."

"So?" said Spynie, "Wasn't David Jonathan's mignon? I love the King..."

"You?" laughed Carey, "you don't love anyone except yourself, you limp-pricked coward."

Spynie's face became pinched and mean.

"I do love the King," said Spynie, coming close and thrusting the handle of his whip into Carey's groin and twisting. "I love him more than ye can ever imagine. And I'm not a coward."

Carey's face clenched and drops of sweat ran down his face.

"Ye are so," whispered Carey, "If ye weren't, ye'd fight me. I challenge you to fight me now as I am, my lord, and ye with yer pet whip."

A short flicker of fear went across Spynie's face and he twisted the whip handle again and Carey let out a short cry.

"My Lord Spynie," same a new voice, very cold from behind Carey. "Stop that now." Spynie peered over Carey's shoulder and his lips parted in horror.

The release was more painful than the twist had been. Carey almost blacked out and couldn't think whose the new voice might be although its Scots was familiar to him. But Spynie was up close to him and distracted. He instinctively pushed with his foot down onto the kerbstone, lifted his knee up and kicked Spynie right in the nuts so he fell back and landed on his arse, clutching them.

And now there was someone next to him sawing at the rope until it gave, and he could start lowering his arms carefully, as multiple bruises and grazes told on him. The same knife, Dodd's knife, sawed through the ropes on his wrists and he looked up and saw Dodd's face, grim and angry and he nearly blacked out again.

"I'm glad to see ye, Sergeant," he managed to whisper, hoping that Dodd hadn't betrayed him.

"Stay upright," snarled Dodd, "we're no' out o' the woods yet."

His knees felt rubbery but he straightened them and locked them and saw someone in a plain wool doublet, with the brim of his beaver hat pulled down over his eyes, standing beside Spynie who was still flopping around and trying to breathe. Considering the clamour from his own groin, he rather hoped he'd busted one or both of the favourite's ballocks.

"Can ye hear me, Lord Spynie," said the man in the woollen doublet and at last Carey knew him for the King and stared. The King added to the two of his own men who had come to stand at his shoulders: "Search his body."

They laid hands on Spynie and patted him down. From the breast pocket of his doublet one man brought out a slim wooden box and gave it to the King. He opened it and looked down on it for a long time, his jaw clenched. Then he looked across at Dodd.

"Thank ye, Sergeant," said the King, "I'm sorry I didna believe ye."

Dodd tipped his hat, said nothing.

The King waited until Spynie could talk again. "Where did ye get this, my lord?"

"It's not mine," wheezed Spynie, "I didn't..."

"Then quhy, pray, was it in yer doublet?"

Silence. Spynie licked his lips. "Yer Highness..."

"Shut up. Did ye ken yer pet witchfinder wis a Spanish spy, complete wi' a superstitious hair shirt and an indulgence fra the Pope and a code book in Spanish?"

Spynie's mouth opened like a codfish and he went white.

"He tried tae attack me wi' a poisoned blade in the cellar, but luckily and by God's grace, I was able to fight him off and kill him. Alas for it there was poison in a flagon of spiced wine there, which I drank, and that might have killed me too. It made me ill."

"I... I didna ken." Spynie's voice was cracked with fear as he climbed to his feet, still tenderly cupping his cods.

"Did ye no'?" said the King wearily, squinting at him. "Mine eyes are hurting still. And this... this mammet." He held up the wax doll in its scraps of finery. "This is witchcraft, right enough, and ye have it, not Lady Widdrington whom ye accused."

"It was ainly to bring ye to me," burst out Spynie, "and Lindsay swore it wis Hermetic, not magic."

"Bring me to ye?" spat back the King with his mouth twisting. "BRING ME TAE YE? How dare ye? How dare ye try and make me, yer King, intae a puppet?!"

Finally Spynie dropped to his knees. "But I love ye, Jimmy, I love ye more than words can tell, I love ye more than..."

King James stepped close and gave Spynie a great buffet on the face that knocked him over. "Shut up. That's a fine way to show yer love, using black magic to draw me here so yer witchfinder friend could slit me wi' his poisoned knife! Eh? EH?"

"No... no..."

"Get him out o' my sight," snapped the King. "And never ever call me by that name again, d'ye understand, Alexander Lindsay? Never!"

The King's Master-at-Arms, took Spynie's shoulder and effortlessly moved him away from the King.

It seemed to Carey that there were tears in the King's eyes, but he tilted his face up and coughed, blew his nose.

Carey forced his knees down, so he was kneeling to the King, with only his left hand for modesty. Dodd went down on one knee because he had his sword out.

"Sheath your sword," Carey hissed at him and after a pause Dodd put up his weapon.

"By God, Sir Robert," said the King, forcing a bluff tone of voice, "Ye get intae a power of trouble, don't ye?"

"Yes, Your Majesty." Somehow the right words came out of his mouth without his having to think about them. "I am very happy and grateful to God that you were able to kill the Spanish assassin and didn't take any harm from the poison..."

"Nay, it gave me some strange dreams which I canna now rightly remember, and my eyes are dazzled, but naething worse." He paused thoughtfully. "Would ye like revenge on Spynie?"

Carey paused as well and then decided that even if this was a trick, he didn't care.

"Yes, Your Majesty."

"Well Sir Robert," said the King with quite a nasty smile on his face, "if ye can catch him before he gets to Scotland, ye can do what ye like to him, short of killing him."

"Where are my clothes?"

The King gestured and one of Spynie's men sprinted off to get them.

"These are the rules. Nae horses, nae guns nor swords nor knives, nae armour. It's a running race. Ye can take up tae two men wi' ye and I myself will be yer umpire."

Carey bowed extravagantly and wobbled. Then he pulled Dodd close. "Don't run with me, Sergeant, I want ye here. Ride south to the posting inn and tell Mr Stephenson to lend me Leamus and anyone else who can keep up... oh, and bring a rope. Did I kill Sir Henry?"

Dodd shook his head. "He's rotting inside, he's delirious, he keeps shouting that Lady Widdrington is watching him."

Carey was throwing on his clothes at speed.

"If ye can get a message to Young Henry, tell him I have reason to suspect there's a large raiding party of Grahams either on their way to Widdrington or waiting their chance in the Middle March. He needs to gather his surname and his friends and defend Widdrington."

"Och."

"Spynie's going to send his henchmen north on horseback, ready to defend him when he gets to the Border and attack me."

"Whit's yer plan?"

"Catch Lord Spynie and hang him before the King can stop me."

"Ay, but then ye'll hang yerself."

"D'ye think I care, Sergeant?"

"But sir, Lady Widdrington's not dead. Me and Janet broke her out of Widdrington, along of the King, before ye got there last night, quietly."

Carey went still and shut his eyes for a moment. "Are ye joking wi' me, Sergeant?"

"Nay sir, Ah wouldna do that. My lady's wi' Janet and Jane and they should ha' got to the Fenwick bastle by now."

Carey took a deep breath and then another and then he crowed with laughter, like a boy who's just scrumped some apples.

"Elizabeth is alive?"

"She is."

"She's all right?"

"Ay sir, she drank some of the poison as well as what the witchfinder did tae her, but last I

saw her she was on a hobby and heading for Jane's family's bastle."

Carey could have kissed Dodd's miserable face but didn't. Instead he shook Dodd's hand solemnly.

"Sergeant, that's the best news I've heard in all my life. Maybe I won't kill Lord Spynie after all."

"Well, I would if ye can but get awa' wi' it," advised Dodd sourly, "After all, he's never going to stop being yer enemy any other way, now is he?"

Carey laughed and tied the laces of his boots firmly, stamped his feet and and waved cheerfully at Spynie. Lord Spynie was looking scared. Dodd went and grabbed a hobby from the barnekin and mounted with a negligent steed leap, cantered off in a southerly direction.

***

It took a while to organise the race. Finally the King was waiting in the infield with all the cows gathered in outrage at the other end. Spynie had two men next to him who didn't look very happy to be there. Carey sauntered over, sustained by bread and slightly mouldy cheese, feeling a little light-headed still from the sheer relief of the news that Elizabeth was definitely alive. He felt under-dressed since he didn't have a hat on, but never mind, Spynie would likely start to regret his fashionable high beaver.

He locked eyes with James's ex-minion until Spynie looked away and licked his lips. Carey pointed his finger at the minion playfully and then drew it across his throat.

King James was sitting his horse and enthusiastically writing the book for the bets on the race. Carey put a lot of money he didn't really have on himself to win. He thought about putting a smaller amount at longer odds on Spynie in case the pervert somehow won, but in that case he'd likely be dead so wouldn't be able to collect.

"Where are your Seconds?" asked the King, "Are those the men?"

Carey looked round and saw Leamus and Nick Stephenson cantering towards them, Leamus with his legs and feet bare and his hair unplaited. Behind him came Nick Stephenson, carrying a leather bottle and a rope wrapped around his waist. They were riding quite well, really, and they dismounted and jogged over.

Spynie looked like he was having a heart attack when he saw Leamus, his eyes were on stalks and he remonstrated with the King at length. The King seemed amused.

"Sir Robert, my Lord Spynie is concerned lest yer pet Irish kern uses some Irish enchantment on him."

"What, like Lord Spynie used on you, Your Majesty?"

The King shook his head. "Now, now, my lord was beguiled by the Spanish witchfinder."

"Your Majesty, I don't need magic or witchcraft to beat Spynie. All I need is my righteous desire for revenge for my lady, myself and for you, Your Majesty, that ye were unforgivably endangered by Lord Spynie's stupid treachery."

King James nodded wisely at this. "Ay, yer tongue's a wonder, Sir Robert, but I'm giving Spynie a start on you because I did love him once." Carey shrugged.

"As Your Majesty pleases."

"Oh. Ye don't want to protest?"

"No, Your Majesty, he's a weak and lazy man, there's more sport in the race if he has a start."

Spynie winced and looked sulky but Carey grinned at the King with such a wild look that James found himself wishing again that he could somehow seduce the Englishman into his own bed. Ah well, that was one who would probably never escape from the she-devil's spell, he thought and sighed. God, Carey was more handsome than ever, battered though he was, in the prime of his strength, unshaven and his goatee expanding, and his bright blue eyes dancing. Something had cheered him up and no mistake. There was none of the smell of desperation and rage on him now. Ah yes, Sergeant Dodd would have told him about Lady Widdrington.

Finally, when all six men were standing in the infield, King James stood in his stirrups and let a lace-edged handkerchief flutter to the ground. Spynie was off at once, moving fast, his henchmen a little behind him.

James waited until he was well out of sight and then dropped the handkerchief again. Carey bowed elaborately to the King and then started off at a solid fast pace, not as fast as Spynie's sprint, with Stephenson at his left shoulder and Leamus ahead of him, pulling away and closing on Spynie, his face amused and intent.

The King cantered slowly after them with his ten men behind him and much unseemly whooping and cheering.

For the first few miles, Carey was struggling because he was tired from getting beaten up the night before, he still had a headache, and parts of him were sore from Spynie's whip, but then he realised that he was feeling lighter because he was used to riding and running after raiders in his fifty pounds of jack, and today he was only wearing doublet and hose. Something changed internally and he stopped having to force himself to run and his pace became easier and smoother.

The first time Leamus came back to him, Carey had almost forgotten he was there. Leamus matched paces with him, his big feet slapping softly on the stones of the Great North Road as if they were made of leather.

"The Scot has gone off the road and he's running up the lanes and tracks between the fields."

Carey nodded, jumped a small brook. "The Great North Road bends to follow the coast," he said. "He's trying to go straight for the Scots frontier, a little to the west of Berwick. Hm."

To Leamus' surprise, Carey turned around and trotted to the King's stirrup where he seemed to be explaining something complicated to the King as they ran. After a minute, the King nodded and beckoned one of the younger men to him, spoke to him and off galloped the man north and east.

Carey caught up with Leamus and Stephenson who had gone to a walk, ran past them.

"What...?" asked Stephenson.

"I asked His Majesty to warn the Berwick Garrison and especially the Sergeant-at-Arms there, Hugh Collingwood, that this is a footrace for the settlement of an argument between two gentlemen and not a hot trod and to give him my name in particular."

Leamus and Stephenson exchanged looks. Yes, it was probably a good idea but why had Carey taken the trouble to do it?

Leamus showed them where Spynie had gone off the Great North Road, north-westwards, though the triple tracks were clear enough. They led through farmland, winding muddy lanes and small spinneys near streams. Leamus frowned at the tracks and sprinted ahead while Carey and Stephenson kept on, northwest now.

"Thank you for coming with me, Nick," said Carey after a minute. Stephenson was high stepping over a tangle of small streams leading to a pond. He shrugged.

"You told us to get out of Widdrington as soon as you thought it was a trick, and then stayed to delay the Scotsmen," said Stephenson after a minute. "That's the action of a captain worth following."

Carey smiled. "I wasn't thinking of you, I was thinking of getting my revenge for Lady Widdrington's death."

"I know, sir. But you told us to get out first."

Carey tilted his head and then had to concentrate on following the Scottish boot tracks through another network of streams and marshy bits.

Suddenly he stopped dead and squinted at some bushes. There was a red thread flying from a thorny bramble runner. Very carefully he untangled the thread, sniffed it, stared at it and put it in his doublet pocket. Then he upped the pace, opening his long legs and pumping up a hill, with a plowman ploughing with an ox-plow down below, stopping at the side of the field at the turn to stare at them.

From the hill he could see the King and his men in the middle, and just on the next hill, Lord Spynie in his red doublet with his two men still behind him.

Carey ran down hill, jumping the molehills and laughing like a boy, keeping his stare on Lord Spynie like a wolf on a deer. As they looked, they saw one of Spynie's seconds start heading due north while Spynie and the other second carried on over the rough country. The King hesitated and then continued to follow the favourite in his smart beaver hat, and his henchman.

"Leamus!" Carey shouted and there he was, limping slightly as he padded over the heather. He paused, lifted his foot up at an impossible angle, looked at the sole, brought his foot up higher and put his head down to pull something out of his foot with his teeth, then carried on up to Carey.

They came to the place where the third man had headed off north rather than northwest, the tracks as clear as day, Spynie and one man going northwest, the other man heading due north. Yet there was something wrong with the bootprints. The two men together were both wearing poor men's boots; the single man heading due north was wearing much better made boots, with evenly-spaced hobnails.

Carey grinned and said "Habeo!" Then he started northwards after the single man, running much faster now. Stephenson frowned although Leamus was almost laughing.

"Sir?" said Stephenson questioningly.

"Trust me," sang out Carey, now slightly breathless, "I think Spynie exchanged doublet, jerkin and hat with one of his men."

Leamus had a grin as broad as Carey's and now accelerated past him, pulling Spynie in on an invisible rope. They could see the ex-favourite struggling up the next hill, running half hunched, his fist in his side.

"Of course... It could be a double bluff," said Carey to Stephenson and ran faster. "But I don't... think he had time to... change boots." He could see the running man at the top of the hill ahead, walking.

"Don't kill him, Leamus," shouted Carey, "don't touch him... just use that excellent Irish magic you showed me!"

Leamus looked over his shoulder, paused, then raised his arms and started chanting something foreign.

The man ahead was sprinting again down the hill, tripped and fell over, scrambled up and kept running blindly, his statute cap lost and sweaty blond curls showing.

"T'y il est haut!" sang out Carey, sprinting up the hill and down, past Leamus, speeding up as he got closer and closer until his outstretched fingers felt the man's collar and pulled him backwards and over, punched him in the face. There was a violent scuffle, the two rolled into a gorsebush, there was the thud of fists, a gasp and grunt, more fists.

Carey rose up from the gorsebush and kicked the man in the crotch a couple of times, rolled him out of the undergrowth. Carey was crowing for breath, Spynie clutching his groin again in agony and seeming to have difficulty breathing.

Panting hard, Carey held him down and looked around. There was a tree at the corner of a field not far away, it looked tall enough and had a convenient branch.

Spynie had got some air into his lungs by the time Leamus and Stephenson arrived and was using it to beg for mercy.

Carey smiled at him nastily and gestured for Leamus and Stephenson to pick the favourite up. They did it, breathing hard themselves, carried Lord Spynie by his legs and arms and trotted him to the tree which was when Spynie began to wail.

Stephenson produced the length of rope which had been wound around his waist. Carey began to make a noose.

"N... nay, the King said ye werenae to kill me..."

"Did he say that?" wondered Carey. "I don't remember."

"Ye canna..."

"Shut up," said Carey, looking critically at the noose and testing the rope. "Get his clothes off him."

Leamus and Stephenson stripped the favourite ungently of his servingman's doublet and hose and everything else, even his very fine linen shirt. He had no scars at all and lilywhite skin.

Carey advanced on him and shoved him under the tree while Stephenson threw the rope attached to a log up and over a stout branch of the tree. Now Spynie tried to fight them and it took all three of them to grab him properly again and tie his hands with a bit of his shirt, and once he was standing on a stone under the noose, they heard a farting noise, followed by a nasty smell.

"Jesus Christ, my lord, ye've shit yerself for fear," drawled Carey.

Leamus shook his head and tutted while Spynie snivelled that it wasn't his fault, it was the Irish kern's magic. Nick Stephenson seemed amused.

Carey was staring at him and kept staring until the King's ex-mignon finally shut up and stood goosepimpled in the cold wind, the shit drying on his buttocks. Spynie had a long list of foul bills on Carey's account, including the thumbscrews, but Carey found his thoughts going back again and again to Young Hutchin and the way he had been at the posting inn. There was deep anger still in his belly about that.

It would feel so good to kill him. And he had a small window of time wherein he could do it and improve the world a great deal.

The argument for killing the man was weighty. But there was an equally strong argument for not killing him. When Carey married Elizabeth Lady Widdrington, Queen Elizabeth would be offended with him. In that case it would help both of them considerably if he had the favour of the King of Scotland. He thought he had it now, but he knew that if he killed Lord Spynie he would lose it. His Majesty of Scotland had no idea what a viper the man was, or actually, he did know but still loved him. Carey knew that if he killed the ex-favourite, he would lose the King's favour permanently.

He should have been happy to win the race and kick Spynie's ballocks. Yet instead of feeling triumphant, he felt paralysed. That's a pretty weak excuse for not killing the loathsome Spynie, in't it? said a voice deep inside him. What, are ye sceered of killing him because the King might not like it?

I promised the King I would obey the rules of the race.

Ye were lying, said the voice, and ye know it. Hang him if ye've come over all maidenly and squeamish, not so much blood as cutting his throat.

He looked at Leamus who came of a family that had served the Kings of Ireland, or said he did, and on impulse beckoned him over. "Is it really true that your family were advisors to the King of Ireland once upon a time?"

"It is, sorr," said Leamus, "although I'd not claim to have their wisdom."

Are ye crazy? growled the ugly bloodthirsty voice inside him. Ye're asking an Irish kern for advice?

I'll ask whoever I like, retorted Carey internally, be off with ye, foul fiend or whatever ye are.

Carey tilted his head at Spynie who was shivering now and staring at the ground. Jesu, was he crying?

"I don't know what to do," he said quietly to Leamus, hoping the Irishman could help him. "I want to kill him for... for so many reasons. But something in me doesn't want to as well. Is that cowardly?"

Leamus slowly put his right foot a pace behind his left leg, put his left hand on his chin and his right arm across his belly. He looked hard at Spynie, stared at him from head to foot.

"The man is unworthy of life," he said thoughtfully, "but then so are we all. We are all sinners in the eyes of the Almighty. The man has treated ye badly, he has tried to destroy the life of your true love, Lady Widdrington. His behaviour with his pages is notorious and unconscionable."

"Why isn't it simple? Why can't I just rid the world of him?" asked Carey helplessly.

"Because it isn't simple, sorr. Once he was an innocent child, new come from God, from the place of light, containing within him a spark of light from the Most High. Your own soul recognises that tiny hidden light in him, for it cannot be put out, no matter how evilly we behave. Your soul is troubled at ending his earthly life and it is right. Is killing not a sin?"

Carey was surprised. "Well, yes, I suppose it is."

"If ye kill in battle, if ye kill judicially, that's different, but not so different. You are taking from him the opportunity of living longer, suffering and perhaps amending his sin and so having the chance of going to Purgatory and not Hell."

"I don't believe in Purgatory."

"Ah that's sad, sorr, it's a more hopeful way of thinking than going straight to Hell from this Earth. I also say that the undoubted benefit of killing this poor worm of a man is less than the black sin that you would take upon your own soul by doing it thus in cold blood and against the King's sacred orders."

Carey nodded slowly.

"But in the end, sorr, this is your decision not mine, and I pray to God that you will listen to your own soul and so decide aright."

Leamus bowed, took three steps backward and turned away.

The ex-mignon was indeed crying, tears and snot rolling down his face and off his chin since he couldn't wipe it off with his hands tied.

Do it, came that ugly voice inside him, you'll not get a better chance.

That broke the spell. Carey answered the voice aloud: "Of course I will." He solemnly put his arm round Spynie's neck and choked him so he dropped. Stephenson put the noose where he pointed.

"Hang him up," he said, and they pulled the rope up between all three of them and tied it off to a tree root and left Lord Spynie hanging and swinging in the breeze.

They wiped their hands on the bracken and Carey looked over the fields. The King was visible, far in the distance, galloping forward with his men sprinting behind him, standing in his stirrups, trying to make out what had happened to his favourite.

Carey started running again eastwards, followed by Leamus and Stephenson and Carey was laughing like a boy running for the fun of it.

"Where are we going now?" panted Stephenson as he ran behind Carey who still seemed to be in a hurry.

"We're meeting some Berwick friends of mine," said the Courtier opaquely.

Behind him the King galloped up the hill to find his ex-minion hanging from the tree, stark naked, still covered in shit, but upside down, hanging by his feet not his neck.

***

They ran north eastwards to the Great North Road, turned left and kept running past the people and the pack trains. A troop of men came in sight, riding south at a hand-canter and Carey cheered and sprinted up to the Sergeant-at-Arms who was carrying the Berwick

Garrison's flag. He stopped the whole troop together on a sixpence with one gesture.

"Hugh!" shouted Carey, and the Berwick Sergeant gave the flag to his deputy, jumped down lightly from his hobby and they shook hands.

"Hey Rob," said Hugh Collingwood, "Er... Sir Robert, where's Spynie and his men?"

"I'll explain later, but they're crossing the Border to Scotland in a few hours."

"Ay? That's good news, is that..."

"But we need to get to Widdrington as fast as we can, I've the feeling a West March raiding party is on its way. Mainly Grahams."

"Ah've heard naething..."

"Trust me," said Carey, "I'm betting they're almost there. I'll tell ye about it on the way."

Collingwood had remounts at the back and soon Carey and Stephenson were mounted. Leamus smiled and said he would rather run ahead to see what could be seen. The whole troop turned as one and started a hand-canter again, due south on the road.

SUNDAY 11TH MARCH 1593, WIDDRINGTON

Young Henry was sweating and angry as he came up to the Widdrington castle gate with twenty relatives behind him having travelled for days from the Highlands and Edinburgh. Behind him was Sam the Man, leading four beautiful Irish wolfhounds.

"What is this I hear about Lady Widdrington?" he demanded of Dodd who was sitting on a hobby at the gate.

"Mr Widdrington," said Dodd, "there's a raiding party of Grahams and other reivers on their way here and I'm right glad to see ye and yer kin since Lord Spynie's men have all run awa' and the King took his men north for the running race. All I've got to stop the reivers wi' is thirteen men of Hieronimo's Troop and some guns."

Young Henry looked up and saw a row of ten calivers poking over the battlements with the men behind. One of them raised his hand.

There had been a lot of hard work after Dodd had sent Nick Stephenson and the mad Irishman to Carey that morning. He had rousted out all the rest of Hieronimo's Troop, told them what was likely to happen at Widdrington with Young Hutchin loose for two days. They had decided against using the wagon and the men had found a handcart the alewife used for transporting barrels and borrowed it. They had brought all the guns and powder and especially the shot from the post-inn to Widdrington and got it there in record time. It was well worth the trouble to see Young Henry's expression relax slightly when he saw the guns, but Dodd would have appreciated a thank you. On the other hand, Young Henry wisna a soft southerner either.

"What running race?"

Dodd explained and Widdrington's face became grim. Dodd had to explain what had happened to Young Henry's step-mother and his face became thunderous. "So. How many Grahams?"

"Ah dinna ken, sir, sorry. Ah'll explain more about what's been happening later but now I want tae get the stock in the barnekin and shut the Castle and I havena the experienced men nor the authority."

Young Henry nodded once, called to the eldest of his cousins and gave him orders. Most of his cousins fanned out to the infield to bring the animals in, even the sheep on a high pasture far away. The three men who were already out trying to bring the animals in looked very relieved as the Widdringtons started rounding up the stock.

"Where's my father?"

"I havena looked to see, but he was sick to death in the second bedroom, of the gravel in his bladder. He might be deid now."

Young Henry grunted, jumped from his horse and ran into the castle, followed by Sam. Ten minutes later he was back with the keys.

"Where is everybody?" he asked, looking bewildered. "Where's my brother?"

"Ay, well, when ye accuse a woman like Lady Widdrington of witchcraft, all the women in the castle take fright and leave if they can until they're all gone and then their menfolk go with them. Ah dinna ken about yer brother."

"So that's why Sir Henry sent me off on a wild goose chase to the Highlands to get Irish hunting dogs?"

"Ay."

"He's not far from death and it looks like his stomach is ready to burst open, he's rotting already like someone wi' the plague."

"It isna plague though."

"No, it's his gravel right enough." Widdrington looked into the western horizon. "Jesus Christ." After a while he said, "Why isn't there any food in the place?"

"Lord Spynie and his men were here for a week or more," said Dodd, "Sir Henry invited them. And then the King turned up too, though he brought some supplies."

Young Henry shut his eyes briefly. "There's nothing left. Even the oldest barrels in the provision cellar are empty."

Dodd did his best to look sympathetic – nothing was worse for your land nor your insight, barring a raiding party of Grahams or Elliots, than a nobleman or a King turning up.

"And all this just to accuse my Lady Widdrington of witchcraft?"

"Nay, there was an assassin in back of it. Minister Lindsay who claimed to be a witchfinder, was sent from Spain to kill the King of Scots."

"Oh Christ." Young Henry's eyes widened with enlightenment. "Is that the man who's dead in the provisions cellar?"

"Ay."

"Who killed him?"

The cattle were flowing in nicely with the horses and two of the Widdringtons were setting up the hurdles again, for the pens to keep them in. The sheep were waiting further away, baaing anxiously and looking over their shoulders.

"The King said that he did it," said Dodd, "in self-defence. So it was the King."

"Yes, but the King canna abide blades of any kind..."

"It must have been the King," said Dodd loudly, "since the only other person in the cellar was your step-mother and she had been given poison and was furthermore manacled."

"But the corpse had the marks of..." Dodd glared at him, he stopped and swallowed. "Ay, that'll be it."

There was silence as the sun dropped and the sky began slowly unfurling royal banners of purple and red.

Dodd was squinting into the sun.

"Ay, there they are," he said with grim satisfaction. "See, there in the eye of the sun."

Young Henry gestured for the sheep to come in at the run, went and checked every gate, the dairy postern included, which he locked and barred, came back to stand by the gate while the woolly flood galloped past including the ewes with their lambs. As soon as the last lamb had wobbled in with his anxiously baaing mam, Young Henry locked and barred the gate, told his cousins to get up to the wall, and went to the small gate tower. Dodd was handing out arquebuses to anyone who knew how to fire one, along with inadequate powder and shot. He interspersed them with the calivers, facing west and north. Then he went to stand next to a pile of arrows and bows he had rescued earlier from the old chapel.

The Grahams were clearer now, in an untidy bunch with lances pricking the purple cushions of cloud above them.

Young Henry squinted too and then he said steadily, "There are a lot o' them."

"Ay," said Dodd.

***

Sam the Man took the dogs to the stables and tied them up there. Then he climbed the stairs to Sir Henry's chamber with his hand on his dagger, following the smell of piss and rot.

He found his master across the bed, his shirt soiled, his stomach swollen, his face red with a rash and the smell of shit and rot all around him.

Sam stopped breathing through his nose. "Sir Henry?" he asked.

"Where's... Lord Spynie?" whispered Sir Henry.

Sam shrugged. "Gone to some kind of running race."

There were tears running down the man's face and he snorted. "But... I'm dying..."

"Ay, ye are," said Sam. "Best get ready tae meet God, eh?"

"I want to... see Lord Spynie."

"He's not here."

More tears. "I love him," Sir Henry said, "Love him, love him. Wish I could see him."

Sam stared at him with complete contempt. This man had hanged his son, poor Toad, once called Tom, who was so gentle and so kind and had had such a hard life, partly because of him, and... Why couldn't he just stick his dagger in Sir Henry and get his revenge?

"Hurts," said Sir Henry, "Everything... hurts."

"Good," said Sam, sitting down on a stool by the bed. "I'm glad."

"Why?"

"Because ye hanged my son, Toad."

The bloodshot eyes closed and opened again. "Ye've come to kill me."

"That was why I came," Sam admitted, "but now I don't think I will."

"Why... not?"

"Why should I end your pain?"

Sir Henry rolled his head uneasily, looked up. "She's there. She's hurting me."

"Hmf," said Sam, "D'ye think I care?"

"Please... ye can kill me. Kill me."

Sam sheathed his knife and smiled. "No," he said, and crossed his arms.

SUNDAY 11TH MARCH 1593

Lady Elizabeth had been sitting on the hobby's back for a long time, she had forgotten how long because her head was still full of clouds and her body was slow and felt unfamiliar to her. She was in a narrow lane with Janet pacing sturdily ahead of her, leading the hobby. Elizabeth was grateful she didn't have to direct the hobby or make any decisions although she couldn't think where they were going either. Her memory was full of odd scraps of pictures, as if a Puritan had ripped up an old Catholic breviary, with strange pictures of elongated women and weird animals. There was herself in the cellar for days and days, not knowing what her husband would do to her next, with the branks making her mouth so sore. It was impossible to speak and hard even to pray internally. And the spiced wine Lindsay had brought her when she was desperate with thirst so she had drunk it despite the bitter taste. The world had gone fragile, like an old linen shift full of holes... Some visceral memory was there of enormous heat and strength inside her, strength and a world-encompassing rage that she should be treated like this. She had hated Lindsay, hated him with passion and when he said that she should attack the other man – yet she could smell that other man and knew she mustn't touch him although she couldn't remember why. And the rage had overspilled and she had seen Lindsay as he had turned and drawn his long sticky blade and nearly stabbed the King. And so... what? What had she done? She had felt like a second Sun, overflowing with rage and power.

Had she killed him? Surely not. Surely, she couldn't have done it? But something had made the manacles bruise her wrists terribly. Something she had done with the chains.

She was blinking at them now, the bruises had had time to flower and were red and purple all over her wrists.

She shut her eyes and let her hunched back move with the hobby. No, it must be some kind of nightmare, not reality. But was her husband screaming again with the pain in his bladder, and everyone refusing to help, was that just a nightmare too?

The whole events of the last few days made no sense to her, except that Spynie was involved in it somewhere, him and his corrupt bunch of ex-catamites. And Lindsay as well, the man who had terrified her until she... Until he ended up dead and was no longer frightening.

Her sight was still blurred and dazzled and she wished she had a hat to shade her eyes from the cloudy sun.

"Nearly there, Lady Widdrington," said Janet, puffing a little.

"Where?" she managed to ask, through the stiff clots on her lips and tongue.

"Jane Fenwick's parents' farm," said Janet, "she's run ahead to tell them you're coming to the bastle."

Yes, thought Elizabeth slowly, Jane did come from a fortified farm south of Widdrington. Had she ever been there? She couldn't recall, though she thought that Jane had been brought to Widdrington six years ago by her father in a new and stiff woollen kirtle, too big for her, when Elizabeth had let it be known she was in need of a new dairymaid to replace Susan who had got married to another Fenwick.

She hadn't the strength to ask any more, she still felt ill from the poison. She tried to straighten her aching back but her whole body was aching in chorus and she soon slumped again.

More fragments of memory floated by. Her sleeping in the charcoal burner's hut in the coppice and somehow flying up from there and into Sir Henry's bedroom where she had found Lord Spynie in the bed asleep cuddling a child. She had flown through into the spare room and there she had found Sir Henry blown up like a bladder with urine, his whole body pulsing with fever like her own, but parts of Sir Henry's body had already started to die.

He opened his eyes and saw her and so he started shouting at her not to look at him. But she drilled down through his eyes until she found the boy, the boy he had been once.

She shook her head and roused herself. Well that certainly wasn't true, she thought, she wasn't a witch and couldn't fly. Sir Henry had never once mentioned his long dead mother nor his father who hadn't been a good headman at all.

Had she tried to stop Robin from fighting all Spynie's men at once, had she tried to beat them off him and found her fists going through their misty bodies?

No, that was ridiculous. She had been asleep and as they bore Robin down and piled into him, she hadn't protected him. But Spynie had certainly captured him.

"Mrs Dodd," she said, lifting her drooping head, suddenly urgent. "Is Robin... is Sir Robert all right?"

Janet shook her head. "Ah dinna ken. Sergeant Dodd and the King went back into Widdrington from the coppice where we rested to stop Spynie harming him."

"Will Spynie's men obey the King?"

"Oh ay, they will," said Janet in an odd tone of voice.

She wanted to ask more questions but suddenly felt exhausted and sick. Through the holes in the world, she saw Jane running down the lane towards them, her skirts kilted up and her hobnailed boots splashing the mud, her cheeks pink and a wide smile on her face. And soon she could hear the pelting of the boots in the distance and at last Jane arrived, looking exactly the same.

"Jane!" called Janet, "how far?"

"Only a mile, Missus Dodd," Jane came up on them and went to a walk and pushed her hair back under her cap where it was sweaty. "I brung some ale for my lady."

Elizabeth suddenly realised that the reason why she felt so sick was because she was thirsty.

"Thank you sho much, Jane," she said to her, "Can I have some now?"

Jane beamed again and unhitched the large leather bottle from her shoulder, handed it up to Elizabeth, whose hands were still clumsy because of the terrible bruising from the manacles, but she managed to drink. It felt wonderful, carving a path down her throat like a spring flood making its own banks for itself. The ale was good, nutty and sweet and not too strong.

She gave the bottle back and Jane gave it to Janet who tilted it back thirstily.

Suddenly Elizabeth saw the curve of her belly and how she stood and asked, "Mrs Dodd, is it possible that you're with child?"

Janet looked at her oddly for a minute. Then she smiled. "Yes, my lady, I think it's three or four months."

"Why, that's wonderful news!" said Elizabeth, "Grace and blessings attend your hour and God send you a short labour and a happy result."

Janet gave a small curtsey. "Thank you, ma'am," she said. "We should get on."

It was only a mile, though it seemed like forever. Jane's mother and father came out of their bastle to the fence around their infield to welcome her, the man in his best jerkin and Jane's mother with a new apron. Behind them were their servants, a maid and two cheap Scotsmen. Lady Widdrington lifted her leg with immense effort and slid down inelegantly, almost collapsing at the end of it. Then she stood, wobbling, and tried to respond to Goody Fenwick's flustering about. Jane was the one who saw what case she was in and whispered something to her mother. Moments later, with Jane helping her, she was upstairs in a warm room with a newly made cupboard bed, Janet's kirtle off and hanging up and the petticoat and the turnshoes, and Elizabeth was finally lying between fine linen sheets of Goody Fenwick's own weaving...

SUNDAY 11TH MARCH 1593, WIDDRINGTON

They could hear the gunfire before they came in sight of Widdrington Castle, a steady relentless crack, boom, crack.

They galloped the rest of the way and saw the reivers round the gate back off a little as they arrived. Three men and two horses lay dead or dying. Carey stood in his stirrups and looked well from a hillock with his eyes narrowed. "Right, I can see Jock o'th'Peartree over there. I want to parlay with him. Sergeant Collingwood, do you have a trumpeter?"

Hugh beckoned up a young man with a lance who produced a trumpet from his lance slings, put it to his lips and blew the Call to Parlay very badly.

The reivers turned about and saw the more than fifty men on horseback with the Berwick banner in front, at an easy distance for a charge. Carey was too far away to see Jock's expression but could imagine it and that made him smile.

There was a long pause while Jock o'th'Peartree consulted his men and then found a grubby bit of linen to tie to a lance as a flag of truce.

Carey had no cloth, but Nick Stephenson somehow produced a handkerchief and tied it to a lance. Leamus had appeared from nowhere and was putting on his boots hastily.

"I'll talk to him," said Carey, "I don't want to kill him."

"Why not?" asked Hugh Collingwood with great curiosity but Carey didn't answer as he rode forward under the flag of truce.

He could see two riders with Jock, one small for a man, wearing a helmet over filthy gold hair.

Jock took his time getting near, partly because Young Hutchin was arguing fiercely with him.

"Ay, ay, Young Hutchin, I hear ye. Be quiet will ye, now?"

They met and sat their horses a couple of yards apart. Jock's face was graven in granite and behind him scowled Young Hutchin.

"I have you between the guns in the castle and the Berwick Garrison's Horse," Carey began coolly. "I know why you're here and I can tell you that Sir Henry is nearly dead if he hasn't died already and that my Lord Spynie and his men and His Majesty the King of Scotland and his men have already eaten the place bare. They're now on their way back to Scotland."

"I've a liking to the cattle," said Jock.

Carey examined him. "For the avoidance of doubt, all of the Widdrington herds are locked up tight in the Castle." He hoped that was true, that Young Henry had attended to the most important things. He couldn't see any beasts out on the hills at least.

"Where's Lord Spynie now?" demanded Young Hutchin in a growl, no doubt in terror that he might squeak.

"I chased him nearly to Berwick, caught him, gave him a hiding he'll not forget, strung him upside down from a tree stark naked."

"Why didn't ye kill him?"

"Because King James asked me not to."

"Och," sneered Young Hutchin, "Ye're soft as shite, ye traitor."

"Haud yer tongue, boy," snapped Jock and then said to Carey. "Whit does he get out of it?"

"What?"

"What does Young Hutchin get for being banged up for nae reason?"

"As a blood price for imprisonment and hard treatment?"

"Ay."

It was somewhat daft asking such a thing for a boy, but Jock o'th'Peartree had to be bribed in some way.

Carey thought about this for a few minutes and then he remembered Beaumont, the beautiful black horse that Mr Heron had complained that the Minister had taken from Berwick. But that was far too good a horse for the likes of Young Hutchin Graham. The still small voice that had advised him before spoke again: nonetheless, give it to him.

For a moment Carey was outraged. The horse was probably worth several pounds considering his big bones and powerful haunches. That was ridiculous.

Nonetheless, said the voice.

"There's a horse you might like that should be in Widdrington Castle right now." he heard himself say slowly to Hutchin, "The one the witchfinder rode with a Berwick brand on him..."

Young Hutchin's eyes blazed. "A black gelding, about sixteen hands?" he asked, "wi' a sore mouth fra the Minister's cruelty?"

"Well I don't know about that, but yes. His name's Beaumont and he's a great-grandson of my father's favourite mount when we were at Berwick, when I was younger than you."

"Beaumont," said Young Hutchin thoughtfully. "Ay, it's a good name. Is it Spanish?"

"No, French, it means "beautiful mountain" and his master's dead so he's the spoils of war if I can get Young Henry to give him up."

Young Hutchin looked sad. "He willna want to, he's a beautiful animal."

"Let me try," said Carey, feeling obscurely that this was important. He rode over to the gate and after a certain amount of shouting, was let in. Young Henry shook his hand and thanked him for bringing out the Berwick Garrison and he put the point to him directly. They went to the pen where the horses were standing anxiously, close together and all looking outwards. There was Beaumont, at the head of them, taller than any of the hobbies or other horses. Young Henry went over to him and caught his head by the rope halter, looked in his mouth.

"Ay," he said, "he's had an abscess but it's healed now."

He led the horse forward to Carey and Carey enjoyed watching the nag's movement. He was a little thin still, and he hadn't been groomed but still he lived up to his name.

"Here you are, Sir Robert," said Young Henry with a smile. "My gift to you in thanks for your help to my stepmother and myself."

Carey smiled back, looked at the horse, shook his head and sighed. Then he went to the gate where Dodd was standing with a brow of thunder.

"Ye're not seriously going to gi' that horse to Young Hutchin, sir?"

"I know, Sergeant, it's hard, but I have my reasons."

Dodd's long face drew down sour and sad. "God almighty."

He opened the gate and Carey led the horse out, mounted his own hobby and went past the waiting Grahams and Elliots to where Jock o'th'Peartree was sitting his horse looking skeptical and behind him Young Hutchin with his head down.

Jock raised his eyebrows and nudged Young Hutchin, whose face lit up with joy. He trotted his pony forward and then when the pony baulked at the size of Beaumont, jumped down and came close to caress the horse. Beaumont whuffled at him.

On impulse, Carey dismounted and came up to the lad. "Listen to me, Young Hutchin," he said very quietly, "I ken ye want yer vengeance on Lord Spynie but I want ye to wait. Wait until ye have yer full growth as a man and the bastard has forgotten all about ye, wait until the time is right. D'ye follow me?"

"Ay but..."

"This horse is a bribe for you, though your uncle will likely take him off ye in the end. But ye know I'm talking sense. Will ye do it?"

Young Hutchin nodded.

"Yer word on it, Young Hutchin, man to man."

There was a long pause and then Young Hutchin took a deep breath. "Ay, mah word on it, Courtier. I'll wait ten years before I kill Lord Spynie. A'right?"

"Right."

Young Hutchin did the steed leap to the horse's back and took the rope halter, trotted over to Jock o'th'Peartree.

"Jock o'th'Peartree Graham," said Carey to the old reiver whose eyes were stretching at the transfer of the horse to Young Hutchin. "Ye have what the Elliots had last autumn. I'll count to a hundred and then the Berwick Garrison will charge."

He turned, leapt to the horse's back like any reiver and trotted over to where Hugh Collingwood was sitting impassively under the Berwick banner.

"All done?" he asked with only slight sarcasm.

"Look," said Carey. Jock had turned his horse about, stood in his stirrups and bellowed "Grahams! Tae me! We're going."

The Grahams rallied to Jock and surrounded him and Young Hutchin, followed by the Elliots and rode briskly away north west-wards, presumably to look for trouble in the Middle March.

Carey talked to Dodd and found two interesting things. The first was that Hieronimo's Troop and his own men had only enough powder and ball for one more volley before their guns would have devolved to clubs. The second was that Lady Widdrington was at the Fenwick bastle, twelve miles to the south, to keep her safe from Jock o'th'Peartree Graham.

***

Elizabeth was lying in the cupboard bed in darkness, dozing, blinking at the watchlight. She felt terribly heavy as if her whole body was made of lead. Goody Fenwick had clucked at the sores around and in her mouth and covered them with a salve of St John's Wort which stung and also tasted revolting. She still couldn't eat but had no appetite anyway.

She heard the sound of horses in the courtyard, men dismounting. Who could they be? The clouds in her head were still there though fading slowly. She heard the sound of boots in the bastle kitchen, deep voices – was it Sir Henry there?

One pair of boots came up into the small room above the kitchen where her bed was and it was Young Henry, his spotty face full of concern.

"Ma'am," he said, "My Lady Widdrington, I have to tell you that your husband, my father, is dead."

She wanted to sit up, but she couldn't, she simply felt too heavy.

"Oh," she said, thinking of Sir Henry's screaming. "May God have mercy on his soul."

Young Henry ducked his head. "Ay," he said, "I've taken over as the heir, ma'am, will you... will ye come home wi' me?"

She considered this. She thought she would never go back to Widdrington again. Never. Why return to the place where she had been imprisoned, not only for a week or two, but nigh on ten years. Not even for Young Henry would she do it.

"Not yet," she temporised, "I need to recover here for a few days, if Goody Fenwick will have me."

"She will, ma'am."

Young Henry turned and clattered out. After him and more slowly came a man in a worn jack and a morion on his head, who took it off and bowed low to her and shook out sweaty white and yellow streaked curls, who stared at her as he came gracefully upright again, bright blue eyes but bloodshot and very tired.

She had no idea how she did it but suddenly she was out of the cupboard bed and across the room and her arms around him, feeling the plates of steel between the padding in his jack, breathing in the smell of him, the wonderful smell. He kissed her once very gently on the lips and then he put his head on her shoulder and sighed long and wearily, like a pilgrim who has at last come home.

After a moment he lifted his head and kissed her face and said, "My Lady Widdrington."

Elizabeth put her own head on his shoulder, where it fitted very well, and smiled. "Robin?"

He smiled back and said the word gently. "Elizabeth."

***

Young Hutchin Graham was in a towering rage with his Uncle Jock o'th'Peartree and with his entire surname. In the evening, Jock had casually told him that he might be riding Beaumont, but that Beaumont was well too much horse for a mere stripling like Young Hutchin and therefore Beaumont now belonged to someone more suitable, namely Jock o'th'Peartree Graham.

Furthermore, Jock and the Elliot headman were quietly plotting something while Young Hutchin couldn't sit with them like a man, but had to fetch and carry the pottage and slice the bread like a goddam boy, while his stomach growled and grumbled. They were in a burnt-out disused pele tower, still in the English East March, with Jock's hastily assembled raiding party camping out in the overgrown bailey and Jock and Wee Colin lorded it over him in the main room of the tower, where they'd lit the fire.

And who had it been who had told them that Widdrington was almost empty and easy pickings? Young Hutchin, that's who. That they hadn't been able to take the castle before Sir Robert Carey somehow managed to turn up with half the Berwick Garrison, was hardly Young Hutchin's fault.

And then he half-heard the words "Lady Widdrington" and immediately came out of his resentful grouch.

He took hold of the wineskin Wee Colin Elliot had picked up from a farmhouse close to Widdrington, carried it awkwardly to the busted chairs where Jock and Wee Colin were sitting, and poured wine for both of them, keeping his head down.

"One o' my cousins who works there told me this afternoon that she's in a bastle twelve miles south o' Widdrington," explained Wee Colin, "And she wilna be expecting aught to happen to her now."

Jock o'th'Peartree sucked his wine down from his leather mug.

"And we made precious little fra the raid," he said thoughtfully, "and she'd be worth a fair price on the hoof."

Wee Colin Elliot grinned and wiped his mouth. "Ay."

Almost holding his breath, Young Hutchin took the heel of the loaf – all that was left – and sat himself down in the corner with his back to the two headmen. He munched it slowly and stretched his ears until he almost sprained them.

About ten minutes later he was dozing off despite himself – until Jock spotted it and shouted at him.

"Hey, wake up."

Young Hutchin sat up and then stood and said, "Sorry Uncle Jock," as humbly as he could because his brain was suddenly awake and fizzing with plans.

"Go and see that big horse o'mine has water and hay and gi' him a rub down."

"Which d'ye mean, Uncle? Beaumont?"

"He's no' a hobby any road. Ay, o' course I mean Beaumont. Who else?"

Young Hutchin kept his head hanging so they couldn't see the plans in his eyes.

"Ay Uncle,"

"And gi' us more o' that wine first."

"Ay."

Very carefully Young Hutching served them more wine – a wine skin was always a bit unchancy to pour from and his hands were shaking with excitement. Then he dragged to the archway and scraped his clogs on each step.

And then he ran as fast as he could to the burnt out stables with bones in the corner that Beaumont had snorted and shied at, and gentled the horse who was nervous too. He picked through the rubbish outside and found some more bones and clouts of cloth while Beaumont drank and nibbled the oats he'd been given.

Next moment Young Hutchin was kneeling by the horse, tying the rags over the expensively shod hooves, while Beaumont stood quietly, only blowing his barrel out and snorting every so often.

Young Hutchin said nothing, because Jock o'th'Peartree Graham was notorious for his sensitive hearing. He put a rope halter over Beaumont's perked ears. The horse nickered softly and pushed his head at Young Hutchin, you would almost say he knew what was afoot.

Then Young Hutchin Graham walked the horse carefully over the rubble and the burnt beams and behind a small bothy and took him up and over the remains of the wall, and walked on across the once-upon-a-time infield and through a hole in the overgrown drystone wall and only slid up onto Beaumont's back when he was at least a mile from the barnekin.

Beaumont needed only the slightest push and went to a canter at once, and then to a smooth delightful gallop while Hutchin put his head down by the horse's neck and urged him on with whispers.

***

Carey was sleeping uncomfortably on a settle in the kitchen near the fire at the bastle, an aged blanket over his shoulder. Now he'd got Lady Widdrington he didn't plan to let her out of his sight until they were wed, but he knew he had to be respectable. That was the only reason why he wasn't crammed into the cupboard bed with Elizabeth. The settle was nowhere near long enough for him either. He was more exhausted than he ever had been before, even in France, and his head was still feeling sore.

And he still woke when he heard the hoofbeats because they were from a large horse, not a hobby, and what the devil was anybody doing galloping about the East March at 2 am on a horse like that if he wasn't on a raid or carrying an urgent message..?

Carey got up, left the blanket where it was, put his boots on as fast as he could and drew his sword. Then he hid behind the door.

There was a very soft knock. "Master?" came a boy's voice, whispering.

Carey lifted the bar and opened the door. There stood Young Hutchin Graham with bags under his eyes you could hide a pig in, but as soon as he saw Carey and his sword he smiled.

"What's going on?" Carey asked. Young Hutchin told him.

Just for a moment Carey felt totally exhausted at the thought of more fighting, but then his spirit rose somehow from nowhere and he smiled back at Hutchin.

"I should have known Wee Colin and Jock would try something like that – but one of the reasons for coming here was that they wouldn't know where Lady Widdrington was. The Berwick Garrison is waiting for them at Widdrington along with Young Henry and the rest of Hieronimo's Troop. Damn it. How did they find out?"

Hutchin thought carefully. "One of their servants is a Scotsman and probably an Elliot and he told Wee Colin that told Uncle Jock."

"God almighty, why does anybody have Scotch servants, even if they take half as much in wages. All right Hutchin, go through the house to the stables and wake the men who came with me, Leamus and Nick Stephenson. Don't light any candles, come back here as soon as they're properly awake."

Young Hutchin nodded once and went past him through the kitchen.

Carey went upstairs and quietly knocked on the door of the Fenwicks' bedroom. There was a pause and then Goodman Fenwick opened the door, holding a billhook. Behind him, Carey could see Jane sitting up on a pallet with a scowl on her face.

Carey was expecting a lot of lamenting at the news that Jock o'th'Peartree Graham and Wee Colin Elliot and a selection of their men were on their way, but Goodman Fenwick's round moon face hardened and his wife was scowling too.

"By God," said Goody Fenwick, "I told ye not to take on that bloody Scot."

Goodman Fenwick took breath to answer her and then sighed heavily.

"We'll leave the bastle locked and get out," he said, "That's worked before."

"Ay," said Goody Fenwick, "But what about my Lady Widdrington, she's in no fit state to gallivant around the countryside again, poor lady, what with the ulcers in her mouth and..."

Carey and Goodman Fenwick exchanged looks. That was true.

"I was going to put her on the best horse and send her back to Widdringtom," admitted Carey "and hope she'd make it before Jock and Wee Colin get here."

"Oh that's impossible," insisted Goody Fenwick, "she can hardly get out of bed..."

"Ay," said Goodman Fenwick, "and Widdrington is north of here and Jock o'th'Peartree might cut her off on his way here and then we've done the job for him."

Carey didn't like to admit it.

"Can we fortify..." he began only to be interrupted by an imperious voice behind him.

"Sir Robert, what is going on?"

Carey couldn't help it. He swung round to her only to find his gaze softening and his heart thundering again as he looked at Lady Widdrington's infinitely precious face. Her red hair was sticking up around her face, she had only a shift on and a shawl around her shoulders and for a second he wondered why he was thinking of Her Majesty the Queen and then remembered a time when Her Majesty had been roused from sleep by a dangerous plot against her and he had been lucky enough to be able to serve her and give her aid. Lady Widdrington's expression was exactly like Her Majesty's.

"My Uncle Jock and Wee Colin Elliot are after ye for ransom," explained Young Hutchin's disgusted young voice from the stairs. "Ye should ride Beaumont right back to Widdrington, ma'am, so ye should."

Lady Widdrington lifted her chin and looked from Carey to Goody Fenwick and over them to Young Hutchin.

"I wouldn't make it," she said in a cold voice. "It's twelve miles, I haven't recovered yet from the poison and I might even fall off the horse. No. I will not run."

Even while he was wondering desperately what he could do about Lady Widdrington, Carey was admiring her and longing to kiss her and put her in front of him on Beaumont and gallop through the co untryside... No. Again, if she said she couldn't do it, then she couldn't do it. And small wonder considering how she had been treated by her husband and the witchfinder.

"Uncle Jock will send a small party in the direction of Widdrington," said Young Hutchen, "He always does things like that."

Well, Carey supposed, you wouldn't get the fearsome reputation Jock o'th'Peartree has if you weren't good at strategy and tactics. Damn it.

He counted up in his mind. "There's only five of us," he said worriedly to Gooodman Fenwick. "With you, Hutchin. How many men will your uncle have?"

"Wi' the Elliots, at least twenty, maybe thirty."

Jesu, thought Carey, and most of my guns are at Widdrington as well.

He noticed that Jane was up and standing behind Lady Widdrington with a half-scornful smile on her face.

"Can ye no' count better than that," she sniffed at Carey. "I mek it eight."

Carey stared at her puzzled. "What?"

Goody Fenwick sighed and rolled her eyes. "Me, my lady, and Jane. Eight."

"Well, but… er…"

"How many calivers and pistols have you?" asked Lady Widdrington of Goodman Fenwick.

"Oh now, my lady, you must let us men do the fighting and…"

"He's got four in the house," said Jane, "And shot and powder. Have you got a caliver with you, Sir Robert."

"I've got my pistols in the case on Sorrel's back…"

"Shot and powder?"

"Of course, but…"

Goody Fenwick nodded at her daughter. "Ye're thinking o' the last time the Routledges came calling on the offchance?"

Jane nodded and Goody Fenwick smiled at her lovingly. "Ay ye're right, it might work. Better than galloping up the road to Widdrington any road."

"Ay."

"Off ye go, husband, get the horses out and the cattle off the infield."

Goodman Fenwick hesitated. "We lost the stables last time…"

"Ay, and we'll lose 'em again. Which is better? With the horses in there, or out and hard to catch. The hay's nearly finished too."

"Young Hutchin, come wi' me," said Jane firmly, as her father trotted down the stairs in the dark. "I need ye to carry the calivers, I'll carry the powder and shot."

Carey was staring at the women, feeling rather surplus to requirements, and then he trotted down the stairs after the Goodman to get his horse out of the stables and find his pistols.

He found Stephenson and Leamas already busily clearing the kitchen for action. Carey saw for the first time the painted over marks of fire on the walls and the wooden table and settles. He hadn't noticed that before.

"Did you bring any guns?" he asked and both of them shook their heads. Even a pistol was heavy and a caliver weighed about eight pounds. Carey wasn't sure what he was supposed to do. He caught up with the Goodman who was hauling a barrel of powder and a bag of leadshot out of a cupboard.

"What's the actual plan?" he asked, taking the bag of shot and then another one. "Where do these go?"

"Upstairs. Come back as fast as ye can, I need yer young legs to deal wi' the henhouse, the cattle and the horses."

Carey's young legs were aching quite badly but he said nothing. He carried the bags of shot up the stairs and into the Fenwicks' bedroom where Jane was fastening the shutters and opening up the muzzle holes and sighting holes cut in them. Most of them were blackened by muzzle flash.

Slightly reassured he went back downstairs and out into the yard to help with the stock. The chickens were all clucking in their henhouse which was fortified against foxes and locked against broken men. Goodman Fenwick picked one end of the whole henhouse up like a litter and Carey took the back end and they carried the henhouse all the way into the outfield with the hens protesting all the way and the cock crowing as if it was sunrise. It weighed a ton and the chickens kept fleeing collectively to one side and then to the other side which made it hard to carry in a straight line.

Once they'd got it into a mound of brambles, and caught their breath, Goodman Fenwick lifted a long plank from the roof and sprinkled some grain into the henhouse which shut up the hens, while the cock crowed valiantly on. He bolted the plank back, and they ran back to the stables where Leamas and Nick were leading the horses out. The four nags and Beaumont were also annoyed at being woken in the middle of the night, especially Beaumont who tried a kick at Fenwick and was instantly led in a circle by Young Hutchin who chucked at him until he calmed.

"D'ye think I should ride for Widdrinton, sir?" he asked anxiously to Carey. "Ah dinna ken which to do, stay here and look after Jane or get help."

Her father was chuckling softly. "Ask her lad, she'll tell ye what she wants."

Young Hutchin went up the stairs two at a time and found all three of the women sitting on the bed loading all the calivers and pistols. "Och," said Hutchin, beginning to get an inkling of the plan.

"Young Hutchin," said Lady Widdrington, "do you have Beaumont with you?"

"Ay," he said, realising she hadn't actually seen the beast since he'd knocked on the door.

"Could you take this letter to my stepson, Young Henry Widdrington. Wake him up and explain the situation to him."

"Ay, m'lady," He took the letter, put it safely in his shirt.

Jane was standing close by and staring at him with an odd intent look in her eyes. Her wonderful breasts were very close and the cross-lacing of her kirtle was loose so he could see a bit of them and Hutchin wondered if she'd be angry and slap him if he...

She grabbed his head and gave him a lingering kiss on the lips. "That's my thank ye for fetching the Berwick Garrison and Hieronimo's Troop as fast as ye can. Off ye go."

He dove for another kiss but she dodged him and clouted him on the back.

He scrambled down the stairs and ran outside, leapt to Beaumont's back who finally stopped crow-hopping. He did his best to look debonair as he knuckled his forehead to Sir Robert.

"I'm fetching the Garrison Horse and Hieronimo's Troop," he said, lordly fashion, "I won't take long, sir."

Then he grinned and whacked Beaumont with his statute cap and galloped down the track that led to the Great North Road and Widdrington.

***

Nick Stephenson and Leamus were expecting a siege of the bastle but the Fenwicks had other ideas. As the Goodman explained and Carey stood next to him in support, Nick was thinking that Carey looked like some species of battered scarecrow but somewhere inside him you could still see his cousinship to the Queen.

There were four of them to fight the twenty to thirty men that Jock and Wee Colin had with them and defend the women until the Berwick Garrison and Hieronimo's Troop got there. Which would take at least an hour, more likely two if they weren't awake.

He thought that sending Young Hutchin off on the best horse was probably the right thing to do, even if it would probably take too long for reinforcements to arrive.

Personally, Nick would have kept everybody inside, locked up and sat tight. Until the roof was alight and the ground floor burning and they had to run out into Graham and Elliot hands. As he understood it, Lady Widdrington and possibly Carey himself were the prizes Jock and Wee Colin were dicing for, namely their value at ransom.

Carey and Goodman Fenwick had gone outside for some reason, though all the stock was now scattered over the infield and outfield and getting deeper into the coppices by the minute. Leamus was piling up furniture behind the door, with a small gap so they could get out themselves.

He licked his lips which were too dry and wished for some ale. He'd thought he might die in the battle for Widdrington the day before, had seen his own face with a spear through it. That didn't happen somehow although there were several near misses. But the image of his face turned horrible with a spear said to him that he could die too. Like most young men he still didn't believe he really could die but suddenly, now, he believed it. He felt sick and wanted to piss. He looked at Leamus whose face was intent but otherwise seemed relaxed.

Yes, but what if I die and nobody knows what happened, asked the cowardly part of himself. What then?

The battle for Widdrington hadn't even been a battle as Jock had been scared off by the Garrison Horse. There hadn't been any real fighting, well, a tiny bit. And now here they were in a bastle twelve miles from Widdrington and he didn't see how he could survive. Plus they didn't even have guns – for some mad reason Carey had insisted that the women should have the guns.

And they would be outside the walls of the bastle, not inside like the women. For God's sake! That was insanity.

Nick did his best to steel himself and accept that he would die pretty soon and all that happened was that the cowardly part of him got louder.

He looked at Leamas again and saw that the Irishman was unplaiting his long hair and smearing his face with soot from the fire until he looked like a monster. He grinned at Nick and beckoned him over.

"Let me paint your face," he said and Nick let him because he couldn't think of any other way of distracting the cowardly voice in his head.

Carey put his head round the door. "I think I can hear them," he said, "I need my jack and helmet."

Nick found them in a pile and handed them over to Carey. Jane came down the stairs and Leamas bowed to her which Nick found very strange. She did too, you could see she was wondering if he was making fun of her.

"Get out now," she said, blowing out the single candle, "I'll block the door."

Leamas nodded gravely to her and he and Nick slipped out and into the pitch darkness of the night which was clouded over with the occasional star popping out playfully.

They could hear the piled up furniture shoved up against the door by Jane's sturdy frame, and her boots going quite slowly up the stairs, another pause and then nothing.

Carey was next to Nick, his morion making a monster of him. "Careful," he whispered, "The yard's full of holes now."

They picked their way round the yard to a wattle fence which wouldn't be much use, and then the woods surrounding the farmhouse on two sides, damp and with a few bluebells poking their heads out but not blue yet. He'd seen them as he rode in, he couldn't see anything now. The footing in the yard was unchancy, with a few flat bits.

Outside the fence, Nick and Carey picked places to hide in the bushy bits at the edge of the woods. Goodman Fenwick was nowhere to be seen and Leamas had disappeared as well.

Us two, then, thought Nick uncomfortably, and that's it.

***

Horses were coming along the track and on both sides of it. You couldn't really see them, just large solid lumps in the less solid darkness. You could smell them, and the men on their backs in their leather jacks and iron helmets and their lances. Nick didn't know how long they had been lying full length in the damp next to a drystone wall – had it been an hour, maybe two? Or just ten minutes. He didn't know. The darkness hadn't changed, there had been a couple of owls and some scuffling in the undergrowth and he had been listening to his heart beating too fast and getting colder and colder and more and more scared... When he'd heard the beat of hooves cantering close and closer, the cowardly part of him had screamed "RUN, NICK! Run NOW!" Somehow he had stayed where he was, more because he was cold and stiff from lying still than because he was brave. And he couldn't run now, could he?

Jock's voice sounded so close to Carey, that he nearly flinched. "A'right," said Jock o'th'Peartree in a whisper. "Let's see if they're awake, eh?"

Jock took out his horn and winded it. "Open up," he roared, "We've come for our rights. Giss Lady Widdrington and Sir Robert Carey and we'll say nae more about it, eh?"

There was silence, the deeper silence of no rustling, no calling, every beast thereabouts holding still and quiet in fear, and the rest run or flown away, not even a hedgepig battering through the brambles.

The bastle was quiet as well.

"Have ye all run, ye cowards?" shouted Jock and slammed through the gate to the yard. His horse pecked and nearly tripped and then did it again. Behind him was Wee Colin, eyes narrowed. Jock dismounted and marched to the door, banged on it with his lance.

No answer.

"Bring us a light," snarled Jock, "Carey! We'll fire yer house and yer stables too if ye dinna come out tae us now!"

About half the raiding party was now in the yard, along with Jock and Wee Colin and somebody had got his firepot open and lit three torches from it, and the lights went to the stables and the wattle fence and set them burning with some difficulty since they were damp.

And then...

Then a gun spoke from a shot hole and took down one of the men closest to the door. Another boom and shot bounced off the well and the stone of the house and lodged in one of the ponies and the pony leaped and kicked and screamed and then the other hobbies started trying to get past the men standing close around the house.

In the middle of the yard a part of the floor stood up and there was a ghost, screaming and wailing with a sheet over his jack and his face floured to white and Jock o'th'Peartree stepped back in fear at the sight. Wee Colin struck with his sword and there was a bellow of gunpowder behind him which knocked him down and blew the arm off a young reiver next to him.

Carey was already in among the men standing gawping, with Nick at his heels, cut down through a man's shoulder with his broadsword, spurt of blood like a fountain, very satisfying. He started fighting Wee Colin who clearly didn't recognise him with yellow hair, Nick was fighting another raider and a caliver bellowed from the upper storey and another man went down. Jock o'th'Peartree was fighting Nick which was too good an opportunity to miss so Carey backed Nick up and one of his own pistols fired from the window.

Maybe I should sell those guns and get better ones, murmured a distant and unbothered part of Carey, while he pressed hard against Jock. Some of the Grahams were crowding into the yard to help their headmen and getting in each other's way with the wattle fence alight. Somehow he was shoved to the ground, rolled and jumped up, and he could see Wee Colin on his hobby shouting something he couldn't hear, something about an ambush, and then part of the raiders followed Wee Colin and cantered off. Another caliver fired.

***

Inside the Fenwicks' bedroom there was a terrible lot of gunpowder smoke so the candle in its dark lantern did no good. Goody Fenwick, Jane and Elizabeth were coughing. Elizabeth had appointed herself loader-in-chief and she was doing the loading with her head down and a cloth across her face which Goody Fenwick had insisted on. Elizabeth on her part had insisted on plugs in their ears to save their hearing. The pistols were loud enough but the calivers fairly bellowed as they fired.

Elizabeth took back the two fired calivers, and reloaded them; the pistols with their wheel locks were ridiculously complicated to load and often missed. Jane and Goody Fenwick fired through the shot holes in the two shuttered small windows and more smoke filled the darkness. There were a couple of return shots which pinged off the stone walls. Working by touch alone she reloaded the next two calivers, once their barrels had cooled. Every so often a massive crash told her that Jane and Goody Fenwick were still firing. Nobody could speak because the smoke was so thick. God sakes, she thought, I need air, I'll go downstairs and fire out of one of the downstairs windows with the pistol.

***

Nick was in the centre of a knot of fighting, hand to hand with two men, including Jock. Carey slipped in behind Jock and stabbed him in the back with his lefthand dagger which bounced off a metal plate inside the padding of the jack. Jock turned on him like lightening and Carey brought his knee up just right and got him perfectly in the bollocks.

A bit of fence fell into the yard and there was a crackling sound and then something went boom at the other end of the yard and there was another crackling sound.

A caliver fired again, this time straight into the middle of a knot of them and the pressure eased as Jock fell to his knees. Nick bent and grabbed Jock, lifted him up and put his knife to Jock's neck.

"Stop Nick," shouted Carey. "Keep ahold of him." He shoved through to set his shoulder against Nick's, his back to the door, and facing the now leaderless bunch of Grahams who also stopped.

They could hear clearly through the forest the pounding of horse hooves, all shod. Seconds later the Garrison Horse erupted into the clearing and yard and set about chasing the Grahams into the woodland. There was another crackling and something else went bang.

And Jock turned his face to Nick's and bit Nick viciously on the nose. Nick's grip loosened and the raider elbowed Carey in the side where it was sore and ran round the house, leaped the wattle fence and Hugh Collingwood shouted in frustration as Jock o'th'Peartree Graham leapt aboard a hobby standing there waiting for him, took the tether, and galloped off into the forest with Hugh chasing him.

There was the sound of a lot of men breathing very hard and some groans.

Carey went and stepped on the slowmatch burning across the yard to another wooden mug filled with powder, picked it up and spat on it.

He found Goodman Fenwick lying untouched and completely unconscious near the hole in the ground made by the first gunpowder mine to go off, still dressed as a ghost.

The shutter downstairs opened and he stared at one of his own pistols pointing at him and then Elizabeth took her finger from the trigger and laughed at him and he couldn't help it, he grabbed her through the window and kissed her on the mouth and for a wonder and a glory she kissed him back.

***

Five days later, Goodman Fenwick was bandaged and in bed and didn't seem able to speak. Leamas had turned up with a long string of horses with a variety of brands on them and Goody Fenwick had blown her nose and begun getting the damage mended, pausing every so often to suddenly draw in a breath as if she'd been stabbed and then let it out carefully. And then she carried on. Sir Robert Carey and Lady Widdrington, plus Leamas, Smithson and Young Hutchin had gone to Berwick with Hugh Collingwood and the Garrison Horse.

Jane had found her father sleeping like a baby but she couldn't wake him up. She had been pale and silent ever since. Two of her brothers came home from Berwick where one was prenticed to a blacksmith and the other to a builder and started arguing over who should have the bastle if Dad died until their mother took out a wooden spoon and started whacking them with it until they cried for mercy.

And Young Hutchin came to the bastle wearing a new jerkin and a new blue statute cap and a pair of boots that was only secondhand and asked Goody Fenwick if he could speak to her daughter.

She brought Jane out, still silent and grey-faced and stood behind her daughter.

"Mistress Fenwick," said Young Hutchin with a surprisingly neat bow to her, "I wantae ask for yer daughter's hand in marriage. I havenae a brideprice for her but I will have and I want yer permission to make my suit to her."

"Ye have it," said Goody Fenwick to her own surprise, considering he was just a Graham whelp. What Goodman Fenwick would think of that, she would worry about when he started talking again.

"Jane," said Hutchin, "I ken ye're worried for yer Dad and ye canna give me an answer now but I love ye and I wantae be your man and look after ye and have weans wi' ye and make ye happy. D'ye think we could walk out together until I'm old enough tae..."

And Jane silently put her arms around Hutchin and held him tight.

THE END

This book is the last in the current series of Sir Robert Carey books – but there will be more, I promise.

I think you'll enjoy the James Enys books, starting with DO WE NOT BLEED.

LOOK HERE if you still haven't signed up for my email list – honestly, you'll love the stories about Carey when he was a boy.

AUTHOR'S NOTE

I found the research for this book very difficult – despite having decided on the theme many years ago. It's hard to read about the tortures that (mainly) women suffered at the hands of the men called witch-hunters or witchfinders or to read about the witch-hysterias that often grew from their activities.

There is one point I would like to make. In most of Europe and in Scotland where a magistrate or procurator fiscal would judge the cases by Roman Law, it was rare for women or men accused of witchcraft to be aquitted. Most of them were hanged, some were burned.

In England, where most witches were tried by juries under the Common Law, half of them were acquitted and freed. It seems that the men of the juries had more common sense than the learned magistrates who regarded them as perverse.

If you want more information on witches, read P G Maxwell-Stuart's scholarly books "Witchcraft: A History" and "Witch Hunters."

CAST OF CHARACTERS

At Widdrington

Alexander Lindsay, Lord Spynie

Sir Henry Widdrington, Deputy Warden of the East March

Roger Widdrington, Sir Henry's second son

Mr Anthony Lindsay, Minister of the Kirk

Young Hutchin Graham

Wattie Widdrington

Barney

Jamie's Jock Widdrington, ex-Head Lad

Sam the Man Affleck, Chief Groom at Widdrington

Toad

Jane Fenwick, dairy maid

Bertram

Toby Hogg

At the Scottish Court

Lady Elizabeth Widdrington nee Trevannion

Mary

Ann of Denmark, the Scottish Queen

Mistress of the Sweet coffers

Young Henry Widdrington, Sir Henry's first son

Johnnie Carmichael, friend of Young Henry's

(Lord Maxwell)

Mouse, Rat – Lady Widdrington's horses

<u>At Widdrington</u>

Jane Fenwick, dairymaid

(Susan)

Little May

Fireweed, lead cow

Amelia Widdrington

Miss Widdrington, Dairy Mistress

Fat Malky

Goody Affleck

Scarface

<u>At Carlisle</u>

Nicholas Stephenson, aka Nick Smithson

(Captain Leigh, Jones, Peter Sheffield, Mr Arden)

Sergeant Henry Dodd

Clockface

Garron

Falls off his Horse Perkins

East

Tarrant (Skelly his brother at Berwick)

(Sir Richard Lowther, Deputy Warden, West March of England)

Bessie

Bessie's Wife

Mrs Kate Nixon

Acting Sergeant Andy Nixon

Leamas, Irish kern

Wee Colin Elliot

<u>At Gilsland</u>

Big Clem Pringle

(Richie Graham of Brackenhill)

Sergeant Henry Dodd

Janet Dodd nee Armstrong

Tiddler, Nuts and Benny Armstrong

Ekie (Hector) Armstrong

At Berwick

Cicely Swanders now Hall

John Carey, Marshal of Berwick

Madeleine Hall (Anna and Susan her friends)

Socrates Hall, Tom Hall

Mr Barley

(Danny Swanders)

(Aristotle Knowsley)

James Heron, Head Groom, retired

Hugh Collingwood, Sergeant-at-Arms of the Berwick Garrison Horse

Andy and Archy, ex-dog boys

Cuddy, Sam Dixon, David Trotter, Jonathan Gray

(Thomas Fenwick)

(Kat, Beth, Hugh Collingwood' wife and daughter)

(Father Crichton)

Bugloss, (horse)

Teazle, Bugloss's dam

The Scotchman, Bugloss's sire

Beauregard (horse)

Violet, Beauregard's dam

Beaujoie, Beauregard's sire

(Sir Robert Cecil)

(Lord Hunsdon)

Post inn near Widdrington

Innkeeper Onslowe, his wife

James VI of Scotland, incognito

Cuddy Armstrong

Goodman Fenwick, Goody Fenwick, Jane's parents

Jock o'th'Peartree Graham

GLOSSARY

Apoplexy – a stroke

Arquebus – a large handgun with a long (but unrifled) muzzle

Barnekin – outer fortification of a castle or pele tower

Bastle – fortified farmhouse, often with a wall, common in the Marches

Buffcoat- heavy leather coat with no sleeves, lowest form of armour

Buttery – where you got wine, beer or spirits in a castle

Caliver – lighter musket or arquebus, with a short muzzle

Chalice – elaborate cup used in church

Chantry chapel – chapel where priests used to sing masses for the souls of the dead. After the Reformation they were converted to other uses

Coppiced – a method of cutting down a tree so it grew back multiple stalks from the base; a way of growing much more wood and incidentally resetting the tree's age

Curfew – a metal cover to put over the fire at night so that the coals would stay warm but wouldn't cause a fire

Dag – smallest handgun, basically a pistol

Giants' Road – term for the Roman road along the Anglo-Scottish frontier

Giants' Wall – Hadrian's Wall

Godspeed – more formal way of saying goodbye

Half-testered bed – the tester was the roof on a four-poster bed. Half-testered meant that the fabric roof was half-sized with curtains hanging around it

Henchman – a boy or man employed as security

Horse-leech – horse vet

Infield – grazing close to the house

Jack – a padded leather coat with steel plates sewn in between the layers of leather, a better form of armour for light cavalry

Jack – a leather mug, containing a pint or a quart (about a litre)

Jakes – outside toilet

Jointure – the part of a dowry which a woman owned outright as her support if her husband died before she did

Kine – plural of cows

Kirtle – the skirt which might or might not be attached to the stays or bodice

Laudanum – opium in brandy

Leges Marchiorum – Laws of the Marches, the Borderlands

Levee – the arising of a monarch from his or her bed, a very formal occasion

Lymer – large hunting dog which looked remarkably like a labrador

March Treason – bringing in of reivers

Marcher Law – the very peculiar Law of the Marches

Mass – the Roman Catholic service which transmogrified into various other Christian services

Milch-kine – cows that gave milk

Morion – elaborate helmet with curves and a peak – what Spanish conquistadors wore

Outfield – pasture further away from the house

Pallet – a thin mattress stuffed with straw or hay

Pollarded – a tree that was cut just below the crown, encouraging a thicker growth of branches

Post-inn – an inn that kept post-horses ready to ride by someone riding post. This meant literally from a post in the ground to the next post-inn – normally a distance of around ten miles. That was about the limit that a horse could gallop. Riding post you could make a hundred miles a day, changing horses every ten miles, or better, if you were terrifically fit.

Pottage – all purpose vegetable stew usually with lentils

Pricket – a sharp implement, usually used for bleeding someone or for torture

Refectory – monks' dining room

Scold's bridle/branks – an appalling contraption designed to put a piece of metal in the mouth of an unruly woman and keep it there so she couldn't talk

Secretary script – old fashioned script, quite Germanic

Smock – a linen shift worn by a woman to protect her clothes from herself and herself from her clothes

Statute cap – basic form of hat (rather like a beanie) which all boys older than the age of 5 had to wear by statute, unless they could afford a better hat

Stays – foundation garment made with wooden or steel bones to support and hide the bust

Tenter frame – a large frame like an upside down table which held a piece of fabric stretched in all directions

Tiring woman – the woman who helped a lady dress in the morning

Truckle bed – smaller bed on wheels that went under the main bed for the servant to sleep on

Vennel - alleyway

Vinegar fly – flies were blamed when ale went sour though in fact it was bacteria

whishke be/uisghe beatha - whisky

woad blue – the light blue you get from woad, once so cheap only servants wore it

wood – crazy, wood-wild

Wort – the first stage in making ale or beer, where you dissolve the malt in warm water. First wort was the strongest and then got progressively weaker. Small ale was third or fourth wort.

Wynd – small alley

COPYRIGHT STATEMENT

First published in 2024 by Patricia Finney Books.

ISBN: A TASTE OF WITCHCRAFT ebook 978-1-915169-24-2

ISBN: A TASTE OF WITCHCRAFT print book 978-1-915169-25-9

Milton Keynes UK
Ingram Content Group UK Ltd.
UKHW020729130524
442628UK00001B/16